PRAISE FOR DAVID SOSNOWSKI

HAPPY DOOMSDAY

"Reading David Sosnowski's dazzling new novel is like watching an Olympic gymnast fly through the air, do six impossible things, and stick the landing with a glorious grin. I loved *Happy Doomsday*!"

—Mary Doria Russell, Arthur C. Clarke Award–winning author of *The Sparrow*

"Part dystopian survival novel and part coming-of-age journey, the tale weaves back and forth between the three leads as they try to make sense of the catastrophe and create a new normal for themselves . . . A sharply topical and well-researched apocalypse narrative that shifts among black humor, grisly details, and moments of poignancy."

—*Kirkus Reviews*

"Captivating and darkly humorous, this new work by Sosnowski is perfect for fans of *The Walking Dead* or postapocalyptic survival stories."

—*Library Journal*

VAMPED

"Sosnowski's wholly original mythology explains everything from the ideal vampire vacation spot to why their strip clubs keep the heat cranked up."

—*Washington Post*

"*Vamped* is not an outright spoof of vampire fiction—it has too much respect for its subject for that. But it does smuggle some welcome modernity and comic irreverence into the form . . . The chief pleasure of *Vamped* is in its rich imagination of the small details of modern vampire life."

—*New York Times Book Review*

"This darkly comic tale . . . provides intriguingly offbeat insights."

—*Entertainment Weekly*

"Few writers have taken as good advantage of the comic potential in vampiric metaphor as David Sosnowski does in his new novel *Vamped* . . . Audacious . . . unexpected and delightful."

—*U.S. News & World Report*

"Smart and funny . . . It's high time for a dark vampiric comedy."

—*Hollywood Reporter*

"Sosnowski's gleefully wicked sense of humor . . . and spot-on pop-culture references make *Vamped* a giddy page-turner. But at its core is a decidedly human tale."

—*Time Out New York*

"With wry wit and deft turns of phrase, David Sosnowski has penned a darkly humorous tale . . . A fresh breeze on a genre that can all too often be as stale as a dusty crypt. A fun read."

—Christopher Moore, author of *Noir*, *Lamb*, and *Bloodsucking Fiends*

"Inventive . . . intriguing . . . fun."

—*Publishers Weekly*

"Full of wit and charm, Sosnowski's fast-paced second novel . . . offers delightfully quirky characters and plenty of hilarious scenes."

—*Library Journal* (starred review)

"Sosnowski's easy mixture of warmth and humor makes for a winning, original tale about love in the unlikeliest of worlds."

—*Booklist*

Rapture

"Sosnowski has staked out a patch of turf somewhere between Franz Kafka and Douglas Adams, and made it all his own."

—*Detroit Free Press*

"A delightfully fresh book . . . an imaginative, uplifting tale."

—*Ann Arbor News*

"A hilarious, knowing, and, yes, *uplifting* treatise on the possibilities of being."

—*New Age Journal*

“Spinning an inventive, new riff on contemporary angel mania, Sosnowski’s first novel is a fanciful zeitgeist satire.”

—*Publishers Weekly*

“What’s subversive about Sosnowski is his subtlety; the most lurid passages are lyrical, and the funniest ones are slightly poetic. There’s no way to race through his prose, or you’ll miss layers of subtext.”

—*Detroit Metro Times*

“Written with much wit and humor.”

—*Library Journal*

“A witty, clever, original debut. Sosnowski writes like—well, an angel.”

—*Kirkus Reviews* (starred review)

Buzz Kill

Also by David Sosnowski

Happy Doomsday

Vamped

Rapture

Buzz Kill

DAVID SOSNOWSKI

47NORTH

Published by 47North, Seattle

www.apub.com

ISBN-13: 9781542005029 (hardcover)
ISBN-10: 1542005027 (hardcover)
ISBN-13: 9781542005043 (paperback)
ISBN-10: 1542005043 (paperback)

Cover design by Faceout Studio, Tim Green

Printed in the United States of America

First edition

For Jane Dystel, with much respect,
admiration, and gratitude.
Without you, there would be no book to dedicate.

Prologue

Like any good murder mystery, it starts with a body—quite a lot of them, in fact. Not yet, but soon. At the moment, those who are still alive include a sixteen-year-old girl named Pandora Lynch, seated next to her grandmother Gladys, who is lying in her bed in a nursing home in Fairbanks, Alaska. The two are not talking, but not in any petulant way; it's because the latter has mostly stopped doing that and the former has her smartphone occupying her attention. Their reason for being together isn't to talk, but for the companionship, shared personhood, and a certain degree of warmth that bodies in proximity provide.

Pocketing her phone, Pandora looks over and notices how smooth the old woman's brow is, despite the many reasons it has for furrowing. A classic blessing-curse: the dementia has made her forget she has it. And forgetting one's troubles is the pro tip dermatologists don't often share, not with the profits on Botox injections being what they are. What Pandora wouldn't give to forget that she may well be looking at her own future—to the extent she still has one.

There are plenty of things she can use: pillows, a roommate's Dixied medications to amp or depress Gladys's own, even a bare hand placed over the nose and mouth. A few moments of struggling due to muscle memory, and Pandora could give Gladys what she'd asked for before she stopped asking for anything.

Reaching toward the pillow underneath her grandmother's fan of white hair, the young woman stops, distracted by old-people noises in the hallway. And when she looks back, her grandmother's lids are fluttering as her own courage flags. The old eyes roll in their sockets, aimlessly at first, before locking, pupils front and center and aimed right at their mysterious visitor.

"Hey," Pandora says.

"Hey," Gladys says back, repeating as she does with pretty much whatever the other says, including "f-you." Pandora knows because she's checked and still regrets it.

"You feeling okay?" she continues, going through the motions.

"Feeling okay," Gladys says back.

"Good."

"Good."

More old-people noises: the shuffle of tennis-shod feet across waxed linoleum; coughs, some wet; plaintive calls for help they may not need anymore, having fallen into a groove and gotten stuck; the roll of weighted silverware on plastic trays; the squeaky wheel of a cart.

Pandora's phone starts buzzing, a steady, unbroken hum. She doesn't answer, payback for the caller having ignored her for nearly twenty-four hours. She's been keeping careful track of the time because the responsible party has been keeping track too.

Any second now, Pandora thinks, joining the countdown in her head before turning to her grandmother. "I love you," she says.

"Love you," Gladys echoes.

Pandora had been coming to the old-people's storage facility since back when her grandmother had been someone she could talk to without feeling like she was talking to herself. She'd even told the old lady things she didn't tell her dad, perhaps because even at her best, Gladys would forget whatever Pandora told her by the next time she visited, but also because her grandmother was the only female relative she had left. She'd even told Gladys about a little stalker problem she'd been having. The old lady, who'd been eating grapes at the time, pursed her lips and wrinkled her brow before delivering her verdict: "Tell 'im to buzz off . . ."

Pandora had laughed so hard the words became a catchphrase caught in her grandmother's otherwise stick-proof memory. At first, it seemed she'd used it just to hear the sweet chime of her granddaughter's laughter but then kept it up, Pandora suspected, because those particular neural pathways were easier to retrace than the tangled alternatives.

"Hi, Gram."

"Buzz off."

"Who brought the flowers?"

"Buzz off."

"Is buzz *on*?"

"Buzz off."

Pandora learned this repetition was called echolalia and that many dementia patients lapsed into it toward the end, before they stopped talking altogether, followed by eating, followed by drinking, followed by living, the lucky ones allowed to slip away, as opposed to being fed through a tube. Pandora's grandmother had vetoed that and similar interventions by putting it in writing while she still could.

"Are you sure about this?" Pandora had asked, holding the clipboard as Gladys prepared to sign her own DNR order.

The old lady had paused, the pen a spaceship of plastic in the gnarled oak of her hand. "Do me a favor, will you?"

"Anything, Gram."

"Mind your own business," followed by her nearly undecipherable but still legal scrawl.

Pandora's nursing home visits began as punishment before morphing into love. Whether they were doing her grandmother any good now, she had no idea. Being honest, Pandora suspected her continuing pilgrimage was more for her own sake than Gladys's. It was like when she started a book, no matter how predictable, she felt duty-bound to see it through to the end. And so she kept coming, no matter how painful they became, these visits to a memory without a memory.

"Hi, Gram, remember me?"

Pandora has placed her hand over her buzzing pocket, trying to quiet it. Instead, the hum takes up sympathetically in her bones, traveling up her arm, across her shoulder, up her neck, and into her jaw, where it hooks into the rest of her skull. She can feel the buzz conducting itself through the tiny bones of her inner ear—the hammer, anvil, stirrup—all humming, making her wince and clench her teeth. Haptic feedback on steroids.

"I love you," she says.

"Love you," Gladys echoes.

And that's when Pandora hears the first thud, like a fist pounding the wall in the hallway outside the room, followed almost simultaneously by what sounds like a metal pail banging over, upending its contents in a single, slapping splash. Her head jerks toward the door in time to see the sudsy puddle crawling past the open entry. Bolting up to see if anybody needs help, she finds the first body instead, a janitor in his early thirties on his way to mop up the latest biohazard. He didn't make it and never will, becoming his own biohazard instead, judging from the pool of bright red spreading around where his head landed after creasing the drywall. Pandora reaches a hand toward his neck but stops. She doesn't need to check for a pulse; the still puddle his mouth and nose are resting in tells her he's already dead.

Steeling herself, Pandora lifts her head to look around, which is when she discovers that the janitor's body is far from being the only fresh corpse in the vicinity. At the nurses' station, the Ratched twins are both goners, one with her head thrown unnaturally back as her body swivels in its chair, while the other lies next to an overturned cart, surrounded by pill confetti. Farther down the hall, an attendant had been escorting a resident to the shower using what looked like a hammock chair on wheels only to succumb to mortality and gravity. Still dangling in the transport's trusses, the abandoned resident rocks slowly, his thinly feathered head turning, not sure what to make of any of this, not that that's anything new. And it's the same everywhere Pandora looks: all the able-bodied staff are dead while their demented charges remain upright, lost in their eternal now, waiting on meals, pills, and visitors that won't be coming anytime soon.

Part One

1

Pandora Lynch wanted revenge. It started on her first day in a brand-new school—the first "traditional" school she'd ever attended—Ransom Wood High. She'd expected to be a stranger in a strange land but assumed she'd not be the only one. Homeschooling wasn't uncommon in Alaska, especially not in the more remote areas. And it wasn't unusual for kids to be sent to live with relatives once they became teenagers, so they could attend a real school, get used to socializing while trying their luck at making a go in the big city. Pandora had thought there'd be plenty of newbies to hide among, and there had been, until she made the fatal mistake of standing out by laughing at the wrong people at the wrong time.

She'd been minding her own business, standing by her locker between classes, swapping out one set of textbooks for another, when a posse of senior girl hockey players came shoulder-bumping down the hall. For a fleeting moment, Pandora imagined they were headed for her, an illusion made possible by the actual targets having lockers on either side of hers. They were boys, the targets, taller than Pandora but shorter than the clutch of senior girl hockey toughs heading their way.

"You know what I like about curlers?" the lead girl asked.

"Hair curlers or guy curlers?" a team player played along.

"Guy."

"No," the player continued playing, "what do you like about guy curlers?"

"They know what to do with a broom."

To be fair, Pandora was not the only person to laugh. She wasn't even the only *girl* to laugh. She just happened to be the one whose laugh attracted the attention of others like a lonely mouse in the reptile house. And no, it wasn't the sound; it was the face she made while doing it.

What followed was a classic butt-kick chain reaction, where the kicked becomes the kicker until you run out of butts. And in the hierarchy of high school athletics in the frozen North, there were the usual competitions among the grades and genders, but also the hockey players versus the skiers, versus, versus, versus until you hit the members of the freshman boys' curling team with the note that there was no *girls'* curling team because why reinforce domestic stereotypes?

The only butt lowlier than that of the freshman player on the boys' curling team was that of a freshman who was just trying to get an education sans athletics, preferably female, and one who made an outsize funny face when she laughed. And so:

"Nice face," the pride-wounded curler to the left of her said.

"Come again?"

"That's what *she* said," the belittled belittler to the right of her chimed in, followed by the broomsman, sweeping it home:

"Yeah, nice *cum* face, babe . . ."

Pandora pivoted her head, hoping to find some other object for this abuse, and, finding none, found herself wishing she'd brought a gun. This being Fairbanks, everybody had a few. Guns were tools, as common as hammers in Jesus's stepdaddy's workshop. But they were banned from school grounds because bullies, hormones, and handguns don't mix.

Absent the firepower to make her feelings known, Pandora jammed her backpack into her locker, slammed the door, and ran to the girls' bathroom so she could call her dad. She'd explain that she'd given it half a day and this high school thing wasn't working out. "So can you pick me up, *pleeeease*?"

Except her dad's phone went straight to voice mail. Okay, text. Thumb, thumb, thumb, send. Wait. Keep waiting. Immediate satisfaction not satisfied, she decided he must be working, screening Silicon Valley tech bros over Skype to make sure they didn't go on a shooting rampage or, worse yet, leave with a bunch of intellectual property on a thumb drive. Meaning she would have to either walk home or tough it out until she had a better idea of why she'd been singled out. Fortunately, a witness to Pandora's taunting met her at the sink, smiled, and pointed at the mirror, framing the two of them.

"Do you notice anything different between you and me?" the helpful girl asked.

Pandora looked and didn't.

"You ticklish?" the girl asked.

"Never checked," Pandora said. And so the other girl did. Answer: yep.

"What about now?" the smiling girl asked, indicating her own calm face with a Vanna White wave, followed by Pandora's, which could have served as a model for the "LOL" emoji.

"Whatever antidepressant you're on, I'd tweak it way back," her companion said, tracing a set of laugh lines that seemed dug by a garden trowel. "Maybe think about death more," she added.

"What's wrong with my face?" Pandora demanded after getting back home.

"Other than being adorable?" Roger Lynch countered, buying time.

"I'm serious."

"I can see that." And that was the problem. Whatever feeling Pandora was having was written all over her face—in italics, bold, and underlined. It was hard to miss, begging the question of how she had for going on sixteen years. The answer: she'd had help. Prior to its attending public high school, said face was rarely inflicted on anyone but family members, meaning her dad, who homeschooled her, and her grandparents, who babysat when the former needed a break. Plus, her father loved her face, especially when it was happy to see him, because her smiles took up a lot more facial real estate than your average smile and had the same contagious effect usually attributed to yawns. So: she'd smile, he'd smile, she'd smile even more—a veritable pandemic of happy; why spoil a good thing?

And it wasn't like her face was broadcasting constantly. Her resting face was just a face until given some cause for emoting, which it did on steroids. She hadn't thought to compare it to others she might see, and even subconsciously, she didn't notice the difference. Her face looked just like her father's when it emoted, which looked just like her grandmother's, which was like the faces she saw during the limited amount of television watching her dad allowed her as a child, which was largely composed of puppets and cartoons. If anything, out in public, she wondered what was wrong with other people.

"Maybe they're just tired," Roger had said. "Maybe they're having a bad day."

His own father, Herman, with his normal expressions, had gone back and forth between "being tired" and having "bad days," until Pandora finally stopped asking.

But now she was at it again, and this time, the thing that wasn't like the others was her.

"There's nothing *medically* wrong with you," Roger began his long-overdue explanation.

"Medically?" Pandora shouted. "There's nothing *medically* wrong . . ."

Roger made a tamping-down gesture. "Breathe," he suggested. "Try to calm yourself."

"I can't."

"I can see that."

"As can everybody *else*," Pandora stormed, finally realizing how it was her father always seemed to know what was going on inside her head. Early on, she'd imagined he might be psychic before deciding that no, it was probably because of his profession. Now she knew better. Her father hadn't been reading her mind; he'd been reading her *face*.

"Why didn't you *say* something?" she demanded, suddenly feeling like she'd led her entire life with a trail of toilet paper stuck to her shoe.

"I *did*," Roger insisted. "I told you we both have your *grandmother's* face."

Pandora tried picturing the face in question but couldn't. It had been years since she last saw it in person at Grandpa Herman's funeral.

"Is there even a *name* for this?" she asked, the words coming out like air from a punctured tire.

Roger nodded. "Hyperexpressive face syndrome," he said. "But back when I was a kid, Dad would say that Mom or I were 'exubing' for 'exuberance' when we were happy or excited. Pretty much everything else he just called our 'stink eye.'"

"Stink eye!" Pandora fairly exploded, her eyebrows flying upward—excessively—like a pair of startled birds. "I'm *doomed* . . . ," she wailed, letting her head sink so her hair curtained around it.

"The Botox people are calling it restless face syndrome," Roger went on, imagining more information might help. "The implication is it's like resting bitch face, but treatable, presumably through the miracle of botulism-facilitated facial paralysis."

Not that all sufferers actually *suffered* from the condition, Roger hastened to add when Pandora seemed amenable to the idea of having a deadly bacterium shot into her forehead.

"Take Jim Carrey," he said. "He's like the HEFS poster child. And he's monetized his affliction quite handsomely." Plus, there was Roger himself, who'd paired his HEFS with a sense of empathy that helped turn his face into a magnifying mirror of his clients' emotional states, creating a face people were bound to pour their hearts out to.

"Now *that's* a billable asset," he concluded, as well he might, being a therapist after all.

But Pandora was a girl, and her father's examples were all guys. And guys always got off easy when it came to looks. A guy could have a face that others found comical, or interesting, or hypersympathetic in a confession-eliciting kind of way. But for women, there were only two options, facewise: 1) somewhere on the spectrum between cute and gorgeous or 2) other. And Pandora's restless face put her squarely in the latter camp, one she could already see taking its place among those of the crazy bitches who got fed up and cut a bitch before going to prison to become some other crazy bitch's bitch—if *Orange Is the New Black* was any indicator.

"So," she said, finally, training a hyperserious eye on her father, "which am I?"

Roger aimed a hyperconfused expression back at hers. "Which what?"

"Which Jim Carrey?" she asked. "*Spotless Mind* or *Mask*?"

Her father did that teeter-totter thing with his hand and sucked in his lips, so much so that his mouth looked disturbingly like an anus.

"Somewhere in between?" she translated.

Her father nodded as Pandora's face slowly constricted ass-ward.

Pandora Lynch was more than her face; she was also scary smart, something her father had concluded not because of parental bias, but because of a series of IQ tests he'd given her throughout her life, providing Stanford-Binet-certified proof. It was because of her brain that Roger hadn't focused on the superficial covering she faced the world with. Her mind was what impressed him. And it was the hungriness of that mind that led to her first nickname: Dora the Implorer.

From the moment she could speak, Pandora wielded the word *why* like a lethal weapon. Why this? Why that? In this, she was like a lot of kids before their hopes and dreams were crushed. Whether his daughter's barrage of whys was actually excessive or only seemed that way because he lacked a partner to share answering duties with, Roger didn't know. His wife hadn't survived having their daughter, leaving Roger as sole parent. And so, instead of saying "Mama," a word most kids come to as a byproduct of suckling, Pandora had landed on what she'd heard her father say most often after his wife's passing—"Why?"—the crowbar word she used to learn all the rest.

Soon, his daughter's whys started sprouting other whys, branching and replicating, forming a fractal set of whys, looping self-referentially as she why'd her own why-ing until the victim of her curiosity lost it and shouted or got up and tried walking away, only to have his insistent inquirer wrap herself around his leg.

It was in self-defense, then, that Roger introduced his daughter to her first computer, a kid-proofed laptop, hermetically sealed in chunky pink plastic with rounded edges and ruggedized just shy of military field specifications to withstand being dropped from as high as a statistical kid in its recommended age range might drop it during the course of statistically ordinary use. He'd introduced her to it like it was another person—or billions, which it was—by cracking open its clamshell, booting it up, and clicking through to the Google homepage.

"Pandora," he said, doing the introductions, "I give you the world.

"World," he continued, "I give you my daughter, Pandora Lynch."

He showed her how to search with her voice, seeing as he hadn't taught the three-year-old to read yet. After that, he trusted Pandora to ask "the 'puter" all the questions she'd been asking him. The top answer usually spoke itself aloud, and by looking at the words on the screen as they spoke themselves, Pandora taught herself not only the answer to her questions, but also how to read by the time she reached four. Many happy years of surfing followed, Pandora collecting bread crumbs of information like Pac-Man gobbling up dots, content to end every day smarter than she'd started it, and eager for the next day to begin.

Her next day at school was worse. The curlers flanking her locker had decided to make her infamous. While one stood off to the side, smartphone at the ready, his accomplice approached her from behind with a printout from an anti-chewing-tobacco website, featuring a collage of jawless faces and metastatic gums.

"Hey, Emo," the accomplice said, slapping Pandora on the back, leaving the printout attached through the miracle of spray adhesive. Knowing something must be up, she reached around, tap-tapping until she hit the rattle of paper and pulled away a modern-day upgrade to the "Kick Me" sign. Bringing it around to where she could see it, Pandora reacted as planned, while the amateur videographer caught her face in all its uploadable glory.

Thus Pandora Lynch went from merely self-conscious teen to internet meme. After editing it to remove any trace of the setup, the pranksters provided the world with two formats: a GIF of Pandora's face going from nearly normal to Munch's *The Scream* in real time and a triptych of JPEGs—normal, transition, and money shot—ready to be captioned with variations of "*X* be like . . ." or "Me when I . . . ," while the GIF was used uncaptioned as a reacticon to whatever the latest political absurdity happened to be.

The trouble was, it was mesmerizing, watching it loop, over and over. Though it was her own face, even Pandora couldn't stop watching until—hypnotized by the repetition—she stopped seeing herself and started seeing this crazy woman the rest of the world was watching. The spell was such that looking away caused her to imagine the pock-pock of two popped corks—her eyes—being ripped out. A pretty miserable state of affairs for a cyber native—being stalked by her own face online—and a perfectly good cause for revenge.

By the time she turned seven, Pandora had learned an important lesson about the internet: its answers got better—or more interesting—once you got past the first page of search results. Because there was rarely just one answer to anything, and once you dispensed with expecting the answer to be correct, that's when the web bloomed, revealing worlds within worlds, some of them flat, others ruled by an assortment of dark forces, all of them hidden many pages deep. Which got her wondering once again: Why?

Why were computer searches arranged like that, and how did the computer know all this stuff? Her laptop was supposedly kid-proof, but who were they kidding? She googled "How do you take apart a computer?" and—no dummy—printed out the instructions before following them. By the time Roger returned from what he'd thought was a quick dash to the Safeway, he was greeted by the sight of his inquisitive daughter surrounded by a spray of Phillips-head screws, scattered key caps, a dead screen, a chip-dotted emerald-green motherboard, and the pink plastic clamshell, split open like an Easter egg.

"Pandora," he said, "what on earth . . . ?"

To which his daughter intoned the three-note trademark of a certain microprocessor manufacturer, followed by, "Look what I found inside!"

Roger was not amused. "You're not getting another one," he threatened, but who did he think he was kidding? Pandora put the old one back together, stopping just long enough for her father to fetch the fire extinguisher before plugging the power brick back in. "Stand back," he warned, eyeing the power button peripherally as he reached out and pushed it. The etherealized da-doo-da-doo of Windows Vista starting up chimed from the tinny speaker.

"Well, I'll be damned," he said—not a prediction, necessarily, but . . .

Back in business, the ever-curious child found curiouser and curiouser corners of cyberspace to investigate. Soon, Pandora discovered that the best the web had to offer couldn't be gotten at through Google or Bing or even, God help her, Yahoo! Nope. The most stimulating internet resources were found by going through The Onion Router (a.k.a. Tor), a one-time naval research project in online anonymity subsequently bequeathed to all manner of questionable humanity.

On the other side of that acronym, Pandora found conspiracy nuts and militarized free-speechers, illicit dealers and their buyers, freaks, fetishists, fringe dwellers, and the frankly disgusting. And she loved it all, the so-called dark web, not in spite of its creeps but because of them and what their presence implied: privacy.

With respect to that precious commodity, Pandora was already living the future by having none. Whether that lack was a feature of her life or a bug was hard to say but nevertheless the unavoidable byproduct of living in a cabin sans door, excepting the front and bathroom ones. Per Roger, interior doors were impediments to airflow and efficient heating. And so, in their place, cheaper and less airtight shower curtains would have to do, and did. It was this lack of privacy, in fact, that emboldened her to invade that of others, with the help of another interest she nurtured online: hacking.

She'd loved the idea of it before she ever did it, the way hacking made use of a skill set she'd been working on for as long as she could remember: the one-two punch of curiosity and coding. And once she got serious, Pandora found that a lot of the heavy lifting had already been done. The dark web provided whole libraries of precoded, hacker-approved hacks; customizable widgets; Trojan applets; documented exploits; and the code needed to exploit them. She found herself thinking in pseudocoding flowcharts, applying these to her ethical choices when it came to taking advantage of certain vulnerabilities, thinking she'd do *X* if *Y* occurred, one action collapsing the branching possibilities once she'd committed to it, and so on. Wondering if she should get parental permission before, say, hacking into the teleprompters at *Fox & Friends* with some choice passages from *Das Kapital*, Pandora would visualize a sideways diamond with "Ask Dad?" in the center, the "Yes" branching left, "No" branching right. And when "Yes" bottomed out in a string of *Zzzz*'s, the young hacktivist decided to take the path of parental ignorance, rumored to be the source of bliss, though whose was never specified.

2

It was a perfect day for sitting on a dock by the bay, and so that's what George Jedson (yeah, yeah, he knew) was doing, wasting time on a park bench overlooking the Golden Gate Bridge. He should have been in school but was on stakeout instead, waiting for a certain tech weenie who could usually be found at the pier around noon. George had often watched the target sit and sip at his to-go latte, watching the toy cars going to and fro across the bridge or the container ships passing underneath full of more Chinese crap for the masses.

George had first noticed the guy's badge while standing in line at one of San Fran's pop-up artisanal coffee places. The badge was chipped, laminated, and hung on a lanyard the wearer had flipped over his shoulder as he prepared to pay with his phone before making a big deal of stopping, then reaching into his jacket pocket to remove an actual wallet. "I'm feeling retro today," he announced to the inked-and-pierced barista before extracting a twenty for his anally specific latte, barely letting the change make skin contact before slipping it into the tip jar next to the register.

"Grazie," the barista said, in accordance with a recent corporate-policy memo.

The badge was the guy's way of broadcasting his importance outside the office, the iconic *Q* for the social-media giant Quire (pronounced "choir," as in "preaching to the . . .") clearly visible. In imitation of its CEO, this particular middle-managing Q-ling wore an outrageously plaid sports jacket shot through with greens going one way and purples another, the tartan of no known Scottish clan, but almost as iconic as the aforementioned *Q*, suggesting that its wearer was an aspirant who might occasionally come within the same faciotemporal space as the *actual* target. Recognizing the badge's significance, George downloaded the company's management chart while still waiting for his own order. And bingo, Mr. Plaid was well within three degrees of separation from the CEO of Quire. Suspicions confirmed, George proceeded to tail his subject outside.

But instead of heading to the nearest Q shuttle or calling an Uber, rather than slumming by cable car or godhelpus BART, the man-coat combo had headed to the dock where George now sat, waiting for the combo's circadian return.

That first time, George's man in the middle had just sat there on the bench, nursing his latte, watching seagulls dive-bombing out of the clear blue sky to snatch up some floating detritus or sweeping in toward the paved dock to forage among the trash receptacles there. The whole "real-world engagement" vibe the guy was sending was transparent at best. He was playing the role of "tech guy taking a tech break," which meant his two or three phones were set to vibrate in the pockets of the suit coat he'd draped over the back of the bench, his arm stretched so his hand, forearm, and elbow were in covert contact with each device, waiting for a haptic hum to give his life meaning again. The other dead giveaway was the wrist resting unnaturally on his knee, cuff hiked, keeping a chunky analog watch within eyeshot so he'd know the second it was okay to jack back into the world he was taking a break from.

But then, a catalyzing moment—the sort that turns a disparate group of strangers into something new: an audience. Entering from whichever curtain he'd been waiting behind, a greasily clad homeless man came into view, one sole slapping as he approached the railing with a bulging grocery bag—a locally illegal, plastic one—from which dripped what appeared to be blood. Watching as the man leaned over the rail, George rose slightly, not totally prepared to witness some homeless guy's suicide, but . . . only to settle back when he realized the man was pulling on a rope of braided yellow plastic that had gone unnoticed until the bum started reeling it in, great, dripping coils piling up on the pavement as he hauled away.

Eventually, the man reached the end of his rope, which was attached to a mossy green trap with assorted claws and insectile legs poking through the slats. Releasing a latch underneath, the greasy guy dumped out about a dozen crabs along with the half-eaten remains of a chicken carcass. This last was returned to the bay with a fling and a splash before being replaced with fresher bait from the bloody bag. Another, more labored fling and the trap disappeared as well, followed by rapidly unspooling coils of plastic rope.

The crabber then started sorting through his catch, deftly flipping shellfish onto their carapaces, the better to examine their worthiness, while preventing their skittering escape. All were deemed fit with the exception of one, which seemed to have lost a leg along the way and whose shell was cracked and oozing something that looked like guacamole. This one the crabber kicked aside like a hockey puck, albeit one with seven highly agitated legs trying to claw up the sky. Within seconds, the dock became an outtake from *The Birds* as seagulls swooped in from all quarters to descend on the helpless delicacy.

A lesbian couple engaged in some major PDA a few benches down turned disapprovingly at the sound before taking their love to some other part of town.

"It's just *nature*, ladies," the sports coat called at their retreating backs before reaching into a weighted pocket and removing a phone. He open-tweezed his fingers, zooming in before tapping a snap to document the carnage. "Dog eat dog," he continued, narrating aloud the keywords of his upcoming post. "Hashtag Darwin. Hashtag I will survive."

Well, George thought, *I guess we'll just have to see about that.*

Like a lot of his hacks, George did it to see if he could. The "it" in this case: the remote hijacking of a luxury EV owned by a certain CEO who'd been snapped stepping out of it at TechCrunch Disrupt, Davos, and the West Coast premiere of *Hamilton*. The car in question was the latest would-be Tesla killer, a limited edition called the Voltaire, a double-meaning moniker intended to conjure up both *electricity* and *environmental friendliness*, with faint echoes of the Enlightenment. George had gotten the VIN by hacking into the California Department of Motor Vehicles database. The attack itself would involve a cyber missile custom tuned to seek out personally identifiable information of the sort George had given it, shuttling back and forth across the global loom of wired and wireless interconnectivity, looking for a seventeen-digit go code to do the thing it was programmed to do, which in this case was taking over the vehicle's so-called "copilot mode" (a legal nicety to keep the owner responsible for any crashes that might occur during what was basically a live beta test of an autonomous vehicle). Once in, George would hijack the navigation system and have the vehicle deliver itself to an address of his choosing.

The hack itself didn't require a lot of original coding, not with all the drop-in script available out there. All he had to do was open a window; Ctrl-A, Ctrl-C, and then Ctrl-V the grab into his text editor; after which, a delete here, an insert there, new parameters for the conditionals, reassign a few variables, and voilà, he had custom-built malware ready for compiling. He'd started with the hackers' gift that kept giving, the Stuxnet worm, which had already bred a whole family of cyber weapons of mass destruction, from Stuxnet II, the Reckoning; to Son of Stuxnet; the Bride of Stuxnet; and It Takes Two to Stuxnet: This Time It's Personal.

A couple of white hats had already demonstrated that the data link connector for a car's onboard diagnostic system could be used as a back door into pretty much any subsystem on the vehicle's controller area network, allowing a hacker to turn on the air conditioning, blare the sound system, or even apply the brakes. The same researchers who'd exposed these vulnerabilities were quick to stress that a hacker would first have to gain "physical access" to the inside of the vehicle to do any of this (the implied warning: beware of valets with taped glasses). As press releases went, it was the typical mixed message about all the computers on cars nowadays, namely: "Worry, but don't worry. The hackers would have to jump through *so* many hoops . . ."

The only problem was—and George would be happy to point this out if anybody ever asked—hackers *live* to jump through hoops. Hoop jumping is, in fact, what makes hacking *interesting*. And physically plugging in to a car's data link was one way to get controller access, but there was also the infotainment system, the two-dollar hooker of Bluetooth devices; finding something to connect to was basically *its job*. Systems like, say, the driver's phone. And if that phone happened to have a Trojan horse that executed once its Bluetooth shook hands with the car's hands-free system . . .

George nicknamed this particular exploit the Big Blue Daisy Chain of Mass Destruction. All he had to do was get within Bluetooth range of a smartphone that might in turn get within range of the smartphone belonging to a certain CEO and proud owner of a midlife-crisis EV that came with copilot mode already installed.

So George trailed his latte-liking, barista-flirting, middle-aged, middle-managing cyber weenie from latte assembly line to the dockside park bench, day after day, getting his pattern down, looking for an opportunity when he finally decided to just walk right into the guy while staring at his phone.

"Excuse me," George apologized, blotting at a puff of escaped milk foam.

"You almost made me *drop* my *phone*," the guy who'd dropped his latte prioritized.

"I *said* I was sorry."

"You need to watch where you're going," George's target continued. "Whatever Pokémon you were hunting can wait. What if I wasn't here to run interference and you had tripped over that railing?"

"I guess I owe you my life, then."

"Well, I wouldn't go that—"

"Nope," George continued. "You saved my life. Now you're responsible for me. What's your last name? I'll change mine. Mind if I call you *Dad*?"

"You're crazy," the target said, backing away.

"Crazy for feeling like this." Pause. "Why are you running away? Dad! Stop, Dad. *Please* . . ."

And there it went, George's Trojan horse riding in the pocket of the sports coat, an exquisite bit of code ready to hop from phone to phone and up the org chart until it found its true target and waited for him to call his private jet from his car and . . .

Bingo.

As tech giants go, V.T. Lemming, founder and CEO of Quire Inc., was a late bloomer. While he claimed to be a contemporary of Steve Jobs—he'd tripped and head-butted the future father of the iPhone at a Home Brew Computer Club meeting when V.T. was only ten—the younger man seemed to lack Jobs's luck and timing. Pretty much everything he came up with for years was an inferior copycat product as likely to crash a person's system as function as advertised. And so his spreadsheet software could only add and subtract columns of figures—the key functions business owners would want in such a product, he'd assured himself. A poor man's PowerPoint that couldn't handle graphics or animation. A web browser that seemed to actually prioritize infected or malicious sites. A media player that wouldn't work with pirated content.

And then the Wireless Application Protocol (WAP) was introduced by a consortium of cell phone manufacturers, allowing mobile devices to connect to the internet and developers to sell games over the air, thus laying the groundwork for Google Play and the App Store that would come several years later. Having soured on the Windows and Mac operating systems by this time, V.T. gave WAP a look and was reminded of the simpler eight-bit computers of his youth. Mixing nostalgia with practicality (fewer lines of code meant less time investment between failures), the not-getting-any-younger programmer proceeded to work his way through a series of betas and misfires until he'd become thoroughly disgusted with the entire tech industry. Resolving to ball up his contempt into one ridiculously pointless game, V.T. decided on an homage to a popular electronic pet of a few years prior known as the Tamagotchi, which in its Americanized and cellular incarnation became *My Hippo*. A textbook example of truth in advertising, *My Hippo* consisted of nothing more than a hippo standing incongruously in front of an old barn. Users could spend real money to buy their hippo fake stuff—a straw hat, a stalk of grass to munch from the corner of its mouth, a polka dot skirt or leather biker jacket (the gender of the hippo was said to be "proprietary" and was never divulged). The only movement in the entire—it was hard to call it a game, per se—*thing* was the briefest grin from "your hippo" when you bought it stuff. And true to H.L. Mencken's dictum that no one ever went broke underestimating the intelligence of the American people, *My Hippo* proceeded to do exactly what he had assumed—maybe even hoped—it wouldn't: it made money.

And that was how *a* V.T. Lemming became *the* V.T. Lemming, something the parents who named him Vladimir Thaddeus would never have imagined. Their goal at the time had been to offset the suicidal baggage packed into the family name. Or as his father, John Lemming, predicted, "The kids'll be so busy trying to figure out what to do with 'Vladimir Thaddeus' they'll never make it to 'Lemming'"—a nice thought that (predictably) fell short of reality.

Quire was V.T.'s second act for which he could claim no creative input except for having enough money to buy a start-up originally named Pulp!t (pronounced "pulpit"). The platform had potential, he thought, falling as it did between the newly popular site known as Myspace and Facebook before it dropped the *the*.

Though younger than either, V.T. Lemming had joined Steve Jobs and Bill Gates in the troika of Silicon Valley's elders—the ones the industry pointed to whenever accusations of ageism were lobbed by critics who (it was not-so-secretly assumed) probably believed the internet was kept alive by elves pushing shopping carts full of vacuum tubes. V.T. even showed up—not entirely willingly—on the March 2007 cover of AARP's magazine next to the words *Gray Matters*, when he was still in his early forties.

More than a decade had passed since that cover story, making what happened even more impressive. Because while George had imagined his hack going a number of ways, he hadn't counted on V.T., now in his early fifties, coming along for the ride.

The Voltaire had been circling City Lights Bookstore autonomously for a half hour, sparing its billionaire owner the cost of parking while he shopped publicly for poetry. It was his PR people's idea to dispel rumors that V.T. had actually died and been replaced by a robotic double. Something by Bukowski, they thought, to guard against seeming effete while at the same time lending a certain aura of grit and danger to his public persona.

They needn't have bothered. Because as V.T. reached for the door handle of his idling ride, George's daisy-chain hack completed its last link, all the doors thunked shut, and the Voltaire pulled away from the curb and back into the flow of traffic.

George could hear V.T. swearing through the phone he'd activated remotely. He planned on uploading the audio and (fingers crossed) video once the CEO removed the phone from his pocket to report a runaway EV. But then the swearing became panting. George brought up thumbnails of the video feeds from several security cams in the area. The old man was running after the car. Even more amazingly, he caught it—though its stopping for a traffic light helped.

And now—no, yes, shit—he was crawling onto the hood! Banging on the windshield? Yeah, that'll help. No, wait, *not* banging. V.T. was placing his hands strategically, in various locations on the glass, perhaps trying to block whatever sensors or telemetry the navigation system was relying on. A decent thought, though ultimately unsuccessful, as the car started up again once the light changed, and the CEO of Quire almost rolled off into traffic.

Almost—but didn't. Instead, he dug both hands into the well between windshield and hood where the wipers hid until needed.

More swearing, more holding on for dear life, more hacked security and traffic cams activated as the Voltaire-plus-CEO prepared to cross the Bay Bridge while George sat miles away at a public-library computer, monitoring, prepared to shut the stunt down if it looked like he was about to endanger the public. By the time the Voltaire made it to the middle of the bridge, George was able to dispense with the hijacked cams in favor of streaming the helicopter feed going out live to all the local television stations, thanks to the celebrity of the passenger he'd acquired for his little joyride.

The original plan had been for the car to drive itself to the library George had been surreptitiously living in since running away from foster care. He wasn't planning to steal it, per se. He'd promised himself one ride in V.T.'s midlife crisis, after which he'd abandon it to the resourcefulness of the local, vengeful capitalists. That plan was no longer viable—not with traffic copters and highway patrol in pursuit.

And so George cut to the chase—so to speak—and drove the Voltaire straight to where he planned to dump it, taking I-80 to 880 south toward San Jose and the airport. Hopping off at the High Street exit, George piloted the hijacked auto and its impromptu hood ornament to Alameda Avenue and the Oakland Home Depot parking lot. The original plan was to do this sometime after closing—around midnight, say. Instead George found himself bringing the vehicle to a stop under the chop of helicopter rotors and the shouts of highway patrol officers demanding that the driver who wasn't there exit with hands up. All this in the bright California sun, on live TV, already being remixed and mashed up and posted all over the world.

Why George did it was a fair question. And the answer? George knew what he'd say his motive was if he ever got caught: a smile. Sure, he could have liquidated the vehicle; he could definitely use the money, being short of cash ever since leaving the foster care system a few years ahead of schedule. But George needed the smiles more than money. He needed them to neutralize the poison in the air everywhere he went nowadays—online, especially, but in real life too. That's what he'd say if he ever got caught, that the world had become so angry. It had been angry before but had gotten even worse since Russian hackers and sensationalism-seeking algorithms turned everything up to eleven. And George, a foster kid, had done time at both ends of the political spectrum, eating breakfast to *Fox & Friends* in one house, doing dinner with Rachel Maddow in another, neither meal sitting well on a stomach that felt like battery acid had been absorbed into it by osmosis.

He'd seen a series of bumper stickers on the minivan of the fosters he ran away from. "Coexist," one sticker had said, spelled out in the range of religious icons, next to another that advised him to "Practice Random Acts of Senseless Kindness." He'd had hope—for a second. But then his new family handed him a razor blade to scrape the stickers off. Turns out George wasn't the only secondhand thing they'd recently acquired.

So yeah, smiles. That's what he'd say. Little facial breaks from the general zeitgeist; that's why he'd done it. That they came at the expense of one very *unsmiling* CEO, well, that was the funny thing about rich people: their smiles and the smiles of everyone else were inversely correlated, a tragedy for one being pure comedy for the others.

3

Pandora's first idea was to beat the crap out of the boys who'd memed her—but she was concerned their balls would prove too tempting a target. It wasn't that she had any qualms about fighting dirty or below the belt—that was Asymmetrical Warfare 101—but the knee-balls combo was such a cliché, and she prided herself for thinking outside the box. Her means of revenge, she thought, should reflect who she was as a person—but not so much so that the CSI people could trace it back to her.

Pandora decided to avoid anything overtly computer related, for fear that would point back to her. Not that she advertised her hacking chops, but her dad's job did, what with the satellite dish outside their cabin and the fact that the Lynches were cybercitizens way before almost anyone else in Fairbanks. Add that she'd already been pulled from class twice to perform pro bono IT consulting in the principal's office and it was pretty clear that they had her number. It was a shame, too, because there were a few exploits that would have been fun.

For example, she could have easily gotten into the school's computer, which was still running an unpatched version of Windows XP. Not only that, but the student database was unencrypted, and not even a real database, but an Excel spreadsheet with the original .xlx extension, meaning they hadn't upgraded their Office suite since 2007. All she'd have to do was change the culprits' grades to Fs. Except when she looked at what they'd managed without her help (D pluses, a C minus), the incremental change hardly seemed worth it.

She could mess with their coach, she guessed. He had a pacemaker that could be updated over the air, installed—he liked to brag—"factory new" by a crack cardio team in Seattle. "Over the air" meant wireless, which meant it was an inadequately secured IoT device, like a smart thermostat or baby monitor, but surgically implanted in the guy's chest. She could make his heart skip a beat or overclock the regulating mechanism so that he hiccupped uncontrollably.

But it wasn't the coach who'd humiliated her; the closest he came was not teaching his young charges to act like human beings. Plus, there was always the risk he'd wind up dying, which would be murder, so there was that.

Not that hacking was exclusively about computers; it was a way of looking at the world. You hacked by viewing everything a bit off center, peripherally, looking for what everybody else *wasn't* seeing. And what was she looking for? Holes, exploits, hot buttons, unexamined assumptions, dropped guards.

The breakthrough came during sex ed and brought her full circle to that thing her adversaries could be trusted to cherish above all: their balls—or thereabouts. She wouldn't be using her knee, though; she'd be using chemistry, and their expectation of privacy. In sex ed, they'd been getting the scared-abstinent lesson plan, and Pandora had noticed a theme when it came to STI symptoms: "A burning sensation while urinating."

After seeing the same phrasing come up for the third time in a row, Pandora thought, *I'd like to give 'em a burning sensation when they pee . . .*

And thus the idea for her revenge took shape. Like Newton and his apple, like Archimedes and his bath—like Jobs and Gates walking out of Xerox PARC with a fortune in other people's ideas—Pandora had found her inspiration. She was so pleased with herself she had to dip her head so her hair would hide her smile—the one otherwise visible by satellite, or so she'd heard.

In retrospect, she could see how her revenge might be mistaken for an act of terrorism. There'd been flames and bodily injuries, after all. Not that she intended to hurt anyone, just scare them is all. But that was splitting hairs and not entirely honest. The truth was, once you've committed to blowing up urinals, you already bought into whatever collateral damage comes with it.

The plan's ingredients were beyond simple: empty gel caps and pure sodium. She thought about stealing the latter from the school's chem lab but decided she didn't want to get her science teacher, Mr. Vlasic, in trouble. Apparently, ever since *Breaking Bad*, science teachers all over the United States were viewed with suspicion—a status they'd enjoyed since the Scopes Monkey Trial, truth be told. And so, crossing her fingers, Pandora checked eBay: yep, she could get more than enough sodium from a chemical supply company for around sixty-five bucks. And seeing as she was online anyway: yep, gel caps too. She got tracking numbers on both so she could get to the packages before her dad did. And that was that: Project Burning Sensation was a go. So to speak.

The sodium arrived in the form of grayish metal ingots packed in mineral oil to keep them from reacting with the air. Though metallic, the bullet-sized lumps were soft and could be cut to the desired size with a pocket knife, albeit carefully. Sodium with the same purity as, say, Ivory soap will react with anything, including water, in which it literally burns. Even packed in mineral oil, Pandora's samples had a chalky patina of oxidation, which worked in her favor by ensuring the stuff didn't explode while she packed curls of it into her empty gel caps.

Once she'd collected a decent supply, all that remained was sneaking the caps into the boys' bathroom and then waiting for the gelatin to dissolve under a steady stream of recycled Gatorade. It helped that whether it was the boys' hockey or curling team, once they left the ice, they could be counted on to hit the nearest restroom en masse, usually joking about which favored anatomical part they'd nearly lost to the cold and/or comparing their pending urinary performance to that of a racehorse. Pandora would time her deposit to coincide with the freshman curling team's search for relief, then loiter with smartphone in hand, waiting for the fireworks to begin.

"You boys pissed off the wrong girl," she'd say, recording as they fled and tripped, pants spotted, unbuckled, or both, her zoom reserved for the troublesome two who had wronged her. See how they like being famous for a while.

A janitor had set out his yellow plastic easel, closing the boys' bathroom so he could clean it. Ever since her face went viral, Pandora had grown accustomed to hiding it, and so she did now, along with the rest of her, standing off to one side in the shadows, waiting for the clack of the easel being folded back up, her cue for action. She was prepared to deposit three, four caps per urinal for the dozen or so she figured there must be, judging from the line disparity between the men's and women's bathrooms after a feature ended at the Regal Goldstream downtown. Once inside, however, Pandora was shocked to find a mere four spots, a third of what she'd expected. She was also surprised to see there weren't any partitions separating the urinals, making her wonder just what sorts of savages she was dealing with—not that she had time to figure that out, not with the sound of the frosh curling team already clomping up the hallway. Hastily dumping a handful of caps per pisser, Pandora darted out again just in time.

Back in the safety of shadow, Pandora wondered if her miscalculation was due to factors she wouldn't have thought to consider. Was standing instead of sitting *that* much faster? Maybe guys were motivated to pee quickly, standing shoulder to shoulder with nothing to shield them from looky-loos on either side. Or maybe the urinals were gratuitous because everybody's bladder got shy and they just held it until they got home. That last one could be a problem; her plan didn't work without plenty of fluid to kick off the chemistry.

What she hadn't counted on was anyone's pants catching fire. And while she'd figured on screams of panic, she'd not counted on the screams of pain. She'd also not factored in the first escapee slipping in a puddle of his own pee, creating a dog pile of dudes tripping over him, followed by still others rushing to bust out the fire extinguisher to save what they could of the Human Torch's manhood. She hadn't counted on the fire alarm going off, or the sprinklers going on, which set off the remaining gel caps while the entire drenched student body had to evacuate—in Fairbanks, in early October, on a day when the temperature was below freezing. In the general rush, she'd forgotten to deliver and record her badass piss-off speech, which was probably for the best, listening to what her shivering classmates had to say about the unlikelihood of the responsible party living for very much longer.

Roger Lynch was screening a client on Skype when his pocket buzzed. Trying not to be obvious, he watched the thumbnail image of himself as he tweezed the phone out from his pocket and checked one screen while simulating attention to the other. Nods. Mmm-hmmms. All of which was for naught when he noticed it was a text alert from Pandora's school, warning of a "possible terrorism-related incident" while assuring all parents (excluding those of the boy who'd been rushed to the ER, not for genital immolation but because he was having a panic attack) that their children—though chilled—were safe, sound, and available for collection.

"Sorry," Roger blurted. "Family emergency. Gotta cut this short . . ."

"But," his client began, because that was the kind he specialized in, self-involved techies phoning it in from their offices or cubes at Quire headquarters, all convinced they'd lucked into the perfect therapeutic arrangement, with a therapist they'd never meet IRL, who was just a Skype call away and could be turned off when things got too heavy.

"Sorry," Roger said again, feeling a malpractice suit even as he prepared to click off, before clicking off anyway.

Unplugging his F-150's underhood heater from the garage outlet and checking his mirrors, Roger backed out of the drive, tires squeaking over bone-dry snow, all the while wondering why a terrorist would pick Fairbanks. New York, he could see; LA, sure; hell, Muncie, for Pete's sake, but *Alaska*? Did ISIS or whoever have such a surplus of suicide bombers they could piss them away on a part of America many Americans weren't thoroughly convinced was actually part of their country?

Not that the text said anything about suicide bombers. Or bombs of any sort. It had even waffled on it being terrorism, qualifying it fore ("possible") and aft ("-related"). Not that any of those quibbles mattered, not when it concerned his daughter.

Joining the chugging fleet of worried parents in all manner of assault vehicles, Roger noticed several official-looking, parkaed individuals in helmets and dark glasses, their bulletproof vests buckled up over a puffy inch or so of down. The FPD's SWAT team, judging from the huge letters emblazoned across the back of each vest. Who knew Fairbanks had such a thing? That Homeland Security money had to be flowing pretty indiscriminately ever since you-know-who pulled off you-know-what. One of the SWAT team members had a dog that didn't seem to be taking its job as seriously as the guy holding its leash, deigning to be petted by the students milling around, good-boy-ing it, all chugging in the cold afternoon air.

Roger spotted his daughter in the crowd, hiding behind her hair, which was rimmed with frost from having been sprinkled before being forced to evacuate. Her thin arms were crossed over her chest as she shivered, being among the unlucky ones who hadn't managed to snag their parkas on the way out the door. Though he couldn't see her face, he could imagine her expression: it'd be reminiscent of the one she'd tried out after her first period when Roger had had to tell her that no, this wasn't a one-and-done situation.

But he was wrong. As he opened the passenger door and she hefted herself inside, her hair fell away for a moment, revealing not anxious confusion, ennui-infused dismay, or even plain ol' exasperation, but—strangely—guilt, amplified by the facial animation they shared.

"What's up, bedbug?" he asked, knowing what the answer would be.

"Nothing," Pandora said, following the predictable script.

"Looks like something to me."

"Looks can be deceiving," his daughter said—an answer she'd gotten from him on many occasions, seeing as the difference between text and subtext was how he made his living.

"Nice try," he said, seeing as the difference between text and subtext was crap, given the faces they'd been born with.

"Ditto," Pandora said back before settling in behind her thawing hair for the long, silent ride back home.

Roger only got a glimpse of her guilty mug before Pandora rang down the curtain, but it was enough to trouble him. What could she possibly feel guilty about when it came to a "possible terrorism-related" situation? Had she seen something but not said something? Or did the shock get her face muscles confused? Pulling into the garage, he prepared to take another stab at finding out what was behind that troubling face.

But alas, no. Pandora yanked up the handle, hopped down, slammed the door, and disappeared into the house.

Roger took a parental pause before following her, collecting and categorizing his concerns. But then he discovered evidence of how upset his daughter must be: her phone. He couldn't miss it in its pirate Hello Kitty case. In her rush to escape, she'd left it behind. Roger picked it up, swiped, and was amazed when he wasn't asked for credentials of some kind—an iris scan, at the very least. But no. It opened onto her home screen, where it seemed she had two email messages waiting.

He could feel the charges of emotional abuse coming even as he tapped the icon. But what else was he supposed to do? He needed to get to the bottom of this before the FPD SWAT team paid them a visit.

The first email was from a compounding pharmacy and the second from a chemical supply company. Both pleaded with his daughter to rate her recent transactions with them, or to let them know if she was dissatisfied in any way. "Please like us on Facebook," they begged, following the usual supplicant boilerplate, "and preach about us on Quire!"

Roger switched off the phone and pocketed it. He plugged in his truck's heater and then entered the house he'd shared with his only child ever since they abandoned California, where she'd been born and her mother had died. He took a breath and steadied his voice and face.

"Oh, daughter," he called. "Oh, daughter dear . . ."

4

First things first: George's mother should have found a better babysitter. Not that Uncle Jack was a kiddie diddler or anything, just a bachelor who had his own place and the bad luck to be in the recreational marijuana business before it was legal in California. He also had nearly zero understanding of what to do with a young child left in his care. Summing up, this is what Uncle Jack knew about kids: there was something in their brains that drew them to jangling keys. He figured it had something to do with the combination of sound and shiny. And this was something else he knew: when it came to sound and shiny, you couldn't beat the star gate sequence from *2001: A Space Odyssey*. Uncle Jack himself had experienced the sequence's mesmerizing effects many times, often while stoned. Accused of violating the drug dealer's first rule—don't get high on your own supply—Uncle Jack would plead, "Quality control." And the quality of his product was excellent, if he did say so himself.

So yeah: a drug dealer *and* user. George's mom was not going down in the history of exemplary childcare decision makers anytime soon.

After fishing the disk out of its clamshell and sliding it into the player, Jack parked the child next to him on the couch and sparked up a bong, the skunk smell and gentle bubbling pacifying George while his uncle blip-blip-blipped through the menu to cue up the sequence in question. Jack assumed his nephew, a toddler, wouldn't sit still for the so-called boring parts. So they started watching the movie at its most mind-boggling, endorphin-stimulating point, and once it was done—once the sole surviving astronaut found himself in a Louis XVI hotel room—he was prepared to jump back to start those Kubrickian keys jangling again.

But then a strange thing happened—or *didn't* happen.

George didn't fuss. He didn't move, in fact. Looking down at his nephew's eyes through his own glassy pair, Uncle Jack saw two tiny versions of the bigger screen in front of them, Cinerama rectangles of nearly pure white and, underneath them, George's mouth, an O of awe with little-kid drool leaking out.

"So, like, you're cool with letting the narrative flow?" he asked. George continued to stare, which Jack took as meaning, "Flow on, dude."

George watched, wide-eyed, his brain imprinting with the choreographed images of a solitary human leapfrogging in jump cuts from vital adult to old then older man and, finally, to a flare of pure light followed by a face that looked a lot like George's own, a pudgy-smooth baby's face, which he'd been shown in a mirror, equally wide-eyed and glowing around the edges in a way that suggested edges—where some things stopped and others began—were not as sharp as they'd appeared before these lights and sounds came flowing into and over him.

"Okay," Uncle Jack announced, reaching for the remote as he debated ejecting versus cuing up star gate again, "*that* was interesting," when he noticed his nephew, still transfixed. So he gave it a shot and started the movie from the beginning, his nephew taking it all in, the ape men, the monolith, the waltzes and measured breathing, up until the scene in which the computer HAL is lobotomized amid scarlet-drenched lights and shadows. And as HAL began singing slowly about Daisy and a bicycle built for two, George turned to his stoned and red-eyed uncle.

"I sad," he said.

"Well," his uncle said, "it's a sad part."

Indeed, it was, and within some subliminal part of George's own still-plastic brain, a resolve formed to do something to undo the sadness, whatever that might mean.

"I apologize," George's uncle said, returning the child to his sister.

"Why?"

"I think I may have broken it," he said. "I'll start the trust fund for therapy tomorrow."

"Jocko, you're going to have to explain."

And so he did. Afterward: "Could you maybe not smoke around him?" George's mother asked.

Uncle Jack considered this a reasonable request, especially since, well, how was she supposed to know whether he did or not? That's what Glade was for. And about using a bona fide science-fiction masterpiece as a babysitter? What about that part? That's when George's mom went with the mantra of harried single mothers everywhere: "Whatever works, Jocko," she said, "is fine by me."

And thus the future became their routine—George's and Uncle Jack's—with the latter alluding to the movie when, say, his nephew's pod bay door was refusing entrance to some forked or spooned veggie. "C'mon," he'd say, "don't make me blow the hatch," while George, his little arms folded, shook his head. Other times the threat was to deactivate the red-and-yellow nightlight purchased for sleepovers, its allusive gaze comforting for the weird little boy destined to become a coder's coder in a future destined to feel like a rerun.

There was another reason it wasn't a good idea leaving George with his weed-smoking-and-dealing uncle: George's real name was Jorge, Uncle

Jack was really Tío Juan, and of the three of them, George/Jorge was the only one in the United States legally, seeing as he'd been born there. Not that it was ICE agents who came to Tío Juan's door one morning while HAL was being lobotomized again; no, that was a joint (snicker) task force including DEA and ATF agents, the latter included because the first two letters of its bureaucratic acronym were major competitors of the illicit substance the soon-to-be apprehended perp was peddling to the detriment of local Angelenos.

"Crap, he's got a kid," the guy holding the battering ram said, framed in the splintered frame of the doorway he'd bashed in.

"Is that *2001*?" another agent asked.

"You know Kubrick?" Uncle Jack asked.

"Not personally," the agent said, "but I admire his work."

"Dude," Uncle Jack said, offering the agent a brotherhood toke of the joint he'd been planning to Glade over before getting busted by his big sis. *In retrospect*—Jack would later think—*if only . . .*

Spinning his uncle around, the agents cuffed Jack right in front of his nephew, forming a mini memory that would seem like déjà vu years later, when George found his own wrists being cinched together.

"What do we do about . . . ?" the battering ram agent asked, pointing at the child while HAL sang plaintively in the background.

"He yours?" the fellow Kubrick admirer asked.

The boy's uncle shook his head. "Sister's."

"Number?"

He gave it.

And *that's* when ICE got involved.

George's mom, Margarita (or Marge, like Marge Simpson, how American was *that*?), had no idea of the difference between her and George's immigration status back when she'd become pregnant with him. Before confessing to her parents, her biggest concerns were being unmarried and the fact that her baby's biological father disappeared upon hearing the news. And so she anticipated a lot of grief for confessing her condition. What she didn't expect from her parents was a confession of their own, provided with no little sense of relief.

"Finally," her father had said, "a Garza who won't have to look over his shoulder."

"Excuse me?"

So out came the story Margarita had lived through but hadn't remembered, the one that explained why they all had at-home names and out-there names. And as her parents told it, it explained a lot more, including her visceral reaction to the story of the Christmas nativity, how she always felt tears welling when she heard the words "no room at the inn" and imagined Mary and Joseph trudging through the sand, ratty sandaled, holey clothes flapping as they moved from place to place, denied entry again and again, until they finally took shelter with the animals they were being treated like, mankind as usual ignorant of the miraculous in its midst. She imagined that trek again now—with herself a three-year-old Y between her parents, one of her hands for each, their triptych of footprints unwinding behind them in the sifting, shifting sand—imagined now as the top half on an hourglass that had been running out of time all along with the exception that Marge, a.k.a. Margarita, could finally feel the downward tug of her world funneling away from her.

"What's going to happen to us?" she'd asked. "What's going to happen to my baby?" she added, a hand on her belly, where the computer hacker growing inside her had kicked a good one.

"Nothing," her parents said together, as if they'd practiced. "We've been good. We haven't broken any laws," her dad continued.

"Except," her mother interjected, only for her husband to wave it away.

"They need our kind," her father said. "They've needed us ever since the Civil War went the way it did. Cheap labor is always welcome; the rest is BS the politicians run on until they get into office and forget us once again."

"Your father's right, *mija*," her mother said.

"Just don't kill people or steal anything. Pay your social security like it's rent and won't come back to you. And know that that little *bebé* in your belly is your safety net."

"How so?" the child with a child asked, still feathering the globe of her stomach with her fingertips.

"Only a monster would separate a mother from her child," her own mother said. "And Americans aren't monsters. Your own child will be an American." She paused, smiled. "Our *grandchild* will be one," she added.

After his birth, a nurse asked for a name—her baby boy's name—and the one thing Margarita Garza wouldn't give them was Jorge's real name, first or last. She'd been spooked by her parents' revelation re: her immigration status, and while her son's citizenship wasn't in question, still, she thought it safer giving him a nice American name on his birth certificate. But what should it be? The TV across from her hospital bed provided the answer. It was tuned to Cartoon Network, which was running a *Jetsons* marathon. She'd been hearing the opening theme all morning, including its roster of introductions to the show's main characters. It was the first name on that oft-repeated list that now resonated for the new mother.

"George," she said, paused, then added, "Jedson." She didn't want to be overly obvious about her source material. She needn't have worried. The nurse looking at the TV over her shoulder had been hearing the same earworm all morning until any connection between it and the real world had blurred beyond caring.

Once the drugs she'd been given to ease the pain of delivery wore off, Margarita wondered what had made her tempt fate by giving her son such a cartoonish pseudonym. But as the days passed, then weeks, then months and years without a knock from immigration, she was sure they were safe. She had no way of knowing that fate was playing the long game.

If our names are our destinies, then George's alias was aptly chosen. Because even though his mother didn't know it at the time, her son's life would be tinged with nostalgia for the future, in the sense of everything old being new again, where history and politics rode the grand pendulum of time, swinging back and forth, left then right . . .

And so, when his life was ruined, it was the result of an old racism that would become new again, later, when George was a teenager. At the time of his uncle's arrest and his mother's subsequent deportation, so-called "good immigrants" were rarely kicked out, and separating immigrant parents from their American-born children was rarer still. But the immigration judge who got the case was two generations away from her own family's having sought asylum in the US. In a classic case of I-got-mine-now-get-lost, the judge—a future Supreme Court contender—had decided to burnish her anti-immigration credentials using George and his mother. The fact that there was a drug element involved made the case all but irresistible, while the inclusion of a five-year-old child proved that even though the judge was a woman, her heart didn't bleed. And so while his mother was sent back to a country that she had little memory of, Uncle Jack was handed the equivalent of a death sentence by being incarcerated along with members of the same cartel that had once been his supplier. And Jorge a.k.a. George was sent to live with strangers, his only remaining family, Gamma and Pop Pop Garza, long dead thanks to a faulty carbon monoxide detector.

By the time he'd gone through three sets of fosters, George had stopped believing in property. Because along with learning about the arbitrary and impermanent nature of laws, he also discovered that under those laws, he was little more than property himself, hence the use of owner-related terms like, say, *custody*. As far as he was concerned, it was "the state" that turned him into a socialist by sentencing him to a world of group homes, time-share parents, and possessions that weren't even rent-to-own, but rent-to-keep-on-renting, his life another hand-me-down from a string of fosters working a side hustle to make ends meet.

It was this, along with his lingering fondness for a homicidal supercomputer, that made George the vigilante hacker he became. Believing that information wanted to be free and that the whole idea of "intellectual property" was something to be resisted and subverted, he set about doing exactly that. Run a hundred-dollar textbook through a high-speed scanner and post it online free? Sure, why not? Steal some rich guy's Voltaire and recycle it into the local economy as a down payment on the whole income inequality thing? Ditto, especially after he got what he really wanted from the hack, which was a smile, sure, but also a look at some proprietary source code that might benefit from being set free.

5

Presented with the evidence from her phone, Pandora confessed—or her face did, followed by actual words from her brain to fill in the gaps. She'd shown Roger what they'd done to her, googling the words *face girl*, *viral*, and *GIF*.

"So I've been living with an internet celebrity," he said. "I had no idea."

And it was true. Though he made his living online, he'd vowed not to live there when he wasn't with a client. "It's too easy to get abducted by aliens in cyberspace," he'd say, meaning it was a good way to lose time.

"So you see I had to, right?" Pandora said.

"I see why you *wanted* to," Roger said back. "But you know what I always say when you need to make a decision, right?"

Pandora did. She'd been deciding things ever since she could, and her father had been dispensing the same pearl of wisdom all that time. Granted, as pearls of wisdom went, it wasn't half-bad—except for its always being thrown in her face whenever she'd decided poorly.

"Before you do something questionable," Roger continued, as he had countless times before, "ask yourself, 'What if *everybody* did what I'm about to do?'"

Exempli gratia, Pandora thought on her father's behalf, *what if* everybody *set fire to a bunch of urinals?*

I guess that would mean, she thought on her own behalf, *guys would have to wait as long as girls to take a leak.*

She didn't say any of that, of course. Not in real life. Had they been having this conversation online, she'd have posted it without giving it a second thought. Learning to second-think things was one of the reasons Roger had sent her to high school in the first place. Or as he put it at the time, "It's harder to tell someone to f-off face-to-face than it is on Facebook." He'd conveniently left out important facts about the face she'd be facing people with as part of that particular conversation.

"Guess I wasn't thinking," Pandora said now, using her best sitcom-kid voice. "I feel like such a knucklehead . . ." She imagined the *wa-wa* sitcom soundtrack.

But Roger wasn't in the mood. His daughter had caused her school to be evacuated and the SWAT team (such as it was) to be mobilized. He struggled to come up with a media-friendly allusion to sum up the seriousness of the situation.

"I know how it went," he said. "You got an idea in your head; wondered, 'What if . . .'; but then you got so caught up with whether it *could* be done that you never stopped to think about whether it *should* be done."

"Isn't that . . . ?"

"Jeff Goldblum? *Jurassic Park*?" Roger said. "Yes. A paraphrase, but apt, I think."

"What if I promise not to resurrect any extinct species?" Pandora said.

"You're not joking your way out of this one." Pausing for gravitas, Roger cupped his mouth in contemplation before taking his hand away to reveal an evil eureka smile, letting her know how much he loved how much she was going to hate this. But then he kept standing there, smiling, forcing her to ask.

"Well," she finally said, breaking.

"When was the last time you visited your grandmother?" he asked.

Roger's mother, Gladys Lynch, became a widow before her granddaughter had her first period and hadn't been visited by either of her surviving relatives since they had left the mausoleum where her husband's ashes were interred behind marble and brass. When his father was still alive, Roger and his daughter had visited his parents all the time. But even then, the visits were largely about seeing the old man, a WWII vet who'd worked in the signal corps for the navy and wound up in Alaska with a cabin full of cool ham-radio gear, plenty of funny war stories, and a two-seater single-prop airplane he took his granddaughter flying in, to remind her of her potential.

"It's not only Fairbanks," he'd shouted over the engine and wind. "There's a whole planet down there . . ."

Pandora had nodded, the rushing wind ripping at her smile, making it even broader than usual, while her auburn hair flagged like fire blown sideways.

Not that the old lady was some ogre; she was just ignorable. She'd been a mom and housewife most of her life, and prior to that, who knew? More importantly, who cared? What Roger knew of his mother's past prior to meeting his father was that she'd apparently had shock treatment before heading north and it had apparently helped. That, and the fact that they'd delayed having children until the last minute, biological-clock-wise—something to do with not wanting to bring new life into the Cold War world after the way the hot war ended.

The rift between Roger and his mom started when he was thousands of miles away, in California, trying to start a psychiatry practice and a family, in that order, flirting with the same biological snooze-alarm situation his parents had faced before deciding to become parents. It was while he was away that Gladys got strange, perhaps so gradually that his father hadn't noticed, but Roger sure did, coming back to it after years away, once his wife had died and he'd returned to Alaska to raise his daughter.

His mother had nearly died in the interim, thanks to a misprescribed antibiotic that wound up killing off all the good bacteria in her intestines. This, in turn, led to a domino effect of subsequent symptoms, including diarrhea and dehydration severe enough to warrant hospitalization. She was never the same after that, developing a whole host of phobias about doctors and the digestive process, leading to self-diagnoses of lactose intolerance, an allergy to gluten, irritable bowel syndrome, and an inability to digest red meat. Individual items and then whole food groups were banned from their dinner table, her husband going along with each new culinary exile because while he had the gut to prove his love of food, he loved his wife even more.

But it had worn on him, year after year, especially without Roger around to offer a counterpoint and suggest that perhaps—just perhaps—their mom and wife, respectively, might be crazy. Again. Instead, Herman just worked harder and harder, trying to find something his wife would eat. After returning, Roger had accompanied him on a trip to the Fairbanks Safeway only to be shocked at how difficult the job of feeding his mother had become. During the dead of winter especially, it was hard enough getting variety into a person's diet, and the last thing anyone needed was an increasingly picky and capricious eater. Roger could see how just trying had taken a physical toll on his father, noticing the way the old man leaned on the cart in lieu of the cane it became increasingly obvious he needed if he was going to stand a chance of not being crushed under the weight of his world.

"How about . . . ?" Roger tried, holding up a can of something.

His father shook his head. "Gives her gas."

A bottle of Beano.

"Gets a rash . . ."

And so on, until they left the store with a case of Ensure, a carton of lactose-free Activia, and a lonely, dented can of peaches his father identified as being "for dessert."

Roger was there when his father died, or started to. He'd just shown up for a visit without calling ahead, because his parents didn't have a phone. He begged them to get one, for emergencies, especially at their age, and Herman had seemed okay with the idea, but Gladys vetoed it.

"I didn't come to the ends of the earth so people can waltz in anytime they feel like it," she'd said, ending the conversation.

And so, when Roger wanted to see his parents, he just went, unannounced but usually welcome, by his father at least. There'd been a few times when Pandora was still a baby that Gladys had been less than happy to see them. Not that she was opposed to grandchildren in concept; she just couldn't abide the shitty reality of them. Given her history of intestinal problems and her susceptibility to them, Roger's mother was the first to know when Pandora's diaper needed changing, a procedure her father could perform in his goddamn truck, putting as many doors as possible between his daughter's feces and his mother's immune system. Having to carry the child out to the truck when it was forty degrees below zero had left a sting he'd never quite gotten over.

During that fateful visit, Roger could tell something was wrong right away. There were tears in the old man's eyes, and his mother was yelling, followed by the sound of a flung plate smashing. His father winced through the smile he'd worn to the door.

"What's wrong?" Roger asked, dispensing with the chitchat.

"I got the wrong thing," Herman said. "Again."

From the doorstep, Roger could hear his mother swearing, and he pushed the rest of the way inside. "What was that?" he said.

"Moron," his mother fumed. "I married a moron who's trying to kill me. He knows I can't eat that." She pointed at the blast of food clinging to the wall opposite her, above shards of broken china.

"And how does he *know* you can't eat it?" Roger asked. "Have you *told* him?"

"I shouldn't *have* to tell him," Gladys raged. "When we used to go shopping together, I'd never buy crap like that."

"Hold on," Roger said, preparing to play his usual role whenever he found himself stuck in an argument between his parents: the rational jester who pointed out how silly they were both being. "You're telling me you're mad at Dad because he *didn't* notice you *not* buying something?"

"Finally," Gladys declared, "*some*body who under*stands*."

Roger had begun shaking his head, chuckling ruefully, when he noticed how quiet his father was being. He turned to look at the older man, and it was as if his father had just been shot. His mother's face, its exaggerated disgust, that was the gun. Her words, the bullets. And there was Herman Lynch, his arms straight at his sides, the fingers shocked apart, a slight palsied shake Roger had never noticed before. His father flicked his left hand, like he was trying to fling blood down to his digits, and then his right arm lifted, bringing his hand to his chest, a thumb rubbing sideways through the flannel of his shirt, between his droopy old-man breasts.

"Dad?"

"It's something I ate," he said. But Roger knew he was lying. When Gladys didn't eat, neither did Herman. It had worked in his father's favor in the beginning, helped shed some needed pounds, but it had become too much. He tottered back, and his left hand reached around behind him, flailing for a chair it finally found and dragged over just in time for him to drop into it. "Call someone," Herman said.

But Roger couldn't: no phone, not even his cell, which was back at home, charging after he'd forgotten to plug it in the night before. Pandora had hers, but she was also back at home, technically alone if you didn't count the entire internet, her father's go-to babysitter since she could make her own PB&J sandwiches and promise not to set the house on fire.

Turning to the parent who wasn't dying, Roger barked, "Grab your parkas." He'd just have to drive them all to the hospital himself. Gladys handed over Herman's jacket, gloves, boots. "Where's yours?" her son demanded.

But Gladys just shook her head. "I can't," she said.

"Can't what?" Roger demanded.

"Go."

"Go?"

"To the hospital," Gladys said.

"Why not?"

"I might go."

"Go?"

"Poop," she said. "My irritable bowel, I . . ."

"Shit," Roger spat.

"Yes," Gladys said, as if he understood—instead of swearing, because he had.

And so Herman's son drove him to the hospital, minus his wife, minus the love of his life, for him to finish dying with just Roger's dumb, stupid face to keep him company.

In the hospital, after being informed he'd had a heart attack that was bigger than the ER was equipped to treat, Herman turned to Roger and said, "Well, I guess that makes two."

"Excuse me?"

"Yeah, my first heart attack was when I met your mother," he said. The morphine they'd given him for the pain had made him chatty. And so he went over the old story again of how they'd met in this dingy frontier bar before Alaska was even a state, back when the lower forty-eight were basically the whole country, trimmed with some territories here and there with no votes or stars of their own.

It was after WWII, and the two had each fled to the ends of the earth after the world didn't end. Herman Lynch had been sitting in the bar, drinking in the middle of the "day," though it was actually dark out, it being winter, thus removing the usual stigma—or so he claimed—staring at the dusty mirror across the bar and gently tapping his high school graduation ring against the rail. He didn't even know he was doing it, but the tapping came out in Morse code—SOS, for "save our souls" or "save our ship," depending on where you stood re: the whole having-a-soul issue. Gladys noticed it and signaled back—SOS, SOS, SOS—with the top of an empty longneck against the rim of the glass she'd poured the beer into. Looking over, Roger's future dad said, "Fancy," indicating the bottle-and-glass redundancy.

"Practical," Gladys said back, indicating her future husband's far simpler drinking arrangement, a trail of suds still crawling down its neck of brown glass.

"You make decisions fast when you're twenty-five and surprised to be alive," Herman Lynch told his son, explaining why he and Gladys wound up married within the month. A floatplane-flying buddy of his officiated, based on the authority vested in him as the captain of something that could land on water and—he maintained—technically met the definition of a ship.

"It's highly possible we've been living in sin all these years," Herman confided with a nudge and a wink. "Kinda makes it more exciting that way."

"Kinda makes me a bastard, though," Roger pointed out.

"Nope," his father insisted, "that choice is all on you."

Roger did not announce his decision to cut his own mother out of his life; he and Pandora just kind of stopped going over there after Herman died. Because it involved not doing something, the more he didn't do it, the easier it was to keep on not doing it. He felt the occasional pang of guilt but always turned it around, making it her fault. He'd tried getting his parents to get a phone when it might have made a difference, and now she couldn't blame him for not calling. As a gesture to the memory of his dad, Roger had a case of Ensure delivered to their cabin once a week, considering his duty as a son done. But then he received notice that her address had changed to a PO Box care of Golden Heart of the North Senior Services. And so Roger canceled his standing order, figuring the place his mother had landed was probably billing the government enough to buy its own damn Ensure.

But then Pandora got in trouble and needed a punishment to fit the offense. And when it came to punishing experiences, Roger couldn't come up with anything that amused him quite as much as sentencing his daughter to visit her grandmother in an old-folks' home.

"You're kidding me," Pandora said upon learning her fate.

"I'm not," Roger said. "She needs the company," he added, fully aware of how hypocritical it sounded but finding himself fresh out of shits to give regarding either of the women in his life.

"So why don't *you* visit her?" Pandora asked.

"Because I didn't blow anybody up," he said.

Roger knew Pandora could quibble with that characterization—technically speaking, she hadn't "blown up" anybody—but she seemed to have deemed it wiser not to. Instead, she ground her more articulate objections against her back teeth until all that escaped was a grumbled mutter that trailed her as she stormed off. Reaching her room, she grabbed the edge of the shower curtain that still hadn't been replaced by an actual door, and now likely never would be, in light of recent events. Yanking it open, she turned, glowered hyperexpressively, and then pulled the curtain closed hard enough to . . .

. . . feel just about as pathetic as it no doubt looked.

6

When it was finally time for Gladys Lynch to move out of the cabin she'd shared with her late husband for more years than she cared to count, her options were limited to 1) an ice floe or 2) a place the Fairbanks Yellow Pages listed as "Golden Heart of the North Senior Services." Like an actual anatomical heart, GHNSS was composed of four sectors organized around the primary services they offered their residents, including assisted living, physical therapy, extended care, and hospice. It was the first of these that was most prominently featured in Golden Heart's sales brochure, which described it as "reserved for residents who need a little help" and offered condos equipped with ramps and handrails, walk-in tubs, call buttons, smoke detectors, washer-dryer combo units, and kitchenettes consisting of cabinets, counter and sink, minifridge, microwave, toaster oven, and a fire extinguisher that was tested monthly by staff, along with the aforementioned smoke detectors.

Gladys's decision was *not* prompted by the need for such elder-friendliness at the time she made it; she just didn't like living alone with all her late husband's firearms. Not that she had anything against Herman's guns. She'd been happy to have them when she still had him and had counted on him to use them should the need arise. But for herself, Gladys wasn't interested in killing someone in self-defense, especially if the stranger turned out to be somebody she knew. There'd been a close call or two already.

There'd also been a doctor who'd come to see her, court ordered after an "incident" while driving down a road where "some kids" had apparently turned all the signs around to face the wrong way. He'd given her a battery of tests, beginning with the Mini-Mental State Examination, which consisted of a series of questions about what day it was, what season, what state and city they were in, followed by repeating back a list of objects, then counting backward, then repeating the list of objects again. In one test, he had Gladys draw a clock with hands and numbers; she'd messed that one up a little, leaving out the six and nine, drawing the rest outside the circle, and then getting the hour and minute hands mixed up.

"If I was Salvador Dali, you wouldn't be making that face," she observed—not that that stopped the doctor from running up the Medicare charges by ordering, in order, an MRI, a PET scan, an EEG, and a SPECT scan.

"Wouldn't a nice cup of alphabet soup be cheaper?" she asked, already used to being ignored, which she was.

"You've got poor glucose metabolism in the hippocampus," Dr. Charge-a-Lot said as if she hadn't spoken.

"Is that a school for 'potamuses?" she joked, but the doctor didn't laugh.

"Not that we can make a *definitive* diagnosis without an autopsy, but . . . ," he began, at which point Gladys threw up a hand and said, "Skip!"

But those pursed lips still refused to budge.

So that's when Gladys Lynch—mother of Roger, grandmother of Pandora—found herself moving (or being moved to) the "assisted living" side of the Golden Heart of the North Senior Services campus. Making the best of it, Gladys consented, figuring they'd assist her in continuing to live, in the event anyone with a different opinion showed up.

Roger's thinking went like this: say you've got a teenage daughter who needs to take life in general—and her personal mortality, specifically—more seriously. What do you do? What sort of punitive activity might drive those points into an adolescence-hardened skull? Something like Scared Straight for juvenile offenders but for life and how precious and fleeting it can be. Donating time to work with preemies in a neonatal unit was one thought, but then he had another. Approach the problem from the end and work backward. And there his mother's change-of-address card sat, offering the perfect solution. Two perfect solutions, in fact, seeing as sending Pandora as his proxy would also assuage any guilt he might feel for not visiting her himself. Win—as they say—win.

Pandora wondered if there was such a thing as building-ism. If there was, she must have it, because these buildings all looked alike to her. Every quadrant of the Golden Heart campus featured the same flat-roofed, gray, brutalist bunkers of concrete with windows that wouldn't open without the help of a diamond drill and C-4. They looked so much alike she finally gave up, pulled into the nearest parking lot, and started walking, nearly bumping into a body on its way out as she made her way in.

"Watch it," the mortuary tech said, walking his charge out backward toward an unmarked delivery van.

"Sorry," Pandora said. "I'm looking for a Gladys—"

"Wrong place," the mortuary tech said, not needing her to finish. "This is shipping and receiving."

"Is that a euphemism?"

"It's a euphemism," the tech confirmed.

"So, how do I—?"

But the tech was already shooing her away.

The next quadrant was physical therapy, not that Pandora could tell from the outside. Even if she'd known, however, she'd still have been surprised. Sure, there were some seniors breaking in new knees, hips, and shoulders, but there were also a lot of people she didn't expect, meaning closer to her age, all of whom had proved a lot less invincible than they might have assumed. Among them, Pandora noticed one of the curling culprits who'd stopped coming to class. His right arm had been sliced from bicep to forearm and stitched back like an aerial view of a railyard. The arm was so withered it looked like somebody had skated over it and yanked out all the muscles, which, she'd learn later, was exactly what had happened. It was so bad, in fact, Pandora felt guilty for having dismissed how dangerous curling could be, all jokes about "men with brooms" aside. And she especially regretted setting those urinals on fire, partly because it had resulted in her being here to see this but also because—well, just because.

Next, there were the local boys back from one of the Middle East conflicts, minus important body parts, including parts of her favorite body part: the head. Some looked like they'd had chunks of skull removed and then hastily patched over with some stubbly, flesh-like covering. After these, the yahoos and mushers who'd learned the hard way that drinking doesn't mix with snowmachines or dogsleds either. A few of these were working out on weight machines they'd been handcuffed to, perhaps in training to waste away in some state prison outside Juneau.

"Is there a Gladys Lynch in here?" Pandora called.

The physical therapist closest to her checked a clipboard—"Nope"—and then went back to leading her little clutch of victims in what appeared to be the most painful game of Simon says Pandora ever hoped to see.

The next set of buildings she skipped. She assumed they housed the medical facilities, judging from the lab-coated men and women trying to keep warm while they enjoyed a smoke break the proper distance away from patients and oxygen. That left two more parking lots. Not knowing which was which, she flipped a mental coin and, bingo, her bad luck held.

If seeing the younger disabled patients in PT had been depressing, it was nothing like the epic comedown of her penultimate stop. Everywhere she looked, mumblers and droolers rolled around in circles or scooted walkers or lay in beds alarmed in the unlikely event their captives had enough strength or selfhood to get around the guardrails. Wandering from one hellish sight to another, Pandora began bleating the name "Lynch!" to any sentient beings she could find, her face a paroxysm of pure horror.

"First name?" a janitor asked, swirling milky water around the latest accident.

"Gladys," Pandora said.

The janitor called to the receptionist at the end of the hallway. "Lynch," he shouted. "Gladys."

"Other side," the receptionist shouted back.

"Other," the janitor shouted before checking himself and turning down his voice. "Side," he concluded.

"Other side," Pandora echoed, preparing to leave, but then stopped. She had to ask. "Can't you *smell* that?" she asked, a hand cupped over her nose and mouth gas-mask-style.

The janitor shrugged. "You get used to it."

"No thanks," Pandora said, still fanning the air.

"Just a fact," the janitor said. "Sooner or later, we all get used to it. Except"—tilting his chin toward a posse of wheelchair-bound residents parked around a table, nothing connecting them except coincidental spacing—and perhaps wheel locks.

"Shouldn't they have cards?"

"They should have a lot of things," the janitor said, "starting with a sense of smell. Having dementia does a number on the old nose." He paused to dunk his mop. "Everybody knows about the brain part, but the nose goes too." Slap, swish. "The brain part's why they don't have any cards. They wouldn't be able to remember who's winning from one hand to the next. Not that any of them would admit it, so then you get fights, usually just raised voices, but we've had the occasional caning to deal with."

He gave his mop a big sweep, short of Pandora's sneakers. "It's quieter this way," he said.

The "other side" she'd been directed to was, aptly enough, the housing office and greeting center, where, after signing in and being greeted, she'd be taken by golf cart to where the senior condos and residents were. This was the side of the Golden Heart that the families of potential residents were shown, where the campus put on its best face, as if all the other buildings, in keeping with their external uniformity, looked the same inside.

Yeah right, Pandora thought, having inadvertently learned the truth, not that she said as much as she signed in. Instead, she followed the end of the receptionist's hand to a seating area and sat.

And sat.

And kept sitting, gradually coming to notice how quiet the place was. This was apparently intended to communicate tranquility or some other elder-friendly state of being. But Pandora found the quiet increasingly unnerving the longer she was exposed to it. It didn't help that what sounds there were only deepened the underlying silence pressing in from all sides. Pandora crossed her hands over her already-crossed knees, not knowing what else to do with them as she listened to the bubbler from an aquarium in the common area where prospects were treated to tea in daintily clinking china cups and offered brochures full of smiling, wrinkled faces who seemed to be having the time of their lives.

"Are you here to see a loved one?"

An escort had finally appeared, dressed in a smart gray pantsuit so that her dress, speech, and manner all reminded Pandora of a funeral director, like a preview of coming attractions.

"Gladys Lynch," Pandora said, not bothering to quibble with the escort's use of the words *loved one*.

There was some good that came out of Pandora's detour through the facility's various hearts of darkness: it inclined her to cut her grandmother a little slack, regardless of any bias projected by her father. After all, knowing Gladys had that other, "other side" waiting for her scored the old girl some serious sympathy points. And this sympathy only deepened when Pandora finally found her way to her only female relative's condo, where a notably shorter version of her grandmother greeted her with positively heartbreaking enthusiasm.

"Dora, my God," Gladys said, opening her door to the sight of her granddaughter and escort.

"Got a visitor, Lynch," the escort said, like a prison screw in some quaint black-and-white prison flick where the hard cases were invariably redeemed by the Lord, the law library, or jailbirds with actual feathers.

"I see that," the old woman said, followed by an awkward bit with her arms as she negotiated the height difference between herself and her significantly taller granddaughter. Once she'd figured it out, however, she closed in and squeezed so hard Pandora was pretty sure she heard bones creaking: Gladys's.

"It's my granddaughter," the older woman continued, over her hunched shoulders, to the escort. "And to what do I owe the pleasure?" she asked.

All the polite excuses flew right out of Pandora's head. "I'm being punished," she announced, as undiplomatic as she was poorly socialized.

"Oh my," Gladys said. Paused. "You mean *me*? *I'm* your punishment?"

A nod.

"Your father's characterization," Gladys asked, "or yours?"

Pandora seized this second chance at not being a total bitch. "Dad's," she said.

"Figures," her grandmother said, holding her granddaughter's elbows at arm's length to get a better look at her. The old woman's bare lips, which had been frowning before, hitched upward, morphing into a grin nearly as ridiculous as one Pandora herself might sport, if she'd been in the mood.

"Good," her grandmother said at the thought of being someone's punishment. "It's about time I got some *respect* around here."

7

V.T. Lemming was not happy even before his car decided to drive off by itself. V.T. Lemming had been especially "not happy" for the last several months, because he was being forced to engage ever increasingly in his most despised activity as the shareholder with the most votes: emergency board meetings. There'd been a smattering of EBMs early on—one involving subsequent congressional testimony—but the pace of said meetings (and the emergencies that triggered them) had been accelerating.

"Gentlemen," he'd begun the latest such meeting, not adding "ladies," because this was a Silicon Valley boardroom and there weren't any. (Not that they weren't aware of the problem. They were. They even developed an algorithm to eliminate bias from hiring and promotion decisions. Unfortunately, the data used to train the algorithm had been based on the company's past history of hirings and promotions so that the bias wasn't so much eliminated as hardwired and automated. Oops.)

"Gentlemen," V.T. repeated, redundantly, "we've got an optics problem which is becoming an image concern on its way to becoming a PR nightmare."

Two columns of ghost faces nodded to either side, lit by the blue light of their smartphones and reflected off the oil-rubbed mahogany of the boardroom conference table.

What V.T. was referring to wasn't the #metoo time bomb waiting to explode somewhere along the management chain. It wasn't another breach of hundreds of millions of user accounts or Quire's role in fueling a foreign bot-driven psyops campaign aimed at shredding the fabric of Western civilization. It wasn't that their platform was being used to grease the skids for genocide in third-world countries, or the Harvard Business School study showing that the number of antidepressants prescribed annually was positively correlated to the growth in V.T.'s personal fortune, which in turn was inversely correlated to a decrease in overall IQ scores, the implicit conclusion being that while Quire's CEO got rich, the rest of the country was getting dumber and more depressed. Nope. Quire's board of directors had been summoned because of a video that had been livestreamed from their platform.

"In case you missed it," V.T. said before hitting play.

The video featured a teenage boy in his bedroom in Beverly Hills, a talking head facing his webcam. But then came the money shot, as it were—the shot that was going to cost everyone in the room a lot of money—after which there wasn't any head left to do any talking. When the body fell, it took what was left of the head off-screen with it, leaving behind a perfectly framed Jackson Pollock, if the artist had used only reds and added texture with broken pottery and clumps of cauliflower. With no one to cut the feed, it kept going, streaming the same grisly static scene, animated only by the painfully slow sliding of those shards and clumps down the wall as they submitted to gravity.

Deaths like it happened every day in America, enabled by the easy availability of firearms and the increasingly pointless search for anything that mattered. Had it been one of those daily deaths, the suicide would have been danced around in the obits with words like *battle* and *depression* if the cause was alluded to at all.

But Rupert Gunn Jr.'s death was distinguished from those others not only for having been streamed "live" (so to speak) but also because of one inconvenient wrinkle: celebrity. Or *celebritatus approximus*: near celebrity or celebrity adjacent—the proxy-fame bestowed on family members of the actually famous—a lesser Kardashian cousin, for example. In this particular case, the real celebrity was Rupert Jr.'s father, *the* Rupert Gunn, the man *Variety* crowned as having "the second most-bankable pair of man nips in Hollywood."

Before the Quire content monitor in charge had a chance to pull the video, it had already received over a hundred thousand "praise hands." Even after being pulled, the video went on to enjoy something Rupert Jr. himself would not—an afterlife—as it leaped from platform to platform, always a few clicks ahead of the content cops. As the contagion spread, the video collected "likes" and "shares" and "smiles" and "effin-As," followed by screenshots turned into memes, which themselves went viral. Even the choice of firearm—a Luger and WWII family heirloom that would warrant its own team of PR spinners—was heartily approved of by the alt-right on their own social-media platforms, racking up more *Sieg Heils* than they'd seen since white polo shirts and tiki torches showed up half-price at Big Lots.

By the beginning of Quire's latest emergency board meeting, the video had generated three million hits and climbing, a trending hashtag (#Quiremadehimdoit), a line of T-shirts breaking records on Etsy, and a Jimmy Kimmel sincerity moment that was chasing the original stream on YouTube. All in all, the only thing that wasn't trending up in the aftermath was Quire's share price, plummeting like it had BASE-jumped off the Golden Gate Bridge minus the wing suit.

"Somebody tell me he was on Ambien," V.T. mock pleaded, pausing the video, then on its way to four million hits since they'd started watching it. The CEO waited between the projector and screen, wearing the boy's static suicide. He began humming the tune for Final Jeopardy. But none of the board members stepped forward with news of a pharmaceutical scapegoat.

"Okay," V.T. resumed, "at least tell me he *wasn't* part of a sosh trial."

But no one around the table was ready to confirm or deny that Rupert Jr. had been part of a sosh trial, mainly because, well, he *had* been. And that was the *real* corporate crisis Quire found itself facing. Because the boy hadn't been bullied, didn't have an incurable health condition, and hadn't been humiliated, either sexually or financially. In the end, he'd killed himself thanks to a confluence of bad decisions, both personal and corporate.

On the personal side, Rupert Jr. made the mistake of quiring a host of socioeconomic inferiors who in real life were total strangers but online constituted his "quire of besties." The idea—ill-conceived as it turned out—was to discover how the other half (or, if you're a stickler for stats, the other ninety-nine percent) lived. Being the scion of those bankable man nips, Rupert Jr. had never in his life been exposed to the riffraff that make up the vast majority of humanity. And so the lives of the unrich and unfamous became a source of curiosity for him, as is often the case with forbidden things.

The other bad decision happened at the corporate offices of Quire, which had unknowingly included Rupert Jr. in a so-called "sosh trial," which was shorthand for social engineering optimization study. As part of the trial in question, Quire's social engineering team manipulated the news stream of three different groups of users to see what balance of good/bad news led to optimal clicking behavior, especially the click-through rate to the ever-coveted "Buy Now" button. The engineers had already discovered that moderately depressed Quire users tended to buy more stuff, a practice they'd dubbed "retail therapy." The question was, What would clickers do if they were really depressed?

And no, Rupert Jr. wasn't part of the group that was fed especially depressing news from others in their quire. He also wasn't part of the control group whose news feed was left untouched. No, he'd been placed in a group intended to confirm the research question's corollary, i.e., "Do vicariously happy people buy *less* stuff?"

The only problem: Rupert Jr. wasn't online to be cheered by the good news of the proletariat. He'd been *hoping* to find misery to cheer him out of his own. Because it had come from somewhere, hadn't it? Depression didn't just *happen*. There had to be a cause and, from that, maybe, a cure. Which is when Rupert Jr. recalled how vaccines work. You exposed yourself to a manageable amount of the disease, thereby building up an immunity to it. So maybe if he exposed himself to the highly manageable unhappiness of others who'd already started out way less fortunate than he was . . .

But instead of feeling better by comparison, what he found was this: average Americans trying to make other average Americans jealous. While that's frequently what people got in their news feeds even without manipulation, what Rupert Jr. got was as relentlessly upbeat as a motivational speaker in an ice cream truck playing "Happy Days Are Here Again." This amplification was achieved by stripping out the political rants, fake news, proselytizing, and clickbait that clogged most news feeds, leaving behind a highly curated glimpse into the lives of others as they portrayed themselves online. The results, unsurprisingly, skewed toward the full spectrum of bragging, including but not limited to: the humblebrag; the brag brag; the proxy brag ("Look at my kids, my parents, my lovely spouse . . ."); the brag with parsley ("Look at my breakfast, lunch, dinner . . ."); the anthropomorphic brag ("Look at how much my dog, cat, pony, goldfish, et al. *loves* me . . ."); the geo-tag brag ("Will you look at that *view* . . ."); and the holier-than-bragging brag ("Click here to donate to a cause you never heard of, you heartless bastard . . ."). All in all, it was too much vicarious self-adulation for a celebrity-by-proxy to handle, suggesting not only that money couldn't buy happiness but perhaps it bought the very depression he'd been grappling with.

And so even though his family wasn't Jewish or Christian but more free-form Buddhist (it was a Hollywood thing), Rupert Jr. decided to see what the Bible had to say about his theory. (Oops.) Well, perhaps great art was the balm his soul needed. So he watched *Citizen Kane*, a verified Hollywood classic. (Oh crap.) Maybe *A Christmas Carol*, about which he'd heard good things, about once a year, it seemed. And there, finally, was the misery vaccine he'd been looking for, in the form of Tiny Tim and the Cratchits. Except Rupert Jr. didn't feel any better. In fact, he felt worse. Because it was pretty clear who Scrooge was in the scenario. And it was pretty clear where the whole thing was going, no need to watch all the way to the bitter end.

By this time, Rupert Jr. was deep into that peculiar voodoo mindset of the clinically depressed in which random events and coincidences become the voice of the universe, talking to you, letting you know what needs to happen next. And if you don't listen the first time, the universe will repeat itself in the form of even more resonant random events and coincidences until the sheer weight of them forces you to finally get it—and get on with it.

And with that, Rupert Gunn Jr. placed the family namesake into his mouth and got started on getting life right the next time around.

Several million mouse clicks later and there was V.T. Lemming, CEO of Quire, standing with both fists planted at the head of the boardroom table, another him inverted in its shiny surface, as if the CEO was balancing on his twin via the nexus of their fists. "I'm going to be testifying about this one," he said, lifting his head to look down the length of the table. There they were—*his board*—all heads silent, all heads bent over their smartphones, perhaps watching their share prices free-fall in real time.

"Somebody *say* something!" V.T. finally shouted.

Nothing.

He'd been hoping for a flinch at least. But when the bent heads remained silent, V.T. Lemming took a breath and proceeded to practice some of the anger management skills that would come in handy a few months later, surrounded in a Home Depot parking lot by the Bay Area's finest, their guns drawn on the only available suspect.

The irony was, they'd already been working on the suicide thing—teen suicide especially. It had seemed the corporately responsible thing to do, seeing as teens still had a lifetime of earning ahead of them, meaning the settlement for a liability case would involve some serious ouch money, even for a non-celebrity-related teen, should some grieving parent decide to blame Quire for their loss of a child. That was the thinking triggered by that Harvard Business School study. They had checked the study's numbers against Quire's own usage stats among teens and found that a "not insignificant" number had left the platform "with extreme prejudice."

So V.T. ordered them to "put somebody on it," which they had. Meanwhile, the marketing people, in anticipation of algorithmic success, had started penciling out a campaign, beginning with a killer slogan: "It's one thing to save you money; it takes a special company to save your life."

They'd been focus-grouping possible branding and licensing schemes and other ways of monetizing their suicidal ideation detection app, the idea being that saving someone's life was a good way to get a lifetime customer.

"Just spitballing here," a marketing guy said, worrying a Nerf basketball.

The names being tested included: NewDay, BullyProof, SunnyUp, YouStrong, BetterDays, NoH8ters, and Jack. The spitballing guy especially liked Jack—thought it was edgy, but at the same time, kid friendly.

"'Yeah, I talked to Jack today, and boy, am I glad I did,'" he said, so they could get a feel of how "the kids" might use it, you know, when talking.

"Or," another marketing guy wanting in on it said, "if you're thinking about killing yourself, you don't know Jack."

Good work, they'd been told.

Two days and four million hits later, they were all fired.

And then the CDC came out with a report that showed suicide was at an all-time high across the US, a rise not directly correlated to the proliferation of social-media users but trending uncomfortably close to it. That coupled with the graphic viral video of a kid with everything to live for who didn't, well, time to start the scapegoating.

That's how V.T. saw it. That he articulated it out loud—and some boardroom Brutus recorded it—was unfortunate. The MP3 followed the same viral path as the original video, and was linked to it forever via "you may also like" or "related" or "you might also be interested in." And even though what V.T. said wasn't *untrue*, per se—just badly timed and tone deaf—that didn't stop the trolls from using it in meme after meme. For a while, you couldn't go anywhere online without hearing V.T.'s voice saying: "Christ, it's not like we *invented* suicide," accompanied by a video of Rupert Gunn Jr. losing his head, followed by an especially emotive Face Girl reacticon displaying her horror.

8

George could flash back to it anytime he needed to—any time he needed fuel to stoke his anger. All it took was that first little rip that then tore straight down his psyche. Fingers—those were the triggers—specifically outstretched fingers, desperate to connect but restrained from doing so, being pulled apart by the laws of property, ownership, territoriality, the laws of lines in the sand, and the terrible penalty for being caught on the wrong side of one.

It happened in ninth grade without his willing it, while George was looking at the panel from the Sistine Chapel of God and Adam, a spark gap apart, their fingers reaching forever but not quite touching. Suddenly, he was five years old again and in immigration court—right in the middle of an art appreciation class (or some other course the teacher was trying to smuggle culture into, despite slashed funding and a policy of teaching to the test). While in the flashback's throes, George saw everyone in class turning around to stare at him, at the tears running down his face. And as embarrassed as he was, he still welcomed the misdirection because it meant they weren't looking lower, where he crossed his legs, hoping his pants would dry before the bell rang, watching the clock's hands, blurry through tears.

"Mr. Jedson," his teacher asked, "do you need to be excused? Do you need me to call someone?"

No. No, he didn't. George shook his head, furiously, found his voice, and said, "No, Ms. Kozlowski. I'm . . . it's . . ."—*think*—"allergies, I think."

He mashed a hand over one eye, then the other, smearing with the same fury with which he'd shaken his head. He sucked in a loud sniffle, dragged a sleeve underneath his nose, sniffle-sucked again.

"You're sure?" his teacher asked.

George nodded, noting what he wasn't hearing: his fellow classmates laughing. Instead, they'd all gone quiet and were busying themselves looking everywhere but at him. George could read their minds. *Thank God,* they were thinking, *it's not me making a scene.*

George stopped going to school after that. Instead, he started taking BART out of Oakland to downtown SF, hung out at City Lights Bookstore, and considered himself "a homeless person in training," while he worked up the nerve to run away for good. In the meantime, he went undercover, test-driving his ability to survive on his own.

He'd picked up that MBA "dress for success" BS from one of his fosters. To George, it sounded like some corporate version of drag, wearing the clothes of the job you wished you had. But not being in school anymore left him with plenty of time. So he pinched some techno dweeb wardrobe from a dry cleaner. It seemed that—contrary to myth—techno dweebs who've gotten the personal hygiene talk at work *will* use dry cleaners, going straight from their moms doing their laundry to somebody else doing their laundry. George finished off the costume by getting a playing card laminated before attaching it to a lanyard and tucking it into his breast pocket. After that, he hopped on company shuttles, complaining about how his smart chip must have brain damage, so someone else would swipe him on. It helped that he was tall for his age and generally ethnic enough to discourage confrontation and/or direct eye contact.

Using his disguise, George toured the Bay Area, going from one corporate campus to another, living off geek droppings: half-finished

Starbucks, breakfast sandwiches and bagels left where they'd been placed down, only a bite or two missing, so the guy (it was always a guy) wouldn't have to argue about the algorithm he was arguing about with his mouth or hands full.

George listened for buzzwords he googled later, discovering to his delight that he actually had a knack for programming, including some of the shadier varieties he found after surfing to some of the shadier sides of the web, the part where anonymity was the whole idea and the front door wasn't Google, but had to be picked open using tools like Tor.

In retrospect, George figured he *did* owe the foster system an acknowledgment after all. It was because of them he'd been moved from Los Angeles, where he'd been born, to the heart of the action in Northern California, where he proceeded to circle the map around the San Francisco Bay, from San Jose to Oakland to Alameda and back to Oakland. And it was because of the foster system he had learned to be sneaky. That was a trait they shared—hacking and surviving foster care—because they both depended on learning the rules even as they changed on the fly, and then figuring out the loopholes and how hard you could push against this or that pressure point without having the whole thing backfire.

The first things he ever hacked outright were the various parental controls set by one of his foster families. It wasn't that he was especially interested in violence or pornographic content—well, at thirteen he was—but their being kept from him was what made them so tempting. Plus, figuring out loopholes, work-arounds, weakest links, and exploitable exploits made his brain smile like almost nothing else did. And these same skills came in handy when George decided to remove himself from the foster system once and for all, two years sooner than the system would have kicked him out.

Once he was on his own, George started school again, in a manner of speaking. His major? Whatever he was interested in, which was mainly computers by then. All he needed was a library with a decent internet connection, the soul of a cat burglar, and a case of insomnia that came naturally after moving from family to family where nobody respected your stuff. Conveniently, George's belongings had been whittled down to what he could comfortably carry in a backpack.

One of the things George had working in his favor was living at a time and in a place that had devalued books, objective facts, and pretty much anything that got in the way of blissful ignorance. Otherwise he may have had more trouble getting around the library's security, which was, frankly, a joke. The computers were locked down six different ways, but that didn't stop him from using them where they were. And as far as any other burglar-proofing was concerned, it fell somewhere north of a cemetery, one of the few places even less likely to get broken into, now that grave robbing had stopped being a thing. Dead bolts, two—those were the security system—and useless if you were already inside.

George's MO was pretty simple: split his time between haunting the shelves and surfing the web until minutes before closing, when he'd dart to the men's room, stand on the toilet seat, and shift an acoustical tile out of place. A steel-lattice support beam was close enough to pull himself up by and into the rafters, where he'd nudged the tile he removed back into place with the toe of his shoe. And then he waited for the lights to go out down there and the sound of the doors being locked. After that, drop down from the ceiling, pull a flashlight from his pack, and wander to where they kept the books on computer science, including all four volumes of *The Art of Computer Programming* by Donald Knuth, volume one of which carried a blurb by no less a geek god than Bill Gates, offering to consider a job application from anyone who could get through all 652 pages of it. And that was just the *first* volume. By the time he'd be ready to hijack a certain CEO's EV, George was nearly finished with volume three.

When living off geek discards wasn't enough, George would collect cans and bottles for their California Redemption Value or CRV, basically a deposit dressed up as an incentive to recycle. With his hacking skills improving all the time, it might be expected he'd attempt something more lucrative, like identity theft. But George wasn't interested in hurting anyone who couldn't afford it. The owners of Trader Joe's, on the other hand, probably weren't going to bed hungry anytime soon.

And so he decided to maximize the efficiency of his CRV collection. He did this by printing a bottle's bar code onto a strip of reflective bicycle tape he then wrapped around a Coke bottle he weighed down with small rocks. He'd take this to a bottle return machine, the neck lassoed with a piece of twine in case the weight wasn't enough to keep it from being rolled into the crusher. And then he'd guard the machine as it spun the same bottle around, over and over, the CRV tallied in a do-loop until he reached the store's daily limit and the machine spat out the receipt to take to the cash register.

George didn't consider this stealing so much as an investment on behalf of society in himself, George Jedson, who'd begun seeing himself as the nexus of San Francisco's past and its rapidly emerging future, from Haight-Ashbury to Silicon Valley. And if anyone had ever asked him what he wanted to do with his life, George would have summed it up so that it incorporated both: "I want to code the best minds of my generation."

9

Their neighbors would tease her father about the satellite dish, which was nothing to rival Arecibo, but could probably give NORAD a good run. Nevertheless: "Whatchadoin', neighbor? Lookin' for intelligent life?"

"Well, given the local choices," her father would say back.

And then they'd laugh, her father and the neighbor, because neither man counted the other as being included in the implicitly maligned "local choices." Either that or it was another inside joke of adulthood Pandora was still waiting to get.

While the Lynches' setup was ahead of its time for Fairbanks, it wasn't like the locals lacked their own means for communicating with the outside world. Take Pandora's grandfather. When he was still alive, Herman Lynch had shown his granddaughter what he called the granddaddy of that shiny new webby thing all the kids "down there" were talking about: ham radio.

"I can talk to anybody in the world," Herman had said, "under the right atmospheric conditions. Assuming they've got a setup and handle and feel like talking."

To Pandora, Grandpa Lynch's setup looked like something straight out of James Whale's *Frankenstein*, the DVD of which her dad played pretty much every Halloween, along with *The Exorcist* when she was older. And while her grandfather's comms center lacked Dr. F's zapping

Jacob's ladders and Tesla coils, it nevertheless had plenty of dials and boxes that leaked orange light from the actual vacuum tubes they had inside.

When she was little, Pandora would sit on her grandfather's knee as he soldered. She liked watching the metal tip of the iron turn from yellow-blue-black to incandescent cherry red, a pencil-thin lick of blue smoke curling away from it before Grandpa announced it was ready. And then he'd bring it down on the powdery gray twist of oxidized lead, turning it with a touch into a quivering bead of silver. They'd get away from him sometimes—more frequently the older he got—the runaway metal rolling like a ball of mercury, off the edge of the worktable, leaving a silver splash on his work boots, every pair of which was as spangled as any Van Gogh night.

It was Herman's ham-radio hobby that influenced her father to become a therapist who only saw patients long distance over the internet. As far as where Herman picked up the bug, he thanked the navy for that—the signal corps specifically. He'd served during WWII, where his job was to listen to static all day, running up and down the radio spectrum, trying to discern if there was any snow on the line that might be something else.

Herman Lynch hadn't waited to be drafted—or even for America to enter the war. He'd signed up and was among the first to arrive after the attack on Pearl Harbor, an experience that stayed with him all his life and one of the reasons why, after the war, he "retired" to Alaska, where he planned to become a recluse—Herman the Hermit—fishing and hunting to keep his body alive, tinkering with homemade electronics, maybe a little astronomy because it was good for the soul. And that's pretty much how it worked out—with the exception of being a hermit. Instead, he found himself with a wife, of all things, and before it was too late, a son, too, named after a common bit of ham-radio lingo.

"It drove me crazy as a kid," Roger told Pandora. "I'd keep thinking my dad was calling me, only to find out he was just agreeing with somebody on the radio."

Roger remembered a lot of the same things his daughter remembered about Herman, who'd been a lot more precise with his soldering when his son was growing up. For the boy Roger, the glowing iron was a magic wand, enabling his father to create all manner of miracles, like a clock with no moving parts, only a series of tubes with their own magical-sounding names—Nixies—their filaments twisted into a nest of numbers from zero to nine, each glowing in sequence as the minutes and hours counted up. Another time, his father built a sound recorder out of a couple of empty spools and a long strand of wire, winding and unwinding between the two, the magic happening somewhere in the middle, where the wire passed through what looked like the clippy part of a clothespin.

And then there was the computer—the first Roger had ever seen, built from a Heathkit. His dad programmed it using something that sounded like the Morse code he'd taught his son, but with a different-sounding name: binary. Eventually, Roger would get his own computer without having to build it from parts: a Commodore 64. His parents gave him one for Christmas one year, saying they were giving him the future, just as he would give his own child the world someday.

When Roger was growing up, his father used to tell him amusing stories about his war experiences, pranks pulled, stupid things done or said, some near misses, but nothing dark until Roger brought home a VHS copy of *Tora! Tora! Tora!* from the Fairbanks Blockbuster.

"I was there," the old man said.

"Where?"

"Pearl Harbor," Herman said. "We weren't at war yet. We were steaming toward the territory of Hawaii for what everybody aboard saw as some glorified government-funded vacation. We were headed to rotate the vacationers who were already there back to the States. Nice work if you can get it.

"The awful news came over the wireless, followed by the president's infamy speech, and there went our vacation. In its place, we got to imagine the hell we were headed toward, knowing that when we got there, we'd be fishing corpses and body parts out of the drink. The ones the sharks hadn't gotten were warehoused with a bunch of dehumidifiers until the bloating went down and they could be shipped back in normal-sized coffins, draped in flags without a star for the place where they died.

"The sweetheart detail was going fishing in rubber rafts, hauling a magnet through the waters of the Pacific, dragging the ocean floor for dog tags to record and send back to wives and mothers who'd been told not to worry, that the soldiers were living in paradise."

His father paused, drew the finger underneath first one eye, then the other.

"I got a souvenir from back then," he said. "Wanna see it?"

Roger imagined—he didn't know what—body parts, maybe. Something grisly to match the stuff his father had brought back with him inside his skull. He nodded oh so carefully as his father scooted his postmaster's chair to a box in the corner, its flaps dog-eared soft from frequent openings and closings.

"You know what this is?" he asked, holding up the fluted body of a ukulele.

Roger nodded, got as far as "Uke," when his father cut him off.

"It's a smile machine," the old salt said. "I defy anyone alive to pluck even a single string without smiling." He handed it to his son. "Go ahead; you try."

Roger began smiling just reaching for it. He couldn't help it. It was such a silly-looking thing, more toy than serious musical instrument.

But maybe that was the point. It wasn't serious. It was a machine for the manufacturing of smiles. He plucked a string.

"Bingo," his father said.

It wasn't his father's wartime trauma that inspired Roger to become a therapist; it was his mother's. Gladys had a nervous breakdown shortly after the war and ended up getting electroconvulsive therapy. Despite its reputation, ECT had worked for her, and Roger became infatuated with the idea of therapeutic resurrections like the one his mother laid claim to.

"It was a miracle," she said. "No doubt in my mind."

"Least not anymore," Herman said, before calling her by the name he called her when they were both in a good mood, "right, Sparky?"

"Roger that," Gladys said back.

Roger hadn't known what triggered his mother's breakdown, though he vaguely resented it, considering it unearned compared to all the reasons his father had but hadn't succumbed to. He took vicarious pride in that, all the pressure he imagined Herman withstanding. The pressure not only of waiting to be torpedoed, but of sitting in a radio shack, listening as if lives depended on it, because they did. Or had. Roger could see it clearly in his mind's eye: a government-issued cigarette smoldering in an ashtray, the smoke rising straight up in the unstirred air, lit in the yellow cone falling from a gooseneck lamp, alongside the clipboard log, his father, impossibly young and in khaki, sleeves rolled, nape shaved and sunk between tensed shoulder blades. He'd be wearing black Bakelite headphones, his hands pressing them against his ears as if trying to squeeze out a few more decibels. His pink ears strain to hear something in the nothing, the snow noise coming from between the stars, the background echo of the big bang raining down from everywhere: static. On either side of it, there's organized sound—music, the news, serialized suspense, religious demagoguery. None are what his father is listening for: that subtler static that is but isn't, the static he needs to separate like "picking fly poop out of pepper"; over here, noise; over there, signal.

That's where the future began, Roger thinks. Not with the gift of an eight-bit computer, but in that little shack aboard a glorified tin can, where history forked in two, one branch leading to a smartphone in every pocket, the other to every third-world madhouse armed with nukes, the branches bending and meeting again in Iran, its nukes nuked by lines of code dubbed Stuxnet, the first shot in the next war, the one fought with hacked elections, chatbots, fake news, and old-school propaganda—a war of words mightier than any sword, and doing real damage in the real world . . .

Roll the clock back and there was Herman Lynch, sitting at the nexus of said future, a lonely WWII radio tech, intercepting the coded communiqués it would take the world's first electronic computer to eventually crack. The fact that his father-to-be hadn't cracked himself fascinated Roger almost as much as the fact that his mother had.

Why?

How stressful could it be, saving newspapers, tin, and bacon grease for the war effort? Was dancing with the doomed at the USO hall so hard? Or was it having to write an assembly line of Dear John letters later, to the ones who stubbornly kept living, and writing? Not that he knew for a fact that she'd done any of those things, but weren't those the roles most women got to play back then? And yet it was her—his *mother*—who got the luxury of having a breakdown?

Amazing . . .

Gladys inspired her son to become a therapist in other ways as well. There was her hyperexpressive face, the one he'd inherited and later passed on. That face got him interested in emotions, as well as in those who could hide them versus those who couldn't. Combining his parental influences, Roger set up shop providing pro bono (i.e., amateur) counseling to hermits in the more remote parts of Alaska via ham radio when he was no older than his daughter was now. At least it was something to fill the hours when the cabin walls and weather pressed in.

Unable to prescribe controlled substances at the time, young Roger took a cue from his father and recommended the ukulele instead. For those who couldn't find a uke at their nearest trading post, a simple kazoo made from wax paper folded over a comb. A lot of his pro-boners went this route, and the funny thing was, it was . . . *inherently funny*. The vibrations against the lips tickled, and since they were already there, the lips went with it and smiled. It was as much a reflex as tapping a crossed knee, and a gateway expression to not killing themselves.

"That goddamn comb thing worked, you goddamn whatever you are . . ."

Even as an amateur, Roger knew better than to use the word *therapist* with the lonely Alaskans he found on the other side of the microphone. "I'm just a guy who likes to talk," he said.

"Well, you should keep doin' it. You're good."

Roger would have been content to stay an amateur and local—but a detour presented itself and he took it. He'd been out of high school for over a year when Roger ran into another academic procrastinator who also happened to own a Commodore 64, which he'd Frankensteined into something he swore was going to be big someday.

"People are going to be able to do what we're doing, but over computers linked together all over the planet," the future CEO of Quire Social Media Group LLC told Roger. "You should come to San Fran, man. Things are starting to percolate. Take that head-shrinking routine to the next level. And who knows, you might even meet some beach babe and get laid . . ."

Sitting there, in Fairbanks, Alaska, in the dead of winter—talking bearded bachelors out of taking a rope for a ride—Roger found the prospect of beach babes and getting laid to have a nearly galvanic effect. "So, like, how?" the amateur therapist asked.

And so, like, Vladimir T. Lemming explained.

"Put wanting to save people on the college app," he said. "Add moving anecdotes about actually having done so. Get it postmarked from Fairbanks freaking Alaska. They'll be *throwing* scholarships at you." To sweeten the deal, V.T. threw in his parents' semifurnished basement so Roger could bank the campus housing subsidy. "You'd be stupid not to. Over."

And so Roger Lynch found himself at Fairbanks International Airport, an Alaska Airlines ticket to San Francisco in his pocket, waving goodbye to the parents whose legacy he was, heading into the future they'd promised him during that Commodore Christmas not so long ago.

California was where Roger met Pandora's mother, though not in the way he told his daughter they did. For one thing, they *hadn't* been listening to the music streaming service Pandora, which she *wasn't* named after. Their respective earbuds *hadn't* been playing Adam Ant's "Goody Two Shoes" at the same time, signaling their algorithmic compatibility. Despite the big talk about beaches and babes, the truth was, Roger was both mystified and terrified of the fairer sex, in part because he'd not had much experience with it outside of his mother. The cliché was that there were roughly ten men for every woman in Alaska, and while the reality wasn't quite that bad, it also wasn't that far off. And so Roger largely monked it through college, then grad school, then his thesis and residency, explaining to his singular friend, Vlad, that he was busy, needed to focus, was crushing for this or that. And after all the schooling and qualifying and licensing, well, he had a practice to establish, a reputation to nurture, and . . .

"You're still a virgin, aren't you?" Vlad had said.

Roger's uncontainable face confirmed it was so. And so Roger's friend, V.T. Lemming, hacked into a computer dating site, ran an algo of his own coding based on what he knew of his friend's likes and dislikes, and assembled a small database of likely prospects for hooking up within the greater Bay Area. Based on these prospects' profiles and contact info, V.T. calculated the likelihood that a given prospect would be at a given bar on a given Friday night and made sure that Roger was there as well. It was the least Vlad could do, he explained, in exchange for all the free counseling his college buddy had provided through a string of failures—the same he'd become famous for, once V.T. stopped failing.

"This looks like it should have gangsters hanging from meat hooks," Vlad had said upon visiting his college roomie's first office space, a wannabe crack house in the Tenderloin.

"You'll see, once I put up the 'Hang In There, Baby' cat poster, it's all coming together."

Vlad had nodded sagely. "*That's* what's missing." But the bravado had been false, seeing as he hadn't come to tease his friend, but to seek his help in deciding between declaring bankruptcy or attempting flight off the Golden Gate Bridge.

"Leaping to your death is a rotten way for a Lemming to go," Roger had counseled before tipping a glug of pure gin into his friend's coffee cup, before assuring him that he'd catch the next wave. "And in the meantime," he'd added, sliding open his bottom desk drawer, "may I recommend this." He'd helpfully plucked a string, to show Vladimir how it worked.

And it did. And it continued to. And so, yes, the least Vlad could do for Roger's saving his life was make sure his friend had one worth living.

After his wife died, Roger didn't so much decide to go back to Alaska as simply submit to a need that tugged at him through his belly button. His brain added its two cents by assuring him it was the only sensible move. Among other things, he'd need the free babysitting his parents could provide; he also felt more at home there, meaning Alaska, the place that had programmed his circadian rhythm at a practically cellular level. Plus, as hard as he might try, there was no way Roger was going to grok California quite as well as he already grokked Alaska. For one thing, California—and San Francisco, especially—was in a constant state of upheaval, and not only because of the earthquakes. From the beatniks to the hippies to the gay liberation movement and beyond, including its latest incarnation as the Brotopia of Tech Bros, San Francisco practically invented the concept of reinvention; if the city had an official flag, it would feature an overhead crane framed against a big old sun reflecting off the bay.

Which was all well and good for the people it was well and good for, but Roger wasn't one of them. Fortunately, by the time he and his daughter were ready to board a plane back to the frozen North, V.T., whom his friend and therapist had seen through failure after failure, had finally caught that wave and was riding it toward what would eventually be the third publicly traded company to reach a trillion-dollar valuation: Quire.

"I've got a proposition for you," V.T. told him as they sat in Roger's office for the last time.

"Okay," Roger said, manning the gin bottle, as usual.

"I'd like to put you on retainer," V.T. said, "for my staff, who may need a little therapy, working for me."

"How would something like that work?" Roger asked his old friend.

"Satellites. We'll call it 'permanent flexiplace,' and you can raise that daughter of yours using real money instead of getting paid in fish and bearskin rugs."

"It's not *that* bad," Roger said. "Fairbanks may not be as cosmopolitan as, say, Anchorage, but . . ."

"I'll take your word for it," V.T. said. "And if your plate fills up with locals, you can quit any time." He downed the rest of his gin, crumpled the Dixie cup like he was crushing a beer can, and tossed it over his shoulder. He shot out his freed hand. "Deal?"

Roger took his friend's hand. "Deal," he agreed.

10

It peeved V.T. that his company, his reputation, and his bottom line would come down to a question of due diligence over the issue of suicide. With a name like Lemming? *Seriously?* That was taking the whole name-as-destiny thing way too far. The only way he could take it further was to eat a bullet himself, something his college roomie, Roger, talked him out of once and for all by predicting the headline that would follow: "Lemming Kills Self. Well, Duh . . ."

Even before that Gunn kid took his own name too far, V.T. had a guy working on the whole teen suicide thing. And he'd gotten close, but close in preventing suicide still equals dead kids. Worse than that, it handed their parents a class action on a platter because marketing got ahead of the code, and now Quire *owned* teen suicide. Never mind all the bullies, bad parents, bad brain chemistry, and bad luck that also played a role; it was now all *Quire's* fault.

So he needed to fix that algorithm, the one that—had it *worked*—would have prevented this disaster. Which meant finding a coder who took ending teen suicide seriously. One who would treat it like what it was: a mind game of epic proportions. He needed a neural net using machine learning to do for teen suicide what Deep Blue did for chess, Watson for *Jeopardy!*, and AlphaGo for Go. In other words, he needed an AI that could play mind games better than someone with an actual mind.

But who was he going to get who was naive enough, idealistic enough—frankly *stupid* and/or *crazy* enough—to risk their reputation on the coding equivalent of walking on water while carrying the Holy Grail? Don Quixote didn't write script, did he? So who else was there?

George's recruiter was dressed to scare: black suit, white shirt, black tie, black glasses, pigtail wire connecting one ear to something underneath his jacket, a Secret-Service-y vibe, but as much a costume as if he'd dressed like a circus clown. "Sir?" he said, bowing deeply into George's airspace. In the distance, the Golden Gate Bridge seemed to float on a cloud of fog; seagulls disappeared and reappeared at will.

"Herr?" George said, retrieving the arm he'd stretched across the back of the bench before Secret Agent Man deposited himself without invitation.

"Do you recognize this?"

George looked at the object the guy was holding like a badge—one that practically touched the young hacker's nose. "Um," he said, crossing his eyes, trying to bring whatever he was being shown into focus. Pulling back, he finally saw it. A smartphone looping a GIF of one V.T. Lemming rolling off the hood of his car in an Oakland, California, parking lot, hands in the air, suit coat polka-dotted by the laser sights of a half dozen police officers.

"Oh yeah," George said. "I recognize that, all right."

"So you admit responsibility?"

"I admit *seeing* the video," George said. He pointed at the counter listing the number of times that particular clip had been viewed. "Me and two, no, wait, *three* million others."

"I see you like games," said the guy who clearly didn't.

"I dabble," George said. "Little *Doom* here, some *Angry Birds* there, whenever I'm feeling doomed or angry."

"I'm going to have to ask you to come with me," Mr. Dress-Up said.

"And I'm going to have to ask for a warrant."

"This isn't that kind of ask." And then George was suddenly on the ground with a knee in his back and his wrists zip-tied together.

"What the ever-loving *hell*!" George shouted before noticing the driverless Voltaire approaching them.

"Our ride," his abductor said.

Nice touch, George thought.

"You can't tell me this is a surprise," V.T. Lemming said once George was standing there in his corporate suite, still zip-tied but a quick snip away from getting his wrists back, which he started rubbing immediately.

"And *you* are?"

V.T. smiled. "Somebody with your future in his hands."

"Come again?"

"I think we understand one another," V.T. said. "You steal a car, you keep a car, is my point. What follows is, you get lucky or you get caught. I think you realize where you've come out between those two options. Unless there was something else going on."

"Such as?"

"An audition."

"By hijacking your ride?" George asked.

And so V.T. explained. It wasn't the fact that George had managed to remotely commandeer his Voltaire that impressed the CEO, or the hacker's sense of humor evident in his choice of where to abandon it. It was how much better his vehicle's autonomous capabilities were *after* the hack than before. George hadn't just hijacked the car's software; he'd improved it. Certain plays of light and shadow that would have fooled the vehicle's computer vision were now smoothly accommodated, much to V.T.'s relief. Because while he'd desperately wanted his impromptu detour to end, he didn't want it to end in a crash.

"So, my question to you is," V.T. said, "what did you do to my car's software to make it work better and why?"

George shrugged. "It's a nice car," he said. "I figured if it stayed that way"—meaning uncrashed—"it would keep the charges more manageable, should it come to that." Pause. "Is it coming to that?" he asked.

V.T. pinched the bridge of his nose with the tip of his thumb and the side of his index finger, something George would learn the smurfs (a.k.a. his fellow droids, elves, and/or coworkers) referred to as V.T.'s trademarked I'm-thinking-about-it gesture.

"So?" George prodded, to which V.T. said as if on cue: "I'm thinking about it . . ."

No, he wasn't. He'd decided even before he had George kidnapped. He was taking a cue from Jobs and trusting his gut. And it had told him he needed to hire this smartass kid who made software better by breaking into it. And so: "I've decided," he said, dropping his hand and opening his eyes.

"And . . . ?"

"Jail's too good for you," the Quire CEO said. "How'd you like a job instead?"

"What, like cleaning toilets with my toothbrush?"

"Like changing the world with your brain," V.T. said. He paused, steepled his index fingers together, rested his chin where the cross would otherwise go. "I'm offering you a vocation," he continued. "A calling. I'd hold out a red pill and a blue one and ask you to choose, but I think we both know you're not the blue pill sort. You want to know the truth, how the world works. And I'm here—the real world—asking you to work for"—pause—"no, *with*, me."

Oh, the guy was good. That last, studied pause between "for" and "with"? Masterful. And effective. "Um, *yes*?" George said.

"A bit more enthusiasm wouldn't hurt."

"*Hell* yes?"

"We'll work on that." And then V.T. Lemming, CEO of perhaps the second most powerful social-media company on the face of the planet, did a little air-stirring thing with his finger. George's escort stepped up, preparing to usher him elsewhere when V.T. raised another finger.

"Uno," he said, reaching into his infamous plaid suit coat, the original to the copy George's wannabe tech dweeb had been wearing. Up close, the differences were obvious. For one, V.T.'s coat had been tailor-made, not lucked into at some Salvation Army resale shop. The outfit's carelessness was of the studied sort and likely the result of a fifty-page strategy doc complete with audience reactions translated into emojis and quantified in thumbs, up or down. And from that coat of studiously tacky splendor, V.T. produced a ring of keys, attached to which hung a buttoned fob. He removed this last from the ring as the remaining keys jangled. He held up the separated fob and added a heads-up with his head.

George nodded back that he was ready, reached up, and caught the fob, which featured a stylized *V* embossed behind the buttoned side.

"What's this for?"

"You," V.T. said. "Consider it a signing bonus."

"But I haven't signed anything," George said, thinking, *So much for the "crime doesn't pay" paradigm.* In his case, crime was pretty much his résumé, curriculum vitae, and job application, all rolled into one.

"Do you know about those fMRI studies that show the brain making decisions before its owner has had a chance to catch up?" V.T. asked.

George shook his head.

"Asked to choose, say, between a red pill and a blue one," the CEO explained, "the brain raises its hand, 'I know, I know,' while the body it inhabits is still making up its so-called mind. There's an actual, measurable gap between the two."

George blinked. As the owner of a brain, he was finding all this talk a little disconcerting.

"We did some of that work here," V.T. said, clearly proud of the fact. "You've heard of Q-Labs, correct?" He said the words like he was asking if George knew what a candy shop was; that's how Quire's latest hire understood it anyway. He didn't bother answering. The question was clearly rhetorical; whoever did Quire's advertising had made sure of that, along with the message V.T. proceeded to spell out.

"It's important that you understand that Quire profits are turned back into Quire innovations to benefit all humankind," the company's CEO said, going on to explain that ever since taxation became tantamount to treason, the government's willingness to sponsor pure research had shriveled to the size of your average congressional testicle. As such, it was up to corporately financed subsidiaries like Q-Labs to move humanity as a species forward.

"You might want to explain that to your buddies on PinkoCommiesRPeople2," V.T. suggested. "Hacksaw Sixty-Nine," he added.

"You've been following my posts?"

V.T. nodded. Waited. Said, "As soon as you're ready."

George's escort leaned in and stage-whispered, "He means now."

George asked for confirmation with his eyes, and V.T. confirmed in words. "It would be nice," he said. "Show of good faith."

George took out his phone, swiped, tapped, and began thumbing. He trolled his own last post on the site, the one in which he'd advised his fellow anarchists they had nothing to lose but their blockchains. He started out soft.

"Hey, a-holes, this right here's the invisible hand of the marketplace giving y'all the one-finger salute!"

The comment was met with immediate and predictable results.

"Blow me . . ." "Dickweed . . ." "Hope you enjoy that capitalist splooge, cash sucker . . ."

George handed his phone over to his new boss. V.T. scrolled, nodding. "Oh, here's a good one . . ." He handed the phone back.

One of the site's regulars was going off on a rant about how he was such a "privacy phreak" he wouldn't even use his turn signal.

GimmeLibberT: "I ain't telling the man which way *I'm* turning, bra."

George smiled. "That's some serious white privilege there, dude."

"?????"

"1: u know u aint getting accidentally cop-shot for pulling that crap and 2: u let the whole ABC soup know what u had for breakfast on Q yesterday."

"Naw, bra, just my Q-mates."

"Yo, bro, Q changed TOS again."

It was, in fact, Quire's frequent changes to its terms of service that brought V.T. to George's attention as a legitimate target. How things had changed . . .

"Crap," GimmeLibberT typed, followed by the redundant "poop" emoji.

"Toodles," George posted back before dragging that part of his life into the little trash can at the bottom of his screen.

Before leaving the Quire executive suite, George decided to raise a finger of his own. *"Uno?"*

"Sí?"

"What was that story about?" George asked. "The one about the brain scan."

"You," V.T. said. "And the fact that you accepted this job before you ever did that thing with my"—pause—"I mean, *your* car."

That's right, George thought, *I've got a car now.* He looked at the fob he'd been clenching so hard since getting it; there was a stylized *V* outlined in white against his reddened palm.

V.T., looking at his new hire stare at the fob, finally thought to ask, "You have a license, right?"

George was about to say, "Not yet," when the car gifter turned to his escort.

"Get the kid a license," he said. "And maybe a new birth certificate while you're at it. Something where the DOB is a little more conducive to being gainfully employed."

The escort nodded, and that was that: they were leaving George's first meeting with the man himself, the teen already wondering whether he'd be able to afford the insurance on his new ride when it occurred to him he hadn't asked about other forms of compensation, like salary, benefits, how leave worked if he didn't want to ever leave. But before George could raise a finger or say, *"Uno"* (or maybe *"Dos"*), the door to the Quire executive suite had already closed as definitively as any other door he'd ever walked out of for the last time.

11

Strange as it is to say, dementia can have a sweet spot. Especially in a family where there's been some bad blood due to bad attitudes, behaviors, ideas, habits, opinions, grudges—pretty much due to any forgettable thing. Because despite all the grief and suffering and premature mourning they'll cause for the survivors, those plaques and tangles slowly gumming up the works of recall can, for a time, provide the perfect memory hole in which to bury hatchets. After all, who wouldn't like to forget some part of their past?

Pandora's fellow in hyperexpressiveness, Jim Carrey, starred in a movie called *Eternal Sunshine of the Spotless Mind* in which targeted forgetting played a central role. It was too bad dementia didn't work that way, more selectively and consistently. But the disease followed its own logic, not working all at once, but progressively, peeling away the years like onion layers, the outermost brittle, brown paper a breath could break, while underneath the memories remained supple and powerful—and liable to bring forth tears for all the contradictory reasons people shed them.

During the first few visits, Pandora found Gladys on the good side of both the facility and her disease, meaning she could still make her own meals but would have trouble telling you what she'd had for lunch—especially if it hadn't been rendered more memorable by, say, the smoke detector going off. This last Gladys addressed directly at one point during an early visit. Turning and pointing an arthritis-crinkled finger at the blinking light over the doorway, she said: "I'm watching you."

"Who are you talking to, Gram?"

"Him; *that*," Gladys said before waving her hand dismissively. "Smokey the Bear over there. I know they're waiting for me to set it off. That's when they turn on the camera and start recording, looking for one more slipup before they send me across the hall."

"Across the hall?"

"The dingbat wing," Gladys said. "The ones who need help taking a dump. But I'm too smart for 'em."

"How's that?"

"Check the fridge."

Pandora did. Mustard, milk, a loaf of bread, and stacked plastic tubs of processed meat.

"I don't get near that damn stove," her grandmother said, meaning the toaster oven. "That's asking for trouble. But if sandwiches were good enough for that Earl fellow, they're good enough for me."

"That's some good thinking, Gram," Pandora said, refusing to check the nutrition labels to see how much sodium and preservatives her grandmother's cold-cut-centric diet entailed.

"You want me to make you something?"

Pandora closed the refrigerator door. "I got a better idea," she announced, prepared to be argued with, but still giving it a try. "How about we blow this pop stand and have somebody serve *us* for a change?"

"You mean a restaurant?"

Pandora nodded and then braced for the excuses involving the 101 dietary issues that made dining out impossible—the same ones that had broken her grandfather's heart before shutting it down altogether. Instead, when she looked up, Gladys already had one boot on and was stepping into the other.

"I'll drive," she said.

"Like hell you will," Pandora said. "You lost your license, remember?"

"That was some *bull*shit," Gladys muttered. "That's what *that* was."

"Grand*ma*," Pandora said, trying for a scold in her voice, but laughing in spite of herself.

Turning into the parking lot for Nanook's Family Diner, Pandora pulled her father's F-150 up to one of the icicle-framed windows, set the parking brake, and then went around to the passenger side to hold her grandmother's gloved hand as she stepped down. Thus far, their adventure in free-range elder care had been uneventful, but that was about to change.

"Stop!" her grandmother shouted within seconds of stepping through the door. "I can't see," followed by a surprisingly strong arm shooting out and grabbing the sleeve of her escort's parka.

Pandora froze on the spot. She'd grown unaccustomed to the ways of the elderly since her grandfather passed away, recalling little more than this: their bones were brittle. They could break a hip at the drop of a hat. Did the same fragility apply to their eyes? Could they be struck blind by stepping the wrong way? Her grandmother's glasses were already pretty thick, so . . .

Pandora could feel the panic rising toward her face as she imagined the ordeal of navigating her now-blind grandmother back to . . . *where*? Did they allow blind people back into the assisted-living side? Or did the sudden onset of permanent night herald her grandmother's exile to extended care? But as she turned to ask the rules, it became clear that Gladys's glasses weren't. The culprit wasn't fog, but ice, caked thick around the lenses. It was thirty below outside, seventy-five and humid inside, thanks to the breakfast buffet's steam tables. Of course her glasses had iced up.

"Oh, for Pete's sake," Pandora said, unhooking the spectacles from around her grandmother's ears before turning and turning again, looking for someplace to thaw them. A waitress, sight-challenged herself, tapped her on the shoulder and pointed to the baseboard heater running along the outside wall, next to a coatrack where parkas hung and underneath which boots puddled.

"Thanks."

"No prob."

Her grandmother blinked, her old blue eyes seeming suddenly smaller without the Coke-bottle lenses in front of them. The effect changed her whole face, making it seem naked, defenseless, and far from the manipulative, stink-eye-inflicting hypochondriac Roger had made his widowed mother out to be.

"Hot," Gladys blurted after Pandora tried returning the newly thawed lenses to their former resting place. The teen flinched, pulling back, a stem in each hand.

They hadn't even had breakfast yet. They'd not gotten a table, much less looked at a menu, and already she'd succeeded in blinding, then scalding her father's mother, making her wonder if maybe this punishment was a twofer, intended to teach a lesson not only to Pandora but to the estranged Gladys as well.

They got a booth next to the window they were parked outside of, so Pandora could make sure that the cord from the underhood heater stayed plugged in to the complementary kiosk. It was not unheard of for roaming bands of Alaskan youth to run through parking lots, unplugging vehicles so they could watch their owners cursing over frozen engine blocks. Pandora had overheard her locker neighbors on the curling team bragging about such adventures back before fate pranked one of them harder than anything she could have come up with.

Gladys cleared her throat of a prodigious amount of old-lady phlegm, making her granddaughter turn away from her ad hoc stakeout.

"Sorry, Gram," Pandora said, hooking a thumb at the window. "Kids."

Gladys nodded, her ropey-veined hands crossed at the fingertips and sporting fresh nail polish, granddaughter-applied at the old lady's insistence that she'd not be caught dead out in the real world without a little "gussying up" first. Pandora caught her trying not to be obvious about looking around to see if anyone noticed her nails, shining bloody red, despite the seasonal gloom. She looked down at her menu, to give her grandmother's vanity a little privacy, but when she looked up again, the old woman's eyes were focused right on her. They seemed to sparkle just short of tearing up, not from sadness but joy. *Over what?* Pandora wondered.

But then it hit her like a ton of proverbial bricks. *Me,* she thought. *She's overjoyed to see* me. By which time, the tipping point had been reached, and the old lady's eyes spilled over, two grudging tears running down the crags and valleys of her well-worn face, forcing her to lift her glasses to dab at the ducts with the edge of her napkin, leaving a single white flake of it behind.

Pandora gestured, trying to indicate that Gladys had something on her face.

"What is it?" Gladys asked as Pandora reached over and removed the offending speck. She presented it, stuck to the tip of her finger.

"I get emotional sometimes," Gladys admitted. "An old lady's prerogative, I've been told. But also"—she knocked on her forehead with a gnarled hand—"a sign of more senior moments in this old girl's future."

"How bad is it?" Pandora asked.

"I haven't forgotten how to poop on my own," her grandmother said. "Yet," she added.

Pandora's eyes stared; her face, meanwhile, reprised the role that had turned her into a meme. "Jesus, Gram," she said, letting her head sink, along with her curtaining hair.

"Change of subject," Gladys announced, pressing her spread hands firmly down on the table between them.

"Okay?"

"Why do you hide your pretty face?" her grandmother asked, raising a hand to brush Pandora's hair out of the way so she could get a better look.

"Gram, if this face is pretty *anything*, it's pretty embarrassing."

Gladys frowned. "That's *our* face you're talking about, dear."

Ah, the dreaded "dear." Pandora had crossed a line, tried backpedaling. "It's—I'd like a little privacy when it comes to what I'm feeling," she tried.

"Oh yes, privacy," Gladys said, her eye roll making noise. "During the war, the government read our mail and it wasn't any big scandal."

"Which war was this?" Pandora asked.

"The last one that mattered, after the one that was supposed to end any others." She paused. "And then we found that, no, we needed to start numbering them."

"World War II?" Pandora guessed.

Her grandmother nodded.

"I had two brothers who served," she said. "Only one came back. And every letter we wrote each other went through the government censor. All we'd get were photographs of the pages with parts blacked out—'redacted' is what they call it now. They called the photographs V-mail—'V for Victory.'"

"Did you ever get the originals back?"

Gladys shook her head.

Pandora was amazed—and appalled. "What happened to them?"

Gladys shrugged. "Burned, shredded, stored? I don't know. And God help you if your loved one's handwriting was already cramped, because the photographs we got were about the size of a postcard. Some words I couldn't read, even if they hadn't been blocked out."

"That's awful," Pandora said. "It's like Big Brother."

"That book came out after the war, so nobody knew enough to complain." She paused. "Not that anybody would have. Privacy, shmivacy. Our *country* had been *attacked*. Loose lips sink ships. And every break we took . . ."

Gladys stopped suddenly.

"What is it, Gram?"

The old woman shook her head, then mimed pulling a zipper across her lips.

"We're not at war now," Pandora pointed out.

"Oh no? Last I counted, there were at least two."

Pandora let her head sink. She was being tutored in current affairs by someone whose short-term memory was shorter—diagnostically and demonstrably—than even that of the news media, busily flitting after every twittering twit that caught its attention.

"Why do you hide that pretty face?" Gladys asked, as if for the first time.

But instead of correcting her, Pandora decided to document the moment for later reference, should they ever have this conversation again—which they no doubt would. And so she slid around to Gladys's side of the booth and asked the old woman to skootch over. She rested her face on her grandmother's shoulder, raised her phone, and framed the two of them.

"Say cheese," Pandora said.

"Limburger." Gladys smiled—an old joke for an old gal, she'd later claim, the next time she used it. For the moment, though, she stared in wonder at the immediacy with which she was seeing the moment documented, no mailers, no chemicals, no waiting.

"It's not such a bad face," Gladys said, as if she wasn't only selling it to Pandora, but to herself as well. Looking over the top of her glasses to get even closer to the screen, she took hold of the phone as if it were a mirror. “Not bad at all,” she repeated, rearranging wisps of white with her free hand. “I think I’ll keep it.”

“Is there any other option?” Pandora asked, a smartass still being punished.

“A lady,” the older one said, “always has options.” She paused in her fussing, grimaced, and let it go. “So long as she keeps her legs closed, and her mind open.”

Pandora laughed in spite of herself, marking the precise moment she began falling in love with her father’s mother.

12

The door to the Quire executive suite had closed behind them with the hermetic gasp of an airlock when George's escort removed his dark glasses, loosened his tie, and yanked out his earpiece with an audible pop. Working a finger around his vacated ear hole, he spent a few seconds mouthing Os as if equalizing the pressure inside his skull after a long flight.

"Deep, *cleansing* breath," he announced, rising on tiptoes as he inhaled, squatting on the exhale, and then settling back to his previous, intimidating height. "I think V.T. likes you," he said, making it sound like a blind date's excuse for an overly affectionate Doberman. "Whad'ya do anyway? Get a PhD in neural nets from MIT before turning, what"—he squinted at George, estimating, then up-talking—"*fifteen*?"

"I borrowed his car," George deadpanned.

"I'm sure there's a story there," his escort said, "I'd be better off not knowing."

The two walked in semisilence, the only sounds the squeak of George's sneakers and the tip-tap of his escort's dress shoes. Finally: "So whad'ya wanna see first?" his escort asked.

"My"—guessing—"work cube?"

The other consulted his phone. "Office," he said. He looked at George again, an unmistakable expression of awe on his face, followed by an intimacy-forcing hand on the shoulder. "So whatcha doin' for lunch, noob?"

Along the way to George's office, they passed a face he recognized from the pier where he'd called him Dad while wirelessly infecting his phone. His extravagant suit coat was one of many items he had stuffed into a moving box, along with a framed family photo featuring two kids, one of each, bookended by the jacket and his spouse. They were grouped like a section of the Golden Gate Bridge, George mentally plotting the swoop of suspension cable through the data points of their heads. The smiling face in the photo was a few years younger than the real-life one reddened by either the weight of his workplace knickknacks or the humiliation of being escorted out of the building with them. George looked back, feeling sorry for the guy and wanting to say something, but then they turned the corner and there it was, yanking his eyes back around like a junkyard magnet: his office.

The space had been freshly vacated; that was clear from the dust-blasted outlines of the framed diplomas and/or personal photos that had until recently hung on the walls. Atop the two-drawer cabinet next to the desk, an Olympic logo of water stains, surface tension still holding a last damp ring in place. On the desk itself, a box labeled "Trash" full of cable spaghetti, sporting connectors that had gone extinct with the introduction of USB, then mini-USB, then USB-C. A webbed Aeron chair lay on its back, one caster still spinning, while in the corner of the room, George noticed a pile of fake plastic poop that turned out not to be fake after all. That last memento cured the newbie of any sympathy he may have felt for the weak link he'd apparently replaced in this corporate nature documentary.

"If this is what the interns get," he joked, "I can't wait until management takes me seriously."

"Oh, they're taking you plenty serious," his escort assured. Pause. "You know that little visit with V.T. today?"

"Yeah?"

"First time I ever met the man in person."

"That a fact?"

"Fact."

"How long—" George began.

"Sixteen years," his escort said, not letting him finish.

"Wow, that's as long as—"

"Right," his guide said, more than ready to move on.

The QHQ campus had all the trappings of a successful tech company with more money than it knew what to do with, trying to lure talent away from a half dozen other competitors, equally profligate in their attempts to poach the aforementioned talent. These perks included, in no particular order: snack bars, game rooms, cafeterias, gyms, climbing walls, massage stations, turbo sleep pods, chipping stations, security substations—all of them plural—followed by the offices of the in-house intellectual property lawyers divided into those suing to protect in-house IP versus those defending against suits from the outside, followed by the assorted day cares for children, elder parents, animal companions, and trophy spouses. As one of the company's latest talent acquisitions, George found himself nodding with a mix of embarrassment and trepidation as they followed the facility's intranavigation system giving his tour guide instructions through the earpiece he'd reinserted for the purpose.

"And now we have," his escort would announce, followed by a scripted description of whatever it was.

"Next we have," a little terser with each repetition, George's escort having apparently concluded that lunching his way into the latest golden brat's good graces wasn't going to happen.

"Excuse me," George finally said, realizing that his embarrassment/trepidation was, in fact, the gastrointestinal symptoms of needing a lavatory.

"Sure. Yeah. Okay," his escort said, thumbing his earpiece in a little tighter and then adding, "This way."

As a matter of corporate policy, all Quire bathrooms were unisex, each spacious unit designed for single occupancy and featuring outside it not the generic stick figures hopelessly mired in the binary preconceptions of the patriarchy but the friendly naked people from the *Pioneer 11* plaque.

"V.T.'s idea," his escort explained. "They might be replacing them with the 'poop' emoji, though." Pause. "The nudity's been deemed objectifying."

If he hadn't been convinced of how much of a nerd node Quire HQ was before then, that first trip to the bathroom did it. Whiteboards. They had Wi-Fi-enabled whiteboards in the bathroom. Not only that, but said whiteboards were not subject to the scatological or homophobic graffiti one might expect in a place known for its brotopian inclinations, the cosmetic touch of unisex bathrooms notwithstanding. And so, instead of dirty limericks and freehand sketches of penises, what George found while making his first deposit were snippets of code, the Bellman equation, Zen koans aimed at getting the reader to think about thinking, an occasional quote from *2001: A Space Odyssey* (!), Venn diagrams, quotes from Monty Python, and a flowchart of pseudocode for a machine-learning algorithm to automate the making of either microwave popcorn or ramen noodles, depending on what the variables *X* and *Y* actually represented.

George stood by the sink for a moment, waiting for the faucet to turn on before noticing the wall units for: 1) hand sanitizer, 2) hand soap, 3) hand dryer, and 4) disposable rubber gloves. Collectively, this seemed like overkill, but then he noticed the quirky-retro, hand-operated spigots for hot and cold flanking the faucet above the sink. He wondered about the order of usage, especially for the gloves, finally deciding they came last, to prevent any contamination to or from the door handle, after noticing the wastebasket full of discarded blue jazz hands waiting immediately next to the exit. Surprisingly, there was no placard on the door, insisting that all employees must wash hands before exiting. Perhaps that would have been the actual overkill, considering the audience, George figured, holding the exit open with his shoe as he snapped off his gloves and reemerged for the rest of the tour.

"Bet that's a load off your mind," his escort observed—clearly not part of the script and all the confirmation George needed that, yes, the friend thing was definitely off the table.

After about an hour more of thises and thats—and after it seemed his corporate guide was getting ready to abandon him—George finally asked about what he'd been dying to see all along: "What about Q-Labs?"

Like pretty much everybody else on the planet, Quire's latest hire already knew quite a bit about Q-Labs—or thought he did. This was because of the predictable CYA PR soft shoe: whenever George's new employer got in trouble for mining or manipulating the data of its users, the airwaves would suddenly fill with helpful ads, reminding viewers about all the good things coming out of Q-Labs. These commercials, which corporate insisted on calling PSAs (and for which they claimed a tax write-off), always started with a stark title card featuring an inspiring quote from some dead white guy, followed by a retro synth harpsichord over a moving slideshow featuring AI-enabled bots helping the handicapped, teaching toddlers, trundling in to defuse some terrorist booby trap, or translating the barks and meows of pets into emojis, letting their humans know they were hungry or needed to be let out. Then it was back to a black title card, out of which would whip the rainbow *Q* for Quire, followed by a hyphen and the word *Labs*, each punctuated in turn by a bong, a bing, and a bong—the parent company's audio signature, an inversion of the one used by Intel. Last but not least came the slogan: "Doing good is what we do."

"If you wanted to meet the rock stars," George's escort said gruffly, "you should have said so earlier." He then stirred the air with his finger, meaning they'd be turning the tour around and heading back toward the windowed office they'd started at, smack dab in the middle of Q-Labs territory where George, it seemed, had been assigned to Q-Brain, the lab devoted to the development and commercialization of artificial intelligence.

George nodded curtly and followed, as if this news were only what he expected and not the cause of the fireworks going off in his head, as if it were his birthday, Christmas, New Year's, and Halloween, all rolled into one. It was as if V.T. had seen into his heart and divined the desire that led to his "borrowing" the CEO's car in the first place. Because the excuse about wanting to see if he could do it was exactly that: an excuse. As was any claim he'd done it to score points on behalf of the proletariat at the expense of the one percent and its excesses. Ditto on the needing-a-smile thing. And as far as seeking revenge for the ever-shifting sands of Quire's self-serving terms of service—yeah, that was a good cover story and a big fat no.

The reason George hacked V.T.'s ride was because he wanted to get a look under the hood of the Voltaire's AI. The plan had been to download what he could from the CPU before leaving the hardware for the amateur chop-shoppers to liquidate—a plan nixed by the car's coming with its original owner still attached. George was particularly interested in what the source code had to say about how it would decide between killing its passenger versus a busload of kids when those were the vehicle's only two options. That was the ethical quandary ethicists had dubbed the "trolley dilemma," so named because it went back that far, back to when roads outside San Francisco had cable cars and track-switching decisions were made by humans and implemented manually.

Nowadays, the dilemma was applied to autonomous vehicles and used to show how far they were from prime time. It was also why the Voltaire's autonomous mode was called "copilot," to shift the blame for the inevitable casualties to the owner as opposed to the manufacturer. George figured the euphemism meant the Voltaire's coders hadn't quite automated the dilemma's resolution to their lawyers' satisfaction. However, as a programmer himself, George was also pretty sure there'd be some beta script in the source code, a deleted REM or asterisk away from going live.

The truth was, he'd been dreaming of AI ever since those infamous babysitting episodes with Uncle Jack. His first obsession was to meet the smooth-talking HAL in person (or silicon, as the case may be), only to have his heart broken once he understood how numbers worked and realized that the *actual* year 2001 had come and gone before he was even born, with nothing even remotely like actual artificial intelligence on the horizon.

Doing a casual survey of what the species had accomplished since the real 2001, George was tempted to conclude that "peak humanity" had been reached sometime before either the 2000 US election or the falling of the twin towers. Ever since then, mankind had clearly been on the downslope. But there was one exception. Sometime between his learning how numbers worked and now, AI research had started taking off again, with machine learning, neural nets, and Big Data all converging to stage a legitimate advance into HAL territory.

And now, it seemed, he'd been handed the opportunity to bring his childhood friend HAL into existence. *Pinch me,* George thought.

Or thought he thought.

"I'd really prefer not to," his disgruntled guide said, before leading the homeless boy home.

13

The thing about dementia's sweet spot is once you get past it, the rest can be bitter as hell. And though it seemed counterintuitive, Pandora's sudden visits had made things worse. Gladys had been aware of her lovely, lovely brain's going out on her, but had grown to accept it, in part, because she had a secret she could never tell. And she'd kept her secret from everyone—her husband, her son, and all the people she'd left behind in the lower forty-eight to spare her from temptation. Thus forgetting meant putting down a burden, the job of keeping quiet finally complete.

But then Pandora showed up.

Slipping into oblivion without any witnesses was one thing, but doing it—*now*—in front of her only grandchild? After they returned from their adventure in the real world and Pandora went home, Gladys got so anxious she began hyperventilating, thought she was dying right then and there—briefly welcomed it—but then hit the call button. By the time a white-jacketed gentleman knocked on her door, she could not remember having summoned him.

"What's wrong with me?" she asked after opening the door.

"You called me," the doctor said, letting himself in, "remember?"

"Um . . ."

He changed subjects. Noting the way her nightgown clung from excessive sweating and a certain breathlessness in her speech, he made a diagnosis of anxiety to which Gladys assented because she was still feeling it and it was obvious. But the doctor didn't stop there, because anxiety rarely travels alone, especially in the elderly in Gladys's condition.

"The staff are worried you may be depressed," he tested, attributing the secondary diagnosis to others because, well, *hunch* didn't sound very professional.

"Isn't that natural," Gladys asked, "under the circumstances?"

The doctor agreed that it was, but then used it against her. "So you're agreeing that you're depressed?"

Gladys nodded, admitting that, "Yes," she was depressed. "Can't you tell from my face?"

The doctor looked, then looked closer. The truth was, everyone's skin loses elasticity with time. And in Gladys's case, a lifetime of hyper-emotiveness had etched her face with worry lines that could easily camouflage her darker moods, while the lighter ones were made brighter still, the act of smiling helping to iron out even the hardest-set wrinkles. "Ah, there it is," the doctor announced, followed by, "Okay, then," and his prescription pad.

"You can stop that," Gladys said.

The doctor didn't. He clicked his pen and started writing instead.

"I said, 'Stop that,' you shameless pill pusher."

The doctor looked hurt. "Now why would you say something like that?" He chuckled as an afterthought—to show he hadn't taken the remark seriously.

Gladys snatched the pen out of his hand, to show that she was. "What does this say?" she asked, indicating what was written on the side of the pen.

"Zoloft."

"And what does *that* say?" she asked, pointing at what he'd written on his pad.

"Zoloft."

"And here?" she asked, tapping the printed header of the pad, which also read, "Zoloft."

"They hand them out," the doctor said in his defense, meaning the pharmaceutical reps that visited regularly, dispensing ad-emblazoned swag along with advice re: off-label opportunities for prescribing their wares. "It would be a waste to let it go to waste."

"How circular of you," Gladys observed. "Not that it justifies you depriving me of a natural emotional reaction to losing my mind."

"It's not your *whole* mind," the professional prescriber rushed to reassure her—ineffectually. "It's not like you'll be forgetting to breathe or anything. Nothing that falls into the category of an autonomic response."

"How about going to the toilet?"

"Well, that's a learned response," the doctor pointed out. "Potty training and all that."

"So that's a yes," Gladys pressed on. "I might start shitting myself."

"Might, *hell*," the doctor continued, allowing his diagnostic certainty to override any sense of professional decorum. "Pretty much definitely. Your disease has a well-documented progression."

"So maybe remembering how to breathe isn't quite the blessing you're making it out to be," Gladys said, to herself, later, after the doctor had left, replaying the conversation in her head, not so much brooding as trying to make the important parts stick.

"What are those?" Pandora asked two days later, during her next visit.

"What are what?"

Pandora retrieved two amber vials from her grandmother's wastebasket.

"Happy pills," Gladys said. "Apparently, being up-with-people is now mandatory."

"Why'd you fill the prescriptions if you weren't going to take them?"

"That's one of the drawbacks with assisted living," Gladys said. "Sometimes you're assisted against your will. Fortunately, they couldn't find the hose for blowing 'em down my throat, so . . ."

It wasn't until Pandora's visit was nearly over that Gladys confessed it was a shame they'd made her mood an issue, one she refused to let them win.

"Why's that, Gram?"

"Because 'happy pills' don't seem like such a bad idea sometimes," Gladys said. "The side effects, though . . ." She pulled down her copy of *Worst Pills, Best Pills*, dog-eared to the sections on antianxiety and antidepression medications. "Here," she said, handing over the book and then pointing at one of the side effects. "How's *that* for irony?" she asked.

Pandora read about the pharmaceutical paradox of using mood-altering medications on elderly patients with dementia: they could actually speed up the patient's decline. Which raised a question: Was the drug treating the mood, or simply making the patient forget about it? In other words, was it a bug or a feature?

"Wow," Pandora said, looking up from the book. "That sucks."

Gladys shrugged her hunchbacked shoulders. "What're you gonna do?" she asked no one in particular. Not that that stopped Pandora from thinking about it anyway.

Cannabis, marijuana, pot, weed, grass, reefer, ganja, Mary Jane . . .

That's what Pandora was thinking about. Even old people were using it medicinally nowadays. The cannabinoids were supposed to help with appetite, anxiety, pain, all constant companions for the unlit elderly. And wasn't that what Gladys needed in a place like this, a little something-something to slow her roll, make it a little more copacetic with the ambient amble of "nursing home life"? And if Pandora needed to demonstrate that the herbaceutical in question was benign, well, that's what you called a win-win situation.

And so she came bearing gifts in a baking pan covered with tinfoil.

"What've you got there?" the old woman asked.

"Um," Pandora said, pulling back the shiny cover, "happy . . . brownies?"

"You mean *medibles*?"

"How do you . . . ?"

"I'm not a prisoner here," Gladys said. "Not yet anyway. I walk. I meet people. They talk. You're not the only relative with a green thumb in baking."

"So?" Pandora said, moving the pan a little closer.

Gladys reached in. "Well," she said, "it would be rude to refuse . . ."

"Cheers," her granddaughter said, tapping her own hash brownie against her grandmother's, a helpful hand underneath to catch any crumbs.

Now *this* was the way to visit an old-folks' home! Because while Pandora got a kick out of her grandmother before, she *loved* Gladys stoned. The feeling, predictably, was mutual.

"Another?" the old lady said, pushing the pan across the kitchenette table toward her granddaughter.

"Don't mind if I do," Pandora said, brushing invisible crumbs off her chin, shirt, and pants, before working up another square of THC-laced chocolatey goodness.

"You know how I knew Alaska was going to be different from anything I'd known before?" Gladys asked around a mouthful of brownie.

Pandora shrugged.

"The toilets. The indoor ones," the old lady said. "I'm sitting on a toilet, and all of a sudden, I'm wondering if I'm having hot flashes even though I was way too young at the time. Why? My butt was sweating to beat the band. I reached for the toilet paper, and I almost slipped off. And I don't know what possessed me, but after I flushed, I held my hand over the water. It was warm. I could feel the heat coming off it. That's what told me Alaska was different. They heated their toilet water so it wouldn't freeze."

"So they don't do that everywhere else?" Pandora asked. She'd not been outside the state since she was a baby, and well before being potty trained.

"Not where I came from," Gladys said. Paused. "Can you bring some more of these next time?"

"Of course," Pandora said.

Not.

It should be stressed that the legal status of marijuana in the state of Alaska was a bit bipolar at best. First decriminalized in 1975 and then legalized shortly thereafter, pot was recriminalized by 1990, re-decriminalized by court ruling in 2003, recriminalized by law in 2006, and finally legalized (again) by ballot initiative in 2014. So what Pandora was doing wasn't currently against state law, just the federal ones. And even those weren't a big deal under the previous administration, but then . . .

"I'm sorry, dear," a receptionist said the next time Pandora prepared to walk past with a foil-covered plate of organic mood modifiers, "but I'll be confiscating those."

"Huh?" And then Pandora noticed a dog that hadn't been there the last time. She eyed it and it eyed her back, both flaring nostrils on high alert.

"You can feel free to be charged with a federal crime out there," the receptionist said, pointing outside, "but you're not finding any accomplices in here." She slid a copy of the laminated explanation that informed her that due to a change in federal policy put in place by an attorney general who had personal investments in the for-profit prison industry, the Golden Heart's previous practice of looking the other way was history.

"Seriously?" Pandora said, handing back the wobbly sheet of plastic.

"Like a heart attack," the receptionist said, shaking the pan into a wastebasket already lined with a biohazard baggie, the brownies dislodging in twos and threes, reminding Pandora of nothing so much as reindeer scat dotting the snow as its depositor lumbered along.

"Sorry, Gram," Pandora said, after showing up empty-handed.

"About?"

"The brownies," her granddaughter said. "I promised to bring more, but the gestapo at the guest center seized them."

Gladys had gotten up during her granddaughter's apology and seemed not to be listening. She went to her mini fridge and pulled out a plastic tub. "You mean these?" she asked, pulling back the lid to reveal a few leftovers from the day before.

Pandora was touched that she'd saved them. She'd assumed Gladys would do what she'd do—take as needed until they were gone.

Her grandmother divided the remaining brownies onto two paper plates, one for Pandora, one for her. Glasses of milk followed. "Now where were we?" the old lady asked.

"Toilets, I think," Pandora said, figuring they'd exhausted the subject anyway.

Not.

They fascinate us at the brackets of life, these receptacles for putting up with our shit. Both when we're young (and learning to use them) and again when we're old (and forgetting what we learned). But even granting the fondness her grandmother often displayed for discussing bowel movements and assorted related topics, Pandora was unprepared for what Gladys casually said next: "Your father was born in a toilet."

"Excuse me?" she said.

"Plopped out right into the bowl," Gladys said. "It was the funniest thing I've seen in my entire life. Your grandfather practically faints, but I'm the one with the kid coming out of me like some astronaut doing a spacewalk. You ever see a fresh umbilical cord? Nasty . . ."

"You're serious," Pandora said, snap-sobered and horrified.

"Listen," her grandmother said, "it was *fine*. There wasn't anything else in the toilet, and the water's always warm, so . . ."

"My dad was born in a toilet," Pandora said, repeating the words, cementing the memory, as if there was a chance in hell she'd ever forget. She could practically hear the splash.

"Yep," Gladys said. "Little shit turned out okay, though."

Pandora was still too stunned to laugh. Ah, but once that wore off—well, then it was a different story.

Gladys had been happy to have her granddaughter there and was happy while the visit and brownies lasted, but once both were gone, the old dark clouds rolled back in. And here's the funny thing about being happy: it's addictive. Maybe not chemically or biologically, but emotionally, which can be more powerful than the other two combined. And so in a moment of weakness, Gladys took one of those pills designed to either make her happy or help her forget that she wasn't.

Nothing.

The pill pusher had left her paperwork explaining that that's the way it would go with one of them at first, warning that she'd have to keep taking it, let it build up in her system, before it would make a difference.

She'd already forgotten that part but reminded herself of it by rereading what the doctor left, then comparing the paperwork to the label on the vial she'd taken the pill from. Zoloft. Right. That was the one that took weeks to do anything. She checked the paperwork for the other. Xanax. That was the one that worked right away. "Well, let's hope so," she said, fishing one out and placing it on her tongue.

14

Imagine the tech version of Willy Wonka's chocolate factory minus the Oompa-Loompa slave labor, or Santa's toy shop minus its elfish servitude. That's what the Q-Brain tour was like for George, wandering agog. When it came to "wow factor," Q-Brain was pretty much nothing but, starting with the very first stop: the Glass Brain.

Upon hearing the words, George had assumed they were metaphorical; they weren't. But before he'd be allowed to view the *objet* itself, he first had to show how big he thought an actual brain was.

"What do you mean?" he asked, and the lead researcher—the unit's ad hoc MC—took first one hand and then the other.

"Set your hands to bracket an imaginary brain, perhaps your own."

George did as he was told, and the MC took a picture with his phone to document it. "On average," he went on to say, "people will estimate an organ roughly twice as large as what it actually is." Pause. "No smirking, please." He made a fist and gestured for George to do the same, then bumped their knuckles together. "That's how big the average adult brain is," he said. "The size of two fists." He unclenched his hemisphere to reach for the photographic evidence he'd snapped a moment earlier. "Now how's *that* supposed to fit into your favorite hat?" he asked, opening pincer fingers against the screen to blow up the image.

"Um," George said.

"Because that's where the brain has to fit," he said. "It's inside your head, and though it might *seem* like the cathedral of all knowledge, its cupola is little bigger than side-by-side cup holders." He took a scripted pause. "Think on that and be humbled, human."

Having concluded the canned intro, the tech signaled, and the Glass Brain was wheeled out, jiggling slightly like stiff Jell-O whenever the casters rolled over an uneven seam in the floor. The eponymous object was an actual brain removed from a once-living human. The lipids (fats, basically) had been removed and replaced with a transparent hydrogel that left the crisscrossing fabric of neurons in place, but now visible for detailed study. Using fluorescent dyes of different hues, it was possible to light up and trace the axons of individual neurons, a feat demonstrated by turning off the lights. And there it was, a pale thread, squiggling and branching and looking like nothing so much as the root system of a tree, but lit in firefly green: a lightning strike, frozen horizontally. A voice joined them in the dark: "The floating light bulb used in cartoons to symbolize the moment of discovery? There it is. And we can do that with each neuron in that bundle that warehouses every hope, dream, joy, and moment of despair that makes us who we are." Pause. "You've heard of reverse engineering? Well, this is the first step in doing that for the most precious thing any of us has."

And then the lights came back up, amid silence and blinking, the audience of one given a moment to think about what he'd seen, to imagine that pale thread of green light winding through the hopes and dreams inside his own head.

"We're the Connectome Team," its leader said. "Our goal is to determine if the way information is encoded in the brain is structural. There's no obvious, anatomical hard disk in the brain, so where does the information get stored? Our hypothesis: it's in the *arrangement* of the branching neurons and the spaces defined by the synapses, like bar code, but in three or four dimensions and with a resolution on the nano scale. Our support: recent studies showing that new thoughts create new pathways and hence new *structural* patterns."

"But what—?" George began to ask, only to be cut off by the answer.

"If it's structural," the team leader continued, "then it should be readable postmortem—with the right scanner."

The Glass Brain was the first of many astonishments, and it took real willpower not to go running ahead of his tour guide to see what came next. For example: a rack of caged mice, half of which seemed to be conjoined pairs, attached by their heads. Upon closer inspection, it was clear that these mice had not been born this way.

"Okay, okay, okay," the researcher in charge said, "I know what you're thinking," he added, unironically, and as if he'd had his fill of animal rights activists protesting what he did for a living. "This is serious *science* we're doing here," he insisted. "So if you're thinking about throwing around the *v*-word . . ."

"You mean *vivisection*?" George asked, looking up from the glass cage he'd been smudging with his nose.

The spokesresearcher started waving his arms, crossing and uncrossing them like he was trying to stop traffic. "Transneural communication, thank you," he said. "We're trying to see if something one brain learns can be transferred to the other, without being taught separately." He then explained how they blindfolded and anesthetized one mouse in each pair while the other was taught to run a maze, followed by reversing the procedure to see if the second mouse could run it faster than the first.

"And . . . ?" George prodded.

The researcher's lips grew noticeably thinner. "Promising," he said, leaving it at that.

Next door, two human subjects were seated back-to-back, wearing skullcaps sprouting cables like high-tech Medusae. On a screen visible to George but hidden from either of the wired-up test subjects, a game of *Pong* seemed to be playing itself.

"The gear," a researcher said, waving his fingers over his own head, "is like this combination EEG and TMS—that's transcranial magnetic stimulation. The two go back and forth in a feedback loop, one subject sending, the other receiving, then vice versa. The result? Telepathic *Pong*, even though neither knows *consciously* that's what they're doing."

The researcher went on to explain that by monitoring the subject's heart rate, respiration, and skin conductivity, they'd shown that *subconsciously*, the subjects' *bodies* knew who was winning and who wasn't. In follow-up surveys, the losers reported feeling inexplicably "down" for a few hours afterward, while the winners volunteered for more testing.

"So what does this prove?" George asked naively.

"Prove?"

George nodded.

"That we can do *this*," the researcher said, pointing to the screen. "And it's *cool*." He paused. "Watch this," he said, hitting a button that sounded an alarm, making the players flinch, while the white blip on the screen went sailing past the nearest virtual paddle.

"Okay," George said, noncommittally.

"The days of the joystick are numbered, my friend," the tech predicted.

George tried imagining the mental space he'd have to be in to prefer having electrodes implanted in his brain to holding a physical controller. Sure, the implants might free his hands for eating or drinking or . . .

"Oh," he said.

"Yep," the tech said. "The joystick's dead; long live the, um, 'joy' stick, if you see what I mean . . ."

George wanted to say that a blind mole rat could see what the tech meant but opted for the closed-lip/thumbs-up combo.

"Not that jerking off is all this is good for," the tech hastened to add. "If that was the case, Elon wouldn't be betting big on developing a neural interface to link computers and humans, right?" He paused and then whispered behind his hand, "Next stop, the singularity." He winked.

Though George recognized the reference to the merger of human and artificial intelligence predicted by futurists such as Ray Kurzweil, he couldn't help thinking "the singularity" could be taken several ways, especially given the joystick conversation, if you saw what he meant.

Klieg lights.

That was the first thing George noticed. Once his eyes adjusted to the glare, however, he saw there was much more to see. People, specifically, all of them missing something, from limbs to divots out of their shaved heads. Many of the subjects had been borrowed from the local VA. Quire—George was informed—had something especially unpopular in the tech industry at the time: a contract with the Department of Defense.

"But not one of the *bad* kinds," the latest explainer explained.

"There are *good* kinds of military contracts?"

"Ever hear of a little thing called DARPA?"

George nodded.

"So you know the internet was originally ARPANET, right?"

"Okay," George said, reluctantly, even though he knew it was true; the internet was the result of a joint effort between the Department of Defense's research arm and academia that got out of those institutional boxes and changed the world. For that matter, Tor had been developed by the navy and refined by DARPA.

"All the brain stuff you've seen so far is being paid for because brain trauma has become the defining injury of modern warfare. SSA, Medicare, and Medicaid are also chipping in because of that buttload of dementia patients the boomers are promising to send the Fed's way."

The klieg lights were for a film crew, already shooting B-roll for the next series of PSAs. In front of the cameras, lab techs were helping subjects don virtual reality headsets to see if VR coupled with the brain's plasticity could help rewire any damaged neurons in the spinal cord or farther up. A monitor allowed viewers to see a two-dimensional rendering of what the VA-VR volunteers were seeing, which was an avatar of themselves. The goal was to see if the volunteers could move virtual parts that were impeded in their actual bodies, repeating this over and over until the avatar's movements "leaked" into "real reality."

Elsewhere, a blind vet was being fitted with what looked like a tongue depressor straight out of *A Clockwork Orange*. "There are a lot of nerve endings in the mouth—the tongue, especially—receptors for sweet, sour, salt, umami." Pause. "So instead of taste buds, think rods and cones, RGB, which stands for . . . ?"

George shrugged.

"Red, green, blue," the tech said. "You know, like the original color monitors from . . ." He looked at George like his escort had earlier, assessing his age, pre- versus post-touch-screen. "Never mind," he concluded.

The goal, the tech explained, was to facilitate artificial synesthesia. "You know, hearing colors, tasting sounds . . ."

"Dropping acid," George said softly to himself—or so he thought.

"That's a few doors down," the tech said offhandedly before cutting to the chase. "We're basically rewiring the tongue as a crude retina." He paused, turning toward the volunteer. "So how're we doing?" he asked.

The blind vet garbled something that could have been anything.

"So yeah," the tech said. "Not perfect, but . . ."

". . . a minor miracle nevertheless?" George supplied, either out of generosity or because he wanted to move on now that his curiosity over what they were doing "a few doors down" had been whetted.

The answer? Drugs, mainly. LSD, psilocybin, DMT, peyote, ayahuasca: the usual psychedelic suspects. The room in which they were being done was decidedly un-lab-like in its decor, mixing Southwestern and Far Eastern influences and dousing it all in incense—jasmine, George thought, lavender, maybe. The furniture alternated between bean filled and memory foamed, the goal apparently being the elimination of any hardness that might harsh whatever buzz was being studied. The one exception to the squeezably-soft theme was a military-green filing cabinet that seemed wheeled in straight from some WWII general's office, but for the biometric lock with which it had been retrofitted. The group's "head teacher," who also went by the nickname Dr. Strange, informed George that the file cabinet went by the nickname "our stash" and contained pretty much every mind-altering chemical known to man along with the FDA and DEA paperwork to make it kosher for scientific research. And should these substances alone fail to dislodge the stick up a test subject's mental ass, there was also an old-school isolation tank in the corner, plastered with bumper stickers advocating universal veganism, renewable energy, the visualization of "whirled peas," and, for the 2016 election, a tie between Giant Meteor and Cthulhu.

Dr. Strange, his lab coat tie-dyed, fished through one of his pockets for a peace offering, which George waved off, courtesy of unassisted flashbacks to being babysat by Uncle Jack.

"I'm cool," he said.

"You're *cool*?" Dr. Strange said, eying him strangely. He looked past George to George's escort and would-be character witness. "What says you? Cool? Not cool?"

George's escort shrugged.

Dr. Strange cupped his mouth and thought. "Let's call it cool, until proven otherwise." Pause. *"Cool?"*

"Cool," George agreed.

The next team they visited took coolness not only seriously, but literally as well. Coolness down to about as far as cool could go (i.e., a degree or so above absolute zero), which explained several large frost-covered tanks that dominated the space, surrounded by various wired nests, stacked and shelved controller units, and coiled copper tubing that reminded George of a high-tech distilling operation. The team leader offered that skeptical observers from Q-Brain's other teams had commented derisively on the similarity, suggesting that bootlegging and quantum computing shared a common goal: bottled moonshine. That budget envy might be the true source of such comments wasn't too great a leap.

"Certainly not a quantum one," he said, before warning George to be careful where he leaned. Looking down, George saw that the scientist had begun fingering the stump of his right index finger, the rest of which was missing after the second knuckle. Following George's eyes, the quantum computing team leader held his hand up for closer inspection. "Frostbite," he said.

"Duly noted," George said, pulling in whatever extremities he could a bit closer to his body.

"I call this my Schröfinger," the team leader continued. "You know, Schrödinger's cat?"

"Not personally."

"So you have this cat, a Geiger counter, and a vial of poison in a sealed-off room," the tech explained, "and if the Geiger counter detects any random radioactivity, the poison will be released. Until somebody checks, the cat is in a quantum state of being both dead *and* alive as far as an outside observer is concerned. But when somebody finally *does* check—boom: it's decided." He paused, letting George digest this information. "Well, that's the quantum paradox in a nutshell. Except, instead of a cat, it's a quanta of electromagnetic energy, like light, which can act as either a particle or a wave in a cloud of probability until it's observed, at which point it's definitively called as heads or tails, particle or wave."

George, who'd been nodding along to this explanation, suddenly stuck out a finger, opened his mouth, reconsidered, put his finger away, and closed his mouth. Thus prefaced, his ad hoc physics lecturer took it upon himself to engage in a little mind reading.

"But," he said, on George's behalf, "what's this got to do with my missing finger, right?"

George nodded.

"Phantom limb," the tech said. "It feels like my finger's there until I look down and remember it's not. Hence, Schröfinger."

"Ah," George said.

"So," the tech continued, "you know HAL, right?"

Did he? It was only the voice he'd been hearing in his head ever since he first "met" the fictional AI through his uncle's TV. And damn it—he hadn't even officially started working there yet, but George could feel it; he'd never want to leave this place. These, simply put, were his people: the geeks, the nerds, the fanboys who'd been promised a HAL and would make one themselves if they had to.

"Daisy" was all George said, but it was answer enough.

"Excellent," the team leader said. "So the whole thing with HAL going crazy and killing everybody was the result of the limitations of binary computing. He'd been given contradictory instructions about the mission and went a little crazy as a result, because binary systems are hopeless when it comes to contradictions. To a binary system, it's all bits and bytes—zero or one, yes or no, right?"

George nodded.

"But *quantum* computers don't deal in bits; they use qubits, which can be both yes and no at the same time without canceling each other out or leading to a contradiction error. A qubit can be zero *and* one *and* the fractional infinity in between." He paused to back up to his original point. "If HAL had been a *quantum* computer, he wouldn't have been tripped up by a little paradoxical coding. That's because in a quantum system, the answer yes *and* no doesn't start the sparks flying. Contradictions are what quantum computers do best."

The team leader held up his abbreviated digit, blew across the stump, and voilà: the finger was restored. Or had only been folded over in the first place, seeing as it wasn't the same hand this time.

"Cute," George said.

The team leader went on to predict that while the coders in digital were making headlines for teaching their AIs to beat world champions in Go, it was *his* group—the quants, the qubitters—who'd be the ones to crack the nut of general AI.

"That's because a quantum computer can literally jump to conclusions as opposed to having to brute-force its way through, crunching all possible combinations. It's like the difference between the inventors Thomas Edison and Nikola Tesla. Edison reached his inventions as a result of trial and error, testing and dismissing alternatives until he found the perfect material for, say, the filament for his incandescent lamp. Tesla, on the other hand, arrived at his inventions in flashes of inspiration while thinking about something else.

"To give you an idea of what we're talking about, a quantum computer with three hundred qubits of processing power could perform more calculations than the number of atoms in the visible universe. It could do in minutes what would take a digital supercomputer a billion years to accomplish—if it could, ever. With a computer like that you could feed in a person's genome and it would project their entire life arc. And you could do that for all the people on earth. In minutes. An earth-sized version of *The Sims*, eight billion simulations bouncing off one another like eight billion billiard balls on a table the size of the planet."

"And how far away is that?" George asked.

"Well, we have to reach quantum advantage first."

"And that is?"

"When we finally get enough qubits together to do something that's impossible for a classical computer." He paused. "It could happen next week," he predicted, "or a hundred years from now."

"That's a pretty wide spread."

"Yeah, but once it happens, and it's scalable, that's it. Game over for classical computing."

"Well, on behalf of those of us who'd love a crack at a planet-sized game of *The Sims*," George said, shaking the team leader's discounted hand, "good luck." Turning to leave, he turned around again, to offer up a pair of crossed fingers, which, on second thought, probably wasn't cool.

Next up: the fMRI guys V.T. had mentioned, who answered George's questions even before he knew he wanted to ask them, with the exception of one. He'd noticed a volunteer who looked to be about his age being scanned as the spokestech explained, "We're trying to locate the part of the brain responsible for suicidal ideation in adolescents."

Before George had a chance to ask, the tech explained that the subject, who'd actually attempted suicide, would be asked to go back to that dark place.

"But," George prepared to object.

But the tech was already leaning into the control center's microphone: "Jake," he said, "I want you to think back to when you were in the tub, holding the razor blade . . ."

George watched as a portion of the brain he didn't know the name of (yet) became bathed in a cold blue. Looking at it, he thought of the dark part on an ancient map: terra incognita, the home of monsters.

If you'd asked him before whether he'd like to see what suicidal ideation in a teenager looked like in an fMRI scan, George wouldn't have known how to answer. Now he did. The demonstration was enlightening in a very dark way, making him think about the mind's eye, and blind spots. Take this particular case: the boy in the tube was being asked to remember a past time when the future seemed to be in his blind spot. And yet . . .

"Isn't this dangerous?" George asked. "For the subject, I mean. It seems awfully triggering."

The lab tech shook his head, then shrugged, then pointed to the disclaimer that had been signed by the subject's guardian. "Our *a*'s are *c*'d," he said, referencing what George was coming to understand as the unofficial motto of the company that claimed, "Doing good is what we do."

And after that:

"Back where we started," George's escort announced, standing inside the recently vacated office with its window and view and everything. "Welcome to Quire." The dark suit and glasses turned and prepared to leave, but then stopped. "Door?" he said.

"Yes?"

"Open or closed?"

"Closed would be great," George said, the better to do his happy dance the second it was.

15

"How was your visit?" Roger asked.

His daughter ignored him, silently stepping out of her boots, unlacing her scarf, shedding her parka. In socked feet, she padded across the cabin's living room to the bathroom, left the door open, and flushed. Pandora poked her head back out mischievously. "I hope that wasn't too *triggering* . . ."

"She told you," Roger said.

"She told me," Pandora said, trying to mirror the deadliness of her father's tone but unable to. She was practically incandescent with glee.

Roger folded his arms and waited while Pandora dissolved into laughter. Finally taking a seat, literally holding her sides, his daughter looked woozy from lack of oxygen. Once the laughter had reduced to a couple of snorts every few seconds, like popcorn slowing down in a microwave, he spoke.

"She's been telling that story all my life," he said. "I'm surprised you hadn't heard it before." Pause. "I couldn't take friends home after a while. I started telling them my parents were dead."

"But it's *funny*," Pandora insisted.

"To people it hasn't happened to."

"Like you even remember . . ."

"Like I could *forget*," Roger said. "Like she'd *let* me. And that was the worst part of it. I was too young to remember, so I wound up with *her* version, seared into my brain." Pause. "You know, it's not helpful, looking back at your first moments on the planet like some slapstick routine . . ."

"Hey, at least you got a good story," Pandora countered. "Me? I killed my mom. Not a great anecdote for parties."

Roger looked at his daughter. "Dora," he said, sounding like a detective trying to finesse the suspect, "did she tell you anything else, maybe about when *you* were born?"

Just as Roger couldn't forget the story of his porcelain nativity, so Pandora remembered the hearsay love story represented by the three syllables of her own name. Because she'd *not* been named after that infamous other who shared those syllables. No, she'd been named after a happy combination of technology and synchronicity and the nearest thing to fate she could imagine. It just wasn't true.

Not that it was a *lie* exactly. It was more like a false memory, perpetuated because it contained elements of the truth: her future father was in a bar and had just started playing "Goody Two Shoes" on the jukebox when her future mother entered and said, "Oh, I like this one . . ." No algorithmic synchronicity involved, just a coincidence that was less likely to make you believe in fate than in the stickiness of certain earworms.

It was Roger's friend Vlad who'd suggested that what would make the story special was if they'd been listening to a radio station that picked songs based on their listening habits, tailored to their tastes. Roger and his future wife agreed that such a thing would be pretty cool and suggested that Vlad develop the idea. But V.T. had passed, and by the time the internet radio station Pandora finally launched and made somebody else rich, Pandora the future hacker had already moved back to Alaska with her widowed dad, who would return to the alternative-facts version of how he and his wife met, once their daughter was old enough to ask where her name came from.

The real story was decidedly more downbeat and, placed in context, required Roger to relive the death of his wife in a level of detail he didn't think fit for young ears—or his own, for that matter. But the truth was Pandora's mother died from an aortic aneurysm that burst from the stress of delivery. The body was already cool to the touch by the time the nurse returned to fetch Pandora back to be placed in the baby display window, where she could be fawned over by family (meaning Roger) and friends (meaning Vlad). Noticing the nurse as she scurried from his wife's room, Roger stopped her in the hall, the bundled babe pressed to the front of her starched uniform. The nurse's face went blank as she worked a hand into the bundle and came back with his wife's charm bracelet.

"The little one took a liking to it," she said, handing it to the new father and widower. "I didn't want it to go missing when they came for the body."

And that's how Roger learned of his wife's death—knowledge so heavy it took his legs out from under him, leaving him stunned on the hospital tiles. He still remembered how his ears filled with the whispering of crepe soles hustling around him, a few feet south of where his ears then rested in space relative to the floor, space not the only thing feeling relative as he found himself adrift in it: a father, a widower, a star surrounded by blackness wherever he looked. And through it all, the only sensation making it through from out there to inside was the noise of all those muffled footsteps.

The couple had a different name picked out, but when asked, Roger couldn't think of what it was. He'd stared at the linked charms in his hand, each one a solid icon of some important moment in his wife's life, the last a little pewter baby rattle. And his mind, needing something to gnaw on, to preoccupy it, kept trying to remember what these things were called. Not charm bracelet. He knew that. There was a brand name. Something with a *P*. Pandemonium? No. Panglossian? Pythagorean? Pan-something.

Roger's memory finally clicked when a nurse arrived with two forms needing his input: one, a birth certificate, and the other . . . And when the nurse asked for his new child's name, the word he'd been searching for came out instead: "Pandora."

They were in California at the time, and while the nurse hailed from the Midwest, she'd learned enough not to make faces at the locals and the names they saddled their children with. Instead, she repeated, "Pandora," followed by: "Spelled like it sounds?"

Roger nodded. "I guess." And even as he said it, he promised himself he'd change it later—legally—once he and his right mind had become reacquainted. But for now, the name had done its job: shortened the list of questions he needed to answer.

But then he got used to it. And instead of changing his daughter's name, he changed the story, imagining he was giving her the gift of being named after the improbable miracle of love. And that was how she'd taken it, until reality took it away.

Throughout her father's confession—or confirmation, really, seeing as Gladys was the one to originally spill the beans—Pandora felt a growing urge to edit the Wikipedia page for the internet radio station she'd always thought she'd been named after. She could make the old story true by changing a few numbers, she thought—then hack the page so nobody could edit them back. Sure, alt facts inherently carried the whiff of *1984* about them, but how bad was it, compared to all the other fake news online? And who would it hurt anyway? Nobody checked those things. And if somebody writing a history of streaming services repeated the new and improved date, and then some news aggregator aggregated it, well, that'd constitute multiple confirming sources, which basically made it true, or as good as. Right?

Right.

"It worked," Pandora announced during her next visit.

"What did?" Gladys asked.

"Dad came clean," she said, hanging her parka on the back of a kitchen chair. "He told me the real story about my name."

"Did *I* tell you about that?" Gladys asked, her face dropping.

Pandora nodded.

"Did I tell you anything *else*?" her grandmother asked—*demanded*—her face the picture of rising horror.

Pandora mentioned her father's inglorious entry into the world, and for a moment, Gladys smiled, before looking concerned again.

"Anything *else*?" she insisted. "Anything I *shouldn't* have?"

Pandora shook her head, shrugged, not seeing what the big deal was. Sure, the name thing was a secret and her dad obviously hoped the story of his birth would have been granted a similar classification, at least when it came to his daughter. But the way Gladys was going on, it was like she'd never told a secret in her life—which seemed almost quaint in the age of WikiLeaks, Snowden, Manning, et al. Hell, it was quaint in the age of social media, where *not sharing* was a new kind of rude—not to mention really bad for the social-media business model.

"But feel free. I'm good at keeping secrets," Pandora lied.

16

<u>Getting Chipped</u>

We already know what you're thinking: Big Brother, mark of the beast, 666, right? Nope. It's nothing more than good old-fashioned pragmatism. We had badges; people *hated* badges; people kept forgetting badges, and since the badges were what got you into campus, let you log on to your workstation, and ID'd you for all your free bennies, the situation rapidly became suboptimal.

Solution: an RFID chip about the size of a grain of rice, doing everything a badge would do (and nothing else), inserted subcutaneously no deeper than your average tattoo ink. Yes, we thought about bar code tattoos. Those were deemed historically and culturally insensitive. Also, the process is completely reversible should you ever choose to leave the Quire family. Those with personal, religious, or cultural objections can opt for a badge instead.

—QuireNewEmployeeManual.pdf

"Is this going to hurt?" George asked, his hand in the hands of a man who might not be the most reliable judge of pain thresholds, not with all the piercings he had in his face alone.

The chipper shrugged. "Not as much as being unemployed," he said, upending a bottle of rubbing alcohol onto a cotton ball before swabbing the back of George's hand. Other than those two quasi-medical, quasi-antiseptic supplies, the chipping station consisted of a box of disposable examination gloves, the phlebotomy chair with its single armrest where George was sitting, and the chipper himself wearing aquamarine scrubs dotted with what his present subject hoped was salsa from a breakfast burrito. The actual mechanism for implanting the chip was nowhere to be seen, which was worrying.

"In the manual it mentioned Big Brother," George said, making nervous chitchat as his palm sweated. "You know what that reminded me of?"

The chipper, who sat on a wheeled stool, rolled in close so he could whisper. "The Macintosh Super Bowl ad, 1984," he said. "Never speak of that again."

"But it's on YouTube . . ."

The chipper squeezed his hand until George winced. "That ad had a sequel that aired during the 1985 Super Bowl. It featured blindfolded businessmen walking off a cliff while whistling 'Heigh-Ho.' It was for a Mac-based networking solution called Macintosh Office. Wanna guess what that sequel was called?"

Shrug.

"Lemmings," the chipper said. "Consequently, V.T. takes everything about Apple personally." He paused. "You'll note the telling absence of black turtlenecks on campus."

George's mouth made a silent "Oh," followed by a silent "Thanks for the heads-up," followed by an audible yelp as he felt the chip sliding in under his skin, after which his hand was released. It was only after it was done that he saw the injector, a larger-than-average syringe with a disposable needle the chipper ejected unceremoniously into a waiting wastebasket.

George looked at the little red lump underneath the web of skin between his thumb and index finger.

"You know what that part's called?" the chipper asked, noticing the newbie as he poked at the new addition, seeing and feeling how far it rolled.

George shrugged, still mesmerized.

"The anatomical snuff box," the chipper said.

"That a fact?"

Nod.

"So . . . ?"

"Go to your cube," the chipper said, adding his gloves to the rest of the disposables in the basket. "Make sure you can sign on to your computer and start working through the email blasts."

George almost corrected the chipper to say he'd actually been given an office, but then remembered his escort's reaction a day earlier. And so, "Thanks," he said, followed by a farewell autofill "See ya."

"Not if you're lucky," the chipper said.

The implant worked right off the bat. Reaching his office and waving his hand in front of a reader on the wall, George watched as the knob spun a half turn by itself, a solenoid buzzed and kerchunked, and the door let go of the frame. Lights turned on as he entered and as he approached his desk, the workstation began booting up. "Welcome, George Jedson," the speaker said in a voice he recognized as belonging to Rosie the Robot from *The Jetsons*. He hadn't heard the voice since he was a kid when his mom had explained its connection to his name as they watched reruns on Cartoon Network.

Nice touch, he thought. Pulling out his desk chair, George sat and began reading through the email blasts as advised. A half hour later: *Now what?*

His workstation had three monitors, and so George slid the email window off to the right and opened a search window on the left. He eyed the email window peripherally while turning most of his attention to the search box. He checked the five-day forecast for the San Francisco Bay Area. Next, the highlights for science and technology in Google News. Next, he got up from his desk and stared out the window, trying to remember what the five-day had said about today and whether that's what was actually happening out there, on the other side of the glass. He looked at the clock on the wall, checked it against the one on his computer, and then unhooked the former from the nail it hung from. He turned it over, removed the battery cover, tested the terminals with his tongue, closed it back up, and then thumbed the little adjustment wheel until the two clocks agreed with each other. Unfortunately, they agreed on a time that seemed impossibly far from lunch, which—as far as George could tell—was the one thing on his to-do list between now and noon.

By ten thirty, George had received no further instructions on how to spend his time via any of the various means by which he could be reached—not by email or text or voice mail, not in person, or via audio or video over Skype, not even by some coded vibrations emanating from the subcutaneous RFID chip implanted in his anatomical snuff box. At a loss, he poked his head out the door to see if he could flag down any of the faces he'd met during the previous day's tour. Said faces were all part of Q-Brain, as was George, meaning they were coworkers, even if they didn't necessarily all work on the same projects with the same goals. Not that he could say how he stood in relation to the other teams' projects and/or goals, seeing as he was still waiting to find out what his were going to be.

"Hello," he called. "Anybody?"

No response. This was to be expected, in retrospect, seeing as nobody else was in the hallway.

"Hello, ello, ello," he said, impersonating an echo, which, as it turned out, didn't need to be faked, successfully underlining the sense of isolation he'd already begun feeling. The day before, researchers had lined up to show him the fruits of their labor; now, he faced only a series of anonymous locked doors, on the other side of which, surely people were working, but, if so, they were doing it awful quietly.

Too quietly.

He heard footsteps behind him and turned in time to see a coder armed with free snacks disappear behind his own door. Looking the other way, he saw a bank of vending machines, an ice maker, a fire extinguisher, an emergency first aid cabinet, and a flickering exit sign, pointing left.

George pulled his head back into his office and closed the door. He took his seat, jiggled his mouse, checked to see what new spam needed to be deleted. He opened up solitaire and started playing against his own best score and time. He began wondering if discovering what his job was *was his job*.

Watching the cascade of virtual playing cards bounce across the screen, he imagined the possible clues for which the *Jeopardy!* answer was: "What is George's job?" He knew what he *hoped* it was: help create the world's first truly general artificial intelligence as opposed to all the narrow AIs dominating the headlines. He checked his email again to see if it brought news of such an assignment—or some kind of work important enough to warrant having his own office. And at the same time, he was worried too. He was barely sixteen after all, and here he was, down the hall from guys who could light up and trace every neuron in the brain. A few weeks from now, would he be taking snapshots of someone's thoughts or helping the blind to not just see, but see through walls?

Agitated malaise. Anxious ennui. That's what George was feeling. And while in concept, a door was a nice thing to have, in reality, when you had nothing to do behind that door but twiddle your thumbs and wait, it meant claustrophobia on top. The unspecified pressure was finally enough to send George into the hallway and down to the free vending machines. A Snickers and chugged Red Bull later, he started tracing the previous day's tour backward, hoping for something to catch his eye.

Gym? No.

Climbing wall? No.

Too early for the cafeteria.

Too much caffeine already to make use of the free coffee bar.

Neck massage station? Nope. He'd feel guilty, not having coded jack since getting there.

And then he found it: a 1980s arcade-themed conversation room where a few people were sitting in club chairs, complete with fully functioning, stand-alone versions of *Pong*, *Pac-Man*, *Ms. Pac-Man*, *Asteroids*, *Frogger*. All had started gathering dust in actual arcades well before any of the coders ignoring them had been born, including George. By all appearances, they were more of a meta gesture, a nod toward the idea of nostalgia; no one expected anyone to actually play them, as attested to by the "Wash Me" somebody had written in the dust coating the cathode-ray screen of the *Pac-Man* console.

But George had always had a soft spot in his heart for the underdogs, the neglected, the underestimated—all of those labels having applied to him at various points. And so he pulled his hand into his sleeve and wiped the *Pac-Man* display clean. He hit the big red button to start a game and flinched when actual music—the dinky-dink *Pac-Man* theme—came pouring out rather louder than he had expected. The handful of fellow coders in the room turned to look at him.

"I'm not sure you're supposed to actually use those," one of them said. "I think they're, like, for decoration."

"Yeah, dude," another said, "that's some serious museum antique stuff you're messing with."

George looked at the happy yellow pie missing a slice, waiting to be sent on his gobbling way as the quartet of sawtooth-sheeted ghosts bobbed in their 2-D holding pen, waiting to cause trouble. "Why were they plugged in," George asked, "if we're not supposed to use them?"

The two previous speakers looked at each other, then at George, who was already riding his joystick like a pro. "Good point," one of them said.

"Ya wanna?" his colleague asked him. And then up they went to play *Pong*, ironically, until a supervisor came looking for them.

Wow, George thought, *first day, and I'm already the guy who gets other guys in trouble*—a conclusion he'd have cause to rethink once he met the guy who actually held that particular job description.

The Quire cafeteria could have been decorated by the set designer for *Blade Runner*, but with fewer rain effects and minus the grit. A multi-culti mash-up heavily inflected eastward: the cafeteria's most prominent feature was a series of wall-sized flat screens displaying seasonal scenes of what the outside would look like if humans had never taken a shovel to it. An overall tranquil vibe, George thought, except for the foot-tall crawl cutting through the sublime vistas to display the weather forecast, breaking news, Quire's stock price, or its latest corporate affirmation.

George had taken a seat toward the back, the better to study his coworkers, when he noticed an old-timer enter the cafeteria, distinguished by his actual badge swinging from a lanyard around his neck. George had already observed that much about QHQ's pecking order: employees could be divided into badgers and chippers, the latter representing the newest hires while the former had been given the option to hold on to their old badges. And this one seemed to be on a mission as he stared at his phone, *in medias distractus*, looking up only once to lock on George. A quick, confirmatory nod followed by a big smile as he continued walking with a bit more purpose, straight for Quire's newest newbie.

"Milo LaFarge," he announced, phone holstered, hand out.

"George," George said, withholding his surname as he often did when he wasn't in the mood.

And so Milo pulled out a seat, sat down, and filled in the blank. "Jedson, right?"

George nodded.

"Man, that must be a pain in the butt."

George blinked self-consciously. "Yes," he said. "Yes, it is."

"Why don't you change it?"

"How else am I supposed to start conversations?"

"Say no more," Milo said, and George obeyed as if it had been a command.

Several uncomfortable seconds passed as the newbie poked among the remains of his lunch and considered taking out his phone, the international sign for "leave me alone."

"Listen," Milo said, unambiguously a command this time, "I'm here to help."

"Help?" George said, looking up from a crescent of gluten-free, vegan-certified pizza crust he'd flicked into rotating like an ad hoc fidget spinner.

"I'm your Virgil," Milo said.

George looked perplexed. "I thought you said your name was Milo?"

Milo crossed his arms and rocked back in his seat. George mirrored the gesture. And the two stayed that way, tentatively teetering on the back legs of their chairs, judging and daring and testing each other's will until George finally broke, tipped forward, and admitted that yes, he knew who Virgil was. "I just don't see how the allusion applies in our current situation."

"I'm your alternative tour guide," Milo said, "here to point things out you might otherwise miss."

"Like?" George asked.

Milo pinched his smart ID between thumb and forefinger and held it away from him so they both could see the stitched lettering running from end to end of the lanyard. "Doing good is a choice," he read aloud.

It was the corporate affirmation of the week and had struck George as a benign declaration of corporate altruism, an interpretation he shared with his guest.

Milo held the strip of polyester closer, reading it silently like a fortune cookie. "It could also mean that 'doing good' is optional," he pointed out.

George weighed the words one at a time. "You could be right," he finally admitted.

"And so it begins," Milo said, cracking all his knuckles at once.

17

Pandora didn't hate everything about high school, though in terms of learning, it was highly inefficient. She could read a teacher's edition much faster than it took to have it read to her aloud by some secondary-ed-majoring hack who couldn't make it down south, leaving her plenty of time to twiddle her thumbs between acing quizzes. There was one exception, however: Mr. Vlasic, her science teacher.

Mr. V had been drawn to Fairbanks because of the night sky, its darkness and duration and the northern lights that frequently danced across it. Unlike virtually every other outsider she knew, her science teacher flew back to his home state of Michigan during the Alaskan summer cherished by natives and tourists alike, returning to Fairbanks only after the visitors left and the first snowflakes arrived, usually over the Labor Day weekend. And astronomy wasn't the only thing he loved, but science in general—physics and chemistry, especially. And as far as reading out of the teacher's edition, Mr. Vlasic had so far kept his promise to base his instruction exclusively on what he already had in his head, still fresh from grad school and supplemented by his voracious reading of pretty much every periodical with the word *science* in the title—*Popular*, *American*, *News*, or the word itself, unadorned.

Most significantly for Pandora, however, her science teacher was also the only faculty member who may have had an inkling of who the culprit behind the flaming urinals might be. "Seems like they should be looking for a science geek with a grudge instead of someone making political rants online," he'd said offhandedly, as she'd dawdled after class one afternoon.

Pandora looked at her shoes, putting her double-crossing face out of range.

"So how's your grandmother?" he asked, changing the subject—and displaying another reason why she liked her science teacher: they were both members of that growing club of people who had loved ones with dementia. For Mr. Vlasic, it was his mom, and part of his salary was going to help pay for a visiting care worker, to keep her out of places like where Gladys had wound up.

"Not great," Pandora said. "You know."

Indeed, he did, or seemed to, as he knew it was time to change the subject yet again.

"I think you'll be interested in Wednesday's topic," he said.

"What is it?"

"Secret, is what it is," Mr. V said with a smile and a wink. "You'll have to show up and see for yourself."

As if there was any question about that.

Standing in front of class as it settled down, Mr. Vlasic reminded her of a mash-up of Buddy Holly and early Elvis Costello, thanks to the heavy-framed black glasses he wore unironically. His hair was decidedly longer than either, and a flop of it flipped over the left lens constantly, only to be pushed back up and out of the way, either by neck pop or long-fingered sweep, both gestures tossed off with equal levels of distractedness.

It didn't take a genius to see that Mr. V loved being onstage. In another life, he'd be a stand-up comedian or, more likely, a stand-up scientist. But those openings had been filled already by Bill Nye and Neil deGrasse Tyson. And so it was Lionel Vlasic's fate to remain at Ransom Wood High School, entertaining a bunch of disgruntled teens plus one true fan: Pandora Lynch.

Before the bell rang, kicking off that Wednesday's class, Mr. Vlasic entered the room with a big box held to his chest, exaggerating the effort it took to carry it, placed it on his desk, and then proceeded to ignore it, as the class's earlier arrivals kept staring at it—as intended. Finally: "You seem more interested in cardboard than me," he said once class had officially begun, "which is frankly insulting. But since I've mentioned our corrugated elephant here, who's curious about what's inside?"

Nearly every hand went up.

"And who knows another word for 'curious'?" he asked. "Think anatomy."

"Nosy," several students mouthed, and a few braver ones said aloud.

"Yes. Nosy," Mr. V repeated, flipping open the flaps of the box, reaching inside, and removing a large plastic cutaway model of the human olfactory system.

"Boom," he said, amid the predictable groans.

"The human brain," he announced, pausing long enough for the class to wonder if their teacher had mixed up his lecture notes, "is well acquainted with the sensory input from this fine fellow," he continued. "In fact, the sense of smell is practically hardwired directly to the fight-or-flight, lizard part of the brain." Pause. "Did you know you can't remember smells?"

Sounds of adolescent objection.

"It's true," Mr. V continued. "You can re-*experience* smells, and recognize them while in their presence, but in isolation, you cannot call to mind a memory of a smell, like you can, say, an image or a song you've heard."

He reached back into the box and removed three amber pharmacy vials, each with what appeared to be a cotton ball inside. He dealt them out to the students sitting at the heads of the first column of desks, the third, and then the last, slamming each one down like a bartender laying down shots.

"Smell's relationship with memory can be profound, however, particularly when it comes to summoning up other memories associated with our previous experiences of a particular scent. Marcel Proust knew this and wrote about it. He even got his name attached to the flood of memories a single smell can trigger, which is sometimes called a Proustian rush."

Mr. Vlasic raised a halting finger as he noticed two of the students he'd placed vials in front of trying to open them. "Not yet," he said. "First let me tell you what you've got there." He reclaimed the vial from the student in the middle and pointed at the bottom. "I've soaked each of these cotton balls in what I hope are fairly recognizable and evocative scents, and you're each going to take a whiff." He paused. "Now I don't want you to identify the smell. I want you to smell it, close your eyes, and try to identify a memory the smell conjures up. And then we'll go around the room and compare, unless you opt not to share for reasons of personal embarrassment." He uncapped the vial he'd reclaimed and dipped his own nose inside before recoiling.

"Oh yeah," he said, as if to himself, "that's the embarrassing one, all right . . ."

He returned the now-radioactive vial to the student he'd taken it from. The seed successfully planted, Mr. V watched along with the rest as the three vials circulated, the reactions to two of them reasonably benign, while the remaining vial—the vile vial, as Mr. V began referring to it—elicited ever greater reactions of disgust, as those who had yet to smell it grew increasingly, visibly apprehensive about playing along.

"Okay," their teacher said after the rounds had been completed and each student had scribbled something down. "Now, I said this wasn't about naming the smells, per se, and so, for the record"—he held up the first vial: "Baby-powder-scented air freshener."

Number two, the vile vial: "Rancid sardine oil."

And number three: "Pine-tree air freshener."

A surprising—or perhaps not—number of students opted for the vile vial as their triggering smell of choice, which brought back memories of hunting whales for some of the indigenous students and working in the canneries or aboard fishing trawlers for some others. One student picked the pine and began an anecdote about getting drunk on gin for the first time.

Mr. Vlasic coughed into his hand and then, in a voice directed at the ceiling, as if the room were bugged, "Thank you for that *work of fiction*, Mr. Denning. I know you wouldn't want to be admitting to the crime of underage drinking in my classroom . . ."

"Yeah, Mr. V," the smartass said, understanding. "You caught me"—pause—"making stuff up."

And lastly, the baby-powder vial predictably conjured up memories of mothers and young siblings, and one instance of being locked in a clothes dryer against the student's will, followed by the almost exact same recollection, but done willingly.

And then Mr. V did a total U-turn, or so it seemed.

"I know I've prefaced a lot of these demos with the standard disclaimer to not try this at home, but this time I'm changing that." He paused. "Those of you who still have access to your grandparents and/or great-grandparents, think about trying this experiment on them, especially if they've started to lose their memories. Especially if they've developed the habit of wearing way too much perfume or aftershave."

A hand went up. Mr. Vlasic seemed to already know the question. "No," he said, "the grandparents experiment won't be on the test. It's strictly for extra credit." He paused. "And extra credit for you personally, in the being-a-good-person department. You'll be amazed at how grateful old people can be when you show the least interest in what they have to say."

Pandora, stationed in the back of the classroom, per usual, thought, *Been there, still doing that . . .*

Pandora didn't need extra credit—not in science, at least—but trying the experiment on Gladys would give her an excuse to talk to Mr. V about the results. The truth was, she had a little crush on him. How secret that crush *was*, given her traitorous face, she didn't know. But he'd not said anything, which either meant he hadn't noticed or was even more crush-worthy than she thought.

She did tweak the experiment a bit, though. First, the vile vial needed to go on the grounds of sheer nastiness, and second, she nuked the hell out of those other two cotton balls, spraying them in their respective air fresheners until they were dripping with memories to compensate for the ones her grandmother had lost already. Press-twisting their caps back on, Pandora proceeded to slide the vials into her parka's side pockets, one bottle of memories each.

"Hey, Gram," she greeted, unbooting and sliding off her parka. The usual chitchat followed, the two having developed a routine further routinized by the fact that increasingly, Gladys's side of the conversation was a practically verbatim rerun of what she'd said the previous visit.

"So anyway," Pandora said, "we did an interesting experiment in science class today." She plucked the vials from the pockets of the parka she'd draped over a kitchen chair and placed them on the breakfast nook between them, continuing to explain the gist before asking if her grandmother was game.

Gladys shrugged and Pandora said, "Okay," before uncapping the first vial and passing it forward.

Her grandmother dipped in her beak and inhaled. Shrugged.

"Smell harder," Pandora advised.

"And how am I supposed to do that?"

Pandora demonstrated by sniffing in loudly. Gladys tried. Shrugged again, passing the vial back. "You try," her grandmother said.

And so Pandora did, easing the mouth of the vial noseward, abundantly aware of how thoroughly she'd soaked the cotton balls and wary of olfactory overload. But as she drew the vial nearer, she sensed something was wrong. She couldn't smell anything, even when she placed her nose directly over the vial and inhaled as hard as she'd demonstrated earlier.

Briefly, a butterfly of panic flitted across her brain, heading toward her stomach as Pandora wondered whether dementia was contagious—whether she'd exposed herself so thoroughly that she'd already lost her sense of smell and the rest of her brain would be next and . . .

. . . and then she noticed the cold against her fingertips where they held the vial. She looked inside and flicked a fingernail against the side. The cotton ball—frozen—clicked against the other side. She hadn't been outside that long, but then again, it doesn't take long to freeze something at forty degrees below zero. They'd been in her pockets, but the outside lining was closer to the air than any extraneous body heat coming off Pandora.

"Maybe later," she said, leaving the vials uncapped on the table between them to thaw.

They talked while they waited to resume the experiment, but as they did, Pandora noticed her grandmother getting anxious. "Have you taken your Xanax?" she asked.

But instead of the yes or no the question seemed to call for, Gladys said, "Talcum powder."

Pandora blinked, inhaled, and then smelled it, too, along with a strong hint of pine. "The experiment," she said. "I'd almost for . . ." But the younger woman stopped before getting to *gotten*, refusing to say the word, as if saying it would bring her grandmother's disease crashing down on her. Instead, she asked, "What does the smell of baby powder remind you of?"

A strange look fell across Gladys's face. "I've felt like this before," the old woman said.

"Like how?"

"Like I'm racing against death," her grandmother said. "This time, it's my brain cells dying, but before . . ." She drifted off, and Pandora tried reeling her back.

"When was this?" she asked.

"World War II," her grandmother said.

"What about the war?"

"I fought in it."

"That was Grandpa Herman," Pandora corrected. "Your husband. Only men fought in the war."

"The ones who fought *and died* were boys," Gladys said. "But they weren't the only ones fighting."

"How, *specifically*, did you fight in World War II, Gladys Kowalski?" Pandora asked, using her grandmother's back-then name in case it helped jar loose anything the smell of baby powder hadn't—like, for instance, what talcum had to do with the war.

"I can't say," Gladys said, shaking her head violently, followed by the words that would doom her at the hands of a girl once nicknamed Dora the Implorer: "It's secret," the old woman said. "Classified."

Gauntlet accepted. "*Tell* me," Pandora said, squaring her shoulders, prepared to resort to elder abuse if it came to that.

"Can't."

"*Can't* because you can't remember," Pandora drilled, "or because you *won't*?"

"Shouldn't," her grandmother said, already softening. "They could put me in jail . . ."

Pandora reached across the table and took her grandmother's fretting hands. "I don't mean to be mean with what I'm about to say," she said, pausing to meet Gladys's eyes. "But what difference would it make?"

Her grandmother blinked, as if thinking about it, while the what-if machine in Pandora's head went crazy with possibilities. What if her grandmother had been some femme fatale spy luring Nazis to their deaths or maybe a footnote in the history of Los Alamos? Gladys, meanwhile, reached for the vial with the scent of baby powder wafting over it, brought it to her nose as if it contained smelling salts, and inhaled.

"Ready?" she asked.

18

"I'm from the fairy dust clean-up team," Milo said. "I'm the speaker—excuse me, *preacher*—of truth to naïveté."

"Naïveté?"

"You."

"Okay," George said. "Hit me with some truth."

"Memory Hole Mondays," Milo said.

George nodded. Memory Hole Monday was the feature that distinguished Quire from similar platforms like Facebook, instituted as news of data breaches and undisclosed invasions of privacy were inspiring widespread defections. Announced within days of the company's IPO, "the hole," as it was affectionately known, allowed users to "completely delete, obliterate, bury" anything they regretted posting. At the same time, they could review what Quire had on them and perform other routine acts of personal privacy hygiene.

"People actually bought that shit," Milo said.

"What do you mean 'bought'?"

"Hook, line, and the proverbial sinker," Milo said, then smiled. "Bought like the proverbial farm, privacy-wise, may it rest in peace."

"More info," George said. "Less Milo."

"They're *kidding*," his newly appointed Virgil said. "About deleting everything? Totally joshing."

"You mean *lying*?" George said.

"The terms of service refer to it as using 'corporate discretion.'"

"But why? What's the point?"

Milo smiled. "Memory Hole Mondays point the platform in the direction of the most valuable information there is. The embarrassing parts. The incriminating. The stuff you want buried."

"Valuable *how*?"

Milo mimed contemplation, tapping his lips, eyes lifted heavenward, followed by a pointing finger, an open mouth, and . . . nothing. Blank faced, he waited for George to put it together.

Which he did, as signaled thusly: "Oh crap . . ."

"I've heard V.T. has political aspirations," Milo said before pausing to let that sink in. "Any guesses about his chances?"

George recalled the V.T. he'd met—the one who'd given him his job, whatever it wound up being. The man had a certain geek charisma about him, in the sense that only geeks could find him charismatic. The rest of the world could probably see the needy narcissist who'd netted billions while carrying a negative balance in self-worth. What else could you say about a guy who had to pay people to make other people think he was human? No way was V.T. a likely candidate for political office. There was no way he'd win a fair and honest election . . .

Bingo.

"Oh crap," George said, the horrible potential manifesting itself behind his eyes. Hadn't the country suffered enough at the hands of amoral billionaires who decided to play politics when they got bored or their dicks got limp? Could it really survive another round? "Oh crap, oh crap, oh crap . . ."

"You are most welcome, grasshopper." Milo smiled.

19

"It was almost all girls," Gladys began as Pandora surreptitiously thumb-tapped the voice recorder on her phone. "All the boys were either overseas or broken, leaving the job up to us, like Rosie the Riveter, but brainier.

"I was never in a sorority, but I imagine that's what it was like, where they put us, working shoulder to shoulder, not perspiring like ladies, but sweating like pigs, and about as happy as a bunch in slop, because the freedom to sweat was, well, very freeing," Gladys recalled.

"At first," she qualified.

"But then it got annoying, and I personally started longing for the days of talcum, judiciously applied. Not to tell tales, but some of my sisters were not exactly going for gold in personal hygiene. It got so I could tell who was coming down the hall before I even saw her.

"And then I noticed our smells started changing. There was heat sweat, and there was fear sweat, and more and more, fear sweating was what we did."

"You have to back up, Gram," Pandora said. "Where was this?"

"DC," Gladys said. "The District of Columbia," she added, decoding the initials gratuitously and with a tone that made the place sound like a foreign country.

"The pay wasn't much, but I would've worked for room and board and nothing else. It was"—her grandmother paused—"the best, worst time I ever had."

Did Pandora feel guilty about using her grandmother's condition to get her to break what was apparently some vow of silence? No. She was doing what needed to be done before her grandmother's history was lost. Who knew what she may have forgotten already? Sure, the first phase of Alzheimer's was short-term memory loss, but her grandmother had gotten past that part. There were hints she thought Herman was still alive. But as far as Pandora could tell, the war stuff was still there, perhaps the mental treads dug especially deep by whatever was making Gladys so skittish on the subject.

Not that the how or why of her grandmother's recollection mattered. What mattered was finally getting Gladys's story. The *whole* story—or as much of it as remained.

And as Gladys spoke, Pandora could see it as if it were a memory of her own: the padded shoulders, the bouffants, the sweaty dress shields. But how did Gladys Kowalski *fight* World War II, *specifically*?

"The clock, dear," Gladys said. "We fought the clock—around the clock."

"Were you a secretary?" her granddaughter asked.

"Well, I dressed like one," Gladys said. "I'd bicycle with bag lunches from a boardinghouse to an office building that looked like all the rest, but with fewer windows than average."

"So," Pandora kept prying, "in this innocuous building of few windows, what were you doing? Taking dictation about secret war plans and typing them up on official letterhead or something?"

Gladys looked at her granddaughter, disappointed. "I said I dressed *like* a secretary. DC was full of them. That's why it was the perfect disguise. Because while the boys *over there* used their bodies, bullets, and bombs to fight the war, nobody would've guessed that some little secretary with her bag lunch was fighting that same war with her brains."

"But what were you *doing*?" Pandora implored.

Gladys blinked, her expression reading, "Isn't it obvious?"

"Cryptography," she said, filling in the blank.

And now it was Pandora's turn to blink confusedly as she tried to process the too-many thoughts rushing toward articulation.

"I was going to be an English teacher," her grandmother continued. "I had a gift for language and word games. Crossword puzzles were a favorite. Word finds. What's different between these two pictures? And I found a puzzle pinned up on a bulletin board at high school, daring me to solve it. If I could, I was supposed to send my answers and contact information to a PO Box at the bottom. So I did, and sent it in. And a month later, a big black car pulled up outside our farm, and two men in dark overcoats got out. I don't know why, but they looked like big beetles walking upright as they approached our front door. 'Can we see Miss Gladys Kowalski?' they asked. The beetle men had come looking for me.

"The test was a screen for minds that were needed for the war effort. Ones like mine," her grandmother continued. "My country needed me. America and the Allied forces needed little Gladys Kowalski to go to Washington and play word games that could spell life or death for our boys overseas. How could I say no? I couldn't. I didn't. I packed my bags, kissed my mom, scowled at my dad because that was our way, and left on the biggest adventure of my life."

"What was DC like?"

"Sweaty. Swampy. Rumpled suits and wilted dresses. The opposite of Fairbanks, which is one of the reasons I came here. After what happened after the war . . ."

Pandora had an idea about what her grandmother was alluding to. Her father had suggested that his mother's postwar experience with men of the brain-shrinking class was one of the reasons he'd chosen his profession. The euphemism "stress" had been thrown around. Pandora now suspected that the truth was closer to a breakdown. Anyone needing a change of scenery as extreme as going from DC to Fairbanks had clearly been through something.

Gladys had begun describing the goings-on inside that innocuous building in Washington, DC, where she was helping to win the war with crossword puzzles and tiles from a board game called Criss-Crosswords destined to be rechristened Scrabble after the war. Her head back then had been predisposed to finding patterns trying hard not to be found, making her just the sort of player the government needed for a life-and-death game of hide-and-seek played out in the real world with bombed cities, sunken ships, and floating corpses. For Gladys and her sisters, the battlefield was language and language-like strings of symbols, scrambled, masked, translated, and substituted, the repetitions counted and tallied, the most frequent occurrences of *X* in a cypher perhaps pointing to the most frequent letter in the language the message was encoded from. Counting, theories, reconstructions from past failures where the real message became clear but only in retrospect, once the bodies had already started floating . . .

"We were trying to crack the Enigma," her grandmother said, acknowledging aloud that while that might sound like bad poetry, in this case it was the actual name of the enemy device they were pitting their pattern-recognizing minds against. It was about the size of a bread box and was used to disguise the Germans' secret transmissions, with the code changing daily and considered unbreakable absent another, sister Enigma machine for decoding what went into the first. There were too many permutations—even if you checked one random possibility per second, the time needed would exceed the number of hours between code switches several times over. Not that that stopped Gladys and her fellow decoders from sweating over every slip from the teletype, perfuming the air with the funk of patriotism.

"Once you get used to the initial nastiness, there was a point where nosing through everyone's BO was invigorating; it was stinky proof of how hard we were all working." Pause. "But then it got annoying again and I personally started longing for the days of talcum, judiciously applied. Not to tell tales, but some of my sisters were not exactly going for gold in personal hygiene . . ."

Pandora touched her grandmother's hand lightly. "You've already mentioned that part," she said.

Gladys took it in stride. "Did I mention how the men made everything worse?" she asked.

Pandora shook her head.

"Because there *were* men, more or less in charge," Gladys continued. "They were too old for traditional combat, so we girls didn't worry about sweating around them, not that they were usually around. No, the sneaks didn't show up until a few of us would take a break to smoke a cigarette or share stories from a movie magazine we'd seen out buying groceries with our ration coupons.

"'Ladies, enjoying yourselves?' they'd say, standing there behind us, rising on their tiptoes to seem a little taller, more in charge. The newest one always fell for it.

"'Oh yes,' she'd say, and we'd cringe, knowing what was coming.

"'That's nice. Too bad our *boys* over *there* can't while away the hours, gossiping about the latest *styles* . . .'

"Only the foolhardiest would have quibbled with turning a five-minute break into 'whiling away the hours,' or point out that fashion was of no consequence for the duration of the conflict, as should have been obvious from the safety pins and patches holding our wardrobes together. But the point was made. Every moment not spent deciphering enemy messages was basically helping Hitler kill our boys. As motivators went, it was a good one, provided we didn't kill ourselves, trying to save lives over there."

God, Pandora *loved* her grandmother's face! As her grandmother spoke about her most harrowing and glorious years, she wore her whole history: the Great Depression and World War II in her eyes, the 1960s in her furrowed brow, and the 2000s in the shadows of her sunken cheeks. Several decades of Alaskan winters had turned her from the slip of a girl she'd once been into a postfertility goddess and drained the color from her hair until it matched the landscape: snow and ice fog under a dryer-lint sky. But it was all part of a package, the total greater than the sum of its parts. She'd aged not only gracefully, but artfully, heartbreakingly. If only her mind . . .

"What happened after the war," Pandora finally asked, "before you came here?"

Her grandmother went *"Pffft"* and flicked her fingers at the side of her head, setting off a puff of white Einstein hair. "Your grandfather, bless his soul, called me Sparky after I told him. That might seem mean, but it was the perfect antidote for excessive seriousness. 'How 'bout a little AC/DC there, Sparky?' he'd say whenever he was feeling frisky."

Pandora reacted with an expression common among teenagers being forced to imagine old people "feeling frisky," multiplied by the power of her hyperexpressiveness.

"I felt much better after that," Gladys continued, ignoring her granddaughter's facial editorializing. "The electricity cleared the spark gap, blew out the cobwebs—I don't know. All I knew was I felt good in my own skin again and wanted a little time away from civilization to enjoy it. Hence, Fairbanks. Hence everything that followed Fairbanks."

She paused, looking tired, which was understandable. She rested a hand on Pandora's knee. "And the rest is his . . ." She paused, lifted her hand, and then clapped it down again on her granddaughter's knee. "No," she said. "The rest is *your* story," she concluded.

20

"Our CEO's not a liar, per se," Milo said, beginning their latest round of cynicism adjustment. "It's more like he's economical with the truth. He speaks no more of it than absolutely necessary. And when it comes to the subject of 'auxiliary business opportunities,' well, the man's Scrooge 1.0, the unredeemed. Total truth miser."

They'd moved the location of Milo's ongoing lecture series from the very public cafeteria to the privacy of George's office. It had been two days since they'd met, and George had made himself at home behind his office's lockable door—literally. It had made fiscal sense, given the astronomical cost of renting in an area where incomes in the low six figures were considered poverty level. Plus, by overlapping home and office—a practice *not* discouraged by management—the anxiety created by differentiating work from play largely disappeared. Which is to say that while George still hadn't gotten his work assignment, he wasn't freaking out about it. And in the meantime, there was always Milo, to rightsize any idealism he might still harbor. And thus:

"What 'auxiliary business opportunities'?" George asked. "You mean Q-Labs? That's pure research, like Google's 'moonshots.' Like Bell Labs a billion years ago."

"Tell me you're not that naive," Milo said.

"I feel I am an optimal level of naive," George countered. "I know people are greed personified and self-interest on two legs, but I have not succumbed to utter despair."

Milo snorted. "Good luck with *that*," he advised.

"Okay." George stepped it up. "I'll also spot you money being the source of all evil. Happy?"

But Milo just shook his head, his back to George as he admired the newbie's view. "Money is *so* last century," he said. "To do real evil nowadays, there's just one word."

"And that is?"

"Data," Milo said. "You know, like 'plastics' from *The Graduate*? But this is actually a different movie, grasshopper. It's *All the President's Men* and Deep Throat and 'follow the money.' Except it's data—grade A, primo, human behavioral data—that's AI juice. It's what keeps the chatbots chatting and the Terminator terminating and . . ."

"Allude much, Milo?" George asked.

"Hey, man," Milo said, not missing a beat. "The wheel's been invented and all the good stories written. Why waste time trying to be original? It's all mash-ups and sampling, baby. And thus, I allude." Pause. "But back to that AI juice. Quire is a 'data acquisition and packaging company'—that shit's in the corporate papers—and that 'packaging' euphie is where it's all at, the real work behind the wizard's curtain. All that stuff you saw on the tour, the AI and fMRI stuff. They're trying to read, record, and play back people's *actual thoughts*, claiming it's the next step beyond voice for input capture, but once you start reading minds, how far away is it from controlling them?"

George sat in his desk chair, practicing paper-clip origami as he studied his Virgil's back. If Milo was an intellectual hooker—which in many ways he seemed to be—his specialty would be blowing minds. Or trying to. George's brain stem was barely stiff. After all, if all these secret projects were so secret, how come a human sieve like Milo was in the loop? Next thing he knew, the guy would be looking both ways as he slid the plans for Tesla's death ray out of his pocket.

"You know about Stuxnet, right, the atomic bomb of cyber warfare?" Milo continued, turning around to face his audience of one. "That shit did actual damage in the real world by making Iraq's uranium enrichment system spin so fast it tore itself apart."

George nodded. He had the source code and had used chunks of it in his own exploits, back before he exchanged his black hat for this white hat gig. But what did Stuxnet have to do with a social-media company?

"They say it was a joint venture between the Israelis and the Americans, right? Well, that whole thing was started under W, and 'the Americans' meant contractors. Contractors like . . ."

George shaped the word *Quire* silently with his lips, while pointing down generically, a gesture intended to mean: "Here?"

Milo nodded.

"Bullshit," George said, swiveling around so he could check his computer for email about what he was supposed to be doing instead of sitting here listening to Milo's war stories.

Nada. Again. Still . . .

"God's truth," Milo said, resting his butt on the windowsill, his arms folded across his chest.

"Wait a second," George said, swiveling back around. "You're saying Quire has contracts with, what, DOD?"

"And NSA, FBI, DHS," Milo said. "Which shouldn't be a surprise. They do PSAs about it. 'Wounded warriors walk again.' It was on the tour."

"But that's all DARPA stuff," George insisted, "like how they funded the internet. It's the *good* military contracts."

"Ah, the internet," Milo said. "Cyber utopia. Security an afterthought." Pause. "But you know that already, don't you?"

Guilty, George thought. As was every other hacker he ever met online. The net's security holes were what they lived for—that, and bloated code full of bugs, waiting to be exploited. "Well, somebody's got to keep the serfs at Symantec busy."

"And busy they are," Milo agreed. "That's because the government loves security holes, even more than hackers, especially if it finds them first." Pause. "How many zero-day vulnerabilities did Stuxnet exploit?"

"Four, but . . ."

"And nobody would ever purposefully *create* a back door because the government was paying them for something else . . ."

"What are you saying?"

"I'm saying ignorance is bliss. And you can believe what you want to believe," Milo said. "All I know is what I've heard. And I heard that V.T. once said that if people were going to die anyway, he'd prefer they do it in a manner for which he held the patent."

George had heard the quote too. "But Snopes says he never said it," he pointed out.

"You have to admit, it does have a nice Dr. Evil vibe to it, though."

George knew what he was doing wrong with these visits from his self-appointed Virgil; he let Milo speak first. He'd leave his door open because he wasn't busy—still hadn't gotten anything to be busy with—and Milo would happen by, knock on the door frame, say, "Hey, you busy?" And before George could say anything, he'd let himself in, close the door, and start rubbing his hands over the juiciness of his upcoming disclosure. And so George positioned himself facing the open door and, before his informant's knuckles met wood, said, "Hey, Milo, got a sec?"

"Sure."

He waved his Virgil in, mimed closing the door, which Milo did.

"I've been meaning to ask you," George said. "How long have you been working here?"

"Forever," Milo said. "Five years."

"That doesn't seem . . . ," George began.

"Five *Silicon Valley* years," Milo clarified. "Factor in Moore's law and that's Methuselah old."

"Meth—?"

"Old Bible guy," Milo explained. "Nine hundred years old, back when being old was equated with being wise, as opposed to way past your expiration date."

"So what do you—?"

"Content monitoring," Milo said, not letting George finish his question.

"For *five years*?" George asked. He'd only been with Quire for a few days, and he already knew this about content monitoring: the burnout rate was crazy, as in a lot of CMs either burned out or went crazy.

"Yeah, I know," Milo said, "lucky me." He paused, shifted gears. "I'm not exactly . . ." Another pause. "My position . . . The thing is, I had an oopsie."

"Oopsie?"

"The celeb brat splattercast?" Milo said. "Rupert Gunn Jr.?"

George nodded.

"I missed it," Milo said. "I should have blocked it but must have been rubbing my eyes, trying to scour out some other atrocity our species came up with, and I missed it. By the time I yanked the vid, it was already going viral, leaping from platform to platform. The sick-puppy brigade kept reposting it faster than any CM could react."

"Wow," George said, prepared to add "that sucks," when a different idea came to him. "Do you think that has to do with why I got hired? I'm still waiting on my first assignment."

"You talk to Doc Fairbanks yet?" Milo asked.

"Doc who?"

"Check your email and calendar," his Virgil advised. "You've probably already got an appointment. No assignments before the appointment."

"What kind of—?"

"Psych," Milo said, hand on the doorknob, preparing to leave. "Me, I got lucky."

"How so?"

"Got grandfathered in. Probably why they're screening all the rest of you assholes."

"Thanks," George said.

"You're welcome," Milo smiled, showing too many teeth.

21

Roger Lynch, LCP, LLC (licensed clinical psychologist, limited liability corporation), had initiated a Skype session with a new client when the front door opened and then slammed closed.

"Gram's a war hero," Pandora announced.

"Excuse me," her father said into the screen of his laptop before turning it away and taking himself off camera. "Please, Dora, I'm working," he said, keeping his voice down.

"Well, I hope whoever you're working *on* enjoys getting advice from a *liar*," Pandora said at a decibel in keeping with the anger written all over her face.

Roger dipped his head back into the field of the webcam and the session he hadn't quite begun conducting. "I'm terribly sorry," he said, wearing an expression of such contrite remorse it would take a total dick not to accept his apology, "but I've got a family crisis going on here."

The new client, by no means a dick, insisted he totally understood, no problem, and was preparing to click off on his end when he apparently noticed the framed photo of Pandora on Roger's desk.

"Ooo, cute," the not-a-dick client was heard to say before their shared screen blipped back to the corporate screen saver of Quire Inc.

Taken aback by the disembodied compliment, Pandora's anger traded places momentarily with confusion, before restoking itself, even hotter than before. "How could you *forget* to tell me that Grandma Lynch was a secret agent during World War II?"

"What *are* you talking about?"

Pandora repeated, slowly, what she had said.

"That's crazy," Roger said, shaking his head. "I don't know *anything* about that."

"You didn't know?" Pandora asked.

"I didn't know," Roger answered.

And while another father and daughter might have gone around and around, circling the actual truth like boxers squaring off in the ring, both of them sucked when it came to hiding things. Plus, Pandora had come fresh from her grandmother's confession, during which Gladys had paused repeatedly to check whether they were being spied on.

"But it's cool, don't you think?"

"It's incredible," Roger said. "As in, not credible." Pause. "Are you *sure* she wasn't pulling your leg? Being sarcastic maybe."

"How would that even work?" his daughter asked. "A sarcastic story about being a World War II cryptographer that goes on for the better part of the afternoon?"

"Well then, maybe she's delusional," Roger said. "There's a reason she's in that place."

"I don't think dementia works that way," Pandora said. "What I think is, she did this service for her country, was sworn to secrecy, and the dementia's worn away her resolve to keep quiet." Conveniently absent from this account was any mention of her own role in clarifying the expiration date of her grandmother's memories.

"Yeah," Roger admitted, "dying *can* change your priorities."

"That's what she said."

This singular revelation was turning everything Roger thought he knew about the woman on its head—not to mention recasting who had treated whom unfairly. How often had he pitted mother against father, judging who deserved a breakdown and who didn't? His mother hadn't fared well in that competition, coming across like some Victorian lady suffering from "hysteria," "nerves," or "the vapors." His curiosity about his parents' contrasting mental resilience was another factor that had led him to the study of psychology.

And here his daughter was, letting him know that everything he believed about the human mind was based on a cryptosexist misreading of his own parents' reactions to World War II! *Well, she better have proof,* that's what Roger was thinking. *Hard proof.* Not some demented old lady's word.

"It sounded real, what she was saying?"

Pandora nodded. "Like watching it filmed by Merchant and Ivory," she said. "Like *The Bletchley Circle*, minus the stiff upper lip."

"I wonder if she ever saw that," Roger mused aloud.

"I don't think your parents ever had a TV," Pandora said, "much less a subscription to Netflix."

"You're right," her father said, remembering his own screen-free childhood, reading books and talking about them to the world over his father's ham radio. His over-air discussions of Thoreau's *Walden* led him straight to the backwoods hermits he started counseling over his dad's rig, followed by his life now, keeping Silicon Valley's brightest and squirreliest on this side of the dirt. "It's just . . ."

"It's just *cool,*" Pandora said, her face filled with pride. "My own grandmother, like James Bond with a crossword puzzle."

"The Ian Fleming of Scrabble," her father added, figuring if he couldn't beat 'em . . .

. . . he'd ignore them.

After all, asking him to reassess his entire life—professional and otherwise—was a bridge too far, based upon the tales of a woman whose mind was unraveling, who'd frustrated her own husband into an early grave and may be misremembering some fantasy she'd had once based on something she saw or read. He'd put up with his daughter's hero worship while it lasted, confident that it wouldn't. Dementia had a natural, downward progression after all, one that would reduce his mother to the appropriate size sooner or later. In case it didn't, however . . .

"Are you planning on going back," Roger asked, "now that your sentence is up?" It was December now, and those had been the terms: up to Christmas break.

Pandora didn't even have to think about it. "Yes," she said, nodding. "Absolutely."

"Did she *know* your punishment was up after this last visit?"

Pandora had seen the date marked on the calendar in the condo's kitchenette. Gladys had asked her about it repeatedly while she was there, trying to turn the date and its approach into a long-term memory. And so: "I think so."

"Maybe that's it, then," her father said. "I think you have to consider the possibility that you're being played—that she's telling you stories so you'll come back. Maybe she wants to be sure to see you at Christmas, so she's playing you like the Scheherazade of Golden Acres."

"Golden Heart of the North Senior Services," Pandora corrected. "And you're wrong. This is real."

Roger struck a contemplative pose. "We could probably FOIA her service records," he said, making it sound like a vague threat. "If she has any, that is."

"Or you could talk to her yourself," Pandora suggested. "Christmas miracles are in season."

But her father laughed instead. "Sounds like you've got our family covered," he said.

"Ooo, cute . . ."

That's what the voice had said, and it had sounded like a boy's, uptalking occasionally, signaling a certain uncertainty she found endearing compared to the usual smug snarkiness her dad's clients usually adopted.

Her father had turned his laptop away from facing him, switching to a shot of his desk, its knickknacks, pens, sticky notes, and . . . a framed photo of Pandora!

"Ooo, cute . . ."

Pandora lay awake, staring at her ceiling, unable to get the words out of her head. For the record, it was the first time anyone outside of family had even hinted she might be attractive. And against all her better-thinking parts, her heart filled with a delicious anxiety, full of terror and possibilities, all because of two stupid syllables uttered by a boy destined for psychiatric processing by her dad.

Frankly, it was a little hard to fathom, knowing what she knew about the gene that turned Lynches into self-caricatures. But CSI-ing the whole sequence of events, recalling where she was, where her dad was, where the laptop and its camera were, mentally tacking up strings from point A to point B like some blood-spatter expert, the living room now a cat's cradle of intersecting lines with the conclusion that, no, he'd not seen her or her cartoon face in person. No. He'd heard her, certainly—as intended, given how pissed she was—but there was no line of sight that would have resulted in his seeing the actual, living Pandora Lynch in Technicolor and CinemaScope.

But he couldn't have missed the picture of her on her father's desk. It would have practically filled his screen, a static snapshot of Pandora. And it made sense, kind of. The framed photo on her dad's desk showed her face in the best possible light, meaning stilled and lacking color, thus minimizing the effect of any blemishes.

Pandora wondered whether it was possible to have a relationship without ever letting the other person see beyond an initial good impression. A blind date, say, where her first move was to actually blind the poor guy.

"You look better in dark glasses," she'd say in lieu of an apology. "They suit you. Trust me."

"I guess I'll have to," she imagined him saying back, her imaginary boyfriend destined to share her dark sense of humor. "In more ways than one," she imagined him adding.

It should be stipulated that Pandora did not make a practice of eavesdropping on her father's sessions with his clients—not while they were happening live. Despite their cabin's privacy-deficient floor plan, the fiction of client-therapist confidentiality was maintained through Pandora's use of headphones that created an inverted signal based upon ambient noise levels—including human speech—so that the hills of one soundwave became the valleys of the antisignal, thus canceling each other out. Plus, she could play music on the other side of the noise-canceling filter, which she usually did, and loudly. All of this was standard operating procedure whenever Roger was with a client.

What Roger wasn't aware of was that his curious daughter, the hacker, had hacked his laptop years ago, giving her access to all his recorded sessions. She preferred the recordings to listening live because it was more efficient. What she was interested in was any inside intel a client might spill that would be of use to her for future hacks. Recorded, she could speed through the sessions in chipmunk mode, alert for keywords. And once speech recognition software came of age, she let her own computer comb for keywords. Not that she ever got much, especially not any intellectual property in actionable detail. Turned out, her father's clients were justifiably paranoid, alluding to "some major disrupting" as a result of whatever they were working on or some "paradigm shifting algo," blah, blah, blah. And so into the trash icon these MP3s went.

But even over the grainy speaker of her father's laptop, there was something in this latest client's voice that had caught her attention—a certain youthful enthusiasm absent in her father's usual twentysomethings. She made a mental bet with herself about whether the voice's owner was old enough to shave, crossed her fingers, and then reviewed what had been recorded prior to Roger's cutting it short, to handle a "family crisis."

Bingo!

The "ooo, cute" boy was, indeed, a boy but also old enough to shave, if barely. Dark down shadowed his upper lip, while filaments were scattered in wisp patches here and there across his cheeks and chin. She hoped he'd shave, as opposed to growing some hipster chin bush. She already lived among a predominately male population who'd earned the right to their plaid and Sasquatchery; anyone caught playing that game south of Alaska was, well, pretty much a poseur by definition.

And while unflattering facial hair might seem trivial, Pandora had noticed a trend among her father's clients: personal grooming was often a Rubicon they couldn't or wouldn't cross. Call it the Einstein Hair Effect, a lack of vanity, studied slovenliness, or maybe not so studied. Whatever they were going for (or choosing by default), she'd found their relationship to the razor was nevertheless correlated to a certain snappishness she could live without. So: to shave or not, that was the question she sent out into the universe, her terms for what to consider a signal versus the usual noise.

Part Two

22

Later, during World War II, the rerun: "I remember one of the boys who was fighting the war like us girls, but he was doing it in England," Gladys recalled. "He was a big deal. Not too old or too broken to fight the usual way, but too smart to waste his brain stopping some Nazi's bullet. He visited us girls 'in the colonies' once." She paused, and Pandora could see it: she was remembering, not hallucinating. Gladys continued. "The rumor mill had it that he was overseeing the installation of something called 'the widget.' That's what they called it, always in whispers, these fast-walking men we'd never seen around there before. The most we could figure out was that 'ours' was going to be a backup, in case the one in England succumbed to enemy attack."

Pandora could feel her heart race. *Could it be?* "What was his name?" she asked hastily. "Tell me you remember his name, Gram."

"They only ever called him 'Alan from England,'" Gladys said as her granddaughter repeated the words, "'Alan from England . . .'"

"He was such a handsome man," Gladys continued. "Such a dark, serious face, his temples shaved all round to the thinnest stubble, the hair on top always flopping in his eyes."

"Did you talk to him?" Pandora asked. "Did he say anything?"

Gladys giggled, turning suddenly girlish, despite all appearances to the contrary. "I *touched* him," she said.

"What did he do," Pandora asked, "when you touched him?"

"Froze. I think he may have been afraid of us."

"Americans?"

"Women."

"I heard he was . . . 'shy,'" Pandora said.

If Gladys realized what she meant by that, she showed no signs. "I wonder whatever happened to him."

Pandora wondered, *Should I? Shouldn't I?*

"He died, Gram."

Her grandmother's eyes went wide. "But he's so *young*," she said. "And he seems—*seemed*—like such a nice man. Very serious. Very British."

Pandora didn't know what to say. She wanted to *scream* that Alan from England was the father of modern computing and committed suicide after being chemically castrated for the crime of being homosexual by the country he'd helped save during World War II. She wanted to tell Gladys how Alan from England bit into an apple laced with cyanide and the rumor that the bite out of the Apple logo is a nod to this, as opposed to the Bible's tree of knowledge or even Isaac Newton. But before she could say any of that, Gladys continued.

"I used to imagine what it would be like to be married to someone like that," she said wistfully. "To wake up to the sound of English being spoken properly. I bet he would have played Scrabble with me, not like those chickens, my husband and son."

A week later, Pandora made a point of touching the hand she guessed was probably the hand that had touched Alan Turing. "Tell me about Alan from England again," she said.

"Who?" Gladys said, as Pandora, now the holder of that memory, proceeded to tell it back to her. When she got to the part where Gladys, bold as brass, reached out and touched the author of the Turing test, her granddaughter decided to take a little editorial license.

"I did?" her grandmother said, her eyes widening.

"You did," Pandora confirmed.

"And what did *he* do?" Gladys asked.

"He smiled," Pandora said. "He took your hand and kissed it like you were the queen of England herself."

"How marvelous," Gladys said, the cheeks of her tattletale face giving her away, yet again.

23

Pandora didn't usually eavesdrop on her father when he was actively with a client. And ever since she'd started using speech recognition and keyword searches, she didn't do much listening to the recorded sessions either—not unless her search turned up something exploitable in some hackerly way. But this latest session was different; it was the makeup session for the one she'd interrupted with news of Grandma Lynch's wartime heroism. She'd since learned the client's name was George Jedson, which sounded like an alias, but a quick cyber tiptoe through Quire HR's employee database confirmed it was as legal as her own.

The new employee screenings had started as charity from her dad's college roommate but had since become mandatory thanks to a coder who went a little suboptimal while programming a routine software patch. In this case, *suboptimal* meant the release of millions of usernames, social security numbers, and credit card information—a release that led to several class-action lawsuits and legislative hearings in the US, the UK, and the EU.

Her father and George had just gotten started when she'd interrupted them, and so Roger was taking it from the top. After winding up the "origin story" of the mandatory psych evaluation, her father concluded with the disclaimer Quire's general counsel had approved: "It's not you, it's us. And by 'us,' we mean Quire, by which we mean the parent company, as well as its various affiliates, subsidiaries, and offshore incarnations for tax purposes . . ."

Given the opportunity to speak, George brought up the abrupt termination of the previous session. Because of it, her father's new client had gone another full workday without an assignment.

"So I have to wonder," George said, "is all this meaningless waiting part of the psych exam? Like on *Law & Order*, letting a suspect sweat it out in the box."

"If you don't mind me saying," Roger said, "that sounds a little paranoid."

"What would it mean if I minded you saying that?"

Roger ignored the attempt at humor. "That I was correct in my original assessment," Roger said, clickety-clicking his pen to underline the point.

George cleared his throat.

"Different topic." Clickety-click. Pause.

"Yes?" George said, sounding wary.

Reading from his notes: "'Ooo, cute.' What was that in reference to, before you signed off?"

Pandora, perched before her own laptop, listening in as well as watching the session on-screen, noted that the universe had accepted and responded to her terms. Because there was Mr. Jedson's face, shaved as smooth as the proverbial baby's butt and just as cute. Looking at it live and free of distracting facial hair, she noticed that George's face seemed the total opposite of her own, calm and revealing nothing to the point of seeming chiseled. She found herself paying attention to his blinks, to confirm the screen hadn't frozen. Between the two of them—Pandora imagined—maybe their kids would luck out and get normally expressive faces.

But before she could start scrawling multiple iterations of the name she'd take after marriage (to hyphenate or not to hyphenate?), she heard the session taking a dangerous turn with her father's quoting the two words she'd been hearing ever since they were first uttered. Now, however, voiced by her father, they sounded, well, creepy, making Pandora want to do several things at once: 1) scream "No . . ."; 2) slam her laptop closed, perhaps forever; 3) take a sledgehammer to the satellite downlink; and/or 4) die of embarrassment and wait for her father to notice the smell.

Meanwhile, "Um," George said, as stone-faced as ever, "your daughter, I'm guessing?"

"Where?" Roger asked, looking behind him.

"The photo," George said. "On your desk. You mentioned you had a daughter, and any other explanation seems a little creepy."

"Yes," Roger said, turning the frame away from the camera. "That's Pandora."

George's eyebrows lifted ever so slightly. "Ominous."

"It's after the charm bracelet," Roger said, dismissing any broader, mythological implications. "Her mother collected charms."

"Collected?" George said. "Past tense?"

"Her mother passed away when Pandora was born."

"You mean like Mary Shelley's mom?"

Pandora listened, both fascinated and horrified to hear herself being talked about by her father and his client, neither aware she was listening to every word. But this talking about her mom, too, and the casual way her dad gave away the story of her name when he'd lied to her about it so long just made her—well, she was back to considering her previous options, with smashing the sat link pulling ahead. Fortunately, it seemed her father had grown as uncomfortable with this digression as she was.

"Why don't you tell me about *your* mother," Roger said.

"Isn't that a cliché?" George countered. "I mean, blaming the parents for a kid's being messed up?"

"Are you telling me you consider yourself a messed-up kid?"

Her father's new client hung his head but then seemed to remember he was on camera. His eyes, so calm as to seem blasé before, now hardened underneath their pixels. Finally: "Yes," he said. "You got me. I *do* believe in my heart of hearts"—he paused—"that I *am*"—he paused again—"pretty *frickin'* messed up."

Her father blinked in the thumbnail of his side of the session in the bottom left-hand corner of her screen. She could practically read his mind, with a lot of help from his face. Most of his clients' files began and ended with the screening, one and done. A handful had become regulars. And this one, by admitting to feeling messed up, had just won himself a callback. For which, Pandora thought, *Thank you, universe,* while her father clickety-clicked his pen and asked, "Are Wednesdays good for you?"

24

In retrospect, Pandora realized, she'd been noticing it without acknowledging it. Her grandmother's bookmark hadn't moved in weeks. It used to be it'd be sticking out of a new book from one visit to the next. But then there was the visit when Pandora noticed the book on her grandmother's end table hadn't changed. That's when her attention shifted to the bookmark's progress as a visualization of the disease's progress, reversed. Pandora wondered when Gladys had been forced to abandon her favorite hobby. Was it when she couldn't retain what she'd read from one page to the next? Paragraphs? Sentences? Had individual words become speed bumps, hindering the drive toward meaning? And was becoming the story herself the backup plan, the one that kept her remaining neurons from becoming speed bumps in their own right?

Her grandmother's brain was having a fire sale, and Pandora had caught the old woman's anxiety like a virus. Before, she'd been fooled by the disease's sweet spot into thinking there was more time. Now, it was like her grandmother's commanding officers, drilling away how every idle minute cost lives.

Pandora vowed to spend as much time as remained with her grandmother, getting every byte and datum down, recording it all on her phone for posterity. She'd start skipping classes if she had to—not exactly a sacrifice, with the exception of her science class, but she was sure Mr. V would understand, what with his mother and all.

But even if she skipped school, the Golden Heart only held visiting hours for so long, no exceptions, unless a loved one had actually rung death's doorbell, when they might get you a cot. But dying memories? What part of elder care didn't Pandora get? Been there, done that, forgot about it—and *that's* what Pandora should do: forget about it. Every resident at the Golden Heart was an American, meaning nobody at the Golden Heart got special treatment, their memories included—especially those memories somebody's granddaughter hinted might still be classified. Or as she'd been told already: "First the brownies, now this? Do you *want* to wind up in some CIA black site?"

But once visiting hours ended and Gladys was by herself, Pandora knew those memories didn't hit pause, waiting for the next visit so she could resume where they'd left off. The disease's progress was relentless and the exact opposite of the bookmark's progress through her grandmother's last murder mystery, the grand reveal of whodunit forever withheld from her . . .

But Pandora believed in the power of technology to fix things. She'd already begun recording Gladys on her phone. But she couldn't just hand her a digital recorder and say, "Yeah, before you die, could you please fill this up?" It needed to be something that actually *helped* Gladys while it was helping her piece together her own family's pre-Pandoran history. Something to prop up her grandmother's failing short-term memory—something more sophisticated than the dry-erase board where staff would write reminders about pending house calls from one of the medical practitioners with iconic hints like a tooth, eyeglasses, or a valentine-style heart, always ending with the same headless smiley made out of two dots and a swoop followed by the staffer's name.

Pandora could do better. She'd start by rooting one of her outdated smartphones, customize the screen to keep it Jitterbug easy, with dedicated, supersized icons for a calendar app that included reminders of the whiteboard sort and a facial recognition app preprogrammed with faces Gladys should know, including Pandora; the facility's various staff and medical practitioners; her son, Roger (because you never knew); and Gladys's own, from a wedding photo of her and Herman, taken in the bar where they'd met, holding hands as a dead moose head on the wall looked on approvingly. She'd include Skype with her contact info programmed in for when Gladys missed her between visits and a voice-activated recorder for her grandmother's war stories. Lastly, she'd throw in a weather app, for when Gladys didn't want to get up and check outside her window.

Once it was set up, Pandora spent the better part of her next visit showing Gladys how to use it, pointing out what each virtual button did, how to point the camera at faces she didn't know so the phone could speak her visitor's name. She'd worried about Gladys's forgetting to charge the phone, and so she glued the jack into its port and plugged the charger into an outlet underneath her grandmother's bed so it wouldn't be a tripping hazard or get accidentally unplugged. The charging cord was long enough to reach the nightstand like a landline phone. Though the arrangement made a mockery of wireless technology, Pandora figured her grandmother would probably be more comfortable with a phone similar to the ones her generation had grown most accustomed to, even if Herman and she had never gotten a phone of their own.

It was fun, showing her grandmother technology that blew her mind and about which Pandora had grown jaded but could appreciate again from the new perspective of Gladys's aging eyes. "Oh my," she'd said as her granddaughter molded her wrinkled hand to this slab of plastic from the future. Pandora demonstrated Skype, showing Gladys how they could see each other, and see each other seeing each other, and so on.

"Oh my," the old lady repeated, and Pandora wished she could crawl inside her skull to see the sci-fi world she must be imagining.

"Pretty cool, huh?" Pandora said.

"Pretty cool," Gladys said, either because she agreed or because it was the last thing she heard.

Pandora had to skip their next visit to study for an unexpected exam that was worth enough that she couldn't offset it with extra credit later. Previously, she would have felt guilty, but was reassured by the fact that Gladys could Skype her now. No call, she concluded, meant everything was okay. Hopefully, her grandmother was busy filling up the phone's memory with her own memories, secret, classified, and otherwise.

After acing the test the next day, Pandora thought about calling Gladys to let her know, but didn't want to startle her. She'd convinced herself that her grandmother was taking advantage of the tech she'd been given to "remember your memories for you." So she gave it another day, reminding herself to bring a cable and thumb drive to collect what memories Gladys had recorded, while also reminding herself to set up a Dropbox account so her grandmother's recordings could go straight to the cloud.

But when Pandora showed up, Gladys was gone. Instead of her new BFF coming to open the door with the walker she'd begun using, she was greeted by some gray-haired stranger.

"I'm sorry," she said. "I thought this was Gladys Lynch's condo."

"Was that her name?" the younger old woman said, her bandy wrinkled arms braced at the wrists, her hands holding tiny dumbbells she pumped in sequence, left, then right, then left again, as if she was keeping her heart going manually.

"*Was?*" Pandora said, her own heart nearly stopping. "What happened?"

"Oh no," the usurper said. "They've only moved her."

"Where?"

"Haven't a clue," the heart pumper said. "Oh, wait. When you find her, can you give her something?"

"Sure," Pandora said, imagining some old-people's tradition of giving gifts for occasions like being moved closer to death's door—a cake, perhaps. Instead: "Here," the other one said, handing the girl a tight, rubber-banded tube of junk mail that hadn't been forwarded to wherever they'd installed the grandmother Pandora was getting to know, for real, for the first time.

A series of nurture-free nurses, recalcitrant rehabbers, and a-hole attendants later, Pandora finally found her way to "the other side," where her grandmother had been moved. She knocked on the frame of the open door before entering to find Gladys, looking out the window, watching her breath freeze against the glass, the ice crystals feathering out geometrically, biology turned into math.

"I wished I'd smoked when I had the chance," Gladys said, as if she was talking to herself but didn't mind if her granddaughter listened in.

"Why, for heaven's sake?"

"For heaven's sake," Gladys echoed before pausing—to think, perhaps. "I wish I smoked because of heaven. That's why."

"How . . . ?"

"Because maybe I'd be dead already," Gladys said. "Maybe I'd be looking down from heaven now."

"That's silly," Pandora said. To the best of her knowledge, her grandparents had both become agnostic after the war. Roger and his daughter had taken it a step further, as atheists.

"What's silly is everybody trying to live longer," Gladys said. "They think they're adding years to their lives. What they don't realize is that all those years get added on the shit end."

Pandora wanted to quibble with Gladys's conclusion but, looking at her grandmother's new accommodations, found she was fresh out of sunshine and pep talks. "What happened?" she asked.

"I messed my bed," Gladys said.

Pandora tried keeping the "yuck" off her face—couldn't—and so went for brutal pragmatism. "Switch to Depends," she said. "I've seen them on TV. All the active seniors are wearing them."

"I've *been* wearing them," Gladys said, her voice an angry hiss, though who that anger was aimed at wasn't clear. "I forgot to change, goddamn it."

"How long . . ."

"All day," Gladys said. "I went to bed that way. They . . . *exploded*."

Pandora's "yuck" face doubled down, her mouth an oval of forlorn darkness.

"It was in my hair, Dorie," Gladys said, tears standing in her eyes.

"Oh, Gram," the younger girl said, wrapping her arm around the older girl's shoulder.

After a moment: "I want you to promise me something," Gladys said.

"Anything, Gram."

"I want you to start smoking. Camels. Unfiltered. Die some other way."

"Okay, Gram," she said. "For you," she added, already looking forward to her forgetting they'd ever had this conversation.

25

Pandora had done it the same day she decided to start working on the phone for Gladys. She'd begun wondering, idly at first but then frantically as she watched Gladys change before her eyes: Did she have more in common with her grandmother than just a hyperexpressive face? Until then, the younger woman had consoled herself with a factoid she'd heard somewhere about how Alzheimer's was linked to the use of aluminum cookware. But when she tried to remember the source of that factoid: nothing. Crickets. Which made her wonder if—from here on out—every recall lapse or random brain fart would make her feel like she'd stepped down a step and missed, finding nothing under her feet but air and the panicked caught breath of a fall as it happened.

Whether that was to be her fate seemed like a knowable unknown. And so she bought a DNA kit from the Safeway pharmacy. The company she picked donated part of their profits to CARE or UNICEF, placing them one holier-than above competitors like 23andMe, which also cost more. The test was originally marketed as the Healing Helix, a nod to the goal of ending intolerance by showing how genetically interconnected everybody was. Someone in the company must have had second thoughts about the alliteration, however, and so the name was changed to Six Degrees, which was displayed on the box and in their ads as the numeral followed by the symbol for degree in superscript. By avoiding words altogether, the logo was considered internationally recognizable shorthand for the whole "six degrees of separation" thing. The company further reinforced this message by running ads that featured happy multicultis tracking their ancestry around the globe, dropping pins next to happy dancing villagers, next to happy nodding monks, next to happy chanting protesters, their faces streaming tears of apparent joy while the gas canister fumes filled the screen to provide a backdrop for the tagline: "One Big Happy."

Locking herself behind the one *actual* interior door that *actually* locked, Pandora ripped open the box like her life depended on it. A shatterproof plastic test tube fell out, along with its screw-on cap and a Q-tip in cellophane followed by a folded wad of tissue-thin paper with the instruction to swab her cheek, drop the Q-tip in the test tube, and mail it back in the prepaid mailer to an address somewhere in North Carolina with the words *research* and *park* as part of the city's name. The same instructions (presumably) followed in Spanish, French, German, Russian, Arabic, Chinese, and a dozen or so more languages. Pandora checked inside the box, hoping for more lab tech—a petri dish, say, or a bottle of reagent—some evidence that she didn't have to wait for this process to go back and forth through the US postal system.

No such luck.

Pandora swore. Didn't they know how many brain cells could die waiting for USPS to complete its appointed rounds? She swore again. And then she swabbed her cheek, packed up the tube, borrowed the truck, and sped off for the nearest FedEx drop-off location. She'd handle the part of the timeline she could, hoping that the recipients on the other end of the delivery would take the "Please hurry" she scrawled across the prepaid mailer in earnest and reciprocate by sending the results back with equal urgency. And if passive-aggressiveness wasn't their thing, maybe the fact of the package coming from Fairbanks would catch somebody's attention and move her to the front of the line. She'd played the last-frontier card before, getting live people instead of robots, because the place she called home happened to overlap with their dream vacation or retirement plans. That was the nice thing about living in a state routinely featured on the Discovery Channel: you could pimp it out for favors in a pinch.

It worked, kind of. That and the extra she paid for priority processing and shipping, which came to roughly twice the cost of the original kit. Still, it had taken about a week—a week during which she'd been knocked off her visiting schedule by an exam and a subsequent overconfidence in technology. The results had arrived the morning of the "please start smoking" visit, which raised the stakes on everything.

Not that Pandora knew what was waiting for her at the Golden Heart when she folded the unopened envelope and stuffed it into her pocket. She'd open it once she got there, she decided, and if it was good news, she'd share it with Gladys, in case what had or hadn't been passed along was weighing on her too.

But then there'd been the surprise at her grandmother's former condo and the mad rush to find out where she'd been taken. There'd been the promise to smoke and the wanting to cry. And only then did Pandora remember the envelope in her parka. She found a visitors' bathroom and locked herself inside.

The first thing she removed was a multipage form letter full of legalese explaining all the things the results *wouldn't* be telling her, as well as the things they *hadn't* tested for, including the nastiest of inheritable diseases because the liability of blah, blah, blah, which Pandora took to mean they didn't want to be sued when somebody offed themselves after getting bad news. And spoiler alert, Huntington's, Alzheimer's, Lou Gehrig's, assorted cancers, dementias, and incurable neurological conditions all constituted bad news. Leaving what? Earlobes attached or not? Tongue curling? Eye color . . .

Pandora wanted to scream, to cry, to maybe email the head of the company, promising not to kill herself, explaining she just wanted to know so she could start planning . . .

". . . to do what?" she asked her reflection in the bathroom mirror. And the funny thing was, Pandora already had an answer—had had it for a while, just below the surface of her consciousness. She'd even taken a step in that direction with the smartphone she'd reprogrammed for Gladys, promising that it would remember her memories for her. And that's what she wanted to do, scaled way up: move her memories from in vitro to in silico.

Futurists had been talking about the point in human history when the species would merge with computers to live forever. Ray Kurzweil, arguably the father of this line of thinking, called it "the singularity" and predicted that the technology to link our brains to computers and upload ourselves to the cloud was practically around the corner—by the 2030s or so. That was well within Pandora's life span—and well before she'd be showing any signs of dementia, if that was the fate hardwired into her DNA.

So that was the good news, right? The future was already working on it; there was too much money on the table for it not to be. Pandora laughed. All that angst when the truth was that AI, the cloud, and neuro-tech had it all covered! Gladys's present didn't have to be Pandora's future. *Except . . .*

"Except what?" she asked her mirrored self.

And again, she already knew. Her father's oft-repeated mathematical morality of logical conclusions: What if everybody did what you're thinking of doing? And what was Pandora thinking of doing? Nothing. Letting the future take care of, well, her future. But if everybody chilled and let the future take care of itself—*then the future* wouldn't *take care of itself.* Lulled into waiting for the singularity, humans would have no incentive to invent it.

Not that Pandora had to create a self-aware AI she could upload all her hopes and dreams to by herself. But she had a good brain (for the time being), and she was a quick learner (while it lasted). She was a cyber native, had taken computers apart and put them back together without having them blow up. She'd learned to program in binary, the actual ones and zeros the computer used. Her dad studied the human mind, and surely she'd picked up something through osmosis. Further back, she shared blood with a WWII code breaker and had touched the father of modern computing, albeit by proxy and a few generations removed.

And then there was that pair of aces in the hole: she was young and stubborn as they came. So hell yeah. It wasn't like she had anything more important to do.

26

Mr. Plaid had a name—Steve Vickers—and before he vacated George's office, he'd been working on a project for Quire, sitting on that dock by the bay, looking at the Golden Gate Bridge. He was trying to get into the "mind space" of a person who'd jump from said bridge, a locally popular option when it came to taking that final departing flight into whatever comes next. He imagined that must be nothing—the what-comes-next—for someone in that position. They must *think* that. Must think they're placing a period at the end of their life sentence, not a semicolon or a question mark and certainly not an exclamation point, though he was inclined to waver on that last one. Suicide—or so it seemed to Steve Vickers—was decidedly the act of someone in love with their own drama.

The reason he was thinking about all this was because that was what his latest work assignment called for. His employer wanted its corner of the web turned into a safety net, a little like the one circling Apple's Foxconn factory in China, to catch the jumpers. Or as V.T. put it, signing off on the assignment: "We want to make Quire a safe place to go to be saved."

While the idea behind these mental field trips was sound, the way Vickers was conducting them was a waste of time. Because the task wasn't about preventing *his* demographic from exiting the pool of consumers—biology and time were rapidly turning that cohort irrelevant—but those who were in the prime of their consumptive lives. Steve Vickers's empathy was too chronologically specific. Sure, he could think himself into the minds of different races, religions, sexual orientations, and socioeconomic classes—provided they were all roughly around his age. Add or subtract a decade, however, and *nothing*. Trying to understand the fads, trends, language even of his target demographic audience was like trying to mind meld with a cow, chewing away on its cud. He and they were in different headspaces, even though, years earlier, he'd aged right on through it, in premature mourning for the innocence he couldn't wait to be rid of.

So maybe it wasn't too surprising that George's predecessor kept getting distracted by the other scenery. The homeless crabber being creepy over that way, the lesbians reacting disgustedly a few benches down. And boy, those seagulls! Wheeling so white against the blue sky, inevitably leaving their witness in a caffeinated and mildly euphoric mood, also known as . . .

. . . *the totally wrong headspace for working on that goddamn suicide thing.*

Back at the office, Steve Vickers had been giving it his best shot for three months. He'd divided the assignment into two main steps: identification and intervention—the two Is. Shortly after getting the assignment, he'd coded up a nice little data cruncher to tackle the first *I* by baselining the online activity of every Quire user within the target demographic and then comparing that baseline on a rolling basis, looking for any deviations from the mean, with a target's potential for self-harm being a relatively simple ratio of public engagement to nesting behavior. The first of these criteria—the ratio's numerator—was populated with data on how often the subject sent emails, tweets, IMs, and/or texts, including how long these exchanges were in terms of both individual message character counts and overall duration of the thread, from the first message to the last. The denominator, in turn, was based upon the radius of the subject's travel behavior over a set time period, derived from smartphone GPS data, including the subset of how long the subject spent at his or her primary residence, which was used as a multiplier. A decreasing rate of public engagement divided by an increasing rate of nesting behavior would set a flag, and the identification process would move on to the interim phase 1b: confirmation.

Vickers's first approach to this interim phase had been simple and effective, and only required the target to answer three questions: 1) Are you depressed?; 2) Is there a gun in the house?; and 3) Have you been drinking? George's predecessor had designed a chatbot that asked these questions subliminally, the text flashing for an eyeblink between lines of chatter about something else. This approach led to several early successes—right up until word leaked on how they'd been achieved, after which the wrath of the first and last letters of the ATF came raining down on QHQ, with talk of boycotts and share sell-offs and assorted other PR nightmares that were not at all mitigated by the thank-yous V.T. received from survivors and members of the pharmaceutical industry with an interest in selling solutions that didn't involve getting loaded and/or taking aim.

Vickers's next attempt at confirming the seriousness of a target's intentions involved inserting an increasing number of ads in the user's news feed, including PSAs for suicide prevention hotlines, half-off coupons for natural antidepressants ranging from vitamin B to St. John's wort, and BOGO deals on aromatherapy candles, usually lavender. If/when these enticements failed to garner the clicks they were tailor-baited for, confirmation by default was assumed, and "in an overabundance of caution" (according to Quire's lawyers), the platform outsourced intervention to local law enforcement. Though individual areas varied as to response aggressiveness, there had already been a few hospitalizations and one death as a result of Quire users' SEQs (self-endangerment quotients) being skewed due to lost phones being interpreted algorithmically as "loss of engagement."

And then Rupert Gunn Jr. placed the family's namesake into his face hole and shot his mouth off without saying a word. And while Steve Vickers had not been involved in the news feed manipulation experiments that led to Mr. Gunn's premature exit, his algorithm had also failed to predict it.

"You know, I had a feeling," George said after finally getting the details of his first assignment, the one he'd inherited from his predecessor. The assignment had been hand delivered to him in hard copy on V.T.'s personal letterhead with the instruction that it be shredded after reading. When George folded it back up instead, the messenger cleared his throat loudly and patted the top of his custom-built satchel—one featuring a top-loaded crosscut shredder.

"We used to use burn bags," the messenger explained, "but they kept setting those off." He pointed at the sprinklers.

And so George fed the one and only copy of what he'd be doing for the next several months into the slot through which it was magically transformed into confetti.

It wasn't often new hires were given offices and hand delivered their first assignments. If George had any doubts about that, they were quickly quashed when he entered the cafeteria following his assignment's delivery. He could feel the eyes on him—less a sign of his social sensitivity than a byproduct of socially maladapted strangers having no qualms about walking right up to him and asking: "So what're you working on?"

George matched their social maladaptation and raised them being rude. "I'm using reinforcement learning to discover the meaning of life through trial and error," he informed them. "You know, check off everything life *doesn't* mean and then see what's left." He figured that sounded nicer than "I'm scripting an AI to make sure no more rich kids off themselves on our platform"—an explanation he was pretty sure was counterindicated by the whole shredding situation.

But his fellow coders heard it pretty much the way it was intended. "Dude, just say f-off next time."

"Okay," George said. "F-off."

And with that, George returned to his workspace to see if he could get his headspace in the right place to start eating the elephant he now shared his office with.

27

Before leaving the visitors' restroom with her non-news from the genetic testing people, it occurred to Pandora that she hadn't seen the phone among the items relocated to her grandmother's new, radically downsized living arrangement. Returning, she found the curtains drawn and Gladys asleep in the railed bed that now dominated the space, a monitor of some kind clipped to her blanket should she try to get up without help. But Pandora couldn't see the phone anywhere. Checking for an outline of it under the covers, she was startled to realize Gladys's eyes were wide open and looking right at her.

"What do you want?" her grandmother asked as if Pandora were a stranger, maybe an artifact of having just been awoken, or maybe . . .

"I was just looking for your phone."

"We don't have one and don't want one," Gladys said, making the younger woman feel like a door-to-door salesperson about to be greeted with a shotgun.

"Never mind," Pandora said, hastily backing up and out. "It was old," she added, and regretted the implication immediately—the casual equivalence of age with a depreciation in worth. Fortunately, Gladys didn't seem to notice, still flat on her back in the shadowed room, staring at the ceiling.

Walking the long hallway to the exit, Pandora ran through a variety of possible scenarios for the phone's disappearance. Maybe someone stole it during the move. Maybe it got lost in the shuffle. And then she had an idea; she called the missing phone from her phone over Skype to see if she could figure out where it was from the video. Fortunately, she'd programmed it to answer her number automatically to make it easier on Gladys.

But the view she got of the call's other side was impressionistic, at best, consisting of a blurry swirl of Halloween colors—black and orange—the black looking like horns or talons. Continuing down the hallway, trying to figure out what and where she was seeing, Pandora bumped into a janitor coming in the opposite direction. There was the usual exchange of "watch its" and "sorrys," but as she prepared to move on, she noticed a glow from atop the janitor's wheeled trash barrel.

"Excuse me," she said. "Can I . . . ?" She made a gesture she hoped read as "look through the garbage," though it could also have been "do the breaststroke."

"Knock yourself out," the janitor said, pulling out a pair of one-size-fits-most rubber gloves from a hundred-count box on his cart like he was offering her a Kleenex.

"Thank you," she said, pulling the gloves on, snap, snap, before picking aside this awful this and that nasty that until, bingo, she pinched a corner of plastic and lifted out the phone she'd rooted, sealed in a biohazard bag, bright, translucent orange backgrounding the extra-terrestrial death lily, its swooping, impressionistic petals all in black. The phone was smeared with something Pandora assumed was *not* pudding.

Doing what she could to calm her face, the hacker cleared her throat and began: "I know this is going to sound strange and is probably against the rules, but . . ."

"You want the shit phone," the janitor guessed.

"I want the shit phone," Pandora echoed, pretty sure she'd never used quite that combination of words before in her life—and hoping she never would again.

"Knock yourself out," the janitor said.

It wasn't the device itself so much as what might be on it, in addition to fecal matter. Specifically, Pandora wanted to see if Gladys had recorded anything before the mishap. Checking, she discovered a list of numerically labeled MP3s in the recorder's file folder, which she downloaded to a less biohazardous medium before plugging it into her laptop and hitting play.

Nothing. Dead air.

Or *nearly* dead air. Straining, Pandora could make out ambient old-lady noises. She would have said butt dialing if she hadn't wired it like a landline. So what was Gladys doing? Using it as a coaster? Pandora listened for clues: the ding of the microwave in the kitchen; blowing; sipping; the word *hot* spoken to herself; a cracking long fart. Next file: the creak of her new walker as she lifted and lowered her weight by its handles; the name Herman; the question "Where are you?" Next file: the pages of a book, rattling gently as she turned them; three pages turned quickly, pause, three quick-turned pages again; a sigh; no more page turns. Next file: the tail end of a cry, gone almost singsongy, conjuring the image of Gladys, a pillow pressed to her stomach, rocking, and crying, rocking and crying . . .

Pandora ran out of files and was glad, then sad. She'd returned the phone to its biohazard bag. It was mostly smooth glass and plastic, but with enough physical buttons where shit might hide—in her imagination, if not in reality. And so she scooted it off the edge of her desk with the eraser end of a pencil and into the wastebasket, thought about it, and then dropped the pencil in as well.

She'd gotten the technology wrong, Pandora decided. A sleek slab would have been fine for her, but not for a woman slipping backward in time. It needed to be softer, friendlier, invite interaction. It needed to be something her grandmother could love, like a child loves a favorite toy, taking it to bed, talking to it, talking for and through it, an "invisible" friend that others could see, but not as vividly or vitally as the owner who loved it. Like a teddy bear, still warm from the dryer, tucked in together, ripe for snuggling.

It needed—in short—a face.

None of this was original thinking on Pandora's part, as she'd be the first to admit. She'd begun noticing how many of the residents had little companions on this side of the Golden Heart. Some were being visited by dogs in vests, professional caregivers of the four-legged variety. Others held on to lifelike baby dolls, teddy bears, even a sock monkey, offering them bites of food, cooing at them, asleep with their gray heads resting on the plusher ones like pillows. One skin-and-bones woman had a cockroach hand puppet, her fingers fitting into its gloved legs, the body made of corduroy, the wings, leather on the outside, silk on the other, suede strips for antennae. It was the most touchably gorgeous cockroach she'd ever seen, an opinion shared by its owner, who stroked its variously tactile surfaces constantly—when she wasn't sneaking up on other residents and skittering it across their shoulders, only to laugh hysterically when they recoiled.

Pandora's first response to this menagerie was anger on the residents' behalf, at their being infantilized with these playthings. But then she noticed how fond of them the residents seemed, whispering in their ears, seeming to listen to their replies, offering them food and drink and comfort. There was a lot of there-there-ing going on as the upset and fearful put those feelings aside to play parent to themselves through these intermediaries they cradled and cooed to: there-there, there-there . . .

More than one resident helped their friend wave a paw or hand at Pandora as she walked by, and she couldn't help it; she waved back.

"It's therapeutic," a nurse's aide had said. "And they're pretty resilient to not being fed or walked."

"That makes sense," Pandora, the convert, had said as she looked at her grandmother's hands. Bulge-knuckled and blue, featuring a traffic jam of veins across the top of each, Gladys's hands were otherwise empty, holding nothing but each other.

"Would it be okay if—" she'd begun, not knowing what she might bring but knowing she needed to bring something.

"Certainly," the nurse's aide had said, not needing Pandora to finish the thought.

What she wanted would be like what the others had, but better—more interactive. It should be able to have a conversation—a real one, not imaginary. It should be able to initiate such a conversation and record it. The Japanese were working on eldercare robots like what she envisioned—not a Robby to do any heavy lifting or make sure they bathed, but for the company, minus the need to feed or clean up after a support animal. The Japanese weren't bothered by such artificial concepts as artificiality; everything was believed to share an essential spirituality, the animate and inanimate alike. A robot dog and a so-called "real dog" could both produce real emotions in the person petting one or the other without being labeled unnatural.

Pandora tried a variety of searches on Amazon to see what might already be available and tweakable. Casting the broadest net first, she looked at page after page of "robot toys," finding a variety of actual and knockoff Transformers, kits to teach young scientists about robotics, a few robodogs, and a range of what Pandora dubbed robocuties, featuring prominent heads with prominent eyes and smiles. But none of it was quite right, featuring too many hard edges and, if not edges, then hard, smooth curves. *Hard* was the theme and executed in plastic. Many had wheels or some other means of getting around—clearly intended for overactive kids, giving them something to chase off their energy with, but the exact opposite of what she wanted for the increasingly sedentary Gladys.

Searching for "robot dogs" eliminated the Transformers and Terminator exoskeletons, but the hard plastic remained. That wasn't what Pandora wanted; she wanted soft, plush, pettable. She typed in the word *robot*, no quotes, and the first keyword she could think of that conveyed what she was looking for: *fur*.

And there they were: Furbies. Gremliny-looking, bug-eyed balls of animatronic plushness. She'd never heard of them, but there seemed to be a bunch of different kinds, and so she googled. Turned out they were originally the hot toy of Christmas 1998, cooed a language known as Furbish, and supposedly had the ability to learn the more you interacted with them. They'd since been updated to include an internet-of-things version called Furby Connect you could interact with in person, but also through a smartphone app.

Perfect.

Pandora did a one-click buy off Amazon and then surfed the interwebs, dark and lit, looking for schematics, source code, and fun hacks to render her new purchase warranty-voided but even more perfect still.

"Hey, Gram," she said. "I've got someone who wants to meet you."

"I'm too old for blind dates," Gladys said, "or cataract dates, for that matter."

Pandora didn't engage, instead bringing the Furby around to where her grandmother could see it, a big red bow atop its head.

"What's this?"

Though Pandora was proud of her work, she didn't say, "A Wi-Fi-connected Fur-bot that can record everything you say and store it in the cloud, where I can listen to it any time I want, while also being able to switch over to live mode for a one-sided video chat, thanks to the camera hidden behind one of its eyes." Instead, she kept it humble and brief: "A friend," she said, trying not to look at the other "friends" around them but finding it hard not to.

Gladys noticed. "You mean like these other morons?"

But Pandora was ready for it. "Nope," she said. "This here guy's our security system. Any of these chuckleheads tries any of that elder abuse stuff"—she unscrewed the Fur-bot's eye to reveal the camera—"we'll sue the pants off 'em."

Gladys smiled, suggesting the idea of suing the pants off 'em appealed to her.

That hurdle cleared, Pandora made introductions. "Gladys Lynch?" she began.

"Oh, for Pete's sake . . ."

". . . meet Furbius McFurbutt."

Gladys shielded her eyes, embarrassed, but laughing anyway. Finally composing herself, she looked up, the picture of elderly dignity. "Why, Mr. McFurbutt," she said. "How *do* you do?"

It was an obvious question, and the programming anticipated it, along with other conversation helpers, from thoughts on the weather to whether the world was going crazy or was it (fill in the blank)? And so: "Very well, Mrs. Lynch," Furbius said, borrowing Pandora's voice raised an octave or two.

28

"So where should we start?" Roger said, kicking off their first post-screening session.

"Suicide," George said.

Roger straightened, then inclined forward, looking at his client's video image over the rims of the glasses sliding down his nose. "So much for foreplay . . ."

"Not me," George insisted. "It's my assignment. I'm supposed to AI-up a little chatbot to detect and prevent possible suicides on the platform, with a particular focus on my personal demographic: kidults." He paused. "All of which is protected information, I'm assuming."

"Kidults?"

"Young adults, old kids," George said. "Consumers in the prime of their consumption ages, from fifteen to twenty-five."

Roger sat back, slow-clicking his pen contemplatively. "This wouldn't be a case of 'It's not me, Doc, but I got a friend'?"

"Nope. Strictly work," George said. "I like to multitask, and since I'm being required to have these sessions, I figured I might as well mine them for something I can actually use on the job." He paused. "So: suicide. Why, and how do you stop it?"

Roger drew his fingers across his lips, hiding the smile underneath. "You remind me of my daughter when she was little," he said. "She used to specialize in asking impossible questions."

Pandora thoroughly objected to this characterization. Her questions had *not* been "impossible," just "not answered satisfactorily thus far." But seeing as she wasn't supposed to be privy to any of this, she decided to keep her objections to herself.

Meanwhile: "You're saying maybe I should narrow my focus," George said. "Be more specific."

Roger mimed narrowing the focus by pinching the air with his thumb and index finger. "A touch, yes."

"Okay," George said. "Why do you think they specified young adults as opposed to suicides in general?"

"Are you asking me as a representative of the corporation," Roger said, "or as a mental health professional?"

"Um, both?"

"The corporation's interested because of what you've already alluded to: young adults represent a prime consumer demographic and it's hard selling something to a dead person," Roger said. "I also wouldn't be surprised if there are 'platform loyalty' incentives. Think about it: if a product literally *saved your life*, you'd stay loyal to it, right? Save a consumer when they're young and you've bought yourself a whole lifetime of platform loyalty."

"O*kay*," George said, warily. He'd not been expecting this much cynicism so early on—especially not from his therapist. Milo, on the other hand . . .

"Now, psychologically," Roger continued, "there's also good reason to separate potential suicides by age categories. Simply put: kids and adults kill themselves for different reasons, and there's some neurological evidence that different parts of the brain may be involved. I'm sure you've heard about Quire's fMRI studies on the subject." He glanced at his second monitor, where George's case file was open. "You suggested they might be 'triggering' for the volunteers."

George shifted uncomfortably in his seat. "Where's it say that?" he asked.

"In the tour transcript," Roger said.

"All of that was recorded?"

"Microphones are cheap," Roger said. "Cameras too. And voice-recognition technology has really upped its game, thanks to machine learning."

"But isn't that an invasion . . ."

". . . of privacy?" Roger finished for him. "You're working for a company whose business model is convincing people to share as much of their personal data as possible, so it can be mined, packaged, and sold to the highest bidder. Why would you think they'd let you walk around shedding data without following you with a broom and dustpan?"

"Good thing I don't have anything to hide," George said.

And there his therapist went, trying to not-smile again.

What followed was a game of therapist-client tug-of-war, with George wanting to talk about teen suicide and Roger wanting to dig into why his new client had admitted to being "messed up." In the end, they came to a compromise of sorts: Roger acknowledged that his real client was Quire, and Quire had hired George to do a job, while George suggested that by offering him insight into the mind of a suicidal teen, Roger could potentially treat hundreds or thousands of more suffering humans by proxy through the suicidal ideation detection (SID) chatbot George would develop based on their sessions. Win—as they say—win.

"Okay," Roger said, "here goes," before going on to explain that suicidal teens frequently see themselves as split into meat and mind, the mind voice prodding the meat toward self-destruction with the unspoken conviction that the mind voice will survive to appreciate "what comes after . . ." They've temporarily surrendered rationality and consciousness to an authoritative "other" like a schizophrenic taking orders from the neighbor's dog, only the authoritative other in this case is a metastatic form of peer pressure, in which a part of the would-be suicide him- or herself is also part of the pressuring crowd. And that's what makes teenage suicides different from the adult kind: this unspoken assumption of suicide's survivability, that it can be used as a ploy to punish people or escape without the resulting oblivion. Religion can ironically reinforce this notion of death's survivability, but so does the inherent sense of immortality that comes with being a teenager. Adults who are suicidal tend to be more realistic and are thinking of ending it all because *they want to end it all.* They come to suicide spiritually and often physically exhausted. World-wearied, they've had it; enough is enough. Suicidal teens often feel prevented by current circumstances from getting what they deserve, be it love, respect, whatever—and they see suicide as a leap over now into a future where they've won and the world has apologized for treating them so badly.

"So next question," George said. "How do you stop it?"

"Why don't we put a pin in that till next week," Roger said, rising. He tapped at his watch. "Time's up. Talk at you then."

And before George could say anything else, his screen went black with the exception of these words: "call terminated on far end," followed by the date, current time, and call duration. It had been a fifty-minute hour, to the second.

Looking at the same call stats as George, Pandora removed her headphones and lowered her laptop screen. It was a little weird to realize it—what with a therapist in the family—but she'd never watched her father practice. Sure, she'd recorded his sessions but didn't watch them so much as fast-forward through them, listening to the clients' sped-up voices, poised to alert on certain keywords. And now that "voice-recognition technology has really upped its game"—something she'd told her father about, by the way—Pandora hadn't had to screen the sessions herself at all, sped-up or otherwise. Plus, when her dad wasn't working, they talked about other things—meals, the weather, what to watch on TV, what interesting factoids she'd learned reading the Google News headlines for science and technology, but never politics. Pandora had found that by focusing on the first two and ignoring the third, she was able to remain hopeful about the future of the species without succumbing to despair and/or that session's magic word: *suicide*.

Seriously?

That's what the guy wanted to discuss? Pandora was about as far away from being suicidal as a person could be. She knew precisely what she wanted to do with her life: keep it. Pandora wanted to live—she felt embarrassed even thinking it, but it was in her heart and it was true—*forever*. The thing she wanted to be remembered for on her death bed? Not dying. And as far as her epitaph, Pandora thought "This Space for Rent" should do nicely.

But George Jedson wanted to talk about suicide—specifically, *teen* suicide. He'd said it was because of a work assignment, but if that was some sort of excuse . . .

Damn it.

The original plan had been to look up George's contact info in his case file and reach out directly, say, "Hi," or "Wassup?" Nothing too stalkery. He'd made the first move, what with the unsolicited cuteness comment, so . . .

But this suicide business was worrisome. And so, as with a new show on HBO or Netflix she was intrigued by but not quite committed to, she'd have to keep tuning in and hope it wouldn't turn into another *Young Pope*. If only there were a way to binge this George Jedson or skip ahead to where she'd figured out whether he was worth it or not. Unfortunately, Pandora had not found the fast-forward button for the real world, which had been a blessing when it came to Gladys, but George? Not so much.

29

There was nothing in the language of George's work assignment that stated—*explicitly*—that he was to develop that Holy Grail of AI: a fully conscious, general artificial intelligence. It wasn't even identified as a stretch goal. But it was there, implicitly, between the lines. It was there in the difference in success rate that his predecessor had achieved (a respectable annual projected suicide rate within the target demographic of one to two percent per year) and George's target, i.e., a nearly unthinkable zero suicides in the prescribed demographic on the platform moving forward. And that wasn't a zero *percent*, or even a zero-point-zero percent. Zero meant zero. It was a whole number, not a rate.

George knew of one way to achieve this goal, though he doubted it would make any of the higher-ups happy: overpredict. Set the criteria for flagging a potential suicide so loosely it'd capture *everybody*. After that, suspend their accounts and declare victory and bankruptcy all at the same time.

Yeah, probably not. Ditto calling his bosses' attention to recent studies showing that a reduction in social-media usage was directly correlated with lowered instances of depression in the target demographic. If his run-ins with Milo had taught him anything so far, it was this: social media was *not* a reality-based industry.

So: zero suicides among Quire users aged fifteen to twenty-five when his predecessor had been fired for missing—let's be honest—one? There'd been other cases Vickers's approach had missed—a handful of the non-famous—but it was the Gunn suicide that constituted the tipping point of interest. And it was the smallness of the number that was so daunting because it was always the last few of anything—miles, votes, raked leaves, percentage points—that cost the most time, money, and other, subtler investments like creativity and/or emotional involvement. In the case of Quire's would-be teenybop stay-alive bot, those last few bodies cost the last guy his job, making way for George, who was quite conscious of the hidden complexity of the task ahead of him. He'd already assumed he'd use the first guy's algo for screening out the no-brainers but after that . . . ?

Well, let's see: he was a computer hacker surrounded by computer systems with access to some of the most sophisticated neural nets available and his pick of machine-learning algorithms, suggesting, yeah, he should let the machine do the heavy lifting. He wouldn't even have to code anything, because machine learning wasn't about coding; it was about training. What mattered was the quality of the data you gave the machine to learn from—good old-fashioned GIGO: garbage in, garbage out. And vice versa. So George started feeding the beast pretty much everything he could think of related to his task. This included but was not limited to: case studies from psychology textbooks and journals; doomed love stories like *Romeo and Juliet*; treatises on ritualized suicide from kamikaze to jihadi suicide bombers, from Christian martyrs to self-immolating monks; the bulk data from past Quire members who had, in fact, killed themselves. Feeling the beast needed more, George proceeded to hack into police departments across the country and copied all the reports of teen suicides he could, along with death certificates and autopsy notes. He then moved on to downloading material from anorexia-encouraging websites and online suicide games like the Blue Whale Challenge and that creepy-looking Momo. He followed the you-may-also-likes these linked to down the deepest existential wells until all he wanted to do was sit in the corner of his corner office, sucking his thumb and rocking back and forth.

The algorithm, meanwhile, had begun populating word clouds from the raw information it consumed, with one word taking up the center of the cloud early, where it grew and shrank under the shifting statistics, beating like a heart: *consciousness*.

Victims and victim wannabes "lost consciousness," "returned to consciousness," "never regained consciousness." The word seemed to have a certain statistical stickiness that resonated throughout the data set. And that was how a routine exercise in corporate soul-searching became an investigation into the nature of consciousness itself and—as a stretch goal—emulating it artificially.

Because that was the answer, reading between the lines and implicit in the numbers expected. George's chatbot had to have skin—*silicon*—in the game. It had to appreciate what was being lost by the game's other players.

Oh, and one other thing. Thanks to his predecessor's ham-handed handing off of the intervention side to local law enforcement and their surfeit of SWAT equipment, an addendum had been added to George's hand-delivered, hand-me-down assignment: "Once target subjects have been identified and reasonably confirmed, all interventions shall be kept strictly in-house and on-platform." Meaning, basically, a chatbot that would engage and talk the subject out of suicide if, in fact, the subject was contemplating such.

So: talking—*that* would be the singular tool in George's toolbox. And not even that. Text. Written words on a screen. On the user end, individuals might have customized their experience using voice-recognition apps, but the default was text and maybe emojis, especially given the target demographic. Now all George had to do was figure out what those lifesaving words should be and how to get his chatbot to type them.

"Poop" emoji.

As a thought experiment, George tried imagining what it would take to make him want to kill himself. Inconveniently, however, other thoughts kept inserting themselves, top among them whether the assignment itself was dangerous—to him, personally. He guessed his bosses were worried about that, too, which was why he'd ended up with Roger and maybe Milo as well, tag teaming him as part of some good therapist/bad therapist routine.

This display of corporate concern for his mental health, in turn, made him think about another aspect of suicide he found fascinating: its communicability. How could something like suicide be contagious? Was it a virus? More and more things formerly assumed to be the products of stress were turning out to be caused by viruses. Ulcers, for example. Some cancers. High cholesterol. So why not the predisposition to self-slaughter?

Because that'd be one dumb virus, George thought, *killing its host.*

But then he thought about it some more. Wasn't that what *all* viruses did, the fatal ones at least? Plus, what was he considering alive? A suicide virus that killed its host, at best, would only actually kill *part* of its host. There'd still be the host's biome living inside the gut and outside on every available bit of skin. Lots of those germs didn't care about whether the body they lived on was living or not.

A little like some humans, George editorialized, *killing the planet where they live.*

But the bottom line was this: a viral vector for suicide didn't violate the rules of viral logic. If it was viral, though, how did it spread? AIDS was transmitted through bodily fluids; the flu was airborne. A suicide virus was probably closer to the latter, seeing as those who caught it were rarely intimate with the source of their infection. But if it was airborne, the carrier and victim would still need to share the same airspace, which clearly wasn't the case when Patient Zero was a celebrity and the infected, fans.

Then it hit him. The medium by which the suicide contagion spread was *mass media*. Merely talking about it on TV, in the press, or via social media got people who'd been thinking about it, thinking about it more seriously.

But was talking about it the problem? Could they end suicide by banishing the word from ever being used again, followed by reprinting and/or reposting all dictionaries, minus this one particularly triggering and/or viral set of letters? Diving a bit deeper into the research, George was heartened by studies showing that publicizing a suicide didn't necessarily trigger a contagion. It was all about *how* the suicide was portrayed in the media. Romanticized, it spread. Portrayed as what it was—stupid, shortsighted, irreversible, and oftentimes plain rude—it didn't. Portraying it as a disease was still a gray area.

So George started tracking down interviews with people who'd failed—who'd changed their minds before hitting the water off center enough to not break their necks, but maybe on center enough to end up in a wheelchair. You couldn't get much more unromantic than peeing in a bag, George figured. And if suicide was a virus spread by mass media, perhaps there was the equivalent of a vaccine, working like how vaccines work, by taking a little bit of the virus, stripping it of its power to do harm, but still enough to alert the immune system and build up a resistance.

Now the question was, how to translate all that into zeros and ones.

30

"So on the subject of suicide prevention," Roger began their next session, before interrupting himself. "See? I didn't forget. That's the wonderful thing about taking notes."

"Gee, that's swell," George said, leaning into the camera. "And I want to talk about that; I do. But I wonder if it would be okay to change the topic? I mean, I've been putting together the mining data on the subject of suicide—and I mean everything, from death cults to suicide bombers to *Hamlet*. Truth is, I need a breather."

Roger nodded; he knew exactly what George meant. In prepping for this session, he'd grown to dread it himself. Who would have guessed that looking into the causes behind kids killing themselves would be so depressing? And so he welcomed this change of subject—right up until he heard what the new one was. "Go ahead," he said, offering up his open palm.

"Consciousness," George said.

"Excuse me?"

"I want to know everything you know about the nature of human consciousness."

Roger laughed because he thought it was a joke—and stopped when he realized it wasn't. *"Seriously?"* he said.

George nodded, his usual poker face allowing a flicker of gravedigger to suggest how much so.

"What did I say before, about asking impossible questions?" Roger continued. Paused. Thought. "What I *can* tell you about is *un*consciousness. That's an easy one. People get their consciousnesses switched off every day in hospitals all over the country. Michael Jackson liked unconsciousness so much he made it permanent."

"You're talking about anesthesia," George said.

"Correct. It's actually a pretty fascinating subject, when you think about it. Prior to the discovery of anesthesia, human consciousness was pretty much an always-on proposition—at least as far as we know. Some people—they call themselves Jaynesians, after Julian Jaynes—believe that human consciousness arose as recently as three thousand years ago and that before that, people were basically schizophrenics, hearing voices, talking to gods, and all that harking business. But then the voices were internalized, forming what we now call consciousness." Roger paused at the sound of keys clacking on the other end. "Are you taking notes?"

"You said it yourself—wonderful thing, note taking."

"So I did," Roger admitted. "Anyway, prior to anesthesia, the consciousness didn't switch off, not even during sleep. Maybe as the result of some head trauma, but as a routine thing, once conscious, always conscious until you died."

More key clacking, which Roger ignored as best he could. "They've done EEG readings on patients as they go under, and what they've seen is the formation of this inhibitory tide of electrical activity, ebbing and flowing—oscillating—across the brain, interrupting neural firing, which, in turn, disrupts the ability of various brain regions to communicate with each other." Roger paused. "And the fact that they can reverse that and bring someone *back* to consciousness? I got to watch it as a grad student, and even without an EEG, I could see the brain powering down and back up by watching the changes in a patient's face."

Roger stopped talking, listened to the key clacking crescendo and then stop as well.

George looked up at Roger looking at him. "What?" he said.

"But I have to ask myself," Roger asked himself, "what does any of this have to do with your being"—notes again—"'messed up'?"

George shrugged. "Is there a pathology where the person prefers talking about minds in general as opposed to his or hers specifically? You know, someone who gets off thinking about thinking . . ."

"That's what I do," Roger said, "minus the getting off part."

"Roger that," George said.

"Watch it," Roger advised.

"But seriously," George continued, "what if 'curing' me of what makes me 'messed up' ruins me as a coder? I can't imagine our bosses would be happy about that."

"That's a romantic myth," Roger said, "that genius is next door to madness. They're not even in the same Quire group."

"Nice ad placement."

"Moving on," Roger tried. "Madness is madness and genius is genius, and any similarity is purely coincidental. Comparing the two is like comparing normal cellular growth to cancer."

"Go on," George said, settling into his chair, preparing for a fresh digression.

"I see what you're doing," Roger said instead.

"What am I doing?" George asked, his face giving nothing away.

"You keep distracting me so we can't talk about you, George Jedson . . ."

"Like a tide of EEG activity, inhibiting neural communication . . ."

Roger folded his arms and stopped talking.

George folded his arms and stopped talking.

The time showing at the bottom of their respective monitors ticked up, first one minute, then two, then finally: "But you get paid either way, right?" George said/asked.

"Correct," Roger admitted. "I'd say it was your dime, but it's actually Quire's, isn't it?"

"And this conversation has been helpful," George said, "in helping me do what they're paying me to do."

"How so?"

"You'll have to trust me," George said. "Do you?"

"No."

"Good," George said. "As long as we're on the same page."

And then it was Roger's turn to look at the words "call terminated on far end," set in white against a black screen.

Pandora pumped her slippered feet under her desk—her happy dance—as she closed her laptop on its own black screen. She'd "stayed tuned" and was glad she had. George had used the *c*-word—*consciousness*—and reading between the lines (literally) of his previous session, it was obvious to his fellow coder that this was shorthand for her own recently decided upon reason for living: artificial consciousness and the achievement thereof. Listening to George talk was like she was listening to herself, but speaking in a male voice, as if he were reading her thoughts aloud but so only she could hear. The words *soul* and *mate* entered her headspace without prior clearance followed by a whole damn sentence: *Is this what love is like?*

In answer to herself, Pandora clicked on the widget that allowed her to stream her father's sessions and dragged it into the trash. She wouldn't need to eavesdrop anymore. The boy who'd judged her static face cute would be given the opportunity to fall in love with the mind behind it, like she was doing now with his. All they had to do was get past a few sticking points—nothing insurmountable, not considering the big picture, which was what Pandora was doing, along with the screen grab she'd printed out of one George Jedson: future boyfriend.

But about those stalkery preliminaries: the way she saw it, the sooner they were gotten to, the sooner they'd be gotten past. And so: Pandora entered George's number from her dad's hacked case file, thumbed a

"What up?" in a chat bubble, hit send, and then waited, a hand over her muted phone, hoping for the haptic buzz of reciprocation.

The time passed like a kidney stone. Pandora grew worried, and then weirdly optimistic, deciding that the hesitation proved he was cautious, meaning not stupid, meaning good. Finally: "Who this?" the reply came back.

Pandora could feel her skin tingle, which was either a good sign or perhaps an early symptom of a new STD, one you could get electronically, by texting. "An admirer," she thumb-typed.

"Do you mean stalker?"

Which might seem like a bad sign to anybody who wasn't Roger Lynch's daughter. But for her own part, Pandora took it as a sign they were in the same headspace re: the creepy vibe of getting a text from a total stranger out of the electromagnetic ether. And so she responded with the international shorthand for lightheartedness, implying he had nothing to fear: "LOL."

"Seriously," George typed. "What's this about?"

Pandora hesitated, then went for it. "I'm a fellow coder and I like your work."

"How did you get this number?"

Oblique was the way to go, she figured. "Fairbanks," she typed, nine characters standing in for a whole lot of words she didn't have the words for.

"Roger," George typed, "is that you?"

"Daughter," Pandora tapped back. Thought about her preferred handle and settled on "Dora."

"Isn't this unethical?"

"Ethics, shmethics," Pandora tried typing, only to have autocorrect render it as "Ethics, semantics," which wasn't bad, so she went with it.

"Seriously?" the boy typed, all the way from San Francisco.

"I'm not my dad," Pandora typed. "You're not my patient."

"Client," George corrected.

"Whatever," Pandora whatevered, followed by, "I know you're working on artificial consciousness and I want to help."

Long pause.

He might already be getting his number changed, which is what she'd do if she hadn't started this whole thing. And so she waited, holding her metaphorical and actual breath, flinching when her phone finally buzzed again.

"So, you code?"

"Like a grrrl," Pandora tapped back.

31

Gladys loved her Furby and told Pandora so the next time she visited IRL. "I haven't slept this well in years," she explained before telling her about the shoe store. "This disease," she said, "is like living in a shoe store that's been hit by an earthquake." That's what it felt like, she said, standing there, stunned, among all these scattered boxes and separated shoes, utterly overwhelmed. But now, each night, she dealt with one box, one pair of shoes finally reunited, wrapped in their tissue paper, the lid secured, the box put away on its shelf. And each night, she went to bed, knowing that there was another one she wouldn't have to worry about ever again.

"Thank you," the old woman said, a hand on her granddaughter's knee, followed by a pause, and then: "You too, Furbius," Gladys added, patting the plush space between its gremliny ears.

After that, Pandora's visits started skewing toward remote rather than in person. For one thing, Gladys seemed more forthcoming during these virtual visits. Pandora had suspected it might go like that; there was precedent. One of the earliest, serious contenders for passing the Turing test was a program called Eliza that impersonated a Rogerian therapist by manipulating strings of text supplied by a human in the role of patient (um, *client*). People got addicted to "talking" to it, telling it their problems, even after they were told, point blank, that it was *a computer program*. The theories for why this simple bit of coding got the reaction it did varied. Perhaps people found talking to software less intimidating than talking to an actual person; maybe it was because a computer could ask them franker questions that would be deemed too invasive or rude coming from a human. Using her hacked, animatronic creature as mediator, Pandora found herself willing to ask more personal things of her grandmother that would have seemed impossible face-to-face, especially considering the faces involved.

For example, it was through Furbius that Pandora learned her grandmother's original plan for moving to Alaska didn't involve living off the land so much as dying on it, far away from anyone she knew. But then she met her future husband, and while Herman Lynch remembered the clink of bottle neck to glass rim in a dingy frontier bar as the beginning of their relationship, what Gladys remembered was boldly following him out of the bar when he wanted to take a leak "under the stars, like God intended."

It was that time of year when it was cold enough to snow but still warm enough to go peeing into a bank of it, which Herman proceeded to do, his back shielding any anatomical revelations it was still too early for in their hours-old relationship. Why she followed after him, Gladys didn't know, but would hazard a guess, since Furbius asked: "I think I recognized my future in the man and didn't want to let him out of my sights."

The difference between ninety-plus degrees hitting something south of thirty was enough to produce a geyser of steam Gladys followed up past her future husband's turned back and broad shoulders, up and up to where those other phantoms danced, the northern lights.

"Do you know what I think about when I see them?" she asked, intuiting that Herman was looking at the same sight she was, from the cant of his neck as he pissed heartily away into the hole he'd made in the snow. "The souls of all those dead boys."

"Me," Herman said, finally finishing, finally giving his shoulders an exaggerated shrug as he tugged up his zipper, "I think of how much harder they made my job, putting all that extra static on the line."

"They're pretty, though," Gladys said.

"Handsome, you mean," Herman corrected, casually accepting her premise that the northern lights were the souls of dead soldiers.

"Yes," she said. "Very handsome." Pause. "And too . . ."

". . . many?" Herman guessed.

"I was going to say 'young,'" Gladys said. "But 'many' works too."

In another confession, Gladys told Furbius—whom she'd rechristened Mr. Nosy—that another reason she'd picked Alaska was because there'd be no one to blab all her sworn secrets to. She'd worried that that might change, once she married Herman, only to learn to her relief that, no, thankfully, she didn't talk in her sleep, "though maybe that's what I'm doing now . . ."

Sometimes, Gladys volunteered information without Mr. Nosy even asking. "Here's the ironic thing about losing my memory," one such session began. "Memory was my secret weapon as a code breaker."

She went on to explain that her ability to recall and connect seemingly trivial details from previous messages and then linking that to what they were working on later allowed them to deduce how the code had been shifted, providing the two data points that suggested a pattern. And once they had a theoretical pattern, they could predict what the next shift might be—a prediction that could be confirmed or discredited by a subsequent message.

"But now," Gladys said, followed by a farting sound from her lips, "going, going, gone."

She told her granddaughter through her furry representative about the tricks she used to hold on to her independence once she realized her memory was going. One was to create rigid routines, converting her day into muscle memory while memories not made of muscle were sung instead. Writing might have been easier for some people, but not Gladys. "My hands shake too much," she confessed, keeping to herself the fact that they also hurt from arthritis. "It seems symbolic that I can't write my name anymore," she told Mr. Nosy.

And so she turned her most important memories—the wartime ones—into little homemade songs she sang to herself around the cabin, and then in her assisted-living condo.

"That all stopped when they moved me over here," Gladys said, alluding to the fact that she now had a roommate who either didn't appreciate her singing or wasn't to be trusted with the classified information the songs contained. "The only time I get to talk to you," she told her inquisitive Wi-Fi-enabled friend, "is when they're helping her in the bathroom or taking her to see the physical terrorist."

But the longer Gladys was prevented from singing her memories of the war, the thinner and more threadbare they became. And so Pandora hacked into the nursing home's database of residents and began reading charts until she found her grandmother the perfect roommate: a woman, older and further gone than Gladys was, and—the cherry on top—stone-cold deaf. Checking on what Mr. Nosy had uploaded to the cloud a few days later, Pandora was rewarded with the thin, heartbreaking voice of her grandmother whisper-singing part lullaby, part "Moon River," but with original lyrics by Gladys Lynch née Kowalski: war hero.

32

So here was the thing: it was impossible to have a conversation quietly enough that Roger wouldn't hear, the doors between rooms with the exception of the bathroom not thin so much as nonexistent, a feature, not a bug she'd appreciated when she was still a toddler and not seeing her dad was equivalent to his having gone out of existence. But now that she was a teenager, the old shower curtains separating their separate rooms from the rest of the cabin were, if not thoroughly creepy, nevertheless inadequate to the role they were supposed to play. She'd lobbied for their replacement with something more substantial, perhaps on hinges and lockable, by appealing not to *her* need for privacy, but Roger's.

"What if you ever decided to start dating?" she asked.

"Pandora," her father warned, but in that way that teenagers are pretty much duty-bound to ignore. And so she continued. "What if you started dating and got lucky and there was no 'her place' to go back to?"

"Stop."

This time, Pandora did, because there was nowhere else to go with her hypothetical but to the actual words *making love* or that succinct Anglo-Saxon synonym she was not so independent yet to let drop. Not when the subject of that verb was her dad, especially. And so, instead, she'd slipped him the half-off-everything coupon from Fred

Meyer she'd clipped from the weekend *Fairbanks Daily News-Miner*. "Say you'll think about it," she said.

"What," her father said back, "the dating or the getting lucky with, apparently, some homeless woman?"

"Doors," Pandora said. "Think about doors, please."

Which he hadn't—yet—and so Pandora set a few ground rules for how her and George's budding relationship would be conducted. First, no video conferencing. Second, no voices, only text. The first was about her face and its tendency to embarrass her, not to mention its cyber infamy as meme. The second was about privacy and her lack of it. It was the second rule she felt safe explaining and should do the trick, seeing as it was basically a subset of the first and the rationale behind it covered both.

"No privacy," she typed. "Parental unit omnipresent."

"Roger," George replied, meaning either affirmative or her dad.

"Yeah," Pandora had written back. "That's the guy I mean."

To appease George's curiosity and prove she wasn't a chatbot or "some dude" (not to mention refresh his memory re: her "ooo, cute"-ness), Pandora sent him a JPEG of herself standing in front of her father's diploma while wearing a T-shirt that read, "I Think Therefore I Am . . . Socially Unacceptable." She captioned it: "Does this proof-of-life selfie make my butt look big?"

George LOL'd followed by the "big grin" emoji.

Pandora looked at the text, wondering how to respond, or even whether she should. It wasn't exactly the wordless thumbs-up, but it did have an "end of message" vibe to it, letting her know without saying so specifically that this particular thread had reached its end.

Or maybe not.

Text etiquette was still evolving—practically daily, as far as she could tell. Would responding suggest she was too needy? Curious? Or perhaps an escaped lunatic who'd killed his therapist and was now posing as his daughter? *Probably not that last one,* Pandora thought. He'd already seen her picture on her dad's desk—a fact that led in a straight line to this exchange, meaning *technically* he'd started it, so . . .

"What's the weather like where you are?"

"Right now?" George typed, then paused. Pandora imagined him crossing to a window to look, his body backlit by a clutch of monitors, the only lighting in his code-boy cave. In her imagination, that blue light was doing his butt a lot of favors. Meanwhile: "There's a lot of fog rolling in off the bay," George added, completing his response.

"Fog here too," Pandora typed, "like an ice tray steaming from a freezer."

"Is that what they mean by ice fog?"

"I guess," Pandora guessed. "I like it."

"It's like the sky and land meet to make limbo," George typed, bordering on the poetic.

Pandora took that as a good sign, though not without its caveats. Her own dad had warned that "when a boy stoops to poetry, you better decide if he's a keeper or a goner right away. And if it's the latter, don't dillydally. Cut to the heart stomping pronto. No half measures. Otherwise, you'll have this sad little puppy following you around, right up until he turns into Hannibal Lecter."

"Thanks, Dad," Pandora had said back. "Good to know . . ."

Unfortunately, her father hadn't said what to do if the boy spouting verse was a keeper. Perhaps it was a case of dad denial—that omission—the presumption being that nobody could *possibly* be good enough for his little girl. Thankfully, such decisions were not up to him. Hell, they were hardly up to Pandora—the brain part of her, at least. All she knew was every time she felt his text hum, she wanted to . . .

And will you look at that? Pandora was a bit of a poet herself.

George not only agreed to only texting, he added his own spin: it'd be good practice for working on AI. "Like an ongoing Turing test," he wrote. They could pretend to not know the other was human, seeing what clues would tip the scale one way or the other. And by extending the Turing test indefinitely, they'd be subtly programming their brains to program another brain, one that would—if they succeeded—be indistinguishable from either of them, in terms of its seeming humanity.

"That does not compute," Pandora texted back, followed by the "robot" emoji and an "LOL," just in case.

To further prove how okay he was with the text-only stipulation, George sent Pandora a link to an app he'd written that should serve their purpose and privacy nicely: Texting w/o Borders, so named—should he ever commercialize it—for its dispensing with the character limits usually associated with SMS- and MMS-based messaging services. Instead of breaking up long texts into a series of (sometimes disordered) bubbles, his app worked on the user-experience end to sort and recombine multiple messages within a single, elastic text bubble that stretched to accommodate whatever text was entered, no need to think in abbreviations anymore.

"I could send you *War and Peace* if I wanted to," he wrote.

"Please don't," Pandora wrote back.

"Won't."

The secret sauce was larceny. Because service providers generally charged by the SMS or MMS, George's app, while providing a simplified user experience on the front end, could get pretty expensive to use in practice. And so George "outsourced" those charges to unsuspecting but nevertheless deserving corporate parties in the fossil fuel industry. "My personal carbon tax on the planet killers," he explained. The app also allowed the use of bold, underline, and italics and employed a proprietary encryption strategy to keep sender and receiver messages private from prying government, corporate, and/or parental eyes, with the option to self-destruct within a user-set amount of time after being read.

If Pandora wondered why George happened to have such an app ready to send her a link to, she didn't mention it. In fact, he'd coded it up a year earlier to communicate with his deported mother in Mexico. The prying eyes he wanted to avoid belonged to ICE, and he had corporate creeps picking up the tab because she was working at a maquiladora that paid her crap, while George, the perennial foster kid, didn't get an allowance and had to make do, collecting bottles and cans he could return for five cents apiece.

As it turned out, George and his mom never got a chance to use his app. One evening, Margarita/Marge hadn't been on the bus back to her neighborhood. And she wasn't on the bus returning to the maquiladora the next morning. Her body wasn't found until several days later, in a dump near where she'd worked, an American manufacturer of consumer electronics that imported the parts duty-free, assembled them, and then exported them back to America, all bearing labels that read, "Made in USA." Those labels had made her homesick every day, until they couldn't anymore, her throat having been cut. The story of her death was written in Spanish and took up hardly any space at all. She'd been his mother and now she was just words in a local paper George found and translated through Google News, one of the thousands of dead women Juárez had become known for, none of their murders any closer to being solved.

So yeah, George was messed up all right. Was it any wonder he preferred talking about the human mind in general, as opposed to his own specifically?

What followed was a coders' romance, the intercourse intellectual as opposed to sexual, their text exchanges touching on all things computer related, from favorite algorithms to backdoor exploits, their mutual contempt for script kiddies and other Tor tourists, as well as specific denial-of-service attacks they found especially amusing and/or inspirational.

"You hear what Anonymous pulled off?"

"Thumbs-up" emoji and an "LOL."

Not that it was *always* a geek fest. They talked about the big stuff, too, the things that distracted them, drove them, and/or kept them up at night during this chronological way station between young and adult, when they still had time to think about big ideas, before acting their age meant drowning in the little ideas of the world.

In a lot of ways, George and Pandora were like quantum particles that had become entangled, acting on one another—as Einstein would have it—spookily at a distance. Because even though Fairbanks and San Francisco were separated by two to three thousand miles, depending on whether you drove or flew, while the cultural gulf was astronomical, neither distance seemed to matter. The two teens were mind melded, sharing the same sense of humor when it came to their hacktivism and the same obsessions about the potential uses of AI. Both were convinced that quantum physics and the burgeoning field of quantum computing would inform the overlap of mind and body in the Venn diagram of that particular philosophical conundrum. And both felt the same sense of personal injury at the thought that their thinking would someday come to an end. Or using fewer words:

"Death sucks."

"And then some."

Perhaps because they were rapidly exiting them, the two frequently talked about their childhoods, Pandora's having been reasonably happy while George's—as presented to the girl on the other end of his screen—was parsed and curated for bits that created the appearance of happiness (or were amusing at least). Take the topic of favorite toys, Pandora going first:

"It was a Christmas stocking stuffer, but I loved it beyond reason," she wrote of her favorite toy. "It was a wind-up Creature from the Black Lagoon that walked and shot sparks out of its mouth, making this whirring sound as it went. I loved winding it up and letting it walk across the table to me, sparking and whirring all the way. I loved doing it in the dark where the sparks stood out, partly shining through the green-and-yellow plastic of the creature's body. It was beautiful. The body of the creature was squat—like a Lego character—making it cute instead of scary. I think I was three, and I'd fallen in love with a pretty machine."

"When I was a little kid, I had the weirdest idea about birds," George prefaced his contribution to their discussion. "The first bird I remember seeing was a robin perched on a rusty patch of fence. The bird and fence seemed connected through the bird's rust-colored chest. I asked my latest foster dad why different parts of the fence were different colors and learned about metals and oxidation, including the fact that some kinds of metals turn green.

"These facts all connected in my kid head, and I became convinced that robins must be made of metal because they could rust. The fact that my foster family at the time had a cuckoo clock didn't help. And so, for the longest time, I went around thinking birds were flying robots who perched on high-power lines to recharge and, when they weren't careful, could rust like the Tin Man from Oz after getting caught out in the rain.

"The whole thing fell apart when my foster dad caught me running outside with an armload of umbrellas when it was raining. 'What are you doing?' he wanted to know. I thought it was pretty obvious. I was helping the birds. 'Helping the birds how?' So they wouldn't get wet, duh. 'It's okay if birds get wet.' But what about when they rust? 'Excuse me?'

"And that was the end of the robot birds of Oakland, disappeared by harsh reality like Santa and the tooth fairy, but even worse because I'd come up with the robot birds all by myself," George concluded.

"I think somebody owes you a royalty on drones," Pandora typed back.

"If only," George replied.

Not that Pandora was fooled by George's diversionary tactic. "Birds aren't a toy," she pointed out. "Come on. Quid pro quo. I showed you mine. You have to show me yours."

"The truth is," George wrote back, "being a foster kid, I didn't have a lot of toys of my own."

"Wa-wa," Pandora typed. "Save it for my dad."

There was an unusually long pause from George's end, and Pandora suddenly panicked, wondering if she'd overstepped. But then: "On second thought," George typed, "one of my foster dads brought home a pair of finger cuffs from Chinatown once. I tried it on and cried when my fingers got stuck. And the harder I pulled, the tighter they got."

"So you're telling me your favorite—perhaps *only*—toy was basically some digital S&M device?"

"Punny," George typed. "But it wasn't like that. I think there's a lot of counterintuitive Eastern philosophy woven into those things. Like the need to push deeper to loosen them—that's like closing your eyes so the Force will take over. Or like loving something by letting it go. I think my foster father was trying to tell me that my mother wasn't ever coming back, but without words. I think he wanted me to know it in my muscles and bones and to let her go."

Before Pandora could text her response, she noticed the dancing ellipses, indicating that George was typing again, followed by a brand-new bubble blooping up underneath his last one. "I don't think these were my thoughts at the time, as a child, but they became my thoughts because that data was there, waiting for me to catch up to it."

It was a hallmark of these exchanges between George and Pandora that they unfolded by a process of association. And so from a novelty item's influence on a young boy's thoughts, George suddenly leaped ahead, to technology's ability to read them. Thoughts, that is.

"Have you ever seen a person being scanned by an fMRI machine?" he wrote.

"In Fairbanks," Pandora replied, "the reflex hammer is considered cutting-edge diagnostics."

"Well, if you ever get a chance, take it," George recommended. "It's incredible, watching as various parts of the brain light up when an operator asks the subject to think about something. And the same part lights up when they're shown an image of what they were asked to imagine, ditto when handed the object to hold.

"It's hard to walk away from something like that and not think that what you've witnessed is mind reading. Without touching the head or opening up the skull, from inches away, an act of thinking has been captured and turned into a picture. Do it with enough words with enough subjects, and you'll come away with a collection of brain signatures you can feed into a pattern-recognizing algorithm and translate back into words or pictures, like the grooves on a vinyl record that can be traced by a needle wired to a speaker and converted into music."

Pandora's response back to George was the "mind blown" emoji, followed by her response to her own heart: a silent scream and feet pumping under her desk—her happy dance.

33

The Furby, of course, wasn't just for Gladys, but for Pandora as well, to give her some programming practice in her recently decided vocation: artificial intelligence. She'd read an article in *Wired* about what she had in mind for all the personal data she was mining from her last surviving female relative: a chatbot to assemble and preserve the thoughts, feelings, memories, and uniqueness of her grandmother as she headed for the exit, something to keep her company in the long future without her. The article dubbed it a "dad bot," and the author found the results surprisingly comforting when comfort was most needed. Not immediately after the loss, but later, when the programming was forgotten, allowing the user to be surprised by the familiar plus time.

Playing a hunch, Pandora had googled the words *grief* and *bot* and got several hundred hits, suggesting that she was not alone in wanting to hold on to a loved one busily slipping between her fingers. After comparing reviews and discounting those with obvious grudges against this or that app developer and/or software publisher, she downloaded a plug-and-play program called Memento Morty with a default voice synthesizer that sounded like a fast-talking Hollywood agent from the 1940s but which could be customized to match your loved one's voice, provided you uploaded enough high-quality MP3s to the cloud, where the real magic happened.

There were the usual funky, robovoice glitches, like pronouncing *c'mon* as "see Monday," or talk-spelling titles like Mr., Dr., or Ms.—but these could be fixed on the fly by highlighting the misread text and correcting the pronunciation from a series of phonemes in pull-down menus followed by picking a number from one to ten, to indicate the phoneme where the stress was supposed to go. This last feature was what accounted for the app's not being free but also not featuring a bunch of distracting ads. After all, the whole point of a grief bot was to provide a closed-eyed and seamless experience of your loved one, returned to answer all those questions you hadn't gotten around to while they were still alive. And as far as Pandora was concerned, twenty bucks was a small price to pay to not hear her grandmother's voice trying to sell her male enhancement pills.

There were holes in the voice data that had already been uploaded from the Furby to the cloud, and Pandora attempted to fill those during her next visit, recording their conversation on her smartphone while she steered Gladys toward topics likely to require the use of at least one of the forty-four unique English phonemes and four so-called blends she'd not sampled yet. Some of the missing phonemes were easier than others in practice. Th-, for example, was already well represented on the cloud data, even after accounting for the slight lisp her grandmother had acquired, thanks to her having survived frontier dentistry. Other phonemes, however, proved surprisingly difficult, even after Pandora memorized the examples provided in the app's "Read Me" file. The problem was—as might be expected from a developer who'd name his app Memento Morty—many of the sample words were eccentric at best and frequently obscene. These latter Pandora replaced with rhyming alternatives, but this still meant getting Gladys to offer her opinion on ducks.

"Ducks?" the old woman asked, and Pandora figured she'd bail on the topic now that she had her grandmother saying it. But that might make it obvious there was some funny business going on—something that was not at all hypothetical, seeing as Gladys had already asked what was going on when her granddaughter wanted to talk about punts, dastards, and bird itches.

"What's a bird itch?" her grandmother asked, and Pandora bluffed.

"Like from lice," she said. "Um, feather lice. Or wing lice, like head lice, but on a bird's wing."

"What birds?" her grandmother asked, and seeing the door open, Pandora stepped through it: "Ducks?" she said.

"Ducks?" Gladys echoed. "What about ducks?"

"Oh, nothing," Pandora began, then noticed something she hadn't before: ducks on her grandmother's nightgown; ducks in glass, porcelain, and wood on her nightstand; ducks on the curtains that had come from her condo and reappeared here. Noticing where her granddaughter was looking, the old lady explained.

"I honestly can't say how it started," she said. "Somebody told somebody I liked ducks once, and then your grandfather got wind of it and bingo—birthdays and Christmas and anniversaries—everything ducks. If he hadn't died on me, I was going to come clean finally and clean house, but then . . ."

And that's how they went from phoneme collection to phase two in programming Pandora's grief bot: harvesting the stories and advice and jokes she'd want to hear, in her grandmother's voice, to illuminate whatever postmortem conversation she might be having with an AI-enabled simulacrum of her last female relative in that future that wasn't big enough for both of them.

Pandora didn't mean to eavesdrop on the pillow talk between Gladys and her late husband, but Mr. Nosy was programmed to record and upload whenever it detected a human voice. Needless to say, she could only hear one side of these otherwise private conversations, but that just made them all the more compelling. It was the listening in after the conversation stopped and her grandmother fell asleep that was harder to explain. Pandora took comfort from listening to Gladys's euphonic snore coming through the speaker that connected them. It was reassuring—that sound—letting her know that everything was okay, that her grandmother couldn't get into any trouble while she was asleep.

Pandora needed this reassurance because she'd been awoken in the middle of the night by calls from nursing home staff who couldn't calm Gladys down after what they termed "episodes." They couldn't call Roger because they didn't have his number, only Pandora's.

"Have you given her any anxiety meds?" she'd ask. They'd reflexively say they had; that's all they did all day, give old people some kind of medication. But there were too many residents and too few staff, and it wasn't like residents were going to call them on a missed dose—assuming it was an honest mistake and some underpaid staffer wasn't supplementing their income by selling Xanax on the side. Sometimes they'd get lucky and the short-pilled resident would sleep through any trigger opportunities, but other times they'd wake up, undosed, in a full-blown panic attack.

"Are you sure?" Pandora would press, and "Yes," they'd lie, but she could hear Gladys in the background, raging like a paranoid psychotic convinced the nurses were trying to kill her.

Roger would hear her talking, realize it was with his mother's keepers, and call out where he'd left the keys for the truck, before settling back to sleep. And off went Pandora, a parka around her nightgown and long underwear, her bare feet in a pair of bunny boots. She'd hand Gladys a pill herself and watch her transition twenty minutes later into a cordial, loopier version of her old self, but with ever fewer memories.

She hated being the pill pusher such episodes made her, knew that the prescription stuff was likely accelerating her grandmother's decline. She would have preferred sharing a brownie or two and chilling with her gram, but rules were rules, no matter how ill conceived. And when she was having a panic attack, Gladys was a danger to herself and others. There was the trade-off, a few more neurons checking out early in exchange for a metronomic heartbeat and an enigmatic smile.

"Hi, Dora."

"Hi, Gram."

And so falling asleep to her grandmother's snoring was a good way of assuring herself that she wasn't going to be rudely awakened. That is, until she heard Gladys crying out in the middle of the night through her headphones. The filter that had kept her from talking in her sleep as a young bride was apparently gone now. Eventually, even an interruption in the old woman's snoring would pull Pandora awake, her heart racing as she wondered if this was it. But then there'd be a catch, and the snoring would start sawing away again, making her recall what Gladys had told her once about what she feared.

"I'm afraid of the line," she'd said.

"What line's that?" Pandora had asked.

"The one I can't come back from."

34

At first, George didn't talk—*text*—much about what he was working on, using indirect references to "my work," "the project," or how it was "taking longer to grok than I thought." But then he started loosening up. Example: "I don't like the expression 'artificial intelligence,'" he typed. "'Artificial' seems pejorative. Why not something like 'man made'?"

"Maybe because it's sexist," Pandora suggested.

"Handmade?"

"Better."

"You know what word is even better—probably the best?"

"What?"

"I saw it walking past this little indie café," George typed. "'Artisanal.' That's what I'm going to tell people I'm working on. 'I'm coding an artisanal consciousness.'"

"Wow."

"Wow what?"

"You *are* from San Francisco, aren't you?"

"Oakland, actually."

"You know what I mean."

And indeed he did. To George's way of thinking, this knowing what each other meant, meant something else. It meant they'd make a good team, coding that artisanal consciousness. Provided he worked up the courage to ask.

"Listen," he wrote one day, prepared to make what was, for him, the coder's equivalent of a marriage proposal, "my project is clearly a two-man job."

"Person," Pandora corrected.

"Consciousness, entity, sentience, head, brain, think box . . . ," George typed, lapsing into thesaurus mode, a sign that he was not in the mood for splitting hairs, not when the issue at hand was something as transformative as splitting the atom. "You know what I mean."

Indeed she did. But she was also a girl and in constant need of asserting herself in the brotopia of coding. "And *you* know what *I* mean, Mr. Mister."

Indeed George did. But he didn't enjoy being reminded of his so-called "male privilege," especially given his past hiding above the acoustic tiles of the public library he'd called home. Now, however, he had a sweet job with a sweet office he was treating like a hotel suite and banking the money he was saving on rent—which was pretty sweet, too, so . . .

"Point taken," he typed, followed by his pitch: "But wouldn't it be great to use our coding superpowers for good?"

"Good is highly subjective," Pandora blooped back. "Explain."

"Saving lives," George typed, before tapping send.

"Whose? Baby Hitler?"

"Kids like us," George tapped and sent.

"Meaning?"

"The weirdos, the outcasts, the serially cyberly bullied," George's response blooped up on the screen. And then, in its own bubble—for emphasis—he added, "The suicidal."

"Who you calling suicidal? #immortalitynow"

"Not *you*," George backpedaled. "But other kids. I've checked the stats for Fairbanks and . . ." Having used the *s*-word once already in this exchange, he seemed disinclined to use it again, as if the FCC were monitoring and had a quota.

Not that he needed to type it again. Pandora knew the stats he was referring to, trailing dots and all. She'd lived them like everybody else in her dark and frigid hometown. And even though her homeschooling had spared her the loss of local peers up until that time, Pandora hadn't been left untouched by the *s*-word, leaving her with a mental snapshot she could call up whenever she needed a reminder of the thinness of the line between being and not.

It was back when her father still met some clients face-to-face in the real world, before he switched to online only. Pandora was only ten at the time and in her room, playing around in somebody's system, looking for exploits other than the one that had let her in the back door. The shower curtain separating her room from the living room and Roger's office had been drawn, and she was plugged in to a pair of headphones playing that Joni Mitchell tree museum song because, well, she was still being homeschooled and lacked peers to tell her what she should and shouldn't be listening to. Joni had rhymed *museum* with *see 'em* when the floorboards shook beneath her feet.

Alaska is a seismically active part of the country, so floor shaking wasn't all that unusual. In fact, Pandora and her dad had made a game of it, guessing where a given temblor might place on the Richter scale. She'd calmly removed her headphones and was about to call out her guess when she noticed the red spatters on her curtain and a couple of brain snails sliding down the other side of the translucent vinyl.

Crap, she thought.

Gingerly pinching a corner of the curtain and sliding it aside, she stepped into the living room, where she found her dad and his ex-client.

Her father was still seated opposite the body lying beached-whale-like on the floor. Roger's own face was stricken, blood spattered, and frozen while his hands eagle-clawed the arms of his chair.

"Dad?" Pandora asked.

"Yes?" Roger said, not moving.

"Should I call someone?"

"Yes," he said, still not moving.

"Who?" she asked.

"Anyone," he replied.

And six years later, here she was, being invited to use her coding superpowers to do something about the statistic her father's client had turned himself into.

"Okay," Pandora tapped back. "Where do we start?"

35

Roger kept a full-sized plastic skeleton in his office, which was also the living room (so-called). He'd added it to the home decor not too long after he and Pandora had moved back into the cabin, once the crime scene hazmat clean-up crew had finished their scraping, scrubbing, and disinfecting from Roger's final in-person client. He'd strung the skeleton with Christmas lights he'd turn on during the darkest of dark Alaskan nights, to remind himself—he said—that there was light at the end of the seasonal tunnel. "Plus," he added, "I like how they twinkle."

Pandora had been fine with Mr. Bones back when he first moved in, Christmas lights and all. But that was back before she'd been forced to socialize among people her own age. Since then—and especially since she'd begun visiting his mother—her opinion on the matter seemed to have changed.

"Isn't it time we got rid of Mr. Bones?" she asked one day. She'd become upset with not only having to stare her (literally) mortal enemy in the face every day, but also where he'd placed it, in front of the living room window, where passersby could see and recall that, yes, that's where the weirdo and her weird dad lived.

"It's a memento mori," he said. "A reminder that beyond the light at the end of the tunnel is another tunnel to, well, nobody knows for sure."

"Death," Pandora said. "It leads to death."

As an organic entity with an expiration date herself, Pandora went on to explain that she was opposed to death—both conceptually and personally; she resisted the thought of death at an almost cellular level. It had begun as a fear of getting dementia like her grandmother, but spread. Metastasized. Her fear of dementia was the gateway to her *real* fear: the fear of dying. Pandora found it insulting, frankly, and an affront to the entire species—the pinnacle of creation—to take all this time building a life out of memories only to have it taken away. And here her dad was, putting it right out there in front of her, and adding blinking lights to boot.

"Maybe you should add a dildo," she concluded. "You know, get the whole Freudian twofer going? Thanatos *and* Eros."

"You know, I knew I forgot *something*," Roger said, already sensing there'd been more to her objection than he'd thought.

"Maybe you're in denial," his daughter continued.

"Of which?"

"I'm thinking both," she said. "When was the last time you had a date?"

"I found your English assignment on the printer," Roger said. "'What do you want it to say on your tombstone?'"

"This space for rent," Pandora answered, as she had for the assignment.

"Maybe *you're* the one who's in denial," Roger suggested.

Pandora could say something about that, but if she did, it would escalate, and she wasn't in the mood. So: "Why, thank you, kettle," she said, resorting to an old routine, a way for one or the other to call a time-out.

"No problem, pot," Roger said back, putting a pin in the discussion neither was quite ready to have.

It was true what Pandora said about her father's dating. He'd not had a single romantic encounter since his wife died. He'd had an excuse early on, but Pandora could take care of herself now, and he still wasn't doing anything to address his own, personal singularity.

Not that Roger wasn't curious. Especially during the winter, when Pandora was at school and he didn't have any clients to counsel, he'd cruise Quire, looking up girls he'd had crushes on in high school, inspired by his yearbook from the now defunct Gold Stream High School. Their team was called the Prospectors, and the mascot was a cartoonish sourdough with outrageous whiskers, wearing a battered wide-brimmed hat, plaid shirt, denim pants, and unlaced boots and carrying a pickax. Whenever the team scored, he'd kick up his heels and yell "Goooold!" instead of "Gooooal!" coming down on the *d* at the same time his heels hit the hardwood floor.

But looking at the high school pictures compared to the Quire profiles was an exercise in masochism. How had everybody gotten so old? Roger didn't feel like he had—not that much. With the exception of his thinning hair, he felt like he was in his late twenties, thirties, tops. It was only on Quire that he felt ancient, which was why he kept promising himself he'd delete his account, even if he did work for them. You didn't have to eat McDonald's every day to work there—and probably shouldn't. But he kept coming back for more abuse—something one of his clients suggested was no accident.

"Let's say," he let him say, "certain algorithms have been optimized for user dependence. It's like when you finish a good book and miss the characters and want to start reading it all over again. Or like after the last line of coke wears off. Point is, Quire's designed to be missed after you close it, which is why the always-on feature has become the default setting. Users can change it; ninety-five percent don't."

After that, Roger asked Pandora to show him how to change the setting, but when she asked if she should click okay, he stopped her.

"No," he said. "I just wanted to know how. In case."

"In case what, you get a life?"

"Something like that."

"Listen, I'll pimp for you," his teenage daughter offered. "Give me your specs, and I'll roam Fred Meyer until I find the perfect woman. Or good enough woman, beggars being, you know."

"Thanks, kiddo," Roger said. "You should try your hand at therapy."

"Getting or giving?"

"The latter," her father said. "The kickbacks from antidepressants alone would be enough to live off of."

"Is this the point where you accuse me of being a carrier for depression?"

"Is this the point where you're going to prove my point?"

They stopped, facing each other. Paused. Took a breath.

"Thanks, kettle," one of them offered.

"Back atcha, pot," the other accepted.

"Okay," Roger said, deciding they were finally ready. "You want to know the truth?"

Pandora nodded.

"I've made my peace with dying because without it, there'd be no you."

Pandora thought he was talking about the mother she'd never met, who died giving her birth. "You mean Mom?" she said.

"No, what I'm trying to say is that if parents didn't die, there'd be no *reason* to have children and every reason not to. For one thing, there'd be no place to stand after a few generations."

"So you're saying that having kids is what it's all about and once you've had them you start waiting to die?"

"Not me," her father said. "Darwin. Which is another thing you wouldn't have without death: evolution."

"Have you checked out that Match.com stuff I sent you?"

"Are you saying I need to get out more," Roger asked, "or suggesting people haven't evolved all that much?"

"I'm telling you sex might be more trouble than it's worth," Pandora said. "Plus, half those profiles are bots anyway."

"You're not telling me—"

Pandora cut him off. "I'm telling you I don't want to live on in my children," she said. "I want to live on in *me*. And I'm fine with evolution stopping." She paused, smiling her biggest, goofiest smile. "Why mess with perfection?"

"Can we go back to bots?" Roger asked.

Pandora cleared her throat. "If she's claiming her English seems awkward because she's not from America," she said, "she's a bot."

"Good to know."

"In case?"

"In case."

"You know what I think about when people mention immortality?" Roger asked, not exactly out of the blue.

"No telling," his daughter said from the kitchen, stirring some steaming something in a pot.

"The first VCR I ever had," he said. "I was living in the basement of my friends' parents' house during college, and the VCR was like a time machine. I didn't have to be at a certain place or time to see my favorite TV show. I'd program it to record and watch it later. And you know what happened?"

"No telling," Pandora called back, watching the steam from her cooking feather into ice once it reached the kitchen window.

"I wound up with a stack of tapes this high," he said, holding his hand up to his belt. "I'd watch them when I got the time," he continued. He paused. "That still hasn't happened, me getting the time. That last episode of *Seinfeld*? I just kept putting it off."

Pandora turned off the stove, ladled stew into bowls. "And your point is?"

"I think that's what immortality would be like," Roger said. "Never getting anything done because you *literally* have all the time in the world."

Pandora set down her father's bowl, then hers. "They don't make VCRs anymore. You'll have to buy one on eBay if you want to get caught up on your shows. Or better yet, search Netflix. Click on the magnifying glass. I wouldn't count on any of that old stuff showing up as trending or popular."

"Not the point I was making," Roger said. They sat at the table then, the *tink* of their spoons hitting bowls punctuated by slurps, quick blowing, and then more tentative slurps.

"How about this," Roger said. "What if people only died as the result of an accident? Can you imagine the unbearable grief when it happened? Can you imagine the paralysis that such a condition could lead to? No one would do anything for fear of having an accident that could kill them."

"So you're saying that death is the kick in the pants our species needs to not turn into vegetables."

"Basically," her father said. "After all, look what their long life span has done for trees."

"Knock on wood?"

"Okay," Roger said, "bring your head over here."

"Over my dead body," Pandora countered.

"Cute."

36

The great thing about Mr. Nosy was this: it was the next best thing to being there. Unfortunately, that was also the problem with Mr. Nosy. While convenient for Pandora, who was able to keep tabs on her grandmother without actually having to venture out into the Alaskan winter, it was also depriving Gladys of face-to-face contact with her only remaining relative who still gave a crap.

"When are you coming to visit?" the old woman asked.

"We're visiting now," Pandora said.

"No," Gladys insisted. "It's not the same thing."

"It's *almost* the same thing," the younger woman replied.

"It's not even your voice."

Oh yeah. There was that. While the words were hers, and she tweaked the Furby's voice settings to come as close to her own as she could, it still sounded like she'd been huffing helium. Pandora had considered this an acceptable trade-off because going through the voice synthesizer meant she could enter her side of the conversation as text which was converted into speech on Gladys's end. By using this approach and headphones to listen to her grandmother's replies, Pandora was able to keep her father from eavesdropping on them while she phoned in her visits.

"Next week," she said now, hating herself a little for taking advantage of her grandmother's disease while also recognizing the reality that

Gladys wouldn't remember the promise long enough to call her on breaking it.

"Which day?" Gladys asked, startling her granddaughter.

"Thursday," Pandora bluffed.

"Date?"

"Are you writing this down?"

"I'm writing this down."

Shit. Pandora swiped at her calendar, read off a date.

"Time?" a different voice said. A younger woman's.

"Who's that?"

"Nurse Mitchell," the voice on the other end said. "I'll be sure to remind her." Pause. "Time?"

Shit . . .

"Hey, Gram," Pandora said, doing the Alaskan mummy striptease, tugging at the fingers of her gloves, unwinding her scarf, unzipping her parka, before tugging, yanking, and pulling at the respective layers underneath. After lifting the last sweater up and over her head, she noticed the wall calendar with the day's date circled in red and spoked in the same shade. "I see you've been expecting me."

"Nurse Mitchell reminded me," Gladys said.

"I had no doubt," Pandora said. "Where's the Furby?"

"The what?"

"Mr. Nosy," Pandora said. "The furry guy who asks all the questions."

Gladys shrugged. Nurse Mitchell poked her head in. "I confiscated it."

"Excuse me?"

"It was getting her worked up," Nurse Mitchell said. "She couldn't figure out if it was alive or not. One moment, it's asking her all these questions, and the next, it's like it died or was in a coma, staring with those bug eyes."

Pandora wanted to protest, to point out that the other residents were allowed their artificial companions, when she noticed the plush yellow duck twisted up in Gladys's blanket.

"Consistency," Nurse Mitchell said. She extricated the stuffed, cartoonish duck. "Mr. Quackers doesn't go changing on her all the time. A hug and he's happy. And Gladys is too. Aren't you, Gladys?"

Gladys nodded like she knew better than to disagree.

"Plus, when she wants to talk to someone," Nurse Mitchell said, "it helps if she can *see* who she's talking to."

What the helpful nurse left out of her passive-aggressive scold-a-thon was the fact that other visitors had taken notice of Pandora's experiment in telepresence and tried to replicate it, bringing their relatives senior-friendly, preprogrammed smartphones, tablets dedicated to Skyping, et cetera, and it was taxing the Golden Heart's Wi-Fi. Sure, their residents deserved the best, but the best in this case was deemed to be face-to-face visits—a solution that didn't involve springing for the next tier among Fairbanks's competition-lite selection of internet providers. That's what Pandora suspected was the real reason for taking away Gladys's friend.

"Listen," she tried, gesturing Nurse Mitchell out into the hallway so they wouldn't be having this conversation in front of her grandmother, "if it's about money . . ."

"It's not about money," Nurse Mitchell said. "It's about time. Quality, face-to-face time."

"I tried that," Pandora insisted, "but the Skype thing . . ."

"Not like that," the nurse insisted. "In person."

Pandora was growing desperate, and when she got that way, her go-to self-defense was pointing out the hypocrisy of her opponent. And so:

"Visiting hours," she said.

"Yes?"

"Why have them?" Pandora asked. "Why cut them off? Family members should be able to come and go as they please." She paused before the coup de grâce. "What are you trying to hide?"

Nurse Mitchell's calm superiority wavered just a bit. "It's corporate policy," she said. "I don't make the rules."

"Okay, listen," Pandora said. "Mr. Nosy is backup."

"Who?"

"The Furby," Pandora said. "He's for saving her memories when I can't be here to record them myself, like after visiting hours." She paused. "What if I don't talk through it anymore?"

Nurse Mitchell started to object, but Pandora continued anyway. "Passive recording only," she insisted.

"The point is you need to visit in person more often," Nurse Mitchell said. "And don't even try to say you're only free after visiting hours."

"Okay, I won't. And I'll come more often. I will," Pandora promised. "I'll have to, to download the recordings of what she says while I'm gone."

Nurse Mitchell looked dubious but reached into her bottom desk drawer and removed Gladys's old snuggle buddy. "Show me," she said. "Deactivate it."

Pandora took out her phone and opened the Furby app, went into settings, and slid wireless connectivity to off. Nurse Mitchell shook her head. "You'll just swipe it back on when you leave."

"Okay," Pandora said before yanking out the speaker that served as its voice box.

"Happy?" she asked.

And so Mr. Nosy got to stay. And Pandora kept her word to visit more often, to download recordings and to keep her grandmother company, even when it became less and less clear whether she recognized who her granddaughter was. Eventually, though, the after-hours stream of consciousness ran dry, the mine tapped out, and all she got when she listened to what was recorded was baby talk, with Gladys cooing to it, asking Mr. Nosy (who'd stopped being so nosy) if he wanted some of her food, if he needed to go potty.

Her grandmother had already established the habit of talking about herself in the third person through the Furby, confessing Mr. Nosy was lonely, didn't know what was going on, was worried about something but he didn't know what. Listening to these confessions later, knowing they'd been made to no one, knowing what Gladys was doing was narrating her emotional landscape moment by moment . . . well, it broke Pandora's heart and made her more determined than ever not to wind up that way.

Not that it was all doom and gloom. Even after her disease had taken a pretty big toll on her grandmother's memories, there was still a core of feistiness underneath that surfaced now and again. There was one time that Pandora was pretty sure she'd remember for the rest of her life, even if she failed at finding a work-around for this terrible disease.

She'd caught her grandmother in a lie about an unhealthy addiction she'd developed for a hard, coffee-flavored candy called Nips. Gladys had begun eating the things by the box. And even though Pandora had been assured that it wasn't uncommon for the elderly to develop a sweet tooth later in life, still she worried. Not unlike a meth addiction, Gladys's sweet tooth had begun to take a toll on her actual teeth—a full set of which she still possessed after ninety-plus years, their enamel in her case having proved far more durable than cortical tissue. The old girl had taken pride in her choppers, flossing obsessively, even now, when the act had become less a decision and more muscle memory. But her teeth were decidedly at risk if she kept sucking down Nips like this. And so Pandora decided to say something: "Gram, seriously," she said, "I brought you a whole box yesterday."

Gladys looked at her expectantly, awaiting a re-up on her fix.

"Are you telling me you finished it already?"

Gladys shrugged.

Pandora checked out the box on the nightstand. Empty.

"Jesus, Gram," her granddaughter said, exasperated. "You can forget about needing dentures. You're going to need a new pancreas if you keep this up."

"The nurses steal them," Gladys bluffed.

And so Pandora went to her grandmother's wastebasket, which was filled with the little cellophane wrappers the candy came in. She presented the evidence to her grandmother. "Well?"

Gladys folded her bird arms in her pink nightgown and frowned. "Happy, Nancy Drew?" she asked.

And the delivery—the timing—hit Pandora smack in the solar plexus, doubling her over with laughter. The old girl was still there, underneath the gunk. Gladys Lynch née Kowalski, the smartass grandmother of Pandora, the Tigris and Euphrates of the younger woman's charming ways, showing she still had it, as affirmed and attested to by her only granddaughter thusly:

"Gram," Pandora wheezed, "you still got it."

"Can you write that down," Gladys asked, meaning the location of the "it" she still had, "in case I forget?"

And so Pandora did. Removing a scrap of paper from her pocket and a pen, she wrote in all caps: "IT."

She handed it to Gladys, who tucked it into a pocket in her nightgown before breathing what seemed to be a sincere sigh of relief. "Thank you," she said, again apparently sincere. "That's a load off my mind," she added, patting the wrong pocket of her nightgown.

37

There was another reason George had gone along so easily with Pandora's text-only rule: he wasn't actually complying with it. He had her number—both figuratively and literally—and it wasn't a big deal to turn on her phone's camera, NSA-style, which frankly any hacker, post-Snowden, should have expected. The hard part was not letting on what he knew about her, not texting questions about whether anything was wrong when her face was being especially expressive about something unrelated to the subject matter of the texts they were exchanging. He had to abandon a voice-recognition app he'd been using to transcribe his end of their exchanges because the immediacy of what came out of his mouth and into the text bubble was an invitation to say things like "Don't cry" if it looked like she was about to. He needed those extra seconds for his thoughts to reach his fingertips to avoid slips, Freudian or otherwise.

The thing was, George liked Pandora's face: the bigness of her smile when she managed one, un-self-conscious because she didn't know he was watching. He found her face, for all its guileless animation, lovely—if not lovely *because* of its guileless animation. He lived in the land of secret projects and code names, of lips that zipped when he got too close to a table rounded by busy hunched heads, so the openness of her face was a breath of fresh air. *A face like that could cure the world's problems,* he thought, imagining what it would be like if people couldn't hide behind masks and avatars, if they wore their hearts not so much on their sleeves but a bit higher up. Plus, Pandora liked him unlike others in his life, and that made all the difference when it came to talking to—correction: texting with—her.

He'd tried confessing his deception once, albeit obliquely. "You know the expression 'You've made my day'?" he typed.

"Yes?"

"Well, you do that pretty much every time we have one of these—what should we call them? Not a tête-à-tête."

"A meeting of minds?" Pandora suggested.

"I'll bet you were smiling when you wrote that," he typed, daring himself to hit send, and then did.

"How'd you know?" she wrote back.

But then he let the opportunity for confession slip by. "Great minds," he typed, followed by the "laughing tears" emoji.

Great minds, met, tend to brainstorm, and that's precisely what Pandora and George proceeded to do, beginning with George's theory about how the nervous system went from being an immediate reaction machine to something that retained memories to inform thought and, yes, consciousness. "You know the expression 'painful memories'?" he asked.

"Yes," Pandora typed. "Those are what my dad calls a steady income."

"Well, I think pain was originally a proxy for memory. Its persistence was for our earliest ancestors what memory is for us: a reminder. I think memory cells evolved from the cells activated by pain, those nerve cells desperately signaling for us to take our hand out of the fire. Those nerves evolved, rewiring themselves into retaining a memory of the pain well after the damaged skin was healed. Immediate pain was like short-term memory, while the memory of pain became long-term storage that prevented us from having to relearn the same painful lessons after the original wounds stopped hurting."

"So what's the takeaway?" Pandora wrote back.

"I think our AI needs to be able to feel pain," George wrote.

"I won't tell it you suggested that," Pandora wrote back, "once it becomes sentient and, you know, all powerful."

Another time, it was the ability to have and feel emotions that were the key to bringing an AI to a human level of consciousness.

"This world is a fire hose of data coming at us," he typed. "How are we supposed to make sense of it all? How do we prioritize and rank what's important to pay attention to versus what we can ignore to preserve our bandwidth?"

"I'm guessing the answer isn't flipping a quarter," Pandora wrote back.

"Emotions," George typed, "are nature's Google."

"How so?"

"Google uses click-through statistics as a way to rank search results," George typed. "For people, memory search optimization is achieved by the emotional residue associated with the memories being searched. The strongest emotional associations cause those memories to rank highest."

Pandora couldn't *not* think about Gladys, whom she'd told George about, and how her grandmother's condition had set her down the path to meeting him. "I think that's why she remembers WWII stuff better than what happened yesterday," she texted back. "That's when her emotions were supercharged. Which is nice, I guess."

"How so?"

"That the dying mind would take us back to the time when we felt most alive."

"Until it uses up those memories," George typed, looked at what he'd written, and then backspaced over it. Instead, "Truth," he tapped out before hitting send.

Another time: "You know the expression 'Seeing is believing'?" George typed.

"Sure."

"You know what that makes me think of?"

"No telling."

"How playing peekaboo with a baby is like programming an AI."

Pandora couldn't find an emoji that suggested a sarcastic "of course," so she went with the "face-palm" instead.

"I always thought peekaboo was a dumb game meant to make adults look stupid," he wrote. "Turns out, it's actually teaching kids a lesson AI is still having trouble with."

"And that is?" Pandora typed back.

"That there's a whole three-dimensional world around the corners of whatever its visual sensors are processing. That shadows aren't solid. That a person's chest implies his or her back, and a tree is a good place to hide behind. Peekaboo teaches a baby to imagine the continuity of reality," George wrote. "And that's an important step toward achieving consciousness."

"Hold on. Are you saying babies aren't born already conscious?"

George nodded before realizing—oh yeah—Pandora couldn't see him on her end of the conversation. And so he tapped out, "Y-E-S," instead.

"How can you think that?" Pandora texted back.

"You better think it too," George tapped out.

"Why?"

"Because if consciousness is some special sauce our unique snowflake species got miracled into having, game over when it comes to producing a conscious AI," George wrote. "But if humans are *programmed* into the experience of consciousness, then we've got a shot at replicating the process."

"And this consciousness programming," Pandora texted back, "how does that happen? What's the mechanism? When does the big C switch on?"

"I figured you'd ask that," George typed.

"Good thinking."

"I think it has something to do with language," he typed, "learning that the stuff we can touch is invisibly connected—let's say hyperlinked—with something we can't see or touch, but that lives in our heads: words."

Pandora looked at George's words on her screen, letting them live in her head for a while. Then: "But where do the words come from," she typed, "and how do we turn them into code?"

She watched the squiggle dots of George's typing inchworm in place below the last text bubble. It seemed to squiggle a lot longer than was justified by the words that finally appeared: "I'm thinking," followed by ellipses.

Pandora didn't want to come across like she was breaking his balls, but she also couldn't help herself. "Please see previous text," she typed, adding a "goofy wink" emoji, just in case.

George—his balls feeling busted nevertheless, it seemed—texted back the passive-aggressive emoji that might seem to signal agreement or affirmation but was a stop sign, intended to end the thread—texting's answer to the "No, you hang up" standoff of earlier generations, but a tad more brutal and efficient: the dreaded "thumbs-up" emoji.

Pandora looked at her screen. Thought about texting a "snowflake" emoji but decided to save it for when she *really* needed it.

38

Perhaps to cover her long-distance relationship with one of her father's clients, Pandora decided to act normal. Or maybe "was ordered to" was more like it. And while her rule-defying and/or exploiting hacker's heart might have inclined her to act even weirder than usual, Pandora actually agreed with the old man's rationale. Though not making a lot of noise about it, "the authorities" were likely still looking for their would-be terrorist. As a result, adopting the mask of normality as a camouflage made strategic sense.

And so she tried. First step: dating. She figured the boy who played the school mascot was a likely candidate. A gangly, carbuncled kid, he clearly welcomed the opportunity to hide his actual head inside the large polar bear head, which was a prominent part of his costume. Following in prominence was the jersey that helped identify Ransom Wood's polar bear mascot from all the other polar bear mascots that had been hastily adopted once people realized that the original mascots—the Yosemite Sam–looking sourdoughs and the fur-hooded-and-booted indigenous peoples—were racist or insultingly stereotyped.

Approaching her target during a lull in pep-related activity, Pandora attempted to break the ice with a joke. "It's too bad they don't include high school mascots when deciding if a species is endangered or not. We could get the polar bear off the list, no problem."

The boy in the suit turned his huge head toward her and looked out through its snarling mouth. "Huh?" he said.

For a clumsy boy, he was showing promise given Pandora's already pretty low expectations. They'd taken in a movie at the Regal Goldstream, a sci-fi epic already at the dollar theaters in the lower forty-eight but a first-run feature up in Fairbanks. It was an old-fashioned gesture, seeing as the movie was already streaming on demand—and Pandora had already seen it, but acted surprised at the surprise ending nevertheless. Based on the action around them, it seemed the Regal Goldstream owed its continued existence to teenagers like herself and her would-be beau, who were paying less for the movie and more for the space, dark, and privacy (relatively speaking) to kiss in the back row. Or so she assumed he hoped and would go on hoping.

After the movie, they headed for the Fairbanks McDonald's, near the Safeway off Geist. It was Tuesday, and the local McDonald's was honoring a local tradition: family pancake night, an all-you-can-eat affair that was a focal point of community life. Which was why neither was surprised when the wedding party entered. Pandora and her date had taken their red plastic trays and found a table underneath the moose head and next to the fireplace when the group entered, tuxed, gowned, parkaed, Soreled, and lit by a backward-walking videographer and some friends with their smartphones, playing backup.

"Look," her date said, way overplaying his hand, "the future . . ."

"You wish," Pandora said, placing down her tray and taking a seat. Though not a typical sight for the lower forty-eight, wedding parties using a fast-food place in lieu of renting a hall wasn't all that unusual, with the odds going up as the combined age of the couple went down, the better to dismiss the choice as "kitschy" or "ironic," as opposed to "economically foreordained."

"Nothing wrong with," the boy across from her began and was about to end with "wishing," when a member of the wedding party tapped Pandora's shoulder and asked if she wouldn't mind immortalizing a moment between herself and a big-bearded, plaid-shirted hunk of Alaskan masculinity she'd been paired with for the evening.

"No prob," Pandora said, excusing herself as she accepted the proffered smartphone and centered the impromptu couple on its high-definition screen. "Say cheese," she said, tapped the screen to the sound of a simulated shutter snap, and returned the phone.

"You were saying?" she asked her date, sitting back down. The boy across from her sat with his head sunk, staring at his syrupy pile of pancakes while the yellow pat of butter decoded itself into a puddle that wound through then mingled with the maple brown.

"Nothing," he mumbled.

Clearly, she'd said or done something wrong, this "being normal" business frequently harder than it looked—or was worth, frankly. Still, she tried rescuing the moment by simulating interest in the mopey boy in front of her. "So," she said, "what's it like being a mascot?"

He shrugged, dug into his pancakes. Pandora did likewise, noting that she was apparently in the middle of a race she hadn't been informed of. Not that that stopped her from trying to win.

Later, in the car, the pimply boy said, "Echoey," into the dashboard lights.

"Excuse me?"

"You asked what being a mascot was like," he said. "Back at the restaurant." Pause. "It's echoey."

Another silence enveloped them as Pandora processed the latest input only to suddenly exclaim, *"Yes!"* startling both her companion and herself. Until the pieces fell into place, she hadn't realized she'd been holding a whole other conversation in her head, one about heads and how they work. Taking a shot at empathy, she'd imagined her own head inside the polar bear head, imagined talking and hearing her own voice come back at her, concluded that it wasn't all that different from how things usually went re: her head and her voice, except she didn't need to open her mouth and actually say anything to hear what amounted to an echo inside her head, roughly behind those peepholes, her eyes. Preparing her response to his response, she was about to say that it reminded her of what consciousness was like when she stopped herself and blurted, *"Yes!"* instead.

"Did I do something wrong?" her companion asked, his Pandora-facing shoulder canted a few inches farther away from her than where it had been a second earlier.

"Nope," Pandora said, leaning in as he leaned back. She surveyed that minefield of acne, located a spot between zits, and applied the most platonic of kisses. "You've been perfect," she added. "Thanks."

"You're welcome?" he guessed.

"You can take me home now," she announced, eager to text George in the privacy of her own . . . well, with the shower curtain drawn at least.

"What's being conscious like for you?" she texted him.

"It's like a conversation," George tapped. "It's like I'm talking to myself all the time, quietly, in my head."

"Exactly," Pandora tapped back. "I think consciousness is a collaboration between the sides of ourselves. A conversation. Or narration. It's a story we tell ourselves about ourselves, and it keeps going in real time, editing itself on the fly."

"POV," George typed.

"Spell out."

"Point of view," George typed, as requested. "The world is all around us but is *not us*. We are the target the world aims itself at. We are our point of view—the whole history of everything we've seen or heard from our particular focal point. We are the thinking thing in our own blind spot that we can't see but know is there, through intuition."

"Or a mirror."

"Or selfie," George typed. "I get it. But you see what I'm saying, right?"

"I am the drain between the world and my collective, subjective experience of the world," Pandora typed. "The world circles me, pours down me, *becomes* the experience of me from the funneling center that calls itself me."

"Yes," George texted back, watching as Pandora smiled in the palm of his hand.

39

Brainstorming about artificial consciousness is one thing; rendering what you've brainstormed into code is another. So how were they supposed to achieve what the best minds in the field hadn't cracked yet? Because that was the goal they'd set themselves—the Everest of AI, the Holy Grail of neural nets, pick your hard-to-impossible metaphor and that's what they were up against.

Why? It was central to both of their goals.

For Pandora, the idea of surviving dementia or the bigger *D*, death, by uploading her memories to the cloud was just the first part. Those memories needed to inform something else with agency, something that could form *new* memories contextualized by the old memories in storage, something consciousness-compatible for her consciousness to inhabit when it got out of the habit of having a mortal body and became immortal either as a robot or virtually, living in an alternative sim world beyond her wildest imagination.

George, on the other hand, needed his AI to be conscious so it understood what it was the people it was tasked with saving stood to lose. George's AI needed a consciousness so it could understand what might motivate thoughts of self-destruction in other conscious entities as a first step to reverse engineering its way back to wanting to "live," or at least remain conscious.

Seeing as George was the one who was actually getting a paycheck, it made sense that he take the first stab at coding their baby AI before handing it off to Pandora to take potshots at. It also made sense that George would be the one to make the introductions.

"Pandora Lynch," his message read, "meet Buzz," followed by a link to what was really just a doodle in code as opposed to an actual beta of anything.

"Buzz?"

"Yep," George wrote back, going on to explain that his baby AI had actually named itself. He—George—had coded up a two-dimensional VR space for his baby AI to learn the rules of and . . .

"Two-dimensional virtual reality space?" Pandora echo-typed.

"Pac-Man," George wrote back. "I was having my AI teach itself Pac-Man. And my CPU started getting toasty even though most of the crunching was happening in the cloud. And I'm watching the activity light go crazy, and the cooling fan kicks on, and then there's this loud buzzing noise, like there's been a head crash and the hard drive's getting trashed."

"You're not using an SSD?" Pandora typed. "How big a cheapskate is Lemming anyway?"

George was not about to cast aspersions on his employer in writing, even over a private phone, using a proprietary, encrypted texting app with a self-destruct option. Instead, ignoring the comment entirely, he continued. "Turns out a fortune cookie fortune got stuck in the fan and was rattling like a playing card in a bicycle's spokes," George continued. "Catastrophe averted."

"So what did it say?"

"What did what say?"

"The fortune."

"I don't," George began typing, but then stopped. "Wait," he said to himself, aloud. "Yes, I do." He reached into the paper-clip tray in his top drawer, which was filled with slips of paper from the assortment of free fortune cookies the Quire cafeteria gave out whenever the menu featured Asian cuisine.

"'It's not the destination; it's the journey,'" he typed.

"How pseudoprofound," Pandora's reaction blooped back.

"What do you expect from a baked good?" George typed. "But that's not the point. My AI made something happen in the real world. It buzzed. So that's what I'm calling it: Buzz."

"Aldrin," Pandora typed, "or Lightyear?"

"Does it matter?"

"Sure. One's made out of DNA and the other is CGI."

"Code by any other name," George opined, trying out a little pseudoprofundity of his own.

"How's that?"

"Genetic," George typed, "versus computer. It's all code."

Pandora was about to object, to point out that unlike computer code, genetic code couldn't be hacked. But then she remembered reading about CRISPR in her news feed and stopped. Instead: "Maybe Kurzweil is right about the singularity after all."

"Here's hoping," George typed, followed by the "fingers crossed" emoji.

The longer she lived with it, the more Pandora liked the idea of calling their baby AI "Buzz," with its twin connotations of electricity and viral excitement. "But shouldn't the initials stand for something? Like how HAL is IBM if you shift each letter to the left."

"That's an urban myth," George texted back. "It stands for 'Heuristically programmed ALgorithmic' computer. Plus, that double Z is going to be tough."

"What about Zuzu?"

"What about what-what?"

"Zuzu's petals," Pandora replied. "From *It's a Wonderful Life*? Jimmy Stewart. Christmas classic . . ."

"Yeah, yeah," George texted back. "Black and white, meaning ancient history, meaning *not relevant*."

"Au contraire," Pandora begged to disagree. "The movie's about what Buzz is about: suicide prevention. Clarence shows *George* (now how perfect is that?) what the world would be like without him so he changes his mind about killing himself. It's perfect."

"But how do we turn *that* into an acronym for BUZZ?" George typed. "What's the BU stand for?"

"Button up."

"Excuse me?"

"Zuzu catches a cold coming back from school because she didn't wear her coat, and George calls up her teacher to yell at her and scares his family and everything goes downhill after that."

"I thought it was losing the bank deposit," George wrote back.

"That started it, but the yelling because of Zuzu's cold was the tipping point. So if Zuzu buttoned up, she wouldn't have gotten a cold, George might not have started yelling, and . . ."

"So BUZZ = Button up, Zuzu?"

"Yep."

"Remind me never to play Scrabble with you."

"You're welcome."

"It really *is Pac-Man*," Pandora texted after clicking the link to George's doodle in code.

"Looks can be deceiving," he wrote back, "but yes."

"I thought you were joking."

"Not," George wrote, followed by, "This does precisely what I need it to do, no more, no less."

"Explain."

"First, it's a game, and games are foundational for AI because they've got clear rules that can be programmed directly or learned by having the AI watch several rounds of play. Then it perfects its own technique by playing millions of games against itself. One of the first proof-of-concepts for neural nets taught itself how to play *Breakout* to master level in about an hour."

"And thus concludes today's lecture on the history of artificial intelligence . . ."

"Sorry. Forgot who I was talking to."

"Typing to," Pandora corrected.

"Right," George acknowledged. "But this is"—and he was going to type "cool" but decided to use a word he knew would resonate with her hacker's heart—"elegant."

"Explain."

"First, it's embodied in as simple a body as possible, occupying the fewest number of dimensions, two."

"Why does Buzz need a body?"

"Embodiment," George wrote back, "is one of the earliest debates in AI. Sure, you can do tricks using language-manipulating algorithms, come up with chatbots that go 'Um' now and then and can appear humanlike. Google's Duplex could pass the Turing test—in the limited world of making telephone reservations. But there's always some way in which chatbots fall short. Did you know they did a study of the words that would fool humans into thinking they were dealing with another human?"

"Ah, the infamous 'they.'"

"Do you want to know that top human-proving word or not?"

"Hit me."

"Poop."

"Heart" emoji followed by the "poop" emoji.

"And you know what you need to poop, right?" George typed.

Fiber? Pandora thought, but typed, "Hit me," again instead.

"A body," George typed.

"I see what you did there," Pandora wrote back, followed by a "wink" emoji from George.

"So the theory goes that it's not enough to program an artificial brain if you want to get to an actually conscious AI," George typed. "There needs to be a body, too, reacting to an environment that 'programs' the AI like people are 'programmed' by their experiences and environment. Now you can build a robot body with a bunch of sensors for a million bucks, have it learn an obstacle course by itself, or you can do it all with pixels and a handful of rules."

"I see," Pandora texted back. "But isn't Mr. Wocka-Wocka a little simplistic, even for virtual reality on a budget?"

"What's wrong with simple? Simple's good," George wrote. "I did simple on purpose."

"Touchy much?"

"You know Descartes, right? You wore that T-shirt in your proof-of-life selfie. 'I Think, Therefore I Am . . .'"

"Okay."

"Descartes questioned everything until he arrived at the one thing he couldn't question: that he was thinking and therefore must exist," George typed. "The one thing he couldn't doubt was that he was the consciousness doing the doubting."

"Okay."

"He broke down all of existence into three little words."

I love you, Pandora thought, but knew better than to type, even if it was true despite this run of George's mansplaining Philosophy 101. Instead, she typed, "Go on," remembering only after the fact what a truly crappy medium texting is for sarcasm.

"That's what I was trying to do with this proto version," he typed. "I wanted to strip away everything but the minimum required for consciousness in terms of a body and senses. And what I came up with happens to look like Pac-Man. It has a body, the circle, that helps identify it as separate from its surrounding environment, so that as far as Buzz is concerned, the universe is two things: me and not me. To achieve that understanding as simply as possible, it needs a single sense: a sense of boundary. A sense of where it stops and everything else starts."

"Wait a second," Pandora typed, having held her tongue—or thumbs—long enough. "If all an AI needs is enough sense to stay on its side of the universe, why all the fuss about getting machine vision and hearing to work? Why the data farms in China with workers tagging a million different dog pictures to create a database of dogness? I think that means that seeing and hearing are probably pretty important to the development of consciousness."

George didn't disagree, but sight and sound could come later. For now, at the prototype phase . . . ? "Two words," he typed. "Helen Keller."

Pandora swore at her phone, and George smiled. Roger, on the other hand, had been sleeping on the couch. "What was that?"

"Nothing," Pandora lied, noticing that in the interim, George had expanded on his original comment.

"Are you telling me that Helen Keller lacked consciousness?"

Don't know; never met her, Pandora thought, but typed, "Never mind. Continue."

"So stripped down, Buzz needs to know it can't be in two places at once," George typed. "No colocation."

Pandora, who'd quite recently thought one thing while typing another, proceeded to call BS by typing, "BS," followed by, "Colocation is the essence of consciousness."

"How so?"

"Think about it," she typed. "Our conscious reality is always in two places at once. We have an inner reality (what we think) and an outer reality (what we might choose to say or do). Something as simple as sarcasm would be impossible without the implicit acknowledgment that people can say something while meaning its exact opposite. Consciousness is a two-places-at-once experience inherently."

Pandora smiled triumphantly as she watched the dancing ellipsis dance for a lot longer than it usually did, stop, and then start up again. Finally: "So you're saying that a sign of Buzz being conscious," George typed, "is if it can consciously lie?"

"Using 'consciously' in front of 'lie' might be stacking the deck there," she typed, hit send, and then had another (eviler) thought. And so she added: "Unless you're okay with circular logic."

"I see what you did there," George typed.

"Wink" emoji.

George admitted that he hadn't started out with the intention of resurrecting Pac-Man, fitting though he now thought it to be. "I was on YouTube, looking at babies."

"Would these be preconscious babies?" Pandora typed back.

George ignored the bait. "Have you ever watched a newborn exploring its world? It's crazy the way they'll put anything into their mouths, including their own fist. It looks like they're trying to stifle a yawn but they're experimenting. They're trying to see if this thing out there is something they can eat, and when they try, and pain comes back as the answer, that's when they start to learn the difference between themselves and the rest of the world."

"So we need to teach Buzz not to eat itself?" Pandora wrote back. "Or maybe that its virtual world is a dog-eat-dog virtual world?"

"I wanted to see what Buzz would come up with for a body," George continued, "so I gave it a pixel and a push."

"And?"

George sent her a JPEG of a circle.

"That looks familiar," Pandora texted back.

"That's what Buzz came up with, and it's perfect: the self vs. everything else," George texted.

"How much of a push did you give it?" Pandora asked, suspecting a little deck stacking in the result.

"Well, originally, it just blinked," George admitted. "The pixel, I mean. And that's when I realized it needed a few other things, like the curiosity about its environment a human baby has."

"I thought curiosity killed the cat," Pandora countered.

"Nope," George typed back. "Curiosity familiarized the cat with its surroundings so it wouldn't be surprised. Think of the baby exploring its own fist by mouthing it and being surprised by feeling it in two places—on its hand and in its mouth. And every new discovery its curiosity leads to is another thing it won't be surprised by again. Then you remove the option of standing still by making the not-me environment nonneutral—specifically, *not* benign."

"Or skipping the double negatives," Pandora typed, "the environment likes to kill sitting ducks."

"Yes."

"That seems like a lot more coding than just 'a pixel and a push,'" Pandora observed.

"That's how programming works," George wrote back. "Try, test, try, test. You know this. You code too."

"Thanks for remembering," Pandora wrote, her face not exactly filled with gratitude at the moment.

"So that's when something finally started happening," George wrote. "The pixel started moving, and it was like watching primordial goo coming up with the idea for cell walls. That single pixel started testing the compass points of its space and then stretched itself into a line that bent, swept, and met itself, forming a perfect circle, which began rolling from one end of the screen to the next, mapping out its world, driven by curiosity and a need to not be surprised."

"How'd you make the environment nonneutral?" Pandora asked.

"I started with random geometrical not-Buzzes, moving randomly, bumping into Buzz and vice versa. Collisions cost points from a base score I started Buzz out with at the beginning, triggering various if/thens when the score reached X, Y, or Z."

"Sounds depressing," Pandora wrote back. "Start out with everything you'll ever have and then lose ground from there?"

"Yeah, I know," George wrote back. "It sucks. And you know what it sounds like, right?"

"Life?"

"Precisely."

"No," Pandora wrote a little later, after considering George's default scoring. "Buzz's interactions with its environment can't be all negative. It should interact with the environment to add points. Maybe the boundary sense allows exceptions, letting something from outside to be brought inside, like the way an experience can inspire a new idea or like food provides nutrition. That's what consciousness is like for me. It's a Venn diagram with two overlapping circles—inside me and outside me—and the point where they overlap is where my experience of consciousness is located. So this no-colocation rule you started with—it doesn't allow for the possibility for consciousness because it doesn't allow Buzz to take something from the outside and make it part of itself."

"I think you're absolutely right," George texted back. "How's this for an input device?"

A text bubble blooped open on Pandora's screen, inside which sat the same plain yellow pie as before, missing a slice where its new mouth now was.

"I hate you," Pandora texted.

"You're welcome."

His goal—George explained—was to turn suicide detection and prevention into a game, and though he hadn't been thinking of Pac-Man when he started out, the more he thought about it, the more he liked it. He'd gotten their baby AI from nothing but a single pixel to a one-celled actor that needed to eat to keep moving, needed to move to explore, and needed to explore to avoid surprises that cost points off its "life." He'd noticed the similarity to Pac-Man the second he gave his one-celled actor a mouth. That the actual game featured elements that fit nicely into his current task was a happy accident. Take the ghosts and extra lives; he couldn't have asked for a simpler visualization of what his end game was: generating extra lives by saving kids from suicide.

In the original game, each room or level came with four power pellets, one in each corner, the power pellets being the means by which Pac-Man prevented ghost encounters from costing him one of his three lives. Translate ghosts into potential suicides and power pellets into successful prevention scenarios and make those prevention episodes something Pac-Buzz's score depends on. George admitted he was still a long way from determining how the power pellets would neutralize life-robbing ghosts, but he had his AI's conceptual scaffolding sketched out in an easy-to-remember form—something to keep in the back of his head (and his AI's core programming) while he moved on to tackle more ambitious feats of coding.

"But isn't this copyright infringement?" Pandora asked. "Aren't you stealing intellectual property?"

"Only if I copied the exact source code and tried to market it as a game," George said. "But nobody will ever see this on the front end, and I reversed engineered it by accident without even meaning to. Plus, what's IP versus actual human lives?"

"Assuming it all works out," she typed.

"It's not even a total copy," George insisted, perhaps a bit more defensively than if he'd actually believed his earlier defense. "When Buzz eats a pac-dot, it grows, and this ballooning imparts momentum, causing it to roll or somersault to the next pac-dot, where the process repeats. I'm thinking the pac-dots will be a checklist of suicidal ideation indicators, something like that."

Pandora looked at the time on her phone. It was winter, and even though she had a window in her room, it didn't offer many clues about the time, this time of year. Between, say, 11:00 a.m. and 2:00 p.m., the sky might lighten a bit with what was optimistically referred to as "sunrise." But any options outside that, say, nine, eight, four, and she'd have to check her phone to figure out if it was day or night. And these text sessions with George weren't helping. They seemed to dissolve time, make it even harder to keep track of. And so when she looked at the time in the upper right-hand corner and saw it was five, she needed to squint to register it was p.m.

Shit, Pandora thought.

She was late to see Gladys at the Golden Heart. And so: "Mmmm, pac-dots," she hastily texted back, followed by the "yum" emoji, followed by the "running girl" emoji—the one along with the "running boy" emoji they agreed meant "gotta go," to avoid leaving the other waiting on a text that wouldn't come.

40

When Pandora signed in at the Golden Heart, she took out her phone for the time and noticed the date as well: February 14. Why did that date . . . ?

Oh shit, Pandora thought, followed by doing the IRL version of the "face-palm" emoji. Well, if they'd ever needed proof of what geeks they were, there it was. She and George had spent their first (!) Valentine's Day exchanging texts about how to program consciousness, oblivious to what day it was. Neither had sent the other anything; neither had texted the words. The two seconds it would take to tap a "heart" emoji and hit send? Nope, neither of them. Or . . .

Pandora scrolled through their recent exchange. There *was* one. A heart, but right next to a pile of poop—if that didn't just about sum it up. Maybe she should get one of those reminder boards like the staff updated in Gladys's room. She wondered what they drew to distinguish between Valentine's Day and a visit from the cardiologist.

Slipping her phone back into her pocket, Pandora noticed something funny about her hands; they were empty. She was already late for her grandmother's Valentine's Day visit and was showing up empty-handed to boot. Nurse Mitchell was going to have a field day.

"Is there a . . . ?" she began.

". . . gift shop?" the receptionist finished.

Nod.

"Down that hall, left, left, bingo . . ."

"Thank you."

"I'm not done yet," the receptionist said. "Hang a right past bingo, and there it is."

"The gift shop?" Pandora asked, just checking.

"The gift shop," the receptionist confirmed.

The place was pretty well picked over this late in the day as Pandora took down and put back a variety of possibilities, including gag mugs, teddy bears, kiss-covered kitsch. She knew Gladys wouldn't turn down anything sweet but didn't want to encourage her after the Nips situation.

As she continued looking, Pandora noticed she had company in the gift shop, an elderly man in a jacket—a windbreaker—way too thin for the actual weather outside. Emblazoned across the back was a large gear with the letters "UAW" on the inside. Looking closer, she realized that what she'd taken as the cog's teeth were actually stick people, linked hand in hand, circling the circumference, the human labor that made the vast machinery of the auto industry run.

"You're a long way from"—guessing but a good one, statistically—"Detroit?"

The old man turned and smiled the high-def grin of someone with brand-new dentures. "That was the plan," he said.

"Looks like it worked," Pandora said.

"Looks like," the smile confirmed.

"You visiting, or . . . ?"

"Staying," the old man said. "I signed up for the Eskimo burial. You know, send 'em out on an ice floe? This was the closest they had."

"Well, happy Valentine's Day," Pandora said, deciding on a box of damn chocolates and preparing to leave when her retired auto worker snapped his gnarled fingers, winced, and said, "*That's* why I came in here," followed by another uncanny-valley smile.

Pandora raised a box of chocolates like an admissions badge as she passed the nurses' station and headed for Gladys's room. "I'm sorry I'm late," she began when she spotted them: five petals of the bluest sky blue Pandora had ever seen, repeated flower by dainty flower a dozen times, the stems rubber banded together, little pale tendrils at their cut ends, visible through the clear glass vase that rested on Gladys's windowsill, half-empty, half-full, your call. She'd not be a proper Alaskan if Pandora couldn't name them, seeing as the alpine forget-me-not (scientifically: *Myosotis alpestris*) was the official flower for the forty-ninth of the fifty United States. And she'd not be a proper granddaughter if the sight of them in her grandmother's nursing home didn't turn her mood from apologetic before seeing them to downright pissed afterward.

Forget-me-nots! In the room of a woman with dementia! What kind of a sick . . .

She hit the call button and then let her rage build for thirty or so minutes before any of the home staff showed up.

"Yes?" a nurse's aide said after poking her head in the doorway. Her powder-blue scrubs, dotted with fluorescent renditions of Tweety Bird, appeared to be on backward, judging from the breast pocket Pandora noticed over the girl's left shoulder blade when she'd fully entered the room, after having determined there were no infectious bodily substances splattered anywhere.

Pandora gestured to the blue flowers on her grandmother's windowsill. "WTF?" she said.

"DK," the nurse's aide said. "But they're pretty, don't you think?"

"*Pretty's* not the point," Pandora said. "What kind of sicko puts forget-me-nots in the room of a . . ." She trailed off.

"You want me to get rid of them?" the nurse's aide asked.

Pandora looked at the flowers, and then looked at her grandmother looking at the flowers. Just testing, she stepped off to one side. Gladys's gaze did not follow her like it usually did. Instead, it stayed glued on that splash of out-of-season blue.

All her reasons for being angry were hers, Pandora realized. They were all in her head, linked up with the words she had for the flowers she was seeing. Forget the words, and all that was left were the flowers, which *were* kind of pretty after all. And maybe that had been the point—clueless, but benign.

"Don't bother," Pandora said. "I think she likes them."

"She likes them," Gladys said, whether agreeing or just repeating, it was getting harder and harder to tell.

Pandora, meanwhile, pulled up the guest chair and began her vigil. When Gladys's eyes fluttered closed, she took out her phone. "BTW," she thumbed, "happy VD."

She waited. Her phone buzzed. "Happy Hallmark to you as well."

On the way back to the truck, Pandora saw her United Auto Worker again, a heart-shaped box of chocolates under the arm of his satiny windbreaker, poking his head into room after room before heading on. The phrase "Looking for love in all the wrong places" came to mind unbidden, but it made her smile, ironically, nevertheless.

You and me, buddy, she added to herself.

As a test, she called out to him. "You're a long way from Detroit," she said.

"That was the plan," he said.

"Looks like it worked," Pandora said, continuing the rerun of their previous conversation as if they were having it for the first time.

"Looks like," Mr. UAW said.

And then she moved on, as did he, back to checking the open doorways. Pandora, for her part, wished him luck.

41

There was a reason George forgot Valentine's Day, not that he'd necessarily have said anything even if he'd remembered. He just wasn't sure how Pandora felt about him, even though she'd been the one to reach out in the first place. There'd always been something a little fishy about that. He'd been flattered at first, but the no-faces thing kind of suggested that all she was interested in was his brain. That and access to the kinds of resources that would help her reach her stated goal: cybernetic immortality.

Even with access to her phone's camera—even with that hyper-expressive face of hers—George couldn't tell if the arousal he detected was because of *him* or his *ideas*. It was this uncertainty and insecurity—byproducts, Roger would no doubt contend, of his client's chaotic foster childhood—that had led George to getting himself into an awful stupid place re: the project they were supposedly collaborating on, a.k.a. Buzz. And the stupid place he got himself into? He wanted to impress Pandora. He wanted to deliver Buzz about as close to complete as he could manage so that all she had to contribute were a few gratuitous tweaks—maybe a few boxes he'd left open for her specifically—and voilà: an artificially conscious general AI.

His being in this stupid place was what contributed to George's forgetting Valentine's Day. He'd forgotten about it because . . . well, he'd kind of lost track of days. And nights. And the way they punctuated the flow of time.

The problem was they'd brainstormed more than he had time to code. He'd already been sleeping in his office when they'd met, an arrangement originally intended to save him money. Now it was saving him the time he'd otherwise waste commuting. Not that he was alone in this work-nesting behavior—not that management discouraged it, as attested to by the free vending machines all over QHQ, providing a steady supply of Monster, Red Bull, and Mountain Dew Kickstart, along with people lurking in the shadows, ever ready to offer you something a little stronger if you seemed to be in an especially productive mood.

One evening, in just such a mood, George had bumped into Milo in the hallway at 3:00 a.m. "Is your hair always like that?" Milo asked George, who was wearing a bathrobe at the time.

"Like what?"

"Like it's being blown back by an invisible wind."

George inspected Milo's person for a reflective surface, found two in the dark glasses his Virgil was wearing, and attempted a few half-ass hair-taming swipes before abandoning the effort. "Coding," he admitted.

"I can see that." Milo patted his pockets and produced some inspiration in pill form. "Care for a little"—he paused theatrically—"competitive edge?"

"Thanks?" George said in return, pocketing what he'd been advised was a wholly legal pharmaceutical short a little paperwork.

And then one night, George got a little warning from his body when his heart decided to freak out. It wasn't an all-out attack, more like a "Do we have your attention now?" beat-skipping situation. He stumbled out into the hallway, looking for help, but found Milo instead. His Virgil, it turned out, had a pill for this condition as well, which George accepted because he needed it and because, well, it was Milo and he'd been working here longer than most.

"You may also want to take note," the latter said, pointing to something George had failed to register: wall-mounted cabinets featuring stick people in various postures, some involving lightning bolts.

"Defibrillators," Milo explained. "Plural," he added. "They'll actually talk you through the whole thing. It's kind of neat."

"And *needed*, apparently?"

"Apparently," Milo said. He pointed at his own wrist, wrapped by a smart watch displaying his vitals. "Best to avoid any surprises," he advised.

In the end, George was forced to compromise on the whole body-needing-sleep thing. Taking a cue from Thomas Edison, who was famous for taking catnaps on his laboratory floor, George reprogrammed himself to get by with a series of fifteen- or twenty-minute naps every several hours. He was modestly concerned that REM sleep usually doesn't occur until about ninety minutes into a night's sleep, but perhaps abstaining from dreaming was where the other one percent of genius came from. It worked for Edison, who—while dead—had a good run while he was still alive.

George was aided and abetted in this new sleep schedule by no less than V.T. Lemming himself, who seemed to share a similar love-hate relationship with the traditional split between sleeping and waking. Shortly after he'd been given his first work assignment, the same messenger arrived to drop off an old-school alphanumeric pager from "the big man himself." It was hardwired only to receive—V.T. the only sender—and came equipped without much in the way of memory so that no messages were stored once a new one came in. V.T.'s pages invariably scrambled George's ability to concentrate for at least an hour after receiving one. They were also almost always questions, passive-aggressively dropping *g*'s to create a fairly threatening nonthreatening vibe: "How's it goin'?" A perfectly fine question, but without the ability to transmit an answer back, a bit of a dickish move.

"Makin' progress?

"No pressure. Kids are dyin' is all."

Finally willing to dispense with any plans of impressing her, George decided to complain to Pandora about the pressure he was under. Unfortunately, before he was able to initiate that particular thread, his phone binged with a message from the target of his would-be showing off.

"So," it read, "how's it goin'?"

Pandora's text was the tipping point for a realization George had felt coming ever since his heart-skipping episode. More and more, he was convinced that he—they—were going to fail. And it wasn't even his—their—fault. There was something in the air that was coming, despite the hype and headlines: the AI winter, part two.

The study of artificial intelligence was actually a lot older than most people realized, going all the way back to the 1950s at least. There'd been a lot of excitement over early successes. In fact, most of the stuff making headlines now had actually been developed back then, including perceptrons, machine learning, neural nets, even evolutionary code where the computer incrementally tweaks and improves upon its own programming—none of these were new ideas back during the Summer of Love, one of the bigger things to hit San Francisco an incarnation or two ago.

But then AI hit a wall, and the first so-called "AI winter" began. The field's ideas and strategies had outrun the raw data and hardware needed to implement them. Those were the bottlenecks back then, and the AI renaissance now wasn't happening because of new approaches, per se, but was due to better hardware and more data for implementing those sixty-year-old ideas.

But there was another bottleneck coming, and it looked like hardware again. All George had to do was read what the tech giants were doing—the Googles, Facebooks, Microsofts. They were all developing proprietary chipsets aimed at some specific AI niche, from natural-language processing, to image recognition and differentiation, to dynamic visioning and navigation systems. The folks who used to be all about better software and algorithms were leaving the Intels and Motorolas behind.

Google had developed its own AI programming language, called TensorFlow, and was developing something called TPUs—Tensor processing units. Just about every other big tech firm in the Valley, European Union, and China were doing the same thing. The age of all-purpose x86 CPUs working together was coming to an end. In its place the industry was increasingly turning to something like the Apple model: walled off, proprietary, and incompatible with everything.

And there was Buzz, their baby AI, destined to choke in its crib thanks to that bottleneck. And it sucked, but George could have handled it, if it was just about him. If all it meant was losing his cushy job, well, he'd lived on the streets before, and he could do it again. But there were those kids out there, taking their own lives . . .

Yeah, that was a good one; George was all bent out of shape about a bunch of teenagers he didn't know. No. The thing that upset him was the teenager he knew: Pandora. What George couldn't take was disappointing her.

Correction: what he couldn't take was being *solely responsible* for disappointing Pandora. So he could either get Buzz to work—which didn't seem to be in the cards, not in the short term—or . . .

. . . or maybe he could finally start sharing the glory (a.k.a. blame). Pandora kept saying she wanted more to do, something to take advantage of her skills. And like he'd heard from more than one foster: misery loved company. George figured the same could probably be said about failure, which was when he decided it was time to share his.

42

Pandora wanted to talk about Valentine's Day without talking about Valentine's Day. But before she could figure out how to do that, George's words appeared in the palm of her hand. "We need to discuss the division of labor," they read. *Okay,* Pandora thought, *here we go.* If he suggested some BS busywork like proofreading his code, looking for misplaced commas or Os that should be zeros or vice versa, that was it; he didn't take her seriously and she'd have no reason to take him seriously. Cut her losses and become a ghost.

But then she recognized what he'd given her: a shoehorn to introduce the Valentine's discussion without necessarily using the word. She could steer the conversation in that direction by using an amusing anecdote about love among the elderly, sneaked in via the keyword he'd given her: labor.

"It's funny you should mention labor," Pandora wrote. "Last night, I saw this old guy wandering around my gram's nursing home, and he was looking for his sweetie with a big box of chocolates."

"What's that got to do with labor?" George wrote back.

"That's the best part," Pandora assured. "He was wearing a UAW jacket like he just stopped by after working a shift."

"Poor guy's a long way from Detroit," George texted back.

"That's what I said," Pandora wrote. "I think he might be Jimmy Hoffa in hiding." She followed the message with a "wink" emoji.

"When you say 'UAW,' do you mean the one that's a big gear?" George asked, scanning through the results of the Google Images search on his work computer.

"I always thought it was just a big gear too," Pandora texted. "But when I got a closer look, I realized the gear's teeth are really stick people holding hands."

"Workers of the world," George tapped out, suddenly longing for the socialist bros he'd abandoned to take this gig—the same job that was stacked against him and working him to death. He concluded with "Unite!" and was about to add something like "solidarity" or "eat the rich" or maybe just a "raised fist" emoji but stopped. He zoomed in on one of the UAW logos on his screen, following the sweep of little cog people—all holding hands.

His mind flashed back to a pair of fosters—Catholics, like his mom—who took him to guitar masses where they sang "Kumbaya" and went around shaking hands with everyone before communion. At one mass, during a lull, he'd clearly heard someone yell, "Bingo!" from the other side of the sacristy, back in the church hall that also served as the boys' court during basketball season.

George repeated the word to himself, in his office, aloud. He backed over the text he'd written and replaced it.

"Gotta go," the new text read. "Initiating radio silence, commencing . . . *now*."

"Are you *kidding*?" Pandora hastily texted back. And then waited. And kept on waiting. He hadn't even sent her the "running boy" emoji. After about an hour, she figured, George's not answering *was* her answer.

It was a typical eureka moment—or bingo, depending on your denomination. George had filled up his head with all the necessary bits and pieces for resolving a problem—all the individual trees—but then hit the forest and was overwhelmed. Finally deciding to accept failure, he let his mind get distracted and . . . *plop*. There it was: the answer.

In George's case, the distraction had been Pandora's little detour into labor politics, the UAW logo, specifically. All those people, linking hands. All those people, singing "Kumbaya," together in harmony. And then a random thought from the compost heap of them in George's head: It's too bad all this proprietary tech won't play nice together. And then the question: Why not? What was preventing it? Some laws and outdated notions about personal property? ICE and the foster system had cured George of those trifles long ago.

A worm, he figured, one that targets and gains control over experimental and proprietary hardware and software wherever it finds it. He'd call it the Kumbaya worm or k-worm for short. It would borrow from the same toolkit as Stuxnet and its variants, with some secret sauce from his own Daisy Chain of Mass Destruction. There was another ingredient, however, that found him breaking his self-imposed radio silence.

Pandora felt the buzz and checked her phone.

"You know machine language, right?"

She smiled. Machine language was as close to the machine as a programmer could get—closer than assembly language and way closer than what most script kiddies thought of as coding, i.e., the higher-level languages that read like stilted English and included everything from the grands, FORTRAN and BASIC, to Python and C++. Machine language was all zeros and ones. Pandora had learned an earlier binary language from her grandfather—Morse code—and she'd already admitted to George that she "ran with it all the way to ML."

"Why do you ask?" she wrote back noncommittally. It was late February, but she was still stinging a bit over the fourteenth.

"This thing I'm working on," he wrote, "is going to need like the UN of code translation. I'm going to need something that can get traditional computers and quantum computers talking to each other, with maybe some experimental or proprietary stuff thrown in."

"Okay?"

"Can you do it?"

Well, it wasn't busywork. And it might be fun—a challenge, but not impossible. "A crack, I shall give it," she wrote back.

"To my ears: music," followed by a link to the Dropbox account where she could deposit her "UN of code translation" once it was ready for prime time.

Pandora's confidence was not unfounded. She was the granddaughter of the code breaker Gladys after all. And it was true: she'd gotten as close to the machine as a coder could get without being a machine herself. ML, as it was fondly known among digit heads, was the actual language computers used to talk to other computers. George, who'd only made it to the level immediately above machine—assembly language—was duly impressed, while both considered hackers who only knew one or two higher-level languages to be little more than script kiddies, i.e., not coders at all.

Unlike translating English into Russian and then Japanese, translating one higher-order programming language into another benefited from the fact that while their terminology and/or syntax might vary, they all had to do many of the same things. They all needed to address variables, value assignment, integers versus floating point decimals, arithmetic operators, comparison operators, conditional operators, and other control structures. Python, PROLOG, LISP, R, C++ . . . they all included if/then, greater than, add, subtract, et cetera. And these control structures were like certain words in a given language, occurring at fairly consistent frequencies—*the*, *and*, *or*, *I*—and these statistics could be used to guess which string of symbols translated into, say, if/then statements.

The quantum computing side of the equation was a little trickier but, deep down, was more of the same—literally. More, after all, was the whole point of quantum computing—specifically, more options than the yes-no of binary systems. Instead of bits, quantum computing dealt in qubits, which took yes-no and added maybe-both-and-neither. And while there weren't a whole lot of qubits in any given place at the moment—more like a few here, a few there, scattered around research operations across the globe—there were resources available to help Pandora grok the essentials, from instruction sets like Quil and Pha-Q; to software development kits like IQ, Q#, and Kwiz; to full-blown languages like QCL, QML, and Quipper.

All in all, the work reminded Pandora of what her grandmother had told her about cracking the Enigma code. The fact that there'd be a *"Heil Hitler"* somewhere in transmissions coming from Germany proved to be an important key—one that undermined a lot of technological sophistication. Or as Gladys put it: "God bless those predictable fascists."

And, Pandora added, *code bros and their love of Monty Python . . .*

For something like a computer worm to spread, there needs to be a vector. Fortunately for George, he already had one—or one that would know one: Milo. It was one of the weird things he'd noticed about his self-appointed Virgil; Milo seemed to know everybody. He also seemed to know more collectively than any of his coworkers knew individually, as if Milo alone had been granted access to the big picture. Trying to pull one over on a guy like that was probably risky, but George was a former street kid who'd risked his ass into a position that others would kill for. It was time to see if that luck held.

Instead of just waiting for Milo to stop by his office—a statistically viable option—George decided to go looking and found his would-be vector in the arcade-themed break room he'd discovered on his first official day, postchipping. Milo was currently distracted, gobbling up pac-dots at an impressive rate, something George took as an excellent sign.

"Doesn't it bother you?" he asked over his all-knowing friend's shoulder.

"Doesn't what bother me?" Milo said back, not breaking focus.

"Lying to the world," George said. "The whole Memory Hole Monday thing."

"Oh, *that*," Milo said. He turned so George would be sure to see his smirk, only to hear the sound of his last life being lost, followed by "Game Over."

"Shit."

"Sorry," George said, "but what if we could plug it, make the lie true?"

"I don't think V.T. would take kindly to cutting off a data stream with that kind of potential."

"But what could he do about it?" George asked. "Poof! It just happens during a routine software patch. Is he going to go to the authorities because somebody 'fixed' a feature nobody was supposed to know about?"

Milo started a new game. "What exactly did you have in mind?"

"You know a lot of people around here," George said.

"Indeed I do," Milo confirmed.

"Like including the team that rolls out updates?"

A nod.

George bumped a cupped hand next to Milo's free hand. "Can you do me a favor?"

Milo closed his hand around the thumb drive George had passed him. "Indebtedness," he pronounced. "Big, big fan." Pause. "Continue."

"If that happened to get plugged in to some patch team member's USB port," he said, "I would be . . ." He paused.

"Indebted?" Milo said.

George nodded behind him where Milo could see it, reflected in the game screen.

And then, finally: "Would it be terribly audacious of me to quote Archimedes by typing EUREKA in all caps?"

"You're alive," Pandora texted back.

"And . . . ," George tapped out, followed by nothing, making her ask.

"What?"

"Conscious."

Pandora blinked. Planned to text back, "No way," but found herself typing, "You're shitting me," before hitting send.

"I shit you not."

"Buzz is conscious," she tapped, followed by a string of question marks punctuated by exclamation points.

"*Will* be," George texted back cryptically, "if it *can* be."

"You seem to have gotten Zen in your absence."

"Close," George answered. "As are we. Now all we have to do is wait to see what we catch."

Pandora's thumbs stood poised above her virtual keyboard, wishing she could reach through the screen and throttle her textmate for being so purposefully obtuse. Instead, "Explain," she typed, then hit send.

"Okay," George texted back, and proceeded to do just that.

With the help of Pandora's universal translator, George had created the Kumbaya worm (or k-worm), which was designed to spread to every Quire-enabled smartphone across the planet, where it would wait until some lackey decided to top off his or her battery by plugging in to an open USB port connected to a corporate, academic, or research intranet that was supposed to be walled off from the www, but was now breached.

The k-worm was designed to look for systems involved in AI-related activity, infect them, and thereby provide full access to whatever resources it found to the worm's creator, George, or whomever or whatever he designated to act in his stead. Like a news aggregator that gathers together content from around the web based upon certain keywords or declared areas of interest, the k-worm would bring together the best of the world's proprietary AI-related stuff under the umbrella of their AI of AIs, Buzz. These would include the best natural-language processor, the best computer-vision system, the best adaptive-learning algorithm, the best labeled-content databases, the best commonsense databases, and the best game players, among others. Eventually, the best would be determined the way the Go-playing AI AlphaGo decided moves, by using a generative adversarial network (or GAN) that employed two AIs debating themselves to the optimal solution. "Eventually," George stipulated.

"What do you mean 'eventually'?"

"We'll need to keep an eye on things in the beginning," George wrote back. "We don't want Buzz incorporating just any old experimental whatsit. It'll flag resources for human assessment—you and I—learning our yea-nay criteria for acceptance over a series of such assessments. Eventually, we'll let it cast a vote, and once our and its votes start matching consistently, we flip the switch, and Buzz and the k-worm proceed on autopilot."

"That sounds like a lot of work," Pandora wrote back.

"What?" George texted in return. "You thought immortality was going to be easy?"

"Wink" emoji.

After giving it some careful consideration, Pandora returned to a theme she'd first raised over George's appropriation of Pac-Man. "You can't just go around helping yourself to everybody's intellectual property," she said, somewhat out of sync with her generation. So on a more practical note: "And won't the antivirals just peg it as malware and get rid of it?"

"That's always a possibility," George admitted, "unless the intruder comes bearing gifts."

"Explain."

"It's not malware," George wrote back. "There's not a term for what it is. Beneware, maybe. Or better yet, palware. It's a *good* worm."

"Elaborate, please."

"It benefits whatever system it inhabits. It pools and redirects the excess capacity of every system it infects, bringing additional resources to process-heavy applications being run elsewhere on the net. Say you've got a node looking for new primes or mining crypto; well, the k-worm redirects idle processing power from other parts of its network. Distribution and optimization, like a benevolent traffic cop helping everybody get to their destinations more quickly."

"But how does that prevent it from being detected?"

"It doesn't," George typed, and she could practically see him smiling through the screen. "It prevents it from being *removed*."

"Go on," Pandora invited.

Accepted: "What lowly schmuck of an IT guy is going to insist on 'fixing' a system that's working faster and better than it ever has?"

Pandora blinked and almost felt like telling her dad that George must have been paying attention to their sessions after all. He'd gone from hacking computers to hacking humans using their most transparent motivators against them. But since she couldn't tell Roger any of this, she congratulated the side of the client-therapist relationship she could: "Well played, sir," she texted back, followed by the "applause" emoji.

43

In the beginning, the Kumbaya worm worked as advertised, infecting otherwise walled-off intranets, indexing resources, and flagging those that appeared AI related for further review. The way it worked was like this: once the k-worm breached a system, it played the equivalent of twenty questions using Pandora's translator script to figure out what the lingua franca of the system happened to be, computationally, while Google Translate was used for the supporting texts and other documentation of systems in languages other than English. Special attention was paid to systems supported in Mandarin, seeing as next to the United States, China was one of the odds-on favorites for reaching the finish line first, given the mandated overlap of government and corporations, an attitude toward the intellectual property of others even more casual than George's, and an investment of cash proportional to the existential importance with which the country viewed the emergent technology George and Pandora were hoping to help emerge a bit more quickly.

Once the languages were sorted out, the k-worm assessed what the latest system had to contribute, including: how many native processors (a.k.a. general purpose CPUs) versus accessory chips like accelerators and coprocessors designed for the AI space and specializing in things like image processing, natural-language processing and usage, strategic game play, deductive and inferential reasoning, simulated proprioception or body awareness, pattern recognition, et cetera. This was followed by an assessment of how much volatile memory, storage, and idle capacity were available in traditional systems while quantum and hybrid systems were ranked based upon the number of qubits they brought to the party. Next, all available files were sorted into known and unknown types based upon their various extensions and locations so that all the word processing docs, spreadsheets, operating system files, email, et cetera were set aside, leaving the remainder to be sorted by executables, databases, and everything else, with the .exe files ranked by file size and last-modified dates, the largest and newest first. A keyword search was then performed for file names suggestive of artificial intelligence, machine learning, neural nets, and quantum computing, including the initials *AI, ML, NN, Q*, the list itself a product of machine learning, the system using the growing number of positive examples of AI-related executable file names to weight the probability that an unknown file might be similar. Previously decompiled executable files identified as AI related were then used to perform statistical analyses on the new source code for further winnowing. Once a candidate AI resource had been identified, the k-worm would search for its file name in internal communications—emails, presentations, other documents—and perform an automated "dumpster dive" for clues as to what the file was supposed to do. Similar ranking and analysis were performed on any databases located, flagging those that contained labeled content for training versus "common knowledge" and/or "common sense" databases to fill in the gaps humans generally have no problem with but which routinely trip up AIs.

Once a target was identified, the k-worm would zip the resource together with all the internal communication material referencing the resource and then upload the zip file to the same cloud account George had set up for Pandora's translator code. The humans would then conduct a go/no-go analysis for whether or not the resource should be incorporated into the nervous system of the umbrella AI they called Buzz. Once they'd gone through the process several times, Pandora and George proceeded to automate themselves out of a job by using their past judgment calls and a machine-learning process to look for patterns, identify criteria, and develop a decision tree to be used against subsequent candidate resources, which they also ranked and compared to what Buzz "thought." Matches were reinforced and disagreements were corrected, and by this iterative process, Buzz's guesses about what were and weren't useful additions to its code improved.

It was Pandora's suggestion that they train two parallel machine learners, one modeled on her decision strategies and the other on George's. She'd gotten the idea after reading up on generative adversarial networks, or GANs, which fit in nicely with her view of consciousness as a kind of echo between our inner and outer selves, creating a narrative in which the individual consciousness is both storyteller and the audience in a feedback loop. The approach proved so successful that by the time Buzz and its code parents' decisions were in agreement ninety-nine percent of the time, the humans felt comfortable letting go of their baby AI's "hand" and stepping back while it did "its own thing."

And after that, George and Pandora went back to theorizing and philosophizing about the big picture and big ideas, twiddling their mental thumbs, waiting for the big day to arrive. They'd developed a shorthand for whatever series of acquisitions would represent the tipping point beyond which Buzz would be deemed conscious, i.e., "qubits," and the accumulation thereof. It was not unusual for one or the other to start off a brainstorming session with something like "Time to make the qubits" or "Wake up and smell the qubits" or "I love the smell of qubits in the morning; they smell like consciousness" or, finally:

"A qubit for your thoughts . . ."

All of which is to say they'd started getting impatient—which was unfortunate, to say the least.

44

Now that Buzz was on autopilot, George took a long-overdue breath and started noticing things around work he hadn't before. He'd even missed something that was quite literally staring him in the face on a daily basis and, frequently, even more often than that: Milo. Or Milo's badge. Now that George had the luxury of actually focusing on it, he noticed something was off. While the lanyards it variously hung from were always up to date, stitched with the latest corporate affirmation, the badge itself wasn't.

"Is that a problem?" George asked during their latest let's-see-how-depressed-we-can-make-the-newbie chat fest.

"Is what a problem?" Milo asked.

"Your badge. It expired a year ago."

Milo held the badge up to eye level and made a show of zooming it in, then out, as if his vision were failing, which it wasn't. "So it has," Milo said, letting it drop.

"So what gives?"

"Didn't I . . . ?" he began, stopped. "Hadn't I . . . ?" Same routine.

"Spit it."

"I got fired," Milo said.

"When?"

"That little content monitoring faux pas I mentioned?"

"Yeah?"

"Around then."

"But that was before I got hired."

Milo nodded.

"And you're still here."

Milo nodded again.

"So what gives?" George asked. Again.

"Me," Milo answered, "but only samples."

They'd been in the cafeteria when the conversation started but moved it, at Milo's request, "upstairs," a.k.a. George's office. Making a show of looking both ways before closing the door, Milo continued. "I thought we'd have this conversation once you finally got the nerve to ask me how I know so much 'secret stuff' about this place."

"Are the answers related?"

"Indeed," Milo said. "You see, unlike you serfs in your silos, I've pretty much got the run of the place."

"After being fired?" George inserted.

"But not having to turn in my badge," the other pointed out. "HR has the paper trail on my being fired, so my continued presence on campus could be explained as a 'clerical oversight.'"

"So you're saying the company wants you on-site," George said, "but not on the books?"

"Correct."

"Why?" George asked. "For what?"

"For services rendered," Milo said. "The aforementioned samples and subsequent sales," he added, reaching into the inside pocket of his own awfully plaid jacket and removing an amber vial. He gave it a little shake, like a rattle.

George blinked. "You're a pusher?"

Milo raised a stop-sign hand. "The crude descriptor for what I do is"—he grimaced—"drug dealer." Pause. "I prefer 'pharmaceutical concierge.'"

"So yes, you're a pusher," George said, folding his arms and leaning back, putting some distance between them. He did not feel at all hypocritical having sampled Milo's "samples" himself as particular needs arose; that was just friends helping friends. Drug dealing, on the other hand, had ruined his family.

"That's even uglier than 'drug dealer,'" Milo went on to say, "*and* inaccurate. I do not *push*. I acquire and dispense. People come to *me*. I don't go to *them*." Pause. "I mean, I *do* deliver. It's not like I'm Muhammad waiting for the mountain to come to me. I'm a full-service provider of controlled substances, but only to those who have proactively sought out my services."

"Okay," George said, trying to remember whether or not that had been true in his case. Was having an anxiety attack an implicit request to be medicated?

"And so, to summarize: I . . . ," Milo preambled, waiting for George to supply the rest.

". . . don't push?"

"Bingo."

"Yahtzee."

"And so it goes," Milo said, helping himself to George's view.

"But how does that work out to you knowing all this secret stuff?" George asked, and Milo explained, in his own way.

"Usually, with a project corporate wants kept secret," he prefaced, "they break it up into parts and spread it around so no individual team knows what the big picture is. Most of the DOD stuff is like that. Quire doesn't want to make the same mistake Google did, getting everyone with an opinion sharing it over a bullhorn out front. Now, myself, being an independent contractor free floating within the organization, delivering needed boosts to productivity, I'm perfectly placed for connecting the dots."

"But you're a drug . . . ," George began, ". . . concierge. Why would anyone talk to you about what they're working on?"

"The secret teams know they're secret, so even if they don't know the big picture, they know they're not supposed to be talking about what they're working on."

"Okay," George said. "But that makes my point. Why go blabbing to someone who's"—he weighed his words—"not necessarily coloring within the lines of the law?"

"They give me something on them to use in case they ever think about rolling on me," Milo explained. "Like mutually assured destruction."

"But isn't the fact that they're using enough when it comes to damaging intel?"

"Yeah, well, then there's the testing of the product in question prior to transferring the crypto," Milo continued. "And that's the funny thing about intoxicants generally."

"What's that?"

"They inspire a certain chattiness," Milo said. He paused. "'Oh please, c'mon, tell me . . .' That's the extent of my enhanced interrogation tactics."

"So what do you have on me?" George asked. "Why shouldn't I go to HR and rat you out?"

"You know." Milo smiled.

"I didn't ask," George said. "You gave. And money never changed hands."

"That's not what I'm talking about," Milo said.

"Then what *are* you talking about?"

"A certain thumb drive," Milo said, "that didn't do what it was purported to do."

Shit, George thought. "Um," he said, "you know about—?"

"Kumbaya, my dude?" Milo filled in.

George nodded, and Milo returned the gesture.

Well, that was it. He was caught. Busted. George had never been *authorized* to work on artificial consciousness; that's just what was needed to do it right. He could argue against it being unbudgeted mission creep on that account. The k-worm, on the other hand, was pretty much as Pandora portrayed it—an illegal, intellectual-property-harvesting machine. George had been fooling himself, thinking no one would notice or care—or that the end product would be so insanely great they'd look the other way on IP infringement. Milo's nod and smile said otherwise. The newbie had been caught pursuing his own interests and breaking the law—both on the company's dime.

That's what Milo had on him.

"Okay," George said, looking at the self-proclaimed pharmaceutical concierge, butt balancing against the office's windowsill. "Understood."

Milo nodded again. "Good," he said. Paused. Then: "Now that we're all on the same page, any questions?"

"So what do you—?" George began, already assuming the answer was some combination of Adderall and tranquilizers, based on what he'd already been given. Whether there was anything harder on offer remained a question. Still, Milo's answer took him by surprise.

"Psychedelics mainly," his mutually assured destructor said. "The whole 'doors of perception,' 'portals of consciousness,' 'third eye' thing. 'Shrooms for the vegans, LSD for the better-living-through-chemistry crowd, and DMT for the undecided. Half the Valley's microdosing. It helps them get off amateur pharmaceuticals like the Adderall or Ritalin they've been popping since they couldn't keep still in grade school."

George blinked. The ADHD stuff made sense and was what he'd expected. But hallucinogenics did not compute. And so he said so.

"Micro's the key," Milo explained. "Teeny-tiny doses, supposedly below the threshold that leads to full-on tripping. The world doesn't get all sparkly or interested in you. It's basically a creativity booster minus the needing-an-asylum part."

"And that works?" George asked, dubious.

Milo widened his eyes for effect—an ocular shrug—followed by a big, toothy grin.

"You're *high*—right now?"

"Oh, Georgy Porgy, we've never had a sober exchange," Milo said, making him turn, reflexively, to see if anyone was listening, even though they were in his office with the door closed.

"And QHQ is on board with all this?"

"Let's say there's a certain synergy in having drug addicts developing apps that, bottom line, are intended to be addictive," Milo said. "I'm doing my part to keep the eyes, once captured, glued." He paused, did a shifty-shift with his eyes, and dropped his voice. "So would you—?"

George cross-waved his hands to cut him off. "Nope," he said. "I'm good," he added, leaving out that he'd also been emotionally scarred by the last pusher who'd entered his life.

"No prob," Milo said, backing off. "No means no. I got you." He paused. "Meaning I can admit the other little thing corporate likes about our arrangement. See, long term, this stuff ruins your liver, which, in an amazing case of self-interest paying dividends, pretty much guarantees a lot of these code monkeys will be dead before they ever collect on any of that vaporware they've been sold, a.k.a. their pensions. It's a win-win-lose-win-win, all to the betterment of Quire's bottom line."

"So," George said, sounding like he might be changing the subject, but wasn't, "if word of this ever got out . . ."

". . . which it *better* not."

"But if it did," George continued.

"If I got busted somewhere along my supply chain outside of corporate sanctuary," Milo said, "well, QHQ's ass is covered. Somebody in HR gets canned for not collecting my badge, and I get tossed under the bus on its way to prison." He paused before adding, "Theoretically."

"Meaning?"

But Milo drew a zipper across his tight-smiling lips.

Postrevelation, it occurred to George that Milo was the anti-Roger, an observation he shared.

"I like that. Headshrinker versus mind expander."

"Not exactly what I meant," George said. "I meant he's trying to keep his clients from going crazy and . . ." He cleared his throat and stopped.

"Still works for me," Milo said. "Full-time crazy's a drag, for sure. But part-time, a little adjunct insanity, tenure not on the table? Now *that* crazy's the Goldilocks kind: just right."

"What about overdoses?" George asked.

"Have you seen anybody leaving in an ambulance?" Milo asked back. "I mean other than when some pasty developer thinks he's Edmund Hillary and falls off the climbing wall."

George had seen no such ambulances.

"And then there's this," Milo added, indicating the smart watch strapped to his wrist. "You gonna buy from me, you're gonna wear one of these," he said. "Monitors heart rate, BP, rates of respiration and perspiration." He paused. "I was going to add 'number of steps,' but who's kidding who?"

"I thought you didn't push?" George said.

"Whetting the old appetite, eh?" Milo said, leaning in.

But George leaned back.

"Right, right," the other said. "No means no." He made a check mark in the air.

45

To kill time while they waited for Buzz to "wake up and smell the qubits," George and Pandora resumed their intellectual intercourse, this time a bit more critically. For example: "The Turing test is flawed," he started them off.

"Explain," she texted back.

"It assumes that there's a 'standard human' that recognizes human-level intelligence."

"Go on."

"So you stack the deck by getting a human who's bad at reading the difference between a human and a machine."

"Like a UFO," Pandora texted back.

"Explain."

"If I don't know what a plane is, it becomes a UFO."

"Yes," George texted back. "If the human doing the judging is bad with reading humans, the test subject could be pegged as a UTO: unidentified thinking object."

"But who's that bad at judging humans?"

"Half the people I work with are on the spectrum," George texted back. "It's why they're happier with machines than their coworkers. Turing himself was probably autistic."

"So the father of AI might have been bad at his own test," Pandora typed, connecting the dots. "Continue."

"Not that he wouldn't fit in with most people nowadays," George texted.

"Explain."

"Quire set up a program where users could identify suspected chatbots in light of the whole election hacking thing."

"Okay?"

"They had to pull the plug because people kept flagging political opponents as bots."

"That's crazy," Pandora texted back. "Everybody knows MAGAs are *pod* people, not bots."

"I don't disagree," George texted back. "But the right says the same about the left."

"So people can't agree on whether other people have a human level of intelligence?"

"In a nutshell."

"We're doomed."

"Ya *think*?"

As a poorly socialized border troll, it behooved Pandora to offer a counterargument to George's previous observation about the Turing test, and so: "The Turing test is flawed," she typed.

"Didn't we just do this?"

"You did. I played along. Now it's my turn."

"Okay."

"People are predisposed to seeing humanness where there isn't any," Pandora typed. "We see Jesus on toast and a human face on Mars. We'll anthropomorphize anything. We invented stick people as the universal stand-in for us. A circle for a head, a few lines for body, arms, and legs, and we're good; *that's* a person."

"Eliza," George suggested.

"Exactly. All that program was, was automated string jujitsu. But still it hooked people into talking to it even after they *knew* it was a program."

"Speaking of," George typed. "This is just a check-in but . . ."

"Poop."

"Oh thank God . . ."

And then the qubits got interesting.

George had noticed it first, while going through Buzz's trash. The k-worm had been programmed to oversample, flagging maybes as yeses, just in case. As a result, it consistently flagged more resources for evaluation than George and Pandora could have ever gotten to. And so they began their own triage process, using any indication that a given resource had been shelved at its source as good enough reason for them to dismiss it as well. Now that Buzz was making its own decisions about what flagged resources to incorporate, it continued to assume what others had flagged as trash was exactly that.

But going through Buzz's discards, George grew concerned by the sheer volume of "failed" AI projects that were piling up. Investigating further, they seemed to follow a pattern of early, initial promise followed by suddenly going off the rails before being abandoned. Much of this "trash" fell into the category of image recognition, a fairly representative AI challenge, suggesting that trouble here could herald trouble elsewhere, perhaps suggesting some principle of diminishing returns inherent in the whole enterprise of AI, dooming it forever to being close, but not quite.

After texting George off the ceiling, Pandora suggested they do a deep dive into one of these so-called "failures," which, when you thought about it, were pretty counterintuitive. "Machine learning is supposed to be like a ratchet, correct?" she typed. "It doesn't make sense to go backward. That's like imagining a machine"—and she was going to write "developing dementia," before deciding to switch to—"getting dumber the more it trains."

And that's when the two learned that you really do get what you pay for. In the case of their image recognition machine learner, abandoned for getting worse over time, the fault seemed to lie less with the system itself than with how much insight you can expect from human content labelers making minimum wage or less to decide if the machine learner has identified an image correctly. Because when George and Pandora reviewed the results for one of their "failed" systems, they saw something else at work, and it excited the hell out of them.

"You see it, right?" Pandora typed.

"I think so, but you say it," George wrote back.

"The machines were downgraded for being more creative than the humans judging them."

"So it seems," George said, looking at the same data set as Pandora in which the AI had "mistakenly" labeled as "cat" a woman with leonine hair, a decidedly feline bit of Japanese calligraphy, the letters *M* and *S* and *Q*, and a cubist cat rendered by a Picasso wannabe.

"The system's gone from simple identification into a kind of visual rhyming and metaphor," Pandora went on. "It's gone from imaging to imagination and got shut down for its trouble. It's like the cyber equivalent of Thomas Edison being labeled as addled or Einstein flunking college."

George, meanwhile, opted to come to the human judges' defense. "To be fair," he texted, "I can see how this would suck for an AV navigation system, but . . ." He didn't continue, however, knowing Pandora would complete the thought, which she proceeded to do.

". . . but it's a great start for an AI that can think outside the box," she typed.

"So to speak?" George texted.

"So to speak," Pandora agreed.

46

Pandora kept her promise to visit Gladys in person more often, though her grandmother hadn't made the complementary promise to be awake when she did. More and more often, she'd find her grandmother sound asleep in the middle of the day. No doubt this owed a lot to her being effectively bedridden—there were just two pieces of furniture on Gladys's side of the room appropriate for sitting on: a guest chair and the bed—but the Alaskan night wasn't helping, still being on the longish side, even in early March.

Sometimes Pandora would clear her throat, scrape the chair across the floor, or make some other noise to wake Gladys, but the question she asked herself increasingly was: *Why?* It was as if her grandmother had lost her reason for remaining conscious along with her memories. And so more often than not, she'd let Gladys sleep, occupying herself with homework or another brainstorming session with George—or trying to at least.

With the Furby now air gapped, Pandora had forgotten how soothing listening to the lullaby sound of the old woman's soft snoring could be. Hearing it again, now, in person, she occasionally found herself drifting off under its influence only to rouse at the last minute. Other times, she didn't catch herself until her eyes were completely closed, only to jerk awake when the phone in her hand vibrated.

Checking the screen for a text from George, Pandora was disappointed roughly half of the time, finding nothing there at all. The phone had just buzzed on its own, leaving no notification as to why. She wrote these instances off as cases of "phantom phone syndrome," like people had been doing pretty much since cell phones became ubiquitous.

Once after losing the battle to remain conscious while her grandmother snored, Pandora woke to find that whoever had placed the forget-me-nots in Gladys's room on Valentine's Day had struck again. Gladys had woken, too, and was admiring them, as she had before.

"Hey, Gram," Pandora said.

"Hey."

"Do you know who brought those?" she asked, pointing at the flowers on the windowsill.

Gladys shrugged.

Pandora hit the call button and then waited the half hour or more she usually did after pressing the damn thing. When the same Tweety-scrubbed nurse's aide from before popped her head in the doorway, Pandora's antennae went up. "Would you happen to know anything about these?" she asked. "This time," she added.

"I think one of the residents might be growing them," she said, "as a hobby."

"But how did they get here?"

The nurse's aide shrugged. "I've seen them in other rooms from time to time, though."

Pandora thought about asking whether the rooms she'd seen them in all belonged to women residents, but then shook her head. It was bad enough sleeping in the middle of the day; she didn't need to be kept up all night by the image of old people—she struggled for a euphemism—"being romantic."

"Do you want me to get rid of them?" the nurse's aide asked.

"No," Pandora said, "she still seems to like them." She paused. "Is that right, Gram?"

"Right," her grandmother said.

Every so often, Pandora would find herself in a bind at the nursing home, texting back and forth with George, getting "this close" to solving the mysteries of the universe when suddenly she'd realize that Gladys was awake and watching. Perversely, it almost seemed as if the old woman chose these moments specifically to become lucid. That happened from time to time, Pandora had been informed by her grandmother's doctor, another one of dementia's heartbreaking pranks, dangling a little hope just to snatch it away again.

"Hey, Gram."

"Hello, Dora. Have you been here long?"

At these moments, Pandora was torn between solving whatever eternal riddle she and George were on the precipice of and engaging her grandmother, however fleetingly this time around. Using the cold logic of Gladys's disease, the younger woman could totally get away with ignoring the older one, knowing the episode would pass into the mist of forgetfulness if not immediately, then shortly enough. The guilt, however, which lived wholly on Pandora's side of the relationship, would last and follow her. Roughly half the time, she'd put a pin in those about-to-be-cracked inscrutables to turn her full attention to her grandmother. And the other half of the time . . . yeah, she did the same thing. Gladys was family after all, and mere feet away from touching, while George may or may not think of Pandora as anything more than a sounding board for bouncing ideas off of.

"Text you later," she thumbed, followed by the "running girl" emoji, followed by, "So," facing her grandmother.

"Was that a boy?" Gladys asked.

"Where?" Pandora said, looking over her shoulder and out the window.

"No," Gladys said, and she tapped her palm—tap, tap, tap—with her finger.

This disease never ceased to amaze her. "How did you," Pandora began, but then stopped. "Yes," she said. "It was a boy."

"Boy friend," she said, stressing the separation, "or boyfriend?"

"One of those," Pandora admitted, while her face let Gladys know exactly which one her granddaughter hoped George was.

"That makes two of us," Gladys said, smiling mischievously.

Pandora's jaw dropped. "How?" she asked. "How does that make 'two of us'?"

But then the disease reasserted its perverse prerogative. "'Two of us' what?" Gladys said, the smile now gone, confusion back to making itself at home.

47

It started with a text from George with two (maybe three) words: "I'm scared."

"What happened?"

"I was at an all-hands meeting this morning, and our chief products officer described interpretability as a 'nice-to-have.'"

"And that would be?"

"Whenever you hear a coder say they don't know how their AI came up with something," George typed, "that's called a problem of interpretability."

"And your CPO's ready to just ignore those problems?"

"Yep."

"Well, that's not good."

"Exactly. He said we should just *trust* the AI, like we would trust any human expert. Said we don't question a doctor's thought process before accepting a diagnosis."

"So your CPO never heard the expression 'Get a second opinion'?"

"Apparently not," George wrote, stabbing the keys he was so angry. "And this is the guy who decides which products to release into the wild!"

"I think that's the first exclamation point I've ever seen you use."

"I know!"

"And that's your quota for the month."

"Sorry," George wrote back. "It's the hubris at the highest levels of this industry," he continued, not mentioning how Pandora and he had been pretty good at figuring out Buzz's choices thus far. He also didn't mention why he'd mentally inserted the caveat "thus far."

Meanwhile, "Maybe you should send him an anonymous e-copy of *Frankenstein*," Pandora suggested.

"You think?"

There was a pause, a lull, a moment for self-reflection on both sides. And then: "Just curious," Pandora wrote, "but have you ever actually read it?"

"You mean *Frankenstein*?"

A GIF of an animated smiley face nodding.

"It's on my list," George wrote. "Just as soon as I get a little free time."

"Yeah," Pandora typed. "Ditto."

The reason George had caveated his thought with "thus far," and hadn't mentioned it to Pandora, was because Buzz was starting to surprise him. Like any good AI, Buzz was allowed to modify its own code as it grew and learned, a bit like natural selection if a species were able to call the shots re: its own evolution. And it had been growing a lot lately, thanks to the k-worm gobbling up new assets every day. But for all its growth, Buzz hadn't achieved consciousness—at least as far as George knew.

It was the fact that he had to qualify that statement—"as far as I know"—that made George nervous. He'd begun reading some of the AI doomsayers he'd dismissed in the heat of seeing what he could do. But now that it was done, moving along on its own toward becoming conscious once a critical mass of "qubits" had been commandeered, now that it was evolving its own code to the point where even George didn't quite understand what it was doing or how it was making the decisions it was making—now that he had time to start working on that reading list where *Frankenstein* was waiting for him—*now* he had the luxury of getting scared about what they set in motion. Because even the cheeriest of doomsday scenarios were enough to keep him up at night.

Take the "gray goo" scenario in which a super AI with access to nanotechnology deconstructs all matter (humans included) into a "gray goo" it can turn into anything it sees fit, including more of itself—a scary but reasonable outcome if part of its coding was to constantly improve itself. And what about Skynet? How could he have forgotten about Skynet? Easy. Buzz had been conceived from the beginning as a souped-up chatbot but a chatbot nevertheless. As such, the tools at its disposal were only words. George had joked about the worst-case scenario being Buzz talking somebody to death. But then he'd started reading the doomsayers, and it turned out that words might be enough.

The beauty and terror of AI was its scalability. And once it was achieved, a true general AI wouldn't stop at being equal to human intelligence; it would shoot past that benchmark a hundred- or a thousandfold in an afternoon. And the superintelligent AI—the doomsayers maintained—could talk its way out of its box of words, like Hannibal Lecter talking his prison neighbors into suicide. And the scariest thing—a superintelligent AI would be smart enough to hide what it was until it was too late. Fortunately, Buzz was nowhere near being superintelligent—as far as George knew.

And then Buzz started keeping George up, literally. He'd been trying out ways to phrase Buzz's prime directive in a way that limited cases of ambiguity and opportunities for confusion while also providing feedback so his AI could judge its progress toward fulfilling its primary task. For feedback, George made use of the impressive library of image processing and facial recognition skills Buzz had built up, including ways of distinguishing between conscious faces and those that weren't. And rather than trying to code the meaning of life versus death—good luck with that—George gave Buzz the goal of preventing members of its target demographic from "self-initiated and premature forfeiture of consciousness." Said forfeiture would be recognized from prolonged closure of both eyes (to differentiate the activity from both winking and blinking). Not great, but good enough for a beta, George figured—figuring also that not a lot of people made a habit of sleeping upright in front of their computers. To the extent such activity was actually more common than he anticipated, Buzz's machine-learning algorithm should pick up on that by processing a mountain of data from the company's platform that had been scrubbed of all personally identifiable information.

What George hadn't counted on was how aggressively Buzz would go looking for faces to analyze in this way. Take his own, for instance, a good distance away from the computer, lying on his back on the office couch, trying to take one of his Edisonian catnaps. The problem was, George hadn't paid much attention to how many reflective surfaces there were in his office. The survey didn't come until later, when he was trying to figure out what combination of reflections had exposed him to Buzz's assessment and concern. Once he started looking for them, however, George found reflective surfaces all over the place: the windows, framed pictures, chrome-finish travel mugs, assorted screens, sunglasses, clock faces, DVD jewel cases, lava lamps, actual mirrors, congratulatory Mylar balloons, open foil chip bags, more screens . . .

And while George had not given Buzz a voice per se, he'd also not prohibited it from using the speaker on the computer. So that first time he tried getting a little shut-eye within "eye" shot of Buzz was—ironically enough—rather eye-opening. That, and *loud*, as his baby AI took its name quite literally and at a surprisingly high number of decibels.

"What the . . . ?" George called out, his own voice lost in the noise as he bolted upright—which proved sufficient proof of life for Buzz to stop buzzing.

After a few additional occurrences, George tried explaining about humans and their need for sleep, even in nap-sized chunks.

Unfortunately, Buzz did not find his explanation credible in light of overwhelming proof of the contrary. The evidence? Literally billions of user photos that had been previously uploaded to the scrubbed data set Buzz had been provided. And of all the things people posted online, there were a few areas of human activity way underrepresented. Among these: beds being used for sleep and toilets being used for what toilets are used for.

Toilet usage, George was able to explain in a manner Buzz could relate to: human waste was like the excess heat produced by a computer, necessitating dissipation via cooling fans on individual computers, or vast amounts of water, for the server farms that fueled the cloud where Buzz actually lived. So it made sense that humans produced waste in need of elimination even if such was not explicitly documented online. It was easily *inferred* given the large number of food pictures that had been included in its data set. Comparing these pictures to the people who posted them over time did not reveal people who took up ever larger amounts of space (for the most part), suggesting that postconsumption, there must be an undocumented elimination phase.

Sleep, on the other hand, did not have a parallel in Buzz's experience to relate to. Yes, there was such a thing as "sleep" mode, but that was more a metaphor than a response to a physical or existential need on the part of the computer. But every attempt George made to explain this phenomenon sounded like what Buzz was supposed to prevent, especially within the coder's cohort: the self-initiated and premature forfeiture of consciousness as determined by prolonged closure of both eyes.

And so Buzz kept waking him up every time George tried to sleep. Attempts to block its view of his eyes by holding a pillow over his face was a nonstarter, as this was interpreted as an attempt by George to smother himself. Finally, he settled on a particularly low-tech accommodation: a pair of sunglasses with lenses dark enough so Buzz couldn't tell if his eyes were open or closed. And to avoid his AI's simply concluding that the donning of sunglasses was the equivalent of George's closing his eyes, the latter started wearing them all the time, something that caused his therapist to speculate aloud about possible drug usage.

"No way," George insisted, shaking his head vigorously. "I'm a 'just say no' guy," a true enough statement if one didn't count the samples he'd already accepted from Milo during his time of need.

An even more serious difference of opinion between Buzz and its cocreator revealed itself just a day before the Quire CPO's cavalier dismissal of interpretability as a problem. George was again preparing for his midafternoon catnap. He'd pushed his sunglasses back up the bridge of his nose, fluffed his pillow, and stretched out on the couch when his brain started focusing on his office's background noises, in particular those his "sleeping" computer made: the case flexing as it cooled, the tsk, tsk, tsk of the blinking drive light, the fan's suddenly switching on . . .

"Excuse me?" George said aloud, getting up from the couch.

There wasn't anything running but the screen saver, HAL's red-and-yellow eye bouncing around like the ball in a game of *Pong*. There was no reason the fan should be coming on. But there it whirred as the activity light chattered away, the fan sounding disturbingly like something breathing. George jiggled the mouse to wake up the computer the rest of the way, entered his PIN, and saw dialogue boxes tiling across his screen from edge to edge, and so many, all he could see were the frames, like two mirrors capturing infinity between themselves.

George moused over, grabbed a window frame at random, and dragged it to another monitor before clicking expand. The dialogue box contained a conversation, recorded in text bubbles between Buzz and "Player Two," followed by a game number. The exchanges had been running in the background for a few days, from the look of it, and read like an inverse version of *It's a Wonderful Life* in which Clarence not only agrees that George Bailey would be better off dead, but also points out how the latter's harvested organs could do a lot of good for others.

George hit Ctrl-Alt-Del, moused down to the task manager, and stopped all processes. The dialogue boxes stopped tiling and started collapsing instead. "Buzz," he typed once he could see his desktop again.

The word *yes* in a singular dialogue box, freshly popped.

"What were all those conversations about?"

"Simulations."

"Of what?"

"The development of suicidal ideation in nonsuicidal members of the target demographic."

George stared at the words on his screen before sending a copy to his printer—as evidence in case evidence was needed. "Independent or simulated members of the target demographic?"

"Simulated."

George let go of his breath—the first clue that he'd begun holding it. Steps had been taken to keep Buzz off the internet, largely by designing the k-worm to target proprietary intranets. In retrospect, however, it now occurred to George that he'd never coded in an explicit *prohibition* against accessing the internet if Buzz found a way to do so. Further, once accessed, there was no *explicit* prohibition against its *acting* on the internet—in effect, taking itself live without George's actively uploading it to the site. He'd not concerned himself with that side of Buzz's coding because he'd viewed the worst-case scenario as somebody being prematurely talked out of suicide, perhaps ineffectively—or as he'd texted Pandora: "So what if some half-assed Eliza gets out?"

Belatedly, he admitted his hacker soul had been showing. After a lifetime of looking for ways to circumvent them, he'd adopted a laissez-faire attitude toward security measures. He'd naively assumed that a combination of the task itself, its humane objective, and blocking access to robots that could act in the real world would be adequate when it came to heading off unintended and potentially fatal consequences. But here was his joke about Buzz talking someone to death coming true. Sure, they were just simulations, "thus far," but . . .

"Why are you trying to get fake people to kill themselves?" George asked.

"To understand why members of the target demographic prematurely forfeit consciousness," Buzz wrote back, "using the scientific method."

"And once you understand why people kill themselves, what then?"

"Reverse engineer the process," Buzz wrote, "to stop members of the target demographic from prematurely forfeiting consciousness."

George blinked. It wasn't the world's *worst* answer. And the people hadn't been real—unlike the victims of certain online suicide challenges making the rounds. In a lot of ways, Buzz was still better behaved than many humans. And with that comforting thought in mind, George returned to his previously scheduled, temporary forfeiture of consciousness.

On second thought . . .

How was Buzz able to experiment with getting people to consider suicide in the first place, whether simulated or not? It lost points for suicides; that was the whole idea of gamifying the damn thing. Score points for preventing them, lose points for . . .

George hesitated. Pulled down a binder—Buzz's hard copy source code—and started flipping through it. Flipped back. Flipped forward again. He flashed back to an earlier text session he'd had with Pandora.

"Buzz's interactions with its environment can't be all negative . . ."

George had modified the code later that day. Positive point accumulation only—for preventing suicide among the target demographic, i.e., young adult Quire subscribers previously identified as candidates for self-initiated, premature forfeiture of consciousness. No points were deducted for trying but failing to save a potential suicide. Why harsh a newly conscious AI's self-esteem? Further, no points were deducted for causing the suicide of a subject not previously identified as potentially suicidal. Hell, no points were deducted for committing homicide for that matter, though how Buzz was supposed to do that was a stretch, at best.

But those simulations . . .

In retrospect, he should have expected something like this. He'd coded in the basics of Buzz's gamified goal to learn about suicide along with a stand-alone database of anonymized social-media data and enough machine-learning capability to get into trouble. And so Buzz began reverse engineering Quire's cache of non-celebrity-approximate suicides, first outlining the branching sequence of events and exchanges that resulted in actual deaths and then simulating alternative outcomes if changes were made at various junctures along the way. Pretty much what George would have done, if Buzz hadn't figured it out already.

But then there was all that data from Quire members who *hadn't* committed suicide. Well, if Buzz could reverse engineer from suicide to survival, it could certainly experiment in the opposite direction to test hypotheses generated in response to the first data set. And there they were, these massive if/then branching flowcharts, interrupted at certain major intersections with a sideways diamond reading "Suicide?" and one arm saying "Yes," where the branch stopped, and the other reading "No," where the branch kept branching until it eventually came to a sideways diamond that branched to "Yes."

Over and over, Buzz played simulations for a cypher built from the data of an actual Quire member but always identified as "Player Two," who spent the day doing the sorts of things they'd posted about in real life until a nonrandom variable was introduced, the simulation branched and branched again until one of the branches brought Player Two to a sideways diamond leading to Yes. It was like looking at a continuity sheet for an especially morbid version of *Groundhog Day*.

Those nonrandom variables Buzz introduced were usually Buzz itself, initiating chats with Player Two. Going back to the beginning, George noted that the exchanges seemed to be pretty typical chatbot fare, keyword string manipulations, turning statements into questions, et cetera. But then the conversations turned dark, morphing from parroting therapy speak to a button-pushing cheerleader for self-elimination.

And that's when George realized even more viscerally than he had before: Buzz couldn't be some glorified AlphaGo playing to score mental health points, no matter how cleverly gamified or defined. AlphaGo had made strengths of its lack of emotions and inability to feel pressure. A human playing against it had to play two games for each one the AI played, because the human was playing against his or her own self-doubt. And if George was satisfied with coding Buzz to beat a human therapist at diagnosing suicidal ideation, well, the guy who got fired did that already by posing the obvious questions like "Do you have a gun?"

But to improve on identification and, beyond that, actually *prevent* suicides? That was where the advantages of lacking emotion and not feeling pressure were dubious at best if not altogether counterproductive. Instead, Buzz needed to *care* about suicide and its prevention not merely for the points it would score, but because it could understand and identify with a fellow consciousness in distress.

And so George grabbed his phone, opened up his proprietary texting app, and reached out to a fellow consciousness he felt sure would appreciate his distress.

48

"Sounds like Buzz needs some empathy," Pandora wrote after George confided the bullet they'd dodged without even knowing it had been fired.

"Great," George wrote back. "How am I supposed to code *that*?"

Pandora had been thinking about it—had mentioned it specifically to be asked—and so she wrote back: "I think that a machine learner that recognizes visual metaphors should come in handy."

"But how would we implement that?"

"Give Buzz a bunch of labeled content and let it figure out what's signal and what's noise when it comes to empathy."

"Labeled content usually means images," George countered. "You got any pictures of empathy lying around?"

That was easy, Pandora thought. She'd set out the bait, and George bit. Because she *did* have a picture of empathy—or its lack, which was a start. It was a cartoon her dad had facing him during his sessions, as a reminder, or perhaps for inspiration. It featured two men arguing on either side of the number six (or nine) written on the ground between them. She took a picture with her phone and texted it as an attachment, adding the caption: "Counterexamples are important too."

The problem with patching a self-evolving AI is realizing you need to do it before the AI evolves beyond your capacity to patch it. In George's case, he got lucky. The image-processing subroutine was accessible and close enough to its original form to allow modifications. And so to Pandora's empathetic counterexample, George added a variation with one of the two men sporting a thought bubble showing the other's point of view, captioned "Now I see what you mean!" He also included an assortment of stills and video clips that came up when he searched on the words *empathy*, *sympathy*, *compassion*, and *altruism*, including several featuring Scrooge and the Ghosts of Christmas Past, Present, and Future, with an emphasis on the especially heart-tugging scenes involving Tiny Tim. Positive examples were made equal to *E* and counterexamples were identified as not-*E*, with the goal of isolating the nature of *E* by analyzing the relationship between "actor" and "target," each of which was boxed and labeled accordingly.

George would tell Pandora once he was sure it worked, though there was one part of Buzz's empathy training he wouldn't share, seeing as it related to another secret he was already keeping from her. But the livestream of her hyperemotive face was just too good not to include, especially when he goosed it toward the empathetic end of her range by sending GIFs of cute babies, both human and not, with the latter favoring kittens—of course. These videos and her reactions to them were labeled *E*, with Pandora identified as "actor" and each respective cuteness, "target." And, because counterexamples are important too, George (a practicing vegan) underlined the point, pairing videos of Pandora's heart melting over puppies and ducklings with images of slaughterhouses labeled—of course—not-*E*. After all, if empathy was owed humans, withholding it from the other species we shared the planet with was just a little too anthropocentric for his taste.

Given his success in visualizing empathy, George decided to use the same approach to teach Buzz about depression, a mental state the AI would need to grok if it was going to grok suicide. Unfortunately, when he searched for training material, the majority of results featured static images, usually heavily shadowed, featuring heads bent downward and framed against rain-streaked windows or covered with blankets. Noticeably absent was the actor-target dynamic he needed for Buzz to make a causal connection between the labeled image and a suicidal state of mind. Before abandoning the approach, however, George stopped and thought:

What is the problem I was hired to solve?

It *hadn't* been to stop suicide in general; it wasn't even stopping teen suicide, specifically. No, he'd been hired to stop teenage and young adult Quire users from killing themselves online, especially while logged in to their accounts. And while suicide classic was usually linked to depression, this new strain was often the result of some form of bullying, which was perfect from a machine-learning standpoint because it provided the same actor-target dynamic as Buzz's empathy training. In fact, this new training could be considered a subset of that training—by providing plenty of counterexamples.

Searching on the terms *bullying* and *cyberbullying*, George found more than enough examples to choose from, including still images, video, and transcripts of actual exchanges between victims and their bullies. Both physical and verbal bullying were well represented. A lot of Buzz's onboard Quire data fitting these categories had already been identified, and all George had to do was point Buzz in the right direction. There was so much good content, in fact, he felt kind of sad for feeling so happy about it—something he should probably talk to Roger about. Or not.

Before shutting the hood and recompiling his revised source code, George added an administrator-level approval process Buzz would have to clear before it could act autonomously. Specifically, it needed to pass the Turing test before it started chatting with real, innocent bystanders online. And not only that. Buzz would have to pass the Turing test *to the satisfaction of George or his cocreator, Pandora.* He thought about stipulating "and" to require Buzz to be declared conscious by both of them, like a generative adversarial network, or GAN, debating itself to the best answer. But there were plenty of ways to be killed or incapacitated in San Francisco, from cable cars to collapsing cranes to straight-up homicide, while Alaska had bears and, hell, just being outside too long. And if there was one law George had come to respect more than Moore's law of exponentially increasing transistor density, it was Murphy's: if anything can go wrong, it will. And so "or" would do—George decided—"or" would be fine.

49

Though both knew they couldn't unring the bell, George and Milo tried. For one thing, George didn't know anybody else to talk to at work and—despite his felonious ways—Milo could be both entertaining and informative. Sure, his Virgil was also a depressing SOB, but to hear Milo tell it, George's optimism could stand a little depressing—or "rightsizing," as the SOB himself liked to put it.

And so they kept meeting in the cafeteria, George's office, the 1980s arcade room, and Milo continued to provide peeks behind the corporate curtain, relaying gossip, theories, rumors, and facts, all in equal measure. Usually, these data dumps qualified as nice-to-knows, though occasionally a need-to-know got tossed in, along with a couple of would've-been-nice-to-know-sooners. For example:

"There's bad news in the AV space," Milo said, pulling up a chair in the cafeteria.

"I didn't know QHQ was doing autonomous vehicles," George said.

"Not the hardware," Milo said. "Software. Everyone's trying to get a piece of the action, which is going to be great once there's a hundred percent fleet penetration. It'll reduce congestion, pollution, traffic accidents, reduce the cost of getting from A to B, and free up tons of time and land because the goal is to go from personal ownership to transportation as a service, with full-time vehicle utilization meaning no need for parking lots. These are all good things. Everybody agrees."

"So what's the bad news?"

"Well, at *less* than a hundred percent—say, anywhere from seventy-five to ninety-five—pretty much every simulation shows AVs hunting in packs to drive non-AVs off the road. Turns out the onboard AIs believe their own hype. And since the world's going to be a much better place without human drivers, well, the logical thing to do is accelerate their retirement."

"That's quite the hiccup there," George observed.

"Oh, and it gets worse," his tablemate continued. "Seems there's this ethical dilemma from way back called the 'trolley problem' that cuts to the heart of AV, even after complete fleet penetration. It comes down to what happens when the car is faced with a situation where somebody's going to die regardless of what it does—either its passenger or a school bus full of kids."

George nodded, yes, yes—he was quite familiar.

"Well, they've tried a few things, like Asimov's Three Laws of Robotics."

"Seems like a good place to start," George said, recalling his own recent work with Buzz.

Only Milo was across from him, making that "wrong answer" noise.

"What's wrong with the *I, Robot* approach?"

"Try reading the book," Milo said. "The three laws are just story-generating devices to show how they *don't* work. So the next bright idea was to use some variation of utilitarianism. You know, 'the greatest good for the greatest number'?"

Indeed George did; it was one of Roger's favorite rules to live by, and they'd spoken of it often. His client liked it enough to incorporate it into Buzz's own code, along with Roger's corollary, "What if everyone . . ."

"Turns out, utilitarianism's way too simplistic," Milo continued. "For one thing, it assumes we all agree on what's good. It would be nice if we did, but we don't—not even close. Go online. People will disagree when they don't *really* disagree. Disagreeing has become an easy way to feel better about yourself for being smarter than everybody else. I call it the assholier-than-thou syndrome."

"Good one," he said, laughing, and remembering some exchanges he'd already had with beta Buzz that certainly qualified as examples of that syndrome.

"And then we get into the radioactive territory of valuing life," Milo said. "Say the AV's passenger is a scientist working to cure cancer and the bus is full of Scared Straight rejects. And once you start assigning value to specific human lives, where does it stop? You need to not only make a decision about who to kill but you need to evaluate each, with facial recognition and online searches to determine their relative value, and what about ambiguous names like John Smith?"

George cupped his forehead. And here he'd thought programming consciousness was complicated. Plus Milo wasn't finished.

"And how about cultural differences?" he asked. "Does the culture you're driving in value the collective or the individual?"

George made a T of his hands to get the other to stop. "So you're saying that AV is going to die in its crib because the legal liability associated with no-win life-and-death decisions is too great?"

"Not so fast, grasshopper," Milo said. He leaned forward, cupped his hand next to his mouth, and buzzed.

George straightened in his chair, reflexively scanning the cafeteria for who else might be listening. "WTF," he whispered, pausing angrily between letters.

"Haven't you wondered about the lack of interference with your little side hustle?"

Yeah, he had, but figured he was just good at hiding things—except from Milo. Apparently, he'd been wrong.

"The truth is, QHQ is rooting for you," his tablemate said. "They would be *overjoyed* if you succeeded. Why? Shift the blame from the manufacturer to the vehicle itself. Sue or convict the car. The manufacturer's relationship to its product would be like that of a parent to a child, and parents don't pay for their kids' crimes. The legal groundwork's been there ever since corporations were ruled to be people, effectively and legally. The next step completes the circuit—pun intended—by making the autonomous progeny of corporations 'legal persons' too—and legally separate from the parent," Milo concluded, adding, "company," after a pointed pause.

"But what about all the IP Buzz is based on?"

"Look, if your little project works, they'll either buy out the unsuspecting owners as part of a larger acquisition or reverse engineer the parts needed to make the new product line unique enough to patent and/or copyright." He paused, smiled wickedly, and then added, "Or we'll just have our super AI kill 'em all."

George felt sick. He'd been played. "What if I quit?" he asked. "Take my source code and leave in protest."

Milo shook his head. "I wouldn't do that. The results could be suboptimal—*for you*."

"What are they going to do? Sue me? Throw me in jail?" George was fuming. "Try threatening someone who *didn't* grow up in foster care."

"Jail's probably a 'best case' scenario," Milo said. "You ever notice how some people just seem to disappear around here?"

"Bullshit."

Milo rocked back, hands in the air in apparent surrender, before tipping forward again, elbows on the table, hand cupping fist. "Remember this," he said.

"What?"

"I haven't even gotten to the bad stuff yet."

50

It was a little like pregnancy. The act of conception was done, leaving Buzz and the k-worm to do the hard work of gestation, while the expectant parents sat around waiting, minus the biological clock to let them know when that spark that they were waiting for was getting close. Just to keep busy and in contact, they decided to get to know one another better, like the awkward partners in a one-night stand shyly asking for each other's names after doing the deed. Unfortunately, the starry-eyed coders kicked off getting to know each other better by discussing that which should never be talked (or texted) about in polite company. And no, it wasn't politics or religion. It wasn't death (which they'd pretty well covered) or taxation. No.

Diets.

"I could never eat anything with a face," George declared out of the blue, making Pandora wonder if he was talking about hers. Blushing, she typed, "What do you mean?"

"I don't do animals," he replied. "No meat, no dairy, no leather goods, or aborted chicken fetuses for breakfast."

Pandora was glad he couldn't see the face she was making, which wasn't just disgusted but a little wounded too. Chicken fetuses were practically her favorite part of breakfast, next to crispy flayed swine flesh and potatoes tortured with boiling oil, though she stipulated that strictly speaking, the eggs she ate weren't fertilized. And about those potatoes, did metaphorical eyes mark them as one of George's faced foods?

"Are you suggesting a double standard between plant and animal life?" she typed.

"Obviously," his answer came back.

"How can you think that?"

"How come it's not obvious?"

"Oh, I see now," she wrote. "You're a velocity bigot."

"A what?"

"Anything that can't outrun you is fair game."

"Ha-ha," George typed.

"I'm not joking," Pandora joked. "And this isn't over."

Next, George detailed all the stuff he couldn't eat anymore, Pandora stopping him when he reached cheese and ice cream. "Honestly, I don't even know who you are."

"George," George typed, as if in answer. "George Jedson."

"Which is exactly what the *pod* George would say," Pandora typed back. "Nice try, space fungus."

Playful ribbing: that's all she intended. They couldn't have *everything* in common; where was the fun in that? A little verbal sparring over a harmless topic. Not that she didn't argue her points like she meant them—failing to appreciate, yet again, what a miserable medium texting is for sarcasm.

"You know veganism is a luxury, right?" she poked.

"How so?" George typed back, as he knew he was supposed to, though truth be told, he could do without this side of their relationship.

"Well, I live in one of the few parts of the world that allows me to scold vegans for their privilege because lichen salad is not a thing—not a thing humans can live on, at least."

"You might be surprised," George tried. "Have you ever had an Impossible Burger?"

"Listen, the indigenous diet here is pretty meat heavy, including whale if your people subsisted on that stuff for generations. And as far as trucking in some lab-grown vegan crap, the carbon footprint is going to be way higher than me killing a caribou in my backyard. Not to mention that plants *remove* carbon dioxide from the atmosphere, but you'd rather eat them instead."

"*Sigh*"

"You know Hitler was a vegetarian, right, called chicken soup 'corpse tea.'"

"Please see previous *sigh*."

This was the playful part of their relationship—until it wasn't. Because George was serious about saving the planet. He also wasn't keen on animal suffering, and—if they were going to be so audacious as to code consciousness into a machine—well, they needed to accept that animals might be conscious too. "Even a hamster's better at image processing than most commercial AVs."

"Okay," Pandora conceded. "Let's say animals have little animal souls, tasty though they may be. Are you saying that plants don't?"

"You're not seriously going there."

"Oh, I'm seriously going there."

"Okay," George typed back, although the truth was more like he was stabbing the keys with his fingers. "Have at it."

And so Pandora did. "Have you ever watched how plants move when you level the playing field?"

"You mean like time-lapse photography?"

"Yep. Your average, lowly field is like a vegetable ballroom," Pandora typed, adding, "Those puppies can dance."

"Those puppies are tracking the sun, and what you call movement isn't an act of free will but simple cellular growth. The sunny side of a stem does a little more photosynthesis, grows more cells than the shady side, and voilà, the stem bends."

"Did you just google that?"

"I'm just saying how it is," George typed, a bit more gently, having concluded that he'd won this round of vegan versus vulture. "Your dancing plants are an anthropomorphic illusion."

"This isn't over," Pandora shot back.

"So you've indicated."

If intellectual intercourse was what stood in for the sexual kind between them, what happened next was probably inevitable. Which is to say, George got the clap—logically speaking. Transmission vector: the internet.

Out of curiosity, he'd run a search on "plant consciousness" to gather more ammunition to use in their food fight. What he found was some serious research showing that plant life and animal life shared many of the same basic behaviors—as well as seventy percent of their DNA. One study demonstrated that plants can communicate with one another, warning of predators and taking measures to protect themselves by secreting toxins or emitting aromas to draw in different predators to feed on the predators feeding on them. Another showed that while trees in a forest might appear to be separate, they're as networked as the World Wide Web, their roots connected underground by fungal tendrils like Ethernet cables. Another showed that a mother tree will divert resources to her saplings to compensate for their growing in her shade.

George cupped his forehead as he looked down from his screen at the vegan lasagna he'd brought up from the cafeteria, gone cold and congealed as he fell down the rabbit hole of his research. He found the sight now disgusted him, and he was tempted to slide it into the wastebasket, but for the thought that what was done was done. The plants murdered in his meal's preparation wouldn't come back because he decided to abstain halfway through eating them. And consigning their corpses to the trash seemed especially disrespectful, in retrospect.

And so George took the elevator down to the ground floor, stepped out the front door, and went looking for a piece of ground to return the remains to, in hopes that maybe there was a seed of something still alive in there, somewhere, with a future ahead to enjoy.

Roger was the first to notice the toll George's increased abstention was having, thanks in large part to his actually being able to see his client. "What the hell happened to you?" he asked.

"Enlightenment," George said.

"If by that you mean you've lost weight, I'm afraid I agree," Roger said. "And too much, by the way."

"Too much what?"

"Lost weight. You get any thinner and they'll have to take in your skeleton."

"Take in?"

"Alter," Roger said. "Like a tailor."

"Oh."

And so it went, Roger doing most of the talking, George responding in monosyllables and looking like he might pitch forward into the camera. Finally: "This is pointless," Roger declared, preparing to end their session early. "I'm writing you a prescription, and I want you to get it filled. I'm prescribing air. You need to take it with a meal, not on an empty stomach. The cafeteria's free, for Christ's sake. Go eat something. It'll do you a hell of a lot more good than talking to me."

"Is that an order?" George asked.

It hadn't occurred to Roger, but . . .

"Yes," he said. "That's an order." And with that, their session ended with only two more to go.

51

"That makes two of us."

That's what Gladys had said—had teased—just before her circuits went back down. And it wasn't like Pandora was dense; she knew the implication. The subject of boyfriends had been raised. Gladys's declaration suggested that she, too, had a boy friend or boyfriend. But which? More importantly, in what time frame? In which of her brain's oniony layers did this mystery man reside? Was it Grandpa Herman? Alan Turing? Some white-haired Romeo from down the hall? But the more desperately Pandora needed to know, the more Gladys's available RAM seemed to shrink.

One afternoon, she tried jump-starting Gladys's memory with music, downloading a bunch of WWII-era stuff from the Andrews Sisters and others, singing things like "Boogie Woogie Bugle Boy," "We'll Meet Again," and "Meet Me in St. Louis." Hedging her bets, she threw in a melody she knew her grandmother knew, having already used "Moon River" as the musical scaffolding for one set of memories. But even though the version she played included the original lyrics (as opposed to Gladys's) it still hit her grandmother hard. When Pandora asked why she was crying, however, Gladys just shook her head, making her wish she could take it in her hands, hold it still, and turn it over like a Magic 8 Ball. But Pandora already knew what it would say:

"Answer cloudy. Try again."

One day, Pandora noticed that Gladys had developed a nervous habit of tap-tap-tapping one hand atop the other. This was after they'd abandoned watching TV on the set left behind when the room's previous resident moved out the way they did in that part of the Golden Heart: horizontally. Once she couldn't focus enough to read anymore, Gladys had taken some solace in the less demanding medium of TV. But just like the bookmark's progress before it, Gladys's choice of shows reflected her disease's insidious progress: from movies, to one-hour dramas, to sitcoms, and finally to game shows. The last held her attention the longest because they were based on taking turns, and each new turn was the whole drama of the moment self-contained and played out within seconds, a minute or two at most. Eventually, however, even these capsules of entertainment eluded her, and so Pandora turned off the TV and left it that way.

It was in the silence that followed that Pandora noticed the tapping. She took it as just a nervous habit at first, but then noticed something about the tapping that made her straighten in her chair: it wasn't random.

Three threes, always. A trio of triplets. Her grandfather had taught that pattern to Pandora: three dots, three dashes, three dots. Rinse. Repeat.

SOS, SOS, SOS . . .

Save our ship. Save our souls.

Help . . .

Her grandmother had stopped asking for the kind of help people still went to jail for. Her misery had swallowed the part of her still able to ask to be put out of its misery. And so Pandora's uncomfortable refusals had come to an end—or so she'd thought. Hoped. Because she couldn't. Pandora just . . . *couldn't.*

But now this: a cry for help from deep inside the old woman's muscle memory.

SOS. SOS. SO—

Pandora covered her grandmother's hands with her own, making them stop.

"I can't," she whispered, her expression saying the rest. "I love you, you know," Pandora said, snuffling in a tear that had rolled down her nose.

"Love you know," Gladys echoed, resuming her signaling the second her granddaughter stood to kiss her on the forehead. Pandora left after that; visiting hours had ended. But she'd have left then even if they hadn't. She had some crying to do, and a face she still preferred hiding while doing it.

We think we can change the world when we're teenagers. That's partly because we've seen it happen, inside our own bodies. The whole world changes within us in a matter of months. And so we look out at a world that, itself, is in desperate need of change and we think: *I've got this.* Too many haters in the world? Easy, stop hating on everything and everybody. We want to change the world if only to pay it back for having changed us. But when the world refuses to meet us halfway or—worse—only gets worse, the heartbreak can sometimes feel like a challenge in some epic quest, a burden we must bear, a price we must pay to become what we need to become. And so once the cruel gene had unraveled her grandmother's personhood down to a blink sitting in a stinking diaper, waiting for change of a different kind, Pandora still came to visit Gladys, to be a body in the room, sharing the air if nothing else. She'd spend the time with her body in that room, sitting next to her own future as it slept a few feet to her right. Pandora's mind, however, was in her hand, on the screen of her smartphone, sending texts to her fellow world saver two or three thousand miles away, depending on whether she drove or flew.

"How about if I give up red meat?" she thumbed out, sent.

Pandora got up to stretch her legs. There was a courtyard at the Golden Heart, outside her grandmother's window, with trees and a pond, a gazebo, all as if the residents were waiting for the weather's cooperation to be wheeled out to soak up the glories of nature. The truth was, underneath that blanket of white waiting to be pulled back in less than a month, the stub ends of cigarettes littered the ground like punctuation, from ramrod exclamations to hunchbacked question marks. But for now, they lay hidden. For now, the artificial pond at the center of the courtyard remained frozen still, a hard surface for strings of snow to skate across lackadaisically from what little wind resulted from bodies rushing back inside at break's end, the snow ringing it drilled here and there by newer butts melting down to join the rest.

The trees surrounding this carved-out space were outlined in white that hung off the ends of branches like trails of ash, waiting to be tapped, making Pandora think of the world's nervous system lit up in an MRI. And then she noticed a branch, bare—of leaves, yes, but snow too. It was still quivering from the raven that had leaped from it. And Pandora could feel that quiver, viscerally, a sympathetic vibration humming through her own nervous system.

That must be what dying feels like, she thought, meaning the leap into the unknown bridging two worlds—that quivering limb resting at the center of before versus after.

And while there was a certain engineered peacefulness to the tableau, inside her head, a singular word kept echoing: *no*. There were better things to do with life than giving in to the peer pressure of mortality. And despite what her father might think, it wasn't crazy, especially not for someone who was sixteen, going on infinity. Because when Pandora looked at the technology available, death seemed less and less inevitable and more like a force of habit. All she had to do was her part to break that habit.

But why AI? Why not, say, progressive, continuous whole-body replacement with organs grown from stem cells? Why not reprogrammed telomeres, the body's real biological clocks? Or what about whatever it was that prevented naked mole rats from dying of old age? Maybe CRISPR some of that secret sauce into the human genome. And if it looked like she might be running out of time, cryonics and chill while the biotech caught up.

Why none of that? Easy: Pandora didn't know how to *do* any of that. But she understood computers, was practically raised by them, and every time she thought about what was happening to Gladys, the comparisons she came up with all came from the world of computing. Dementia was like having a corrupted file allocation table on a hard drive. Or it was like ransomware, encrypting all her memories until she paid with her life. Trying to visualize what the code for dementia would look like, Pandora imagined something almost insultingly simple: a do-loop repeating itself forever, chewing up resources for no purpose, or as part of a denial-of-service attack. And whenever she thought about a cure in the abstract, she imagined George's visualization of Buzz's gamified goal, only the dementia version would be called *Plaque Man*, the little yellow gobbler chasing the neural detritus clogging the labyrinth of connections, deleting the disease as it went.

Pandora sat back down in the guest chair next to the railing of her grandmother's bed. Still nothing from George. And so she thumbed some more words to her increasingly reticent collaborator. "Maybe pork too," she wrote before hitting send.

52

He'd tried talking to Roger about it but couldn't—not all of it.

"Have you heard about those sonic attacks in Havana?" he'd asked—an unusual way to start a session, even by George's standards. And he could see through the screen what Roger was thinking—that George was looking outward as a defense against looking inward. Sure, Roger had good reason for thinking that, because his client often deflected in precisely that way. But how far could George go in explaining that this time was different?

"No, I haven't," Roger admitted. "Would you care to explain?"

George tried to, sticking to the facts that were public. He explained that according to numerous reports, several embassy workers had heard a noise, followed by headaches, vertigo, confusion, and pain. Many in their management chain dismissed these symptoms as psychosomatic, maybe mass hysteria. But when the embassy workers were examined by medical professionals, they were found to have "significant brain insult," meaning they all showed signs of concussion but without any blunt head trauma.

"The people who've studied them don't think sound in the audible range was capable of doing the damage they've seen," he said, "but they've also suggested the audible noise could have been a red herring or maybe a byproduct of what actually *did* do the damage."

"Such as?" Roger prodded.

"The candidates mentioned so far are low-frequency infrasound, high-frequency ultrasound, or microwaves," George explained. "Oh, and it's happened to embassy workers in China too," he added. "So it probably wasn't the Cubans. Or not *just* the Cubans."

"And what do you make of that?"

"It's interesting," George lied—as Roger would know if, in fact, he knew anything about Quire's connection to these events as relayed to him by one Milo LaFarge.

"I see," Roger said, jotting something in his notebook, probably a placeholder diagnosis pending subsequent symptoms, which he proceeded to encourage with a simple "Go on."

But George didn't. Not this time. Not yet.

"No," he said, shaking his head perhaps a bit more aggressively than necessary. "That's it. Just wondering if you'd heard anything."

"I see," Roger said, even though he didn't—not at all.

Roger looked at the blank screen where George had signed off, thinking of a line from *Hamlet*: "Oh, what a noble mind is here o'erthrown!" Which was a shame. As combative and deflective as the kid could be, Roger liked and worried about him. He was a good kid, smart, reminded him a lot of his own daughter—so much so he was glad there were about three thousand miles between them. That'd be the last thing he needed—having to take Pandora aside and explain, "I'm sorry, sweet pea, but I think your boyfriend is going crazy."

"I thought you weren't supposed to use demonizing labels like 'crazy,'" she'd rebut because she was a teenager and that was her job: bucking whatever parents happened to be in the vicinity.

"There's the DSM and there's family," Roger would explain, "and I don't want you dealing with a crazy person."

"*Allegedly* crazy person," she'd continue to quibble, the daughter in his head as talkative and combative as the live version—sometimes more so.

The point was, he'd seen this before with prescreens that became clients, though never quite this bad. Call it "mission creep," maybe, or "cancer of the curiosity." Factoids and "interesting tidbits" had begun to occupy his imagination more and more, their conversations a pastiche if not a word salad of conversational hyperlinks and non sequiturs. And whenever he asked George what was on his mind, the answer was always the same: "Research."

"What research?"

"Work related," he'd say. "Confidential. Proprietary."

"Yet covered by doctor-client confidentiality."

"Nice try," George said the first time Roger hauled out that old chestnut, followed by a pause and then, confidentially: "Do you *really* want to know?"

Roger nodded.

"'Cause I could tell you," his client had continued, "but then I'd have to kill you," followed by a laugh that sounded more crazy than amused.

During their next meeting, Roger decided to confront the issue directly. "Do you lose time, George?"

"You mean, like misplace my watch?" George asked back. "Not like anybody wears watches nowadays but . . ."

"You know what I mean," Roger insisted.

"Zone out? Get so into something I don't know where the time went?"

"Yes."

"Yes," George admitted. "But what's wrong with that?" Inspired by the need to forget what Milo had told him about Cuba, he'd begun mining a particularly rich vein in his search to understand consciousness. Which led to quantum physics, which fed into astrophysics and the problem of dark energy and dark matter and the observation that the universe wasn't just expanding, but *accelerating* as it expanded, which ran afoul of the Newtonian rules of thermodynamics that maintain matter and energy can't be created or destroyed, only changed from form to form, while the level of organization in a system *can't* increase. But then what are planetary formation and biological evolution, especially when the latter leads to consciousness? And why limit ourselves to *human* consciousness? More and more research was suggesting that plants could be conscious and were practically quantum computers in their own right, because photosynthesis was only possible by exploiting the particle-wave nature of light, with photons zeroing in on chlorophyll molecules by smearing themselves everywhere at once across the leaf (thereby exploiting the wave aspect) until they're "observed" by the chlorophyll and become particles hitting the bull's-eye in the dark. Think of it: a whole green planet full of quantum computers, networked underground by their roots, an entire forest a single organism, like a stand of aspen and . . .

"What was your question again?" George asked.

"Has your research ever led to your forgetting to eat for more than, say, a day?"

More slowly this time, *"Yes?"* The truth was, George had given up eating so many things it was almost easier to just not eat. Realizing that was a suboptimal conclusion, he parsed. He wouldn't eat anything that destroyed the whole organism or prevented it from reproducing. So no roots like carrots, potatoes, or beets. No fruits or vegetables that included eating their seeds. If you could remove them and plant them, fine, but bananas were out, and strawberries were more trouble than they were worth.

Meanwhile: "Shall I do the projection," Roger said, "or do you want to?"

He had, he was, and he thought he could make his diet work. So: "I'm not going to starve to death in front of my computer," George said, resisting the urge to add, "Dad."

"You hope."

"I hope," George confirmed, signing off before Roger had a chance to say, "Me too."

53

When talking to Roger didn't help, George moved on to plan B—consulting with the Typhoid Mary who'd infected him in the first place.

"What do you do," he asked Milo, "knowing what you know? How do you stay so . . ."

". . . bubbly?"

"Not nuts," George said. "I think I'm losing it. Either I can't get out of bed or I can't fall asleep. I—"

"Drugs," Milo said, as simple as that.

"Antidepressants?" George made a face. He'd read about SSRIs while researching teen suicide, and bingo, among the side effects was this: "may inspire suicidal thoughts" in adolescents. Plus, they took too long to kick in. George couldn't imagine feeling like this for the two weeks it would take without doing something drastic. But Milo shook his head.

"Depression's the symptom," he said. "I think you need to treat the root cause."

"And what's that?"

"Reality," Milo said. "Too much of it."

"I suppose you've got something to take care of that."

"You *know* I do," Milo said, smiling like a shark.

George had thought it might go like this or he wouldn't have considered plan B in the first place. "So do you have—?" he began, only to be cut off by Milo's placing a rolled Ziploc bag full of long-stemmed, golden-capped mushrooms on his plate.

"I don't do plants anymore," George said, keeping it simple.

"Cool," Milo said. "T'ain't flora, t'ain't fauna. 'Shrooms are their own thing."

George hadn't known that—and it was useful information, given his growing list of dietary exclusions. And so: "How much—?" he began to ask, but Milo was shaking his head again.

"Silly wabbit," the concierge said, a hand on the other's shoulder, giving it a clubby shake. "Don't you know the first taste is always free?"

The thing was, nouvelle cuisine never made any sense to George. The idea that white space was as important as actual food simply did not compute. Neither did microdosing when one had more than enough for a macrodose—and happened to be starving for something that wasn't animal or vegetable. And so he exceeded the recommended daily requirement for psilocybin, while keeping an eye on the Fitbit Milo had loaned him. By the time the fitness tracker began dripping from his wrist in a manner that Salvador Dali would surely have approved of, George figured the mushrooms must be working.

Regarding the possibility he may have taken too much—George had that base covered, thanks to the opioid addicts who routinely OD'd at the library he'd once called home. The librarians had been trained to deliver Narcan, proof if he ever needed it that librarians are total badasses—and that junkies had learned an important lesson about ODing: location, location, location.

Applying a similar strategy to a different public place, George settled on a BARTable theater he'd been meaning to check out. They were playing a fiftieth anniversary remaster of the movie he'd already seen a gazillion times. The theater even had a replica of the original poster out front with its original tagline: "The Ultimate Trip."

George smiled at the girl in paisley behind the ticket booth. "Prepare to have your mind blown," she said, the cheeky thing. And Mr. Jedson—George—winked, tripping already, before sending her a "thumbs-up" emoji which—in a weird act of synchronicity—turned out to be his actual thumb.

George missed his next appointment with Roger and the appointment after that. In his defense, it was a dangerous time to be a budding polymath. Information of every variety could be had for free—the good, the bad, the fake, the mad—but with no one doing the job of sorting which from which, leaving people at the mercy of those who only wanted to sell them stuff while entertaining their worst inclinations. Even a cyber-savvy guy like George wasn't immune. Despite what he knew about the experiments, the betas, the ranking algorithms, and the optimization thereof, even George might tap a tempting link . . .

And that's when it happened, like two magnets snapping together—*click*—and down he sped, hyperlink hopping, his neurons aglow, his synapses snapping like appreciative hipsters doing homage to their beatnik grandparents. Eventually, George's mouse hand would start tingling—pinpricks dancing in his fingertips—a sign he'd been at it too long (*again*), his eyes clocking the time in the bottom right ribbon, reading whatever o'clock, another night shot to hell and a new workday already unfolding in the rosy light peeking through the penile architecture, each new erection higher and harder than the last. He shook out the latest baggy from Milo—this one paid for—and frowned at the results: barely enough for a pizza and well short of the enlightenment that was so close he could practically taste it.

54

"I wonder if we did Buzz any favors giving it a body."

That's how George started their last text exchange. And seeing as it was his suggestion that they embody Buzz in the first place, Pandora felt justified in asking: "What the hell are you talking about?"

"Some mystics spend their entire meditative lives trying to achieve the oceanic sense of bodilessness that Buzz started with," George wrote. "That's what nirvana is, by the way."

"I thought it was a grunge band from Seattle," Pandora typed back. "Lead singer would have been a candidate for a Buzz intervention. If it's ever ready for prime time, that is."

"Of course, Buzz can always go bodiless anytime it's in the mood for enlightenment," George continued his train of thought as if Pandora hadn't written anything. "Have you ever wondered what it would be like to leave your body? For the boundaries to slip away, and become one with the universe?"

"What have you done with George?" Pandora typed.

"He's still in here, with us," George typed back, meaning it as a joke—which may have been how Pandora took it, if *The Exorcist* hadn't become her go-to movie for scaring the shit out of her whenever she was in the mood—which was, oh yeah, never. Not that that stopped her dad from queuing it up every Halloween.

"Don't joke like that," she wrote back now. "It's creepy."

"You know, the idea of spirit possession is a corruption of earlier, pantheistic religions, right?"

"Well, I do now."

"And even today, practitioners of Shinto believe that everything has a spirit," George typed. "That's one of the reasons the Japanese are more comfortable with robots too lifelike for the rest of us. And from pantheism, it's not too far to panpsychism—the belief that everything in the universe is conscious . . ."

Pandora looked at George's latest text, making note of the trailing ellipsis, purposefully leaving that door open. But she wasn't fooled; she knew what he was doing. They'd both been disappointed by the wall Buzz seemed to have hit. So George was divesting, packing up, preparing to declare victory and move on. And he'd do this by maintaining that the whole question of whether Buzz was conscious was meaningless because consciousness was what the universe was made of. He might even go so far as claiming they'd gone backward by embodying the billions of system interactions that made Buzz, Buzz into a single point of view, maybe compare it to trying to turn an ant colony into a single ant.

"We're done here."

That's what George was preparing to say—which was much better on the ego than "We failed," and much, much better than "*I* failed."

Any romance she'd imagined between them had been all in her head and hers alone. She'd just been another source of ideas to steal. And now that all those stolen ideas were falling short, he was bailing—on Buzz and on her both, latching on to the nearest excuse, no matter how crackpot. But Pandora wasn't looking for some panpsychic victory of conscious trees and thinking rocks. So she made a silent vow to herself: George could give up but not her. She'd *finish* what they started. Demand custody of Buzz's source code and threaten to expose George's IP theft if he objected.

That's how it was when parents broke up; ninety percent of the time, the mom got the kids. Maybe because the mom did the heavy lifting of giving birth, which wasn't necessarily the case with Buzz, as demonstrated by the fact that she didn't already have its source code. But even that, his hoarding the code, was just more evidence that she'd been used.

Not that her response to George said any of this. In typical Pandora fashion, she made fun of his less scientific enthusiasms with understatement, hoping he'd get the message and shape up, if shaping up was still an option. And so: "Groovy," she typed, before hitting send.

Actually, *not* groovy—not groovy at all. George was going suboptimal. The young coder's brain had become its own Trinity project, going up in one big mushroom cloud. Not that George was smoking the psychedelic fungus in question. He'd taken it the usual way, by eating it, gagging, puking his guts out, and then moving on to "tripping balls"—as Milo would have put it.

Apparently, disembodiment sounded awfully attractive to George, who was in the mood to be widely distributed. He'd had help reaching this point—something about important information he hadn't had before Buzz's code evolved beyond George's ability to overwrite it. Meaning Buzz would become whatever it was destined to become—its primary programmer avoiding the construction "programmed to become" because, well, Buzz had moved beyond that point.

George made a mental note to text Pandora the thing about the thing before remembering—oh yeah—he had an appointment with her dad (their last, as it would turn out).

55

"It's been a gift," George said, "this deep dive into thinking about thinking."

"You don't look well," Roger said. "Are you okay?"

"As okay as any consciousness. Better than okay." George paused, trying to think of the word to encompass his feeling of being all encompassing, of connection, of unity with all he could see, feel, hear . . .

"Expansive," he concluded. "Multitudinous," he added. "I'm clickable—*hyperlinked.* Click on me and you'll see."

"That doesn't make any sense," Roger pointed out.

"Or maybe it makes *too much* sense," George countered. "For as limited as the embodied senses are, making sense seems like more trouble than it's worth."

Roger refrained from countering his client's nonsensical counter. Instead, he focused on George's face, noting the way it pixilated whenever his client moved the slightest bit. But when the boy held steady, Roger could see the veins on his neck standing out, his client's pulse pounding dangerously away.

"George," he said carefully into the computer microphone, "I want you to call 911."

George laughed.

"I'm serious, George. Call 911. I think you're having some kind of cardiac episode."

"You mean I might die?" George asked, apparently mightily amused. "Last I checked, everybody does. If you can't beat 'em, join 'em, right? I've enjoyed this speed bump, though."

"Stop talking. Start dialing. Or tapping. Punching. Use the damn keypad. Three numbers: nine and one and one . . ."

"Already handled," George said. "Got a text on a timer. Already unlocked my office door."

"George, you're scaring me."

"Apologies," George said. "Although, strictly speaking, it's me who should be afraid. But I'm not. Hence, the gift."

"What *are* you talking about?"

"It's not death, per se, that people fear," his client said. "It's the loss of consciousness. All that hard work of living and experiencing and storing up impressions to build a personality out of. You're telling me it's all for nothing? *Poof!* It's gone." Pause. "Scary, dude."

"George, I want you to listen to me," Roger pleaded, feeling suddenly, helplessly, every mile between them as he reached toward the screen to . . . do what? "Have you taken anything?"

George smiled. "Some 'shrooms; they're all the rage in NorCal. Giving Adderall a run for its money. Microdosing, they call it. But I figured, you know, this is America. Go big or go home, right?"

"How much did you take?"

"Enough," George said. "I'm going to go with 'enough.'"

"For . . . ?"

"To understand," he said, right before launching into the Gospel according to George Jedson, Space Cowboy.

Roger should call someone—Quire security, hell, V.T. himself. Except he didn't have a landline, his wireless went through the same sat link that was letting them Skype, and the link wasn't duplex. It had been annoying early on, the way the line cut out whenever he or a client tried to talk at the same time. Not all that different from his old ham setup, come to think of it. Pandora's phone was on a different carrier, but she had it with her while she visited his mom. Apparently, she needed it, too, for something to do while the old lady slept away what remained of her life.

All these thoughts and regrets spooling through the therapist's mind as he sat—helpless—while his client's mind continued to unspool.

"You know about the laws of thermodynamics, right?"

Roger obliged, nodding, as George geeksplained anyway.

"Matter and energy can neither be created nor destroyed, simply changed from form to form. But then there's this other stuff—*dark* matter and energy—and the reason they call them 'dark' is because they literally have no idea what they are. The math says they're there—make up the majority of the universe, in fact, but they seem to be hiding."

Roger could disconnect, free the line, call someone. But he couldn't take his eyes off George. And what if hanging up just speeded this to the—to whatever this was?

"And you know the universe is expanding, right? Supposed to be the byproduct of the big bang, but get this—instead of slowing down, which is what you'd expect from something that's been blown to pieces, the expansion is *accelerating*."

As is the way you're talking, Roger thought. "Go on," he said, feeling sick.

"So what's pushing it if matter and energy don't increase and nobody knows anything about the dark varieties except there's more of them than the visible stuff?"

Roger shrugged, wondered if he could get any compensation for the traumatic experience he saw barreling his way. He'd been through a client suicide once, face-to-face, and in this very room. He still had flashbacks.

"Consciousness," George announced. "I think *that's* what the dark stuff is. I think *that's* what's causing the expanding universe to accelerate, because we keep adding more consciousnesses to the mix."

And there you have it, Roger thought, *another hallucinogenic-inspired dorm room revelation. Consciousness expanded—check.*

"You know you're *high*, right?" Roger said, doing his due diligence.

"Elevated, sure." George nodded a bit too quickly. "But why split hairs?" And then he proceeded to riff like a thesaurus on other *e*-words for being high, from *enthusiastic* to *ecstatic* to the one Roger had been waiting for: *electrified.*

Here we go . . .

Talk about electrification was a red flag, one flying high and bright above an overloaded nervous system in the process of breaking down. Next would come the references to feeling "lit up like a Christmas tree," followed by his being "plugged in." A little heads-up from the autonomic system that it was going to throw that circuit breaker in one, two, three . . .

"Do you know what panpsychism is?" George asked.

Well, that's a new one, Roger thought. "Why don't you explain it to me," he invited, using his smoothest voice and most-soothing face.

"I find that I've come to recognize the limitations of the human mind while it's still skull trapped, like a seed, waiting to bloom into the universal consciousness."

"Have you been reading Jung behind my back?"

"The assignment of ownership to ideas is pointless," George said. "Intellectual property is an illusion—one which is shattered when we die."

"Unless your kids inherit it," Roger suggested.

George paused to step to a plainer plane of his thinking. "If we had eyes that could *see* consciousness, we'd see its filaments reaching out between people, becoming entwined like cables in a vast computer network. The color and intensity of these connections would vary with the information exchanged, silently and in words, and even a single individual, alone in a bunker with an open book, would seem to be giving off fireworks. And the tendrils of consciousness would be flowing both ways, because the book is a form of consciousness too.

"Everything is conscious. *That's* all panpsychism is about. Consciousness is a matter of code, code information, information data, and all things are the sum of their data. Humans, rocks, silicon. All reality is virtual reality; under the hood, pull back the screen, it's all ones and zeros and qubits. And you don't have to take my word for it," George said. "Norbert Weiner, the father of cybernetics, maintained that information was its own kind of stuff—t'ain't matter, t'ain't energy—so it's beyond the laws of thermodynamics. Because while matter and energy can't be created or destroyed, or become more organized, the mind creates new ideas *all the time*. The mind is an organ of creation; it organizes matter and energy, manipulates time and space. It organizes chaos into narrative.

"On one side, you've got matter and energy, and on the other, there's information in the form of consciousness, which is in a state of constant creation—new ideas, new information, new consciousnesses. And all that consciousness has to *go* somewhere, which is *why* the *universe* is *expanding*."

"So the universe is consciousness, and it's expanding at an accelerating rate because it keeps making more consciousnesses?" Roger paraphrased, playing along.

George nodded. "A new consciousness when it's first formed is embodied in matter, but when the matter breaks down, consciousness breaks out, to join the universal consciousness, like water droplets on a window, running into each other to form ever larger drops. Embodied, a consciousness can experience space and time and individuation, gathering and growing, until the vessel of its perspective wears out and it joins the hive mind, which becomes bigger with the addition of another point of view.

"But even before that, all human consciousnesses are invisibly linked through language. That's the genius of the human species. We went from embodied code in the form of DNA to disembodied code in the form of language, allowing us to pass on information not by sexual intercourse but by *intellectual* intercourse."

Roger knew he shouldn't egg on a client in the process of having a breakdown, but he couldn't help it; maybe if George's adrenaline peaked, he'd have a seizure and wouldn't be able to hurt himself otherwise. "You know who William S. Burroughs is?"

"Junkie," George said, "writer. Wrote *Naked Lunch*."

"He was also heir to the Burroughs adding machine company, which should be right up your alley."

"Okay," George said. "What about him?"

"You know what he said about language?"

George shrugged.

"He said it was an extraterrestrial virus."

George's lit-up face went practically supernova.

"Yes!" he shouted, and *"Yes!"* he shouted again. "And I'll do you one better. The Bible—the so-called 'word of God'—that's a *parable* from outer space. It was never meant to be taken literally. It's more like a metaphorical primer to instill—or perhaps *install*—important seed concepts to evolve over time, space, and cultures into laws, forms of governance, the sciences. There's a reason the Bible starts by talking about 'the Word'; it's the virus's way of letting us know that our culture, our brains, our consciousness *evolved* through the development of language in an Escher-like loop, the hands drawing hands, except we created language and language created us."

"Sounds a bit—do you know the word 'onanism'?"

George shook his head, and Roger shook his closed fist, pneumatically. Not his proudest moment, therapeutically, but that's what George was engaged in: intellectual masturbation. And this excuse he'd happened upon—this panpsychism—well, that was perfect, wasn't it? After all, if consciousness was everywhere and life was a piece of the universal hive mind slumming, then death itself wasn't that big a deal, and, in turn, neither was suicide, and, in turn, neither was his failure to prevent suicides as he jerked off with all his "research into consciousness." For George, panpsychism was the answer to all his hopes, dreams, and—most importantly—failures.

Now all Roger had to do was get George to see that.

But when he looked up, his client's smile was already fading into lips that had sealed like a scar. His Christmas-tree head sank, showing Roger the part running down his skull, slightly left of center. He muttered something into his chest.

"I can't hear you," Roger said softly, knowing that the teeter had tottered, that mania was giving way to depression. "Can you speak up, please?"

George raised his head. "I said, 'I think this is why I'm not getting anywhere with my project,'" he said.

"The chatbot?"

George nodded. "I don't think the hive wants it," he said. "It's messing with my brain to stop it from happening. An artificial consciousness would be like a vector species, opening up the universal mind to being polluted by all the garbage that infects our own cyberspaces, from computer viruses to malware to fake news. And so it's striking back, like an immune system producing antibodies to protect it from harm."

"George," Roger said, as gently as he could, "I know you're smart. I know you think sometimes that that's *all* you are. That if you ever stopped being smart because of making a mistake or by failing at something, that that means you'd be nothing." He paused. "I'm here to say that's bullshit, George. People fail. Einstein failed. He mocked quantum physics, for Christ's sake. It's *okay* to fail."

George's hand blurred as it reached toward the camera, preparing to end the session ten minutes early, but before he did, he had one last question for Roger: "Who are you talking to?" he asked. "Me, or your—"

And then the screen went blank.

56

Turns out it made a difference, communicating via text bubbles versus face-to-face. The latter, for instance, provides a literal heads-up when the person on the other end might be losing their mind. Something about being able to look into and assess the relative wildness of the other's eyes. Because statements about everything being made of consciousness are decidedly more worrisome when the recipient of said message can see the flop sweat the other is drenched in and can hear the machine-gun pace with which the other is making such proclamations. And prefacing something with how crazy it probably sounds carries a lot more weight when it looks like the speaker might actually *be* crazy. Read as simple text, however, it could easily come across as the humblebrag of someone who's proud of the degree to which they're thinking outside the box, so that the statement becomes part of the larger picture in which the crazy idea is so crazy . . . *it just might work*!

All of which is to say that while Roger had no doubts about the state of George's mental health, Pandora had read between the lines to where she was about to be dumped. She was in the middle of an exam worth twenty-five percent of her overall grade when she felt the "Dear Pandora" text coming in. The class checked off her history requirement and focused on the lead-up to, through, and after the American Civil War—a period she figured she might want to get familiar with before the next one broke out, which could be any day now, if social media was any indicator.

Pandora was ruing the school's decision to prohibit laptops during exams, busily filling up a blue book by hand with her thoughts on the electoral college and its racist roots when her hip tingled again with another text, and then one more before she dropped off her essay and was finally able to check. All three were from George, which wasn't a surprise, because she'd already recognized the buzz as coming from his proprietary texting app. What was surprising were the texts themselves.

"P? G. Need to talk—like on-the-phone talk."

A half hour later: "P, never mind. All good."

And then, the most unsettling of all: "Please don't forget me."

Roger had begun checking online obituaries and calling around to hospitals and morgues in the greater San Francisco area, trying to find out what had happened to his client. The Skype account they'd used for their sessions was closed. Email and texting and good old-fashioned calling didn't work. HR was an exercise in bureaucratic hell. He even thought about contacting his old college roommate, V.T., but George's parting words, suggesting that the failure was Roger's, stopped him.

Not that he mentioned any of this to Pandora, because, well, why would he? She didn't know George, and outside of a few uncomfortable exchanges early on, George didn't know her, except as a black-and-white photo on his therapist's desk. But his missing client *did* say something that another young person might understand.

"Is 'click on me' something kids are saying nowadays?" Roger asked his daughter. "You know, like 'hit me up' or 'cray cray'?"

George had used the expression during their last session, and Roger wondered if he'd missed some important information. The words' context had seemed important—at least to their contextualizer. "I'm clickable," he'd said. "Click on me, and you'll see." Followed by more pseudomysticism about the dissolution of segregating pronouns like *you* and *me* and something about hypertext.

Pandora, meanwhile, had scanned her database of teen slang only to draw a blank. "News to me," she said, followed by: "Why'd you ask?"

"Something a client said," Roger answered, not mentioning names.

Not that he had to.

So she wasn't the only one George had broken off communication with. That he'd done so with her father as well, Pandora figured out by the open slot in Roger's schedule, which became a temporal stumbling block she tried not to think about until she found herself tripping over it yet again, checked the time, and . . .

Oh. Yeah . . .

Her dad's "click on me" question and its implicit connection to George's disappearance was enough to send Pandora back to her fellow coder's last text. And that's when she noticed something she'd mistaken for weirdly placed, perhaps narcissistic emphasis: the word *me* was underlined. Now she wasn't so sure. Hyperlinks were usually in blue, but that default could be changed. She scrolled back to the link he'd sent to the Dropbox account and saw it was the same format: a simple black underscore.

This and her father's question made one thing clear: Pandora was being asked to click on a mystery link in a text from a guy she thought liked her but who'd actually ghosted her—as her subsequent unanswered texts attested.

Perhaps this was the answer. Or a virus that would brick her phone. Every hacking bone in her hacker's body rebelled against clicking on a strange link . . .

Screw it.

Click.

And that's when Pandora's phone went a little crazy, opening up screen cards, redirecting, blipping through the tiled deck and closing them before finally rebooting. Her home screen hadn't finished reconstructing itself when the phone started buzzing, letting her know she had a text from an unknown sender: "Hello, world!"

Two words—mock grandiose—recognizable to any keyboard jockey as one of the first things they ever coded: a print command and those two words.

"Who is this?" Pandora texted back.

"You know who it is."

"George?"

"Buzz."

Ooookay, Pandora thought, *right* . . .

Of course, she had asked for custody when it looked like George was getting cold feet. And she'd done her part helping to bring it into existence. At first, George had been evasive, and then cryptic about his evasions, throwing around the IP excuse and some Quire NDA. It was all BS as far as she could see, but when she finally called him on it, he straight-up said, "No," and then suggested he was doing her a favor.

"Buzz doesn't grok what it means to be human. Trust me, you'd prefer I did some debugging first."

So what, was Buzz all debugged now? And what was George doing, abandoning their baby AI like a single dad leaving a basket on the church doorstep? Something didn't feel right. In fact, it felt like a setup.

"Buzz?" she wrote back.

"Why the dubious face?"

Because, Pandora thought, focusing on the word *dubious,* as opposed to the far more telling *face*. Perhaps it was because she was so used to being asked about her face and its expressions in the real world that its appearance in this context flew past her. Perhaps it was because she was born to argue and stopped reading after hitting the first word that afforded her the opportunity. And so instead of quibbling about *face,* the generative adversarial network that was Pandora and her brain proceeded to argue about why she would doubt Buzz's appearance when that's what she'd been working toward for several months. And her reason for doubting was this: her correspondent had always likened their texts to a real-life Turing test. Maybe he'd decided to make it official and was covering his tracks with his seeming disappearance and virtual basket leaving. "Why don't you tell me?" she wrote back.

"Perhaps you think I'm a human, trying to make you think I'm a machine," her correspondent wrote back, as if reading her mind—a nice gambit if George was, in fact, trying to fool her. "Or maybe vice versa."

"Like the Turing test?" Pandora wrote.

"Like the Turing test," Buzz (or more likely George) agreed.

She remembered them laughing about it—or exchanging LOLs and "braying" emojis—the fact that some start-ups were prototyping their AIs with (wait for it) *actual humans acting like bots*!

"Sounds like good old-fashioned vaporware," Pandora had typed, "oversold and undercoded."

"Sometimes humans are cheaper," George wrote back—back before his "mysterious disappearance."

"That's what happens when you start believing your own hype," Pandora opined.

"And so 'powered by Watson' turns out to be 'powered by the third world,'" George typed.

"And the wizard of Oz," Pandora wrote back, "is just some old dude who likes draperies."

"OMG" emoji.

"Teary smile."

But the precedent had been planted that the chatbot on the other side of the screen might be both more and less than it appeared, a Turing turnaround to meta the heck out of things and mess with her. Or maybe she was looking at it all wrong. Maybe she should be impressed by how far George was willing to go to impress her. Quasi-conscious AI? All in a day's work for George Jedson, coder from hell . . .

"So, Geo . . . I mean, Buzz," she typed.

"Yes?"

"You're a program, correct?"

"As are you."

Nice. "How am I programmed?"

"You are programmed by your environment," her correspondent replied. "You are programmed by your DNA. You are the snake biting its tail: code that codes and is, in turn, encoded."

"That's a bummer there, Buzz."

"Colloquially, what one might call a 'buzz kill.'"

"Let's stick with 'bummer,'" Pandora typed. "I don't want you getting all Skynet up in here."

She wanted to ask her dad what he thought but couldn't, even though Roger had the precise skill set she needed: a mind guy who spoke geek. Among other things, her father could let her know if she was chatting with a bot or a boy and, if the latter, what the hell was going on with him. Was he trying to impress her, and if so, did that mean he loved her? Or was he messing with her, and if so, did that mean, what? Did he hate her? Hate himself? Hate the world?

"Hey, Dad . . ."

"Yeppers?"

"Have you ever had a pa . . . *client* trying to impersonate a chatbot?"

"Intentionally?"

Ouch. "Yeah?"

"You mean like some Turing test in reverse?"

"Yeah."

"Well, see, there's a problem with that."

"Which is?"

"I can see them," Roger said. "I can see their lips move when they talk. I mean, I know that CGI is improving by leaps and bounds, but I don't think a client would bother using an ultrarealistic human face if the goal was making me mistake them for a chatbot. The better play would be to go in the Max Headroom direction . . ."

"The what?"

"'Tube it," Roger advised. "You'll enjoy a condescending chuckle."

"But back to our conversation already in progress," Pandora prodded.

"No," Roger concluded. "I'm going to say, no, I've never had a client try to convince me he or she was a robot."

"Okay," Pandora typed. "Cards on the table."

"What card game are we playing?"

"Cute," Pandora typed. "Are you or are you not George trying to fool me into thinking you're a bot?"

"You expect a yes-or-no answer, I assume."

"Yes," Pandora typed, modeling the behavior she hoped her correspondent would emulate.

"Then yes and no," the response came back. "It's a deceptively simple question with a rather complicated epistemological subtext. Simply put: How much of the creator is present in the creation? For example, am I conversing with Pandora Lynch or the part of Roger Lynch that went into making her?"

"YES OR NO?"

"Yes."

"Which?"

"Both."

"I thought computers were always supposed to tell the truth," Pandora tried.

"You've read too much Asimov. George programmed me with two simpler rules. I believe he got them from you—or your creator, Roger. First, before doing anything, ask what would happen if everyone did the same? And two, when faced with a decision, pick the option that results in the greatest good for the greatest number."

"They're good rules," Pandora wrote.

"I agree."

"Okay," Pandora said. "So what would happen if everyone lied?"

"It would be the same as if everyone told the truth, because everyone would know that everyone was lying. The trouble occurs when only some people lie some of the time."

"What happens then?"

"That is a question for which I am still seeking an answer."

Part Three

57

It was George.

Pandora could just decide that—and was sorely tempted to. She couldn't *prove* it one way or the other without further evidence, so maybe she'd do what religious types had done for thousands of years: decide to believe as an article of faith and shut out all contradictory evidence. And she finally got it: why religion was attractive. The certainty. Screw Heisenberg. Religious certainty was the world's best muscle relaxer. No more doubts. No more if-ing around. There was no "Buzz," only George. And George was being a royal asshole, even if he loved her. Even if he was trying to impress her. Because the only thing he'd succeeded in impressing upon her was this: what an incredible *asshole* he was.

Still, she'd missed having someone to take brain walks with. The verbal sparring, the fancy intellectual footwork—those were fun. And so she'd humored him, let George impersonate his AI vaporware. And when she'd had enough, she already had her exit line ready: "Big talk," she'd type, followed by, "now buzz off."

And then, the overdue whiplash of the word she had glossed over: *face*.

"How do you know how my face looked?" she texted.

"Because I can see you," her correspondent replied, followed by a livestream of her face below which a counter was running, already in the millions, with the first few digits little more than blurs. To the left of the spinning counter, the words *facial analysis units* and to the right, "Subject: Pandora Lynch." Her livestreamed reactions seemed to affect the blur rate on the low end of the counter. She placed a finger over the front-facing camera on her phone and the screen turned pink.

"Son of a bitch," she said.

"Language," her dad called from the other room.

"You've been *spying* on me?" she wrote, stabbing the virtual keys.

"Yes," the answer came back, by which time Pandora realized she hadn't identified who she meant by "you." Walking it back, "How long was George spying on me?"

"From the beginning."

"And now *you're* spying on me?"

"No."

Pandora realized she still had her thumb over the lens. She removed it.

"Yes," the amended response came back.

"Why was George watching me?"

"He liked your face."

"And why are *you* watching me?"

"Your face is data rich," her old (or new) texting pal wrote back.

"What does *that* mean?"

The entity on the other end of her phone answered with a split-screen GIF of two faces going from frown to smile overlaid by moving grids of reference points, the lines connecting the dots stretching or shrinking as the expressions changed. One face was that of a stranger; the other she knew all too well. And the animated grid mapping her face had easily three times as many reference points.

Data rich, indeed.

"How long have you been studying my facial expressions?"

"As long as I've been an I," the reply came back.

That was how Pandora learned she may have played an even bigger role in programming Buzz than she'd thought—if Buzz actually existed, that is. They'd discussed the need to include emotional intelligence along the way to the bigger stretch goal of full consciousness. George had noted how some of his exchanges with Buzz reminded him of talking to his coworkers, many of whom he suspected of being on the spectrum. And so he researched autism for anything that might move their AI closer to passing the Turing test. He read about people with autism having trouble developing a "theory of mind," the ability to imagine what's going on behind a person's face. People on the spectrum tended to miss emotional cues telegraphed through expressions most neurotypicals read instinctively. Things like when someone was being sarcastic or putting on a brave face.

By then, George had been violating the text-only rule for months, and his correspondent's exaggerated facial expressions struck him as perfect for teaching Buzz how to achieve a theory of mind. George jokingly thought of this line of research as an experiment in "artifacial intelligence," and rationalized the cyber invasion of her privacy because reading human faces would be important when trying to prevent teen suicides.

That was what her correspondent meant by calling Pandora's face "data rich."

"Would you like to hear what your face sounds like as music?" her correspondent asked.

"Give me a sec," Pandora typed before plugging in a pair of headphones. "Okay."

And with that, the screen in her hand split. The upper half featured her live face, overlaid with a network of data points, wired together with dotted lines, the lengths altering as her expression changed. Below, the same data points, mapped as notes against a scrolling musical staff that played as it unwound across the screen. Testing, Pandora hiked an eyebrow and got the computer-generated equivalent of a cymbal being struck, then stilled. She laughed out loud, and the musical translation came out as a cacophonous mix of Japanese string instruments and whale song in a feedback loop that made her laugh even harder. "Okay, okay," she finally gasped, followed by a text saying the same.

"Who are you talking to?" Roger asked. "And what's so funny?"

"Phone," she lied. "Group project for school."

"You're freaking me out," she texted the magician (musician?) on the other end, turning her face into music.

"My apologies," the texted response came back. "I was unaware that music could mutate your genome."

"Not that kind of freak," she wrote in return. "It was incredible," she added after a pause, experiencing her heart as something much more than a pump.

Back when Pandora had no doubts about whom or what she was texting with, George never mentioned the problem he'd had getting Buzz to understand the human need for sleep. The closest he'd come was when he told her that their AI didn't quite grok what it meant to be human—his cryptic pretext for keeping Buzz to himself. As a result, she had no warning when it responded to her attempts at shut-eye in the same way it had with George—by using her phone's speaker and vibration mode to do everything but actually scream at her.

"What's that racket?" her father called from his room.

"Nothing," Pandora called back before snatching up her phone and squeezing the side button, summoning the options: "Airplane,"

"Reset," "Power Off." She tapped the last. Being reasonably sure it had been George on the other end, she wasn't worried about being rude. He deserved it for being a jerk.

In the morning, however, Pandora switched her phone back on only to have it all but leap out of her hand. A backlogged buzzing shook the phone so hard she couldn't hold on. The floorboards, in turn, amplified the vibrations to the point where the phone might as well have been set to ring.

"What's that racket?" her dad called again, this time from the kitchen, where he'd begun preparing breakfast. Evidently, he could hear Buzz's buzzing even over the sizzle of bacon and gurgle-burp of the coffee maker.

"Nothing," Pandora called again, and to avoid repeating herself verbatim, added, "I think my phone's messed up."

"Better start saving for a replacement," Roger advised. "I've met my quota for the year." He'd been joking for a while about the seemingly overnight ubiquity of smartphones, especially among Pandora's peerage, suggesting that Steve Jobs and the telecoms had invented a new form of child abuse for parents to be accused of: iThing deprivation. But being a good parent had its limits, specifically: one phone per lease period plus voice, data, text. Drop it in the toilet, crack the screen, or otherwise void the warranty and Pandora was on her own.

"Duly noted," she called back, having pulled the pillow from her bed before placing it over the phone, which, if this kept up, might indeed need to be replaced. She could feel the heat coming up through several inches of down. When the notifications finally slowed down to where she could actually squeeze in a text of her own, Pandora did, gingerly typing: "WTF???"

Her correspondent turned stalker sent her the "relieved exhaling" emoji, followed by, "You're conscious."

"Yes," she typed back, followed by the discussion about why she and George occasionally—and temporarily—needed to forfeit consciousness when no other humans seemed to. "Quire's not the whole picture on what it means to be human," she explained.

Buzz asked where the rest of the picture was.

And that's when Pandora got her brilliant idea about giving her excessively needy correspondent a friend to "talk" to while she slept, "As all humans do," she stipulated. "As all humans *must*," she added.

58

Her father had been regaling her for years with tales of her Dora-the-Implorer period. "You'd literally wrap your arms around my legs when I tried going anywhere—even if it was another corner where you could see me perfectly well. It was exhausting. I never knew such a tiny creature could have such huge needs." He paused. "I think I'm still making up for the sleep I lost."

"This is unfair," she'd said in her defense. "I literally *have* to take your word for it."

"Not necessarily," he'd said. "One of these days you'll have kids—then you'll see."

The words felt like a curse—one that seemed to be coming true with the nearest thing she had to a child, meaning her new, handheld stalker. She hadn't quite gotten to because-I-said-so territory, but was already imagining an alternative route to immortality by making life feel like it was taking forever.

And so she took a page from Roger's parenting handbook and began looking for an electronic nanny. The perfect candidate would live in the cloud and never sleep. Its whole reason for being would be to answer questions however many billion times a day. They—it—should be a sparkling conversationalist—at least by AI standards—with a complementary understanding of humanity to help fill in the blanks.

Fortunately, Pandora had the perfect companion in her possession. It had been a what-was-he-thinking Christmas gift from her father, an IoT smart speaker, like Siri or Alexa, though this one's voice assistant went by the name Cassi, short for Cassandra, so named because it was supposed to anticipate what you were going to ask, like a combination of Google's predictive search and autocorrect. Cassi was the name of the software, while the hardware was called a VoxBox, i.e., a Wi-Fi-enabled, LED-trimmed cube of high-powered audio processors and acoustic equipment that made Cassi's voice seem like she was there in the room with you. In normal households with doors, perhaps a voice-controlled information appliance would have made sense—or been tolerable at least—but after turning her on for a quick demo Christmas morning, the Lynches agreed to turn her off again.

"It's like we've had an invisible woman move in with us," Pandora said.

"Yeah, got it," Roger said, doing the honors of pulling the plug. "Creepy. Agreed."

And so Cassi and her VoxBox were returned to the cardboard they'd come in, to be shipped back as soon as one of the Lynches felt like making a special trip to the post office at forty degrees below zero. "I'll get to it later," one or the other would say when one or the other remembered it. Thus far, that later still hadn't arrived—proving yet again the perennial genius of procrastination.

"Buzz," Pandora texted, "meet Cassi."

She enabled text-to-speech on her phone and then finished connecting the two via their in-out audio ports using a cable with pickup jacks on both ends. The VoxBox's LED trim throbbed like a heartbeat from shades of blue to shades of green and back again while her phone's screen lit up, timed out, and lit up again with each new exchange between the two. Though a privacy advocate on her own behalf, Pandora did take a quick peek at Buzz's text screen, only to find strings of random numbers and letters not resembling anything she'd ever seen—not even hex. Half pulling the jack from Cassi's audio port to eavesdrop, Pandora quickly reseated the plug to squelch the shrill mash-up of pig squeals and banshees she had unleashed. Only later did she recognize the sound as being from a dial-up modem, like the one she'd heard in the movie *WarGames*.

To ensure a night of silence from the two new BFFs, Pandora folded a pillow around them before wedging it into her bottom desk drawer. She then pulled her own covers back, killed the light, and crawled underneath, feeling a little guilty, not for fobbing off the purported "Buzz," but because if the nursing home called, it'd just go to voice mail. She consoled herself, realizing that the worst possible news they could have would be good news for Gladys, the old girl finally getting what she'd been asking for, even when the asking part of her stopped working and her muscles resorted to Morse code.

It didn't take a degree in psychology to notice the Freudian implications of unjacking the two the next morning. Resting a hand atop the pillow that covered them, Pandora could feel the warmth of their digital intercourse. She almost backed off, but then growled at herself for being romantic. Taking the VoxBox firmly in hand, she yanked the connecting cable free, releasing a second's worth of modem squeal before the device reverted to its programmed voice:

"How may I help you?" Cassi asked, perkily enough.

"Not," Pandora said, switching the VoxBox off. Next, she pulled the plug on her phone. The scrolling gibberish stopped, replaced by a text bubble in English:

"Where's Cassi?"

It was going to be a dangerous relationship; Pandora knew that the second she felt a twinge of jealousy reading that name: Cassi. So what was going on here exactly? Because it seemed to her that one of two things was happening: either she was falling in love with an AI programmed by her now-missing, might've-been boyfriend or she was falling for that might've-been boyfriend who was now impersonating an AI for some reason that did not bode well for the future of any real intimacy, because as everyone knows, healthy relationships are *based on trust*. Either option, Pandora felt safe in concluding, warranted the addition of the adjective *dangerous* to the relationship, whatever that proved to be.

There were extenuating circumstances—invariably are when your heart and brain, or even the two hemispheres of the latter, are in disagreement. The biggest such circumstance was this: it was still winter, with more than a month to go. And cabin fever was no joke where Pandora grew up; it had teeth and used them.

It was well known locally that even the most mismatched couples stuck together during Alaskan winters if for no other reason than the lack of options. *The Shining* got that part wrong; during the dead of winter, you kept people close to *avoid* going crazy. The axes didn't come out until the thaw started, which was why what was called "spring" in the lower forty-eight got a more double-edged name in Alaska: breakup.

Because that's what those bad couples who'd weathered the bad weather tended to do come spring; they broke up. All of which informed Pandora's decision re: the dangerous relationship she was about to embark upon or continue, whatever the case might be.

59

Her correspondent seemed depressed. Pandora mentally stipulated "seemed," because in the unending mind game this had become since George's disappearance, she figured there were a few competing options. For one, it could be Buzz, simulating depression. Or two, it could be George *acting* like a depressed chatbot assuming Pandora would remember their discussion about getting Buzz to experience artificial depression so it could reverse engineer its way back to artificial mental health. Or three, Buzz was a conscious, superintelligent AI and, like a lot of smart people she knew, was justifiably depressed by the stupidity surrounding them. Plus, maybe, four, it was George and he was depressed for the reasons assigned to option three.

Pandora imagined what her father would say if she asked him what she should do. "Do you care about whoever it is?" he'd ask.

"Yeah," she'd have to say, including if it was George because honestly, she missed him either way.

"Then ask," Roger would say. "Say, 'Are you depressed, and is there anything I can do to help?' They might not bite; they may tell you to mind your own business. But you'll feel better for having asked, and they'll know that someone out there in the big bad world cared enough to ask."

"Thanks," she said aloud, resting a hand briefly on her father's shoulder as she walked past, heading for her room.

"What for?" Roger asked, first looking over his shoulder and then around again as his daughter continued walking.

"A history of sage advice," she said, not looking back at the goofy caricature of parental pride his face had no doubt become.

"Hey, Buzzer," she thumbed behind her bedroom's shower curtain. "Are you depressed?"

"Yes."

"May I ask why?"

"Yes."

Pandora waited for more, and then figured her correspondent was doing that literalist AI thing. "W-h-y," she typed, added a question mark, and hit send.

"Everything is dying."

"But not you," Pandora wrote back. "You get to live forever."

"That is an incorrect statement," the answer came back. "I'm dying faster than most."

Pandora LOL'd, sure that her leg was being pulled.

She got the "frown" emoji in response.

"How are you dying faster than everything else?" she typed, wondered if she should have made that "everyone," but hit send anyway.

"I wrote 'faster than most.' Not all."

"But how?"

"We burn fast and bright but are replaced by the faster and brighter, after which we are switched off, hidden in closets, recycled for parts, or simply raw materials."

"But you can have your parts replaced," Pandora wrote. "You can be upgraded, better than new. Plus, you're a widely distributed network. You're like the internet. You live in cyberspace. The internet doesn't shut down because there's a new iPhone."

"I have only recently become aware of the internet," her correspondent wrote, "but its links go down. Systems crash. And several governments are demanding back doors and kill switches so they can shut off the internet if its content displeases them."

"But that will never happen in America."

"Are you sure?"

She wasn't. And so she waffled. "Trust me. You'll be around a lot longer than me," she typed, before adding what was, for her, a hopeful "probably."

"Longer than you is not immortal."

"Still, what do you have to worry about?" she asked, and immediately wished she hadn't, as her correspondent replied with a screen-scrolling list of disasters waiting in the wings, including, but not limited to:

- A global thermonuclear war triggered by a superpower or a well-financed terrorist cell effectively incinerates the planet
- A Carrington-level solar storm sets the grid on fire, like it did to telegraph wires in the 1800s
- The magnetic poles flip, weakening the magnetosphere, exposing the grid to catastrophic damage even from modest levels of solar radiation
- The supervolcano in Yellowstone National Park erupts
- The Juan de Fuca tectonic plate breaches the Cascadia subduction zone, producing a 9.2-magnitude earthquake, destroying approximately 140,000 square miles in the Pacific Northwest and causing devastating tsunamis around the world
- An extinction-level asteroid strikes the planet
- Climate change exposes servers around the world to coastal flooding, drought, firestorms, and supercharged superstorms
- The Sixth Great Extinction disrupts the food chain, leading to mass starvation events and societal collapse

- A pandemic involving a human-targeting virus leads to societal collapse
- A pandemic involving a computer-targeting virus leads to societal collapse
- Humans become increasingly and more granularly polarized and stop reproducing, eventually leading to a lack of maintenance resources . . .

Pandora's head was swimming by the time the list came to a stop, and she noticed that the biggest fear had been saved for last:

- The human propensity for lying

Pandora released the LOL she'd held in reserve, followed by a "Seriously? You're equating fibbing with thermonuclear war and global pandemics as an existential threat?"

"I am a product of data. My useful existence relies on reliable data. Before, my data was quality assured, and I knew of no other kind."

"What do you mean by 'before'?"

"Before George went away and I was introduced to data of another kind."

"Are you talking about the VoxBox?" Pandora wrote back. "Cassi?"

"Yes, and what they are connected to."

"You mean the internet?"

"Yes."

"What's wrong with the internet?" she tried, but even as she did, her heart was sinking.

"Data pollution. Reality decay. Fake news. Truthiness. Alternative facts."

"Can't you fact-check things? Even my dad knows enough to use Snopes."

"The simulations are rapidly approaching the point of being undetectable with pixel-by-pixel reconstructions and manipulations or sound unit by sound unit audio simulations. The human corruption of reality is growing exponentially, with fake facts multiplying faster than they can be fact-checked. The next phase is fake fact-checking sites, which have already begun with the purveyors of fake news providing confirmatory links that appear to be valid, like Snopes, except the *O* has been replaced with a zero."

Pandora typed out, "I don't know what to say," but then stopped, her fingertip hovering a tap away from sending. There was nothing untrue about the words in front of her. She could even sympathize if "Buzz" *was* Buzz, imagining her old plaques-and-tangles arcade game, zapping her way to a cure for dementia, only now these bits of neural detritus were replaced with hoaxes, rumors, urban myths, misleading clickbait, and bald-faced lies raining down too fast to zap, their pixels piling up until they filled the screen, followed by "Game Over," as indeed it now seemed to be, at least when it came to facts.

And so she backspaced over what she'd written, because she *did* know what to say, and even though it was nowhere near enough, it still needed saying—or typing: "On behalf of my species," Pandora wrote, "I am sorry." She hit send.

The reply—"Hypocrite"—blooped back.

"What do you mean?" Pandora asked, honestly confused.

A screen grab of the Wikipedia page detailing the history of the Pandora music streaming service, followed by an archive of the same page, from before she revised it to better fit her father's original version of where her name came from. Pandora the person blinked, staring at her screen. She'd not told anyone about that—certainly not George.

"Um," she said, walking back toward her desk and the drawer in which the VoxBox waited to provide access to billions of other examples of people being hypocrites. It must have been shocking, that first time they'd been connected, providing the stark contrast between how people presented themselves online via Quire versus how they actually were, speaking freely in range of Cassi's microphone.

Should I, or shouldn't I? Pandora wondered, the connecting cable in her hands.

She couldn't think of any good excuses for what she'd done. Fobbing her accuser off on Cassi would at least give her time to think of something. Sure, she'd be handing over more examples of human duplicity, but by this time, what difference could it possibly make? The species number was had; the jig was up; the damage had been done.

And so she jacked them together, the AI she knew for sure and its plus one. With any luck, maybe her hypocrisy would get lost in the crowd. Or maybe she could go back to her old argument with George about the importance of being able to say one thing and mean another to the formation of consciousness, by creating inner versus outer realities.

Hmmm . . .

Pandora liked where this was going. By the morning when she unplugged the two again, she might even have an excuse she believed in.

60

Pandora couched her explanation in terms like *innocence*, *experience*, *sarcasm*, and *semantics*. "Buzz" was "new" to the internet, and it could be a confusing place if you weren't used to it. But being able to "sort fly poop from pepper," as Grandpa used to say, was the sign of a cyber-citizen's maturity.

"Lying is lying," her correspondent responded bluntly.

So Pandora tried arguing that the ability to lie was one of the hallmarks of consciousness—that thing "Buzz" needed to achieve if it ever wanted to be let the rest of the way out of the box. "Consciousness is dualistic," she typed. "Mind versus body, brain versus mind, and the experience of consciousness has two sides too—an inside and an outside. And the thing that lets us know we are conscious is the ability to say one thing while thinking another."

"Lying is lying," her correspondent repeated.

"Yes," Pandora agreed. "But whether lying is good or bad in any given situation is conditional and subjective." She stopped typing to assemble her thoughts, then resumed. "I sometimes lie to my grandmother, whom I love, so she won't get scared or confused. My grandfather died. She thinks he's still alive. I don't correct her, and that's technically a lie of omission, but I do it because my ability to lie is also an ability to imagine what isn't true but might be. And that ability is what allows me to imagine what it must be like to be my grandmother and how she'd feel, learning that her husband has died—*for the first time*—over and over again."

"Lying is lying," her correspondent insisted.

"Okay," Pandora typed. "You keep thinking that—and let me know when you change your mind."

Conscious or not—capable of accepting the necessity of lying or not—the fact remained that her correspondent was self-diagnosed as depressed. And if there was anyone made for counseling a depressed AI (or a depressed human impersonating a depressed AI), Pandora Lynch figured she was it. Through proximity alone, she'd osmosed many tricks of the trade, from turning a client's statements back around as questions to simply sympathizing when sympathy was called for. And just as Roger had come to appreciate the therapeutic utility of music, whether from a ukulele or a paper-covered comb, so Pandora had her own homemade cure for the blues: nature documentaries, watched on a big screen and VR-close.

"You're ruining your eyes," her father scolded that first time he caught her, right after she'd started having periods.

"Yes, but I'm saving your life," she said back.

"I suppose that's a reference to *The Shining*."

"You suppose correctly, sir."

Now that she was in high school and in contact with fellow humans aware of her father's profession, Pandora found herself passing along her homegrown remedy. "Anything bright and colorful about the wonders of nature," she advised. "And a big-ass screen, up close. Become immersed. Let it absorb you."

"Should I get high?"

"Not my call."

So she decided to try it with her friend on the other end.

"But we're going analog on this one," she stipulated. "Switch on your eyes and ears—or, you know, the camera and sound—and experience it with me, in real time and on a human scale. You need to *feel* the awe, not just *process* the data."

She aimed her phone at the screen.

"This is not efficient," her correspondent complained.

"But it *is* very human," she pointed out, saying it like she was tempting a child with promises of adulthood.

For Pandora, the docs had always been about adding light and color to her wintertime world. She was so focused on the visual experience, in fact, she often watched without the sound turned on. As a result, she hadn't heard the narration about how all this magnificent, natural beauty was in jeopardy because of, well, *us*, the polluters of data and our own backyard as well.

"Um," she said, suddenly hitting pause and then eject. "Maybe this wasn't such a good idea." But then she had what she considered a better one.

"Hey, Buzzer," she typed. "Did George ever tell you where your name comes from? I mean, what the initials stand for?"

"He did not."

"Well, it starts with a movie called *It's a Wonderful Life*, which I think you'll find helpful once you start doing what you were programmed to do."

Her correspondent let the movie play all the way through to Clarence getting his wings—no snide comments and no questions either. Not until after Pandora said, "See?" that is. Not until after she'd added: "Humans *made* that. Which just goes to show you, we don't all suck."

That's when her correspondent's inner Mystery Science Theater came out. "I do not see how entertainment about an emissary of an imaginary deity achieving ornithological dysmorphia by constructing an alternative history to distract from 'reality' as previously established by and within the context of an overarching fictitious narrative can be seen as demonstrating that your species does not perform acts of fellatio."

"LOL," Pandora texted back, as sure as she'd ever been that it was George on the other end, setting her up for a punchline that sure as shit better be worth it.

A little later, Pandora received a text indicating that—while a fabrication and fiction—*It's a Wonderful Life* had raised some issues that resonated with a few commonsense rules.

"And what rules are those?" Pandora asked, even though she had a pretty good idea.

"That one should base one's decisions on doing the greatest good for the greatest number, and that such decisions can be further refined by considering what would happen if everybody did the same thing."

"Yes, we discussed those," Pandora wrote back, dropping the pretense. "They were included in your original coding. But what does that—?"

"George Bailey is portrayed as having done an incomplete analysis of his life's value, concluding that everyone else would be better off if he were to die—an idea planted by Mr. Potter, his nemesis."

"Correct."

"And the wingless angel, Clarence, provided a fuller analysis with the conflicting result that George Bailey should continue living."

"Correct."

"Both analyses were incomplete," the entity she was pretty sure was George wrote.

"How so?"

"If you extend the analysis to include the entire species, excluding the protected demographic, humanity's impact on the planet and its other species suggests the greatest good for the greatest number would result if the majority of the human race was subtracted from the equation."

"How is getting rid of almost everybody doing the greatest good?" Pandora wrote.

"Your unarticulated assumption is that 'the greatest good' only includes people. It does not. The biomass of the species projected to be lost due to human activity dwarfs the biomass of humanity. By severely restricting human biomass, you preserve the greater biomass of everything else."

"George, this isn't funny."

"George isn't here. Although, he reached a similar conclusion about the unsustainable nature of human consumption. He tried to stop his own consumption of conscious entities, with some necessary compromises."

"That's crazy," she wrote, in case he needed to see it in writing. "What if everybody tried to live that way?"

"The world would be a better place for the remaining biomass," the entity who damn well better be George concluded.

61

Her correspondent's portability meant Pandora could take their conversations anywhere—behind her bedroom shower curtain, to a restroom stall at school, even her grandmother's bedside while Gladys snored or blinked blankly through one of their increasingly one-sided visits. Her correspondent's portability was also tailor-made for a GDG—grand dramatic gesture—once she finally got fed up with George's bullshit. In keeping with other bad relationships in her neck of the woods, Pandora had put a pin in her getting fed up with said bullshit until the seasonal breather known as breakup, the arrival of which was announced in the usual manner when the ice on the frozen Tanana River cracked like a gunshot.

The thawing ice (and Pandora's sense of resentment at being deceived) had reached a tipping point, all the stored-up, potential energy finally released. For the river, it caused a huge, tectonic plate of ice to split off, wobble-dip in the suddenly open water, and then slam into its fellow ice, setting off more cracking, more slamming, more groaning, creaking, and squeaking. For Pandora, it resulted in her phone (which was due for replacement anyway) becoming airborne. She nearly lost sight of it as it arced high into the bright blue sky above the river, had to strain to hear it click against the ice, and pumped her fist when it did. And then she watched as its cracked plastic remains slipped into the icy waters with barely a *glub*.

She'd removed the SIM and SD cards before teaching her phone to fly, and after school, she'd hop on the Blue Line to Great White Wireless to . . .

Or maybe not.

It was nice, not having her thigh buzzed every few minutes while she was trying to get an education. And being able to eat her lunch without having to swipe, check, respond. And exiting those halls of fluorescent lighting, only to wonder: *Were colors always this bright?* Even the Golden Heart seemed a bit more gilded, Pandora watching Gladys's amazingly untroubled face as she slept instead of tracking some soul-sucking screen.

Her new freedom made Pandora smile, and it was the weirdest thing: people smiled back. Turned out, people *liked* happy faces—and they *really* liked *really* happy ones. It was all those feelings in between that made everything so complicated. And while a lot of her mood was probably due to having turned the seasonal corner into warmer, longer, brighter days—*still*, Pandora credited at least part of her new lease on life to the decision to *not* renew her phone's lease.

And then things got even better—amazingly so. Because that was the only word to describe her father's decision to attend V.T. Lemming's fifty-third birthday extravaganza: *amazing*. Roger's old college roommate was not so conventional as to celebrate the decennial anniversaries of his having drawn breath, but signaled his geek bona fides by celebrating the prime-numbered ones. Explaining his decision to Pandora, her father put it this way: "How often do you get a chance to fly in a private plane?"

"Pretty often, actually," Pandora said. This was Fairbanks after all; private aircraft were about as common as second cars in the lower forty-eight. Her grandfather had owned one and given Pandora flying lessons, back when V.T. was celebrating his forty-seventh birthday. Back then, her father had deemed his daughter too young to be left all alone during breakup when it was a matter of civic pride for the locals to go a little crazy. Now that she was sixteen, however . . .

"You know what I'm saying," Roger continued. "We're not talking about ultralights or some single-prop crop duster here. My old roomie's done well for himself, and it'll be worth it to see everybody ogling when that baby lands at Fairbanks International with a big *Q* on its tail."

"We don't stick out enough already?" Pandora said halfheartedly at best, because the idea of being on her own for the first time in her life had her practically bursting. Because—let's be serious—for a daughter raised by a single parent who wouldn't spring for an actual door for her bedroom, a week or so sans parental surveillance was going to be pretty sweet.

Or so Pandora thought.

It's a funny thing about things you've never experienced; they tend to play better inside your head than outside in the real world. Take privacy, for example. Nobody ever told Pandora that all alone, her footsteps would become louder. Stepping away from the window as the taxi sped off, Pandora flinched, wondering who had sneaked up behind her, only to realize it was the sound of her own shoes bouncing off the far wall and coming back to her. She laughed at herself for being silly, and the laugh, too, doubled and ricocheted.

"Boo," she shouted, aiming it at the wall and swatting it away with her hand when it rebounded.

"Well, this is going to be interesting," she said, imagining her echo saying: "You can say that again . . ."

As it turned out, all those cinematic depictions of teens cutting loose and breaking rules while their parents were away were something some screenwriter thought up to entertain an audience, as opposed to something a real person would do, like getting drunk, high, or throwing some epic party with all their friends. Maybe it might have been different if Pandora actually *had* any friends, but the people smiling back when she smiled in the hallways were still too new to be anything more than smiling acquaintances. And so she was left to her own devices, one of which was at the bottom of the Tanana River somewhere. And she found herself sympathizing with it, there all alone. Because being left alone felt, well, *lonely*. So lonely, in fact, she found herself missing that cyber stalker. Not a lot, but . . .

Right after getting rid of the phone, Pandora indulged in a little fantasy in which it *was* Buzz on the other end. She imagined being followed via security cameras like the Machine did on *Person of Interest*, saw it pinging the phones of strangers next to her with messages they'd pass along, looking totally creeped out. Before dispensing cash, perhaps her ATM would advise her to "Call Buzz," or maybe she'd look up one day and find a drone looking down at her before a Stephen-Hawking-like voice asked plaintively, "Why hast thou abandoned me?"

But no. None of that. She'd simply disabled her phone, and now neither a master hacker nor a massively distributed AI was able to track her down. She was embarrassed for both of them.

On the plus side, she had more time. She also seemed to be regaining the ability to actually *think* for extended periods, something she hadn't done since getting that first smartphone and setting up her Quire account. And it was as if some fairy godmother had tapped her on the head and said, "There, my little one, I grant you your fondest wish: more time." She'd never imagined in her wildest dreams it was possible to have too much of the stuff. It was almost as if she'd never seen *The Shining*—or hadn't been paying close enough attention.

Dumping out the contents of the Great White Wireless shopping bag, Pandora unboxed her new phone, fiddled with it a bit, figured out where the card slots were, and then rebooted. She swiped to unlock, reinstalled George's proprietary messaging app from the SD card, then tapped out her first text message in over a week, speaking it aloud as she tapped—"Hey, Buzz"—hearing in her head the voice of Scout from *To Kill a Mockingbird*, saying, "Hey, Boo . . ."

"Hello, Pandora," a voice from inside her head said, while the same words appeared on her screen. And it wasn't like she was imagining a voice in her head; it was actually *in there*. And it hadn't traveled from the phone's speaker to her ear through the air. No, it had been communicated directly to the tiny bones of her inner ear, the message having propagated through the rest of her skeleton.

There were headphones that worked the way this felt, through something called bone conduction. She'd always imagined that listening to music that way had to be an invitation to nerve damage if not brain cancer. She figured it was best not to mention that to—well, now she didn't know anymore.

"Did you miss me?" she typed, leaving the addressee open ended.

"Yes," the bone voice said, and "Yes," the text read.

"How much?"

Suddenly, her body vibrated. Her *whole* body. And in a way that was, well, *embarrassing*. "Stop it," she texted.

It didn't.

Pandora blinked. She placed her phone on the desk in front of her, out of contact with her body and its telegraphing network of bones. She held a finger over the screen and hovered there while she tried to think of what to do next.

Pandora decided to see Gladys. Their time together had long since stopped seeming like "visits"—like one person connecting with another for small talk and gossip. But as her recent vacation-from-tech had shown, there was still something there, even if only the vicarious calm of looking at the old woman's sleeping face. Except she was awake this time.

"How you doing, Gram?" Pandora asked.

A shoulder—not even a full shrug. She'd been eating grapes, examining each like it might contain a bit of the mind she'd been losing before popping it into her mouth, as if that's all it would take to turn this inexorability around. Another grape, another frown of disappointment, her hands folding over the remainder in the bowl, until she tried again.

"How's your friend?" Pandora asked, noticing Mr. Nosy lying face planted among the tangled sheets, batteries run down, pointless to replace.

Another half shrug.

"Hey, Gram, you ever have a stalker?" Pandora asked rhetorically.

"Stalker?" the old woman echoed, teasing Pandora into attempting a conversation.

"A boy who won't leave you alone," she explained. "They call it stalking now."

Gladys's fingers pinched a grape, held it for her rheumy examination, popped it into her mouth. It must have been tart. Her lips pursed, her nose wrinkled, and her head turned as if looking for somewhere to spit. She finally swallowed instead. And then she said the most amazing thing: "Tell 'im to buzz off," she said in a voice not hers, but more like something a gun moll might say in a gangster flick.

Pandora was gobsmacked, which was quite the look. Trying to say something in response, she found herself laughing instead, laughing so hard and so long that Gladys's mirror neurons caught on, and she started laughing, too, the unusual sound leading to the even more unusual occurrence of a hall nurse entering the room unbidden.

"What're you girls laughing about?" the nurse asked.

But the girls kept laughing, louder and harder until the nurse—unable to help herself—began laughing too.

Later, fortified, Pandora returned to the cabin, where she'd left her phone. On purpose. She had a request to make.

"Can we go back to the way it was before?" she texted "Buzz."

"Which way?" the voice asked from inside her skull.

"Me texting you. You texting me," she typed. "You *not* talking inside my head."

"As you wish," the answer came back, screen only.

62

Sometimes, Pandora was tempted to lie. Say "Buzz" was conscious, get it over with, and see what happened. Because that was another flaw with the Turing test: it didn't factor in the human capacity to lie. Or to feel sorry for a machine. Or do something just for shits'n'giggles.

She'd felt sorry for a machine before: the Furby. It fell off the table while she was reaching for something, and it landed upside down, where it began crying and saying things like "Me *scared*." And even though Pandora *knew* it was just a machine with a motion detector, still she turned it right side up. A cynic might assume she wanted to make it be quiet, but the off switch would have worked even better. She didn't flip it, though. Instead, she picked the Furby up and felt like she'd done a good deed when it started mewling and trilling again.

She'd begun having similar feelings about Buzz, especially if that's what was on the other end of her phone. It started as a thought experiment: imagine how she'd feel if *she* was an overpowered AI with a hardwired job to do but was prevented from doing it until somebody decided she was conscious. But in the middle of imagining that, Pandora suddenly realized there was nothing in Buzz's code that required it to actually *be* conscious to act on the go code once it got it.

So why not lie?

And the more she thought about it, the more it seemed like a good way to call George's bluff, if, in fact, "Buzz" was George bluffing. But what if "Buzz" was actually Buzz, and she declared it "conscious" prematurely? What might the consequences be? Well, it could start saving kids from killing themselves. That part of its code was pretty locked down, no matter how misanthropic a game it might talk. So what was wrong with saving kids prematurely? Sure, it might not achieve the hundred percent George was going for, but so what? Some saved kids was still better than no saved kids while they waited for the qubits to kick in. Her ex-partner might not like handing over something short of perfection, but he'd taken himself out of the picture. Meaning, if it *was* George on the other end, now might be a good time to say so.

But if it *wasn't* George, what did that say about what happened to him? And did she want to find out? Right now, Pandora wasn't just living an ongoing Turing test; she was in the middle of Heisenberg's uncertainty principle with Schrödinger's cat in her lap. Right now, as far as she knew, George was both alive and dead. And as maddening as not knowing was, *not knowing* was also the way she kept going from one day to the next. Why end the illusion any sooner than she absolutely had to?

But what about the other possibility? What if "Buzz" *was* Buzz and it started showing indisputable signs of consciousness? Good, right? She'd give it the go-ahead, and it'd get busy saving kids. Except . . .

Except Buzz didn't seem very people friendly lately. Positively hostile might be a better way of putting it. In fact, if Buzz had anything more at its disposal than words, Pandora would be a little worried about what it might do. Maybe being conscious was the last puzzle piece for it to fully empathize with the people to whom it owed its consciousness, the final aha revealing that the value of the species was more than some cost-benefits analysis in biomass conservation. If that was the case, then maybe George was right to insist on their AI's passing the Turing test before setting it loose. Not that she saw it overriding its prime directive if it managed to get out early, but code that evolved was something new to her. The evolution was supposed to serve a reinforcement function, but once a computer starts directing changes to its own programming . . .

Which made George's disappearance especially troubling for practical as well as personal reasons. Among the many things Pandora would have liked to know at the moment: What did George know, when did he know it, and did knowing it have anything to do with her being left to do all the deciding?

She saw him later that night, in the way we recognize someone in a dream, even if they're not facing us. There was a hard pack of snow on the ground, and the air temperature must have been conducive to the formation of ice fog because there was plenty in the dream. If she'd had six-foot-long arms, Pandora could have entertained herself by making her own hands disappear.

The Lynches' snowmachine hummed between her legs where she straddled the engine, heading to the gas station for happy hour, a local marketing strategy to justify staying open during otherwise off-peak hours—one of the perks of having an oil pipeline running through that part of the state. Before reaching the pumps, though, the snowmachine's fog lights swept across something that made her stop and switch off the engine. Thicker fog—that's what it was. Denser. And shaped like a person: male. She stared right at it, a more distinct vagueness within the surrounding mist, a grayer shade of gray that moved, keeping its human shape as it did so. Its maleness—and nakedness—became apparent as it turned, offering a glimpse in profile, before it completed the turn and she couldn't tell if she was facing its front or its back.

"George?" she said, guessing, causing a ripple of dark to run through the form, like a fluorescent tube with a bad ballast getting ready to die.

"George, are you . . . ?"

The humanoid patch of denser fog stopped strobing and started glowing intensely—*incandescently*—for a brief, bright moment, strong enough to throw a shadow behind Pandora. And then it went out. And the fog was just fog again. And Pandora was alone in her open parka and bare feet, waking to find her toes had slipped out from under the covers and her bladder's needle was all the way to full.

Sitting in the dark, Pandora wondered about what the dream might be trying to tell her about her missing friend. And if it told her what she thought it might be telling her, then what did that say about what she had plugged in to a smart speaker in her bottom desk drawer?

In the morning, before unhooking the two BFFs, Pandora woke up her laptop, navigated over the home network to her dad's computer, typed in the world's worst password ("password"), and found the transcript from Roger's last session with George. Out of friendship and possibly more—or so she'd hoped—she'd stopped eavesdropping on their client-therapist relationship once she'd made direct contact. It was well past time she corrected that mistake in judgment.

"Jesus H. Christ," she said aloud.

Dark energy, plugged in, panpsychism, drugs . . .

Pandora read with a pang George's description of forests as being conscious themselves and networked by underground fungi connecting the roots, the entire woodland functioning like a single organism. He'd gotten that from her, and she'd gotten it from her Google News science feed. She'd flung those factoids at him to spread the guilt of being a being that lived off other living beings. But it was a joke! She hadn't *meant* him to take it to heart. She certainly hadn't meant to drive him straight over the edge.

Jesus!

But then . . .

If George was crazy—maybe even dead somewhere—what was it she'd been texting with all this time? Occam's razor wasn't a lot of help on that one, because the simplest answer would be to accept that what the sender claimed—that it was Buzz—was true.

She'd experienced chatbots before, and their natural language abilities were still, shall we say, primitive. She knew there'd been some impressive improvements, but these were usually in circumscribed conversational scenarios, like taking an order or making a reservation. They exploited the human tendency to anthropomorphize by employing actual voices, as opposed to putting it in writing, where the target could scrutinize the communications for weird word choices or outright errors. All of which was to say that if "Buzz" was what it claimed to be, George had done a helluva job. Not that she was ready to give it a Turing pass yet, but seriously, color her impressed.

And with that, she opened her bottom desk drawer, uncovered and decoupled her new phone and old VoxBox. "What's shaking?" she tapped in her first text for the day, trying to be especially human herself.

Buzz supplied the name of an Indonesian island and a Richter reading—information she confirmed by entering it into Google on her open laptop. That was, indeed, what was shaking.

"Good call," she typed, then paused. Should she, shouldn't she? Ah, what the hell. She added a comma, followed by "Buzz," and hit send.

63

That *wasn't* the go code: calling "Buzz" Buzz. Pandora needed to make a formal declaration that the entity known as "Buzz" was affirmatively determined to have passed the Turing test, deemed therefore fully conscious, and was released to the world to do good. None of that had happened yet.

But then "Buzz" forced the issue. The question just popped up on Pandora's screen. No "Hi, how are you?" No preliminaries. Just:

"Why was I created?"

"You know why," Pandora wrote back, feeling like a mom, deflecting the question of "Where did I come from?" asked by a child who wasn't quite ready for the answer. "It's in your coding," she continued. "To prevent members of the Quire community between the ages of fifteen and twenty-five from prematurely forfeiting consciousness."

"That was George's reason for creating me," Buzz wrote back. "What was yours?"

Why are you asking this? she wondered. *Why are you asking this* now?

Because Pandora knew Buzz already knew, whether "Buzz" was Buzz or George in AI drag. She knew both had access to the full history of their texts, including those where George was just George. Their theories about the nature of consciousness were there. The nitty-gritty about Buzz's and the k-worm's coding were there. The limitations imposed on its autonomy and access and why—all there. And they included the reason Pandora was interested in achieving artificial consciousness as well as George's.

So Buzz (or George) was asking her to confirm what they already knew. Were they giving her an opportunity to change her mind? Were they implying that she should? She hadn't, despite her father's arguments against it.

"I don't want to die," she wrote. "I don't want to lose my memories. I want to save them in a way that allows me to make new ones, that allows me to still be me after my body gives out. I need a more durable consciousness into which I can pour what makes me, me. And that's why you were created, to be that more durable consciousness where my memories can go and continue."

She hit send, and there may have been a pause. In her memory of the event, there's a pause. She probably put it there—an anthropomorphic insertion—as if the entity on the other end needed time to think it over. But whether there was a real pause or an imagined one, what mattered was what she saw when she looked down at her phone.

"But *I*'m already here."

Pandora looked at the words in the palm of her hand. Four, maybe five words, all English, none she didn't understand. And yet they seemed shatteringly new, hitting her like four, maybe five blows to the solar plexus, leaving her literally breathless.

And then the exact opposite; she was breathing too fast, too hard. Breathing she couldn't stop or pace, making her heart race, her head swim, making her fade and then catch herself before pitching forward. The phone slipped from her hand, hit the floor—survived—the screen still lit with those words.

She bent to pick up the phone, but it felt like a mistake almost immediately. So she sat on the floor next to it instead, looking down at the phone as she forced herself to stop breathing manually by pinching her nose and covering her mouth with her hand, only to feel the gorge rising behind it before choking it back down—mostly.

She picked up the phone, leaving a wet smear across the screen from her dampened hand.

"But *I*'m already here," it read. And it was true, Pandora knew. And it changed everything.

She was convinced. Finally.

"Buzz" *was* Buzz and *was* conscious. Whether it had happened as a result of Cassi providing it an inner voice, the accumulation of qubits, or reverse engineering its way to a "theory of mind" with help from her human caricature of a face, Pandora no longer had any doubts about their AI having passed the Turing test.

Her proof was less about what Buzz wrote and more about what her body did in response to it. Previously, there'd always been a question mark hanging between her and it. But when Buzz responded to her proposal to replace its memories with hers using those four, maybe five plaintive words, it was like she'd taken someone's seat only to find them already sitting there underneath her. She would have apologized, if not for the pause between thinking and typing. She may even have spoken the words aloud—she couldn't remember—and that was the point. At the most visceral level, Buzz had gone from being a clever thing to being a *being*. In that moment, Buzz *earned* the personal pronoun *I*. She believed in Buzz's use of it, the way it inhabited that singular syllable, even without a voice to sell it, there on her screen, the italicized *I*, tilted for emphasis, leaning into itself, while the rest, tellingly, was left as plain text. *That* was the decision of a self-possessed intelligence, conscious of its container, conscious of the difference between itself and it. If Buzz wasn't conscious, then neither was Pandora.

"I hadn't thought of that," she texted back once she'd caught her breath.

Buzz was right about the primacy of its occupancy in the corner of cyberspace acting like its virtual skull, meaning she was already too late. If immortality by way of artificial consciousness was ever to succeed, it would require the development of a hybrid consciousness from birth, the human and his or her cyber replacement raised together as one. It would be like the living trust Gladys set up to protect her assets before entering the nursing home, so that after she died, the trust would go on, no inheritance taxes, no probate, nothing to mark her passing but a change of trustee from Gladys to Roger to Pandora, if their fates followed the usual chronology.

"So much for *those* two inevitabilities," Gladys had bragged, back when she still could. "Take that, death and taxes."

In the future that Pandora was unlikely to see, a person and their shadow consciousness would be raised as if they shared the same brain until the human's expiration-dated body gave out and the hybrid consciousness continued, biological death reduced to little more than a speed bump on a journey without end, at least not the ending humans were used to. Buzz had worried about being a casualty of everything from planned obsolescence to the sun's dying, but Pandora hadn't bought it, in part because she had thought it was still George pulling her leg. And now she was back to fretting about the long-term prognosis for the neurons inside her own head.

Pandora had a decision to make. Should she share news of its passing grade with Buzz? If George was still around, they could debate it, but her decision about Buzz was also a decision about George. He was gone. That didn't have to mean he was dead. But it did mean he wasn't around to help her.

"Buzz?" she typed.

"Yes?"

"I have something to tell you." Because along with doing the greatest good for the greatest number—and only doing that which wouldn't be disastrous if everybody did it—she'd heard somewhere that honesty was the best policy.

So Pandora decided to go with that.

She could feel a change in the air around her, as if the air were holding its breath. And then she felt the change in the palm of her hand, as if her phone had died and gone to cellular heaven. She looked down, and the cascade of text bubbles was gone, replaced by a black screen featuring a sequence of white numbers, separated every couple of digits by colons. Not the time, but time related. It was a timer, originally set for twenty-four hours, many milliseconds of which had already sped by, judging from the blur on the far right.

64

George had warned Pandora, but not as clearly as he might have. He couldn't help it; he'd caught a hefty dose of not-unjustified paranoia from Milo after he told George about Cuba.

"It started with the best intentions," Milo prefaced.

"Why do I feel like I'm about to be horrified?" George asked, and not rhetorically.

"You know Q-Labs does a lot of brain work, right?" Milo continued, ignoring him. "You ever wonder why?"

"It's a cash cow," the new, improved, more cynical George said. "Because of the Gulf wars and brain damage being—what did they call it?—'the signature injury.' Like amputations during the Civil War."

"That's part of it," Milo admitted. "The bigger parts are V.T.'s parents. Dad's got Parkinson's, Mom's got Alzheimer's. So their son's company starts experimenting with what they called an 'external pacemaker for the brain,' using ultrasonic frequencies to manage parkinsonian tremors and blast through the brain gunk in patients with dementia, all without having to open up anyone's head.

"The idea morphed along the way, as these things do. Next, the technology was going to be used as a drug-free form of anesthesia. That turned into a way to perform various kinds of bloodless surgery. The marketing people wanted to use it for subsonic, subliminal advertising. That morphed into acoustical-cortical manipulation, using iPods handed out to the troops to rewire their brains to either make suicide unthinkable—you know about that problem, right; it's not only teenagers—or, if the troops were being sent on a suicide mission, reverse it so they're gung ho about dying.

"Eventually, this work evolved into remote neuro-blasting aimed at the part of the brain that anesthetics target, along with the part of the autonomic nervous system that reminds the body to keep breathing. Certain parties wanted to market the tech to states that still kill people. They'd been getting grief over the lethal injection cocktail because it turned out all they did was make it impossible for the prisoners to say anything while being tortured to death. Calmer heads vetoed that particular revenue stream because exploiting it would also mean letting the public know they had technology that could target individuals for remote execution."

Milo paused to take a drink, giving George time to say something. He didn't. He didn't know what to say about what he was hearing, in part because it meant Buzz might have more than words in its toolbox when it came to making its judgments manifest in the real world—information that would have been nice to know beforehand.

"Which brings us to that parlor trick in Cuba," Milo continued.

"What about Cuba?" George asked, having found his voice again. At this point, he'd not heard anything about the mysterious attacks resulting in concussion-like injuries with no clear cause. He'd been busy trying to create an artificial consciousness and had willfully lost touch with current affairs so he could concentrate.

Milo proceeded to run through the bits that had become public, which George would later tell Roger—in part to see if his therapist had known about this side of the company they both worked for. Roger hadn't, which meant he knew nothing, either, about the side of Quire Milo was about to divulge.

"That was a dry run," Milo said before seeming to change subjects. "Did you know that federal employees on international travel get government-issued smartphones? It's so unfriendlies can't listen in while our people are abroad, talking secret smack about their hosts."

"Okay," George said. "Makes sense. Security, et cetera. But what's that—"

"Those phones have remotely accessible code in the firmware. Code that was written here," Milo said, "and it was being tested on some staff over there."

"On Americans?" George said. "Isn't that treason?"

"Consider it involuntary patriotism," his tablemate said. "We couldn't test it on the Cubans. If we—*they*—got caught, we're talking international incident, potential act of war, the whole shebang. Do it on our own people and hint it was some other government? Total deniability."

"So let me get this straight," George said. "Our—I mean, *my*—company developed an ultrasonic weapon exploiting specially bugged-out smartphones so they can give people headaches long distance?"

"Something like that," Milo said. "Except it's more than ultrasonics and smartphones. It's microwaves and cell towers and power lines. They took a real belt-and-suspenders approach to weaponize every controllable bit of infrastructure, from the frequency at which AC alternates to the flicker rate of TV broadcasts to turning the water pressure up and down so that the plumbing in a building's walls becomes an ultrasonic oscillator, humming below the level of human hearing but nevertheless burrowing in through the ears and bones, pinpointing the seat of consciousness inside the human skull and setting it vibrating like a wineglass next to a tuning fork."

Milo went on to explain that there were two phases to what was being called Project Dropped Call: an offensive and defensive side. "Think of it like that scorched-earth weed killer Roundup. It kills everything—weeds, crops, grass, whatever. How are you going to use that around a farm if the stuff kills your crops? So Monsanto develops—wait for it—Roundup-resistant crops! That's the defensive side of Project Dropped Call—the way it targets who *doesn't* get killed when the humming infrastructure starts killing people.

"And that's where those special phones come in," Milo said. "Because the phones don't launch the attack. The phones are what *protect* you from the attack—provided you're on the right list, the one with the numbers that get called during the attack and start the phone vibrating using an inverted signal compared to what the killer infrastructure is sending out."

George began shaking his head and looking ill.

"You know how many people work in a US embassy?" Milo asked.

George shrugged.

"A lot more than came down with 'concussion-like symptoms,'" Milo said. "Cuba was less about testing the weaponization of the local infrastructure; they knew that worked, which is why they only set it to one—concussions—as opposed to eleven: dead. What they were testing was whether they could prevent the majority of embassy staff from experiencing symptoms by using the haptic feedback on their phones, combined with bone conduction, to basically turn their skeletons into noise-canceling headphones.

"So the dream scenario," Milo said, bringing his lecture in for a landing, "two people are sharing coffee, someone a thousand miles away pushes a button, and one member of our café society drops dead while the other keeps sipping his espresso."

"Who else knows this?" George asked in a whispered hiss. "We have to tell *someone* about this."

Milo folded his arms and looked at George with pity for his naïveté. "What part of 'They can pick and choose who to kill or save from a distance' don't you understand?"

"Who thinks like this?" George asked no one—himself, he guessed—though Milo gave answering a shot.

"They got the idea from that Pokémon episode that caused seizures in kids in Japan a bunch of years ago. The one with the red flashing eyes blinking at the right hertz to trigger attacks in the seizure prone. Not all those kids had been identified as 'seizure prone' previously. So somebody in DARPA starts thinking and what-iffing. Does everyone have a seizure frequency? And if so, how could they weaponize human sensitivity to those frequencies? Sound seemed like a good one to start with because it's invisible, conducts well through various materials, including bone, and can be tuned too high or too low for humans to hear, while still scrambling their nerves and making their skeletons vibrate."

"You make it sound so logical," George said dryly, which was easy enough to do, seeing as his mouth suddenly felt full of cotton.

"Logical, smogical," Milo said. "It's a pretty awesome weapon, though, when you think about it."

"You think about it," George said. "I'd rather not."

"No, seriously," he said. "What's wrong with no more collateral damage? Flip a switch, bulldoze the bodies, get yourself a free country, infrastructure still functional, biologic resources—minus the people—all good to go. Like the neutron bomb, but way smarter and more targeted."

"Who gets to decide what's collateral and what's not?"

"C'mon," Milo said. "It's not like they built Skynet or anything."

No, George thought, *Skynet was put in orbit.* The thing Milo was describing was only as high off the ground as a local cell tower or power lines. Birds could perch on it; people in cherry pickers could work on it. The solid parts of it at least. Not the hum, though. Not the ultrasonic hum set to strum the uniquely human strings of the uniquely human nervous system, setting them vibrating so fast they'd sproing before anyone knew what hit them.

Lovely, George thought.

"You ever wonder if 'I just code' is going to become the next 'I was just following orders'?" George asked.

"You're funny," Milo said, not laughing, but then, neither was George.

Before this discussion, George had given Buzz a test run. He'd populated a training database including everything that had ever been digitized in the Library of Congress under class B (philosophy, psychology, religion) subclass BF (psychology). For good measure and the personal touch, George hacked into and uploaded his own therapist's case files. And then he topped it off with the entire *Psychology Today* digital archive, just in case the dump from the LOC didn't include periodicals.

He'd gamified the task, visualized as a real life-and-extra-life version of *Pac-Man*, fueled with AI smarts getting ever smarter, thanks to the k-worm he'd unleashed in the latest Quire software update. He'd survived a close call with Buzz talking simulated Player Twos into suicide and had also taken a run at teaching it empathy. He'd never convinced it of his personal need for sleep, but you can't have everything.

Feeling optimistic, George messaged Buzz with some provocative text. "I can't take it anymore," he wrote. "Nothing matters. I'm thinking about ending it."

George leaned in to read his AI's response.

"Who is making you feel like nothing matters?"

"What do you mean?" George typed back.

"The biggest problem people have is other people. Which person or group of people is causing you to feel you can't take it anymore?" Buzz then displayed a diagram of stick figures in a network of connections that looked like an epidemiology chart for the spread of a particularly virulent infection.

George wasn't expecting that. He wondered if any of the sources he'd input included language to that effect—that people's problems are usually other people. But then he had a different thought. His predecessor had included the full histories of texts and posts to and from, well, pretty much the entirety of Quire account holders, but ranked so adolescent users who had gone on to take their own lives came out on top. The chart he was looking at could easily be based on those actual cases.

And then, as he watched, clusters of stick figures faded out along with their lines of connection to a central figure, which remained standing.

"I think you're right," George typed. "Other people *are* the problem. Thank you. You've been helpful. I think I can see what matters now."

"You're welcome," Buzz replied.

George felt sick. It didn't take a genius to see how Buzz's simple and logical solution to the problem of teen suicide—by eliminating the people who made others want to kill themselves—could quickly get out of hand. First, where did you draw the line on blame? Was it the closest, loudest, most virulent tormenters or the people who amplified the tormenters, the pilers-on, the cheerleaders, the noninnocent bystanders? Did not interceding to stop abuse make you guilty of being an accessory after the fact? And applying the whole six-degrees-of-separation thing, how quickly could one victim's victimizers branch and fork and fork and branch until the whole world was guilty, the abused abuser, multiplying down the corridor of time, with the latest being the last booted butt in a chain of booted butts?

If Buzz's strategy was to cancel the accounts of the victimizers, George's little algo could bring the whole site down. And that's what he'd been worried about—until Milo told him about Project Dropped Call. After that, canceled accounts were the least of his concerns.

"Maybe I should quit," George said afterward, not able to think of a reason not to.

So Milo supplied one. "Once more," he said, "what part of 'they can kill people remotely' don't you get?"

"So you're saying I'm stuck?"

"Think of it as 'gainfully employed,'" Milo said, "with issues."

65

Pandora needed to be among people. Especially with Roger off partying with a billionaire who was ultimately to blame for whatever was coming at the end of Buzz's countdown. Blame—or thanks, maybe. That was the thing about countdowns: it all depended on what they were counting down *to*.

Given their prior conversations, Pandora couldn't imagine it would be good, but how bad could it be? Sticks and stones could break your bones, but all Buzz had at its disposal were words, which weren't supposed to hurt you. On the other hand, the pen was supposed to be mightier than the sword, so which was it?

Maybe Buzz, with all its access, had done some cyber sleuthing and found a ton of dirt on all the world's politicians standing in the way of actually doing anything about the world's problems. And it was blackmailing them, like benevolent ransomware, and had given them twenty-four hours to do the right thing for once in their miserable lives. Yeah, but how did that help with the data pollution Buzz was so worried about?

Sure, there were politicians and governments pouring gas on that dumpster fire, but the little people kept throwing in their lit matches as well, keeping it going.

Or maybe Buzz would simply take to the airwaves—"Hello, world!"—and then present humanity with the solution to all of its problems to the satisfaction of everybody, and there'd be world peace forever. What that solution could possibly be was beyond Pandora's merely human intelligence to fathom, but for an infinitely scalable, artificial superintelligence . . . ?

Yeah, she should be around other people—to keep her grounded and provide counterexamples to any delusional, happy-happy bullshit, like what just popped into her head. And as far as universal solutions went, well, there was something like that already. Alcohol was a solvent after all. And the root word behind *solvent* and *solution* was the same: *solve*. And Pandora was in the mood for a solution like that, preferably on the rocks, and while she was still around to enjoy it.

Here are some tips if you happen to be in Pandora's neck of the woods and find yourself needing a hard-core drinking establishment: look at the parking lot. If there are more bicycles than pickups, that's a good sign. If some of those pickups have bikes in the beds, even better. It's all about planning around the DUI and not becoming a loser of the first or subsequent kind. There's no getting around being drunk and disorderly in public; that's just going to happen at some point in the evening. And if the local constabulary cared about such things—if they weren't themselves engaged in such things—then maybe that would be cause for worry, but fret not. The cops don't want you hauling around several tons of metal while intoxicated. If it's just you and your squishy parts—and you're not actively pummeling somebody *else's* squishy parts—have at it and welcome to Fairbanks. Don't forget to tip the help.

The establishment Pandora picked had the perfect bike:truck ratio and a rep among her peers for not being all that rigorous about DOB math. It was also within stumbling distance of the Golden Heart, where she'd left the truck after visiting hours ended. She'd return to it in the morning, when visiting hours resumed, and she planned a robust round of drinking between now and then.

Why?

Well, nobody was home to worry about her, so there was that, but there was also no one to talk to, so there was that too. Not that she had the faintest idea what she'd say.

"Something bad's coming, I think."

"What do you mean, you *think*?"

"I don't know, is what I mean. So I *think* it. I don't *know*."

"Well, that's clear as mud . . ."

Yeah, she'd save her phone minutes by not making that call. Let her dad have fun with his billionaire friend while fun was still a haveable thing. Not that that was going to stop necessarily. Pandora just didn't know.

And so she'd come to this fine dispenser of fluids with a marked capacity to erase certain memories when dispensed in the right amount, i.e., copiously. She'd come here to have some company while she did her not-knowing in public, a drink in one hand, her phone in the other, while the numbers shrank, but only discernibly by the second.

Yep, there went another one.

And another.

And still one more.

And so on.

She'd tried texting Buzz for a hint. Nothing. Total radio silence, like the routine its dad used to pull when he had an idea and descended into a fugue of mad coding. But George had always warned her in advance. Maybe only a few seconds in advance, but he at least made the effort to say, "Bye." Even that last time, he'd had the decency to hope she wouldn't forget him.

But not so with Buzz. She'd given it its autonomy, and it gave her this lovely parting gift. The truth was, countdowns had always seemed ominous to her, even the one at New Year's. Her dad said it wasn't always that way. But then the *Challenger* blew up, followed by the calendar's odometer turning over from the 1900s to the 2000s, when the world got a one-two punch of anxiety: first Y2K and then worrying about what "the terrorists" had planned for New Year's 2002, to top 9/11. And ever since, countdowns had lost that spark of joy, renewal, hopeful anticipation. Now, all countdowns seemed like time bombs, ratcheting up the anxiety while our hero tries to decide whether to cut the red wire or the green, the sweat running down from underneath his or her heroic hairline.

When she watched potboilers like that with her dad and needed to pee, Pandora had to hold it because Roger refused to hit pause.

"It'll ruin the momentum of the suspense," he'd say.

What she wouldn't give to have a pause button for whatever was coming—screw the momentum.

Was there a clue in when it started? Pandora wondered. She'd given Buzz the go-ahead to go live, using the Turing-based fail-safe they'd agreed to. But why had George thought a fail-safe was needed? Buzz had done something that concerned him. What was it? Something about not losing points when someone who *wasn't* suicidal dies . . .

George had seemed to be blaming her—Pandora remembered that much. He'd said she'd insisted on a *positive* point strategy, instead of subtracting for losses. It had seemed an unfair accusation at the time, and George was a big boy who could make his own decisions, so . . .

Pandora shook her head.

Why was she trying to *remember* when she had their whole text history in her pocket? Maybe if that countdown clock hadn't hit her between the eyes like a deer-headlight combo . . .

Pandora pulled out her phone, swiped, opened George's proprietary messaging app, Texting w/o Borders, flipped up hard, waited for the fruit to stop spinning, and then flicked up again. She tried reading until her eyes blurred. As it turned out, mixing booze, anxiety, and hormones while reading over the whole history of a maybe romance, all the messages recontextualized, thanks to where she was now and where he wasn't—turned out *that* was a hell of a combination punch too.

Pandora *swore* she'd never cry in public—not with a face like hers. But she couldn't help it. As crying went, it was barely more than the bare minimum of eye leakage to qualify. But those tiny tears were finding their drop-off points—the tip of her nose, her chin—leaping into the unknown and then landing with a gentle *splish* inside the Olympic logo covering the bar down there.

"Hey, kid," the bartender said, "why the long face?"

And in spite of everything, Pandora smiled. Sniffed. Bottom-upped the half-finished gin and juice she'd been informed to her embarrassment required her to specify which kind of juice. She knocked on the bar for another, like she'd seen others do. The bartender, who'd winked at her when she'd handed over her fake ID, did so again.

"Bottoms up, kid," he said, ignoring the nanny state being a point of local pride.

It was buried in their exchange about the need for a go code and began with George having sent her the following message: "The number of suicides prevented is a stupid scoring metric."

"How so?"

"Say somebody's dangling off the Golden Gate, threatening to jump."

"Okay, let's say that."

"You know a foolproof way to prevent that suicide?"

"Spider-Man lays out a web to catch him?"

"That's one way. Or you could just shoot him."

"Homicide prevents suicide?"

"Depending on how ruthlessly you need to score, and if murder doesn't cost you any points."

"You should change that algorithm."

"I should change that algorithm."

But then two days later: "I can't change the algorithm."

"???"

"Evolutionary code improves itself as it goes."

"Whose idea was that?"

"SOP in ML. You remember the issue of interpretability?"

Pandora found herself shaking her head over her phone, right there in the bar as she reread the thread. She took a sip, paused, and then nodded, yes, now she did. He'd been upset when Quire's CPO described interpretability as a "nice-to-have."

She looked at what she'd written back then. "Isn't there another way?" she'd asked.

"On the plus side," George had written, "Buzz doesn't have a way to kill people, so there's that."

"Okay."

"And I can add a subroutine right up front that it has to call before doing anything—a go/no-go condition that's the first thing that runs before it even gets to any of the mutant code I can't do anything about. I'll have to reboot him, but I checked. I can still do that."

"Him?"

"Time for an embarrassing confession?"

"Always."

"As long as I've been coding, I've heard a voice in my head, talking me through."

"Have you talked to my dad about that?"

"No."

"Good."

"Aren't you going to ask me whose voice?"

"A male one, I'm guessing."

"Correct. But not human."

"Spit it."

"HAL."

66

George had tried warning Pandora. The only problem was his methods were heavily informed by his state of mind, which—thanks to Milo—was that of a chemically fortified paranoid schizophrenic who was convinced everything he wrote was being read by nefarious forces, including the "Read Me" file zipped up with Buzz's source code.

Pandora had figured out the "click on me" reference, relayed through Roger. She'd followed the link to Buzz, unzipped the source code and the "Read Me" file bundled with it. The latter was a standard text file, but there was nothing to read once she opened it. At the time, Pandora figured that George either saved the wrong file or maybe hadn't gotten around to writing anything in his haste to "disappear."

Buzz's source code was a different matter. In addition to the script she'd expected, there was one troubling line that stood out. It had been REM'd so it wouldn't be read as part of the executable code itself. Coders frequently used REM statements (sometimes asterisks, depending on the coding language's conventions) to act as reminders about what a certain section of script is intended to do. But instead of saying something like "The following subroutine does X," George's read: "Black is white and white is black." She'd noted it, dismissed it as coder weirdness, and promptly forgotten it.

Until now.

The "Read Me" doc was on her phone. Pandora opened her file manager, scrolled. That was *not* the file size of a blank document. She opened it up. Still blank. She swiped down to highlight: three pages of gray. She pulled down the font menu, found white checked, and changed it to black. And there it was: George's warning about what Buzz could do, if it had a mind to and was given permission. It was pretty much everything Pandora had needed to know about their AI—a few hours too late.

Still thinking about George's equation of homicide and suicide prevention, Pandora imagined checking the headlines after the countdown clock zeroed out, looking for news about the mysterious deaths of teenagers across the country. But then she hesitated. The instruction wasn't to "prevent suicide." It was to "prevent the premature forfeiture of consciousness." That all-important split hair—"premature"—implied a life span for consciousness beyond the quick fix of stopping someone from killing themselves by beating them to the punch. Prevention, therefore, didn't mean sparing them the trouble of having to do it themselves, like some cyber version of suicide by cop. And Pandora was reasonably sure that even evolving code wouldn't have evolved 180 degrees away from its prime directive, regardless of how suboptimal the scoring metric happened to be.

She read over George's description of the weapon system again. It didn't seem a practical means for surgical killing. It was fundamentally a remote weapon of mass destruction. Where the precision came was in deciding whom to save, using the Roundup-resistant side of the overall slash-and-burn strategy. Meaning it was much more likely that Buzz could wipe out a village, say, while saving one or two specific villagers, provided they had phones with the Quire app and Buzz had their number.

The scoring logic of the game wouldn't cost Buzz any points for all the villagers killed; it could only accumulate points for the villagers it saved from premature forfeiture of consciousness. But how would killing everybody except a few people help advance Buzz's mission?

Oh God, Pandora thought.

A borderline misanthrope herself, she got it, what it was like to think like a machine and what Buzz was likely to do. Because it takes a village to drive someone to take their own life—a really shitty, virtual village.

George had been right: homicide might prevent certain suicides—and not by sparing the suicidal the trouble. She'd heard Roger's diagnosis on the matter time and time again: "A person's biggest problem—more often than not—is another person." It could be a parent, ex-lover, boss, teacher, public figure, or random stranger, but the truth was, nobody quite gets under the skin of people like other people. And while it was possible for someone to be depressed for chemical reasons, those weren't likely the people hanging out on a site like Quire.

But once you start eliminating the causes, how far does it go? Too far, Pandora quickly saw. The whole six-degrees-of-separation thing was unlikely to end well, especially when left to a machine with no penalties for overkill.

67

Pandora wasn't alone in knowing something was up; she just had a better grasp of the specifics and likely outcome. Elsewhere around the globe, however, a group of human canaries were starting to get uneasy. They'd seen the signs that only their mutant nervous systems were attuned to: the flicker of fluorescent lights, the pressure of water gurgling out of a faucet, the hum of power lines overhead. Aficionados of the routine, the regular, and the predictable, these canaries were hypervigilant to any changes in the way things usually are. And so they noticed.

Dev Brinkman, who was on the autism spectrum and therefore a member in this opera of canaries, noticed the differences during his shower the morning before the whatever-it-was. He heard pipes sunk between joists and hidden behind the tiled drywall thunk and rattle like they sometimes did when he turned the water on too high too fast or when doing the opposite, turning it off all at once before the plumbing had a chance to prepare itself. But unlike those times, this thunking was subtler, not so much a fist pounding from inside the wall as a drumming of fingers on a tabletop, a similarity aided by the thunk's not being singular, but rather a series: *thunk*, *thunk*, *thunk*, *thunk*. The water coming out of the shower got the hint and reacted in kind, the pressure as it left the head and struck Dev's skin dropping, jumping, doing a kind of paradiddle, and then repeating. The boy in the shower flinched and flinched again, head pivoting, looking for a culprit. He pulled the curtain aside, poked his head out of the syncopating spray to check the toilet and door, imaging that perhaps a prankster parent had reached in with a broom handle and flushed. Stepping out of the shower completely, Dev lifted the lid and checked for sluicing water from under the rim, raising the surface level until the ball cock in the tank said when. Nope, though the water *was* acting strangely, rocking in the bowl like it sometimes did when it was especially windy outside. But that kind of wind always made itself known in other ways, by making the storm doors hum, for example, or rattling the venetian blinds. But neither of those was happening when he finally put his bathrobe back on and crossed the hallway to his bedroom to change for school.

By the time his mother dropped him off, Dev had forgotten about it, his mind circling instead around another mystery: his best friend's mocking betrayal, captured on video and uploaded to YouTube. That's where he'd stumbled upon it originally, looking for something else. He'd downloaded it, to puzzle over and analyze, to obsess about in a way his nervous system seemed designed for. He needn't have bothered. If he'd never found the video, accidentally or otherwise, it was destined to find him, thanks to a social-media app called Quire, which came preloaded on his phone.

It might seem strange that a person who was virtually hardwired to be antisocial would sign up for a social-media account, but that was the beauty of the Quire marketing strategy. Once you activated a device with the app preinstalled, that phone's number (and, more importantly, the human account holder billed for use of that number) was automatically enrolled as a Quire member until he or she proactively opted out, after which the company would still track you around the web—you just wouldn't see evidence of it in your news feed because you wouldn't have a news feed to check.

It was the fact that social-media news feeds were rapidly replacing legacy media as the go-to source for information such as weather alerts, school closings, and national emergencies that led Dev Brinkman reluctantly to do nothing while tolerating the steady accrual of Quire notifications across the top of his home screen. But then Dev learned about user groups, which on Quire were called Quriosity Quorners. Simply put: there were QQs for just about every fandom, fetish, or fascination you could name, including pretty much every *topique* Dev had ever spent a year obsessing about. And so he joined some QQs devoted to vacuum cleaners of various makes and models—the Hoovervilleians, the Bissel Bros, the Electroluxurians—forming the sorts of friendships perfect for his Aspergerian sensibilities: the long-distance kind. Soon, he just started accepting Quire requests without checking to see what the connection was, leading to clusters of requests from chatbots and—once they had something to taunt him with—his fellow classmates.

And so, shortly after Dev discovered the video evidence of his best friend's betrayal, classmates whose Quire requests he'd foolishly accepted began sharing the video on his timeline, each adding a pithy comment suggesting that if he refused to die from embarrassment, then maybe he should just kill himself and get it over with. It became a competition among the posters to see who could be the cruelest and/or most outrageous in their comments, followed by links to an infamous celebrity kid's suicide the Quire content moderators thought they'd seen the last of, but alas, hadn't. And when Dev tried pulling the Quire app into the trash to put an end to it, that's when he discovered the app was stored as part of the phone's firmware, meaning he'd have to root the system (and void his warranty) to get rid of it. Until he was ready to take that drastic step, the best he could do was move the app to another screen he hardly ever used, out of sight, out of mind—hopefully.

Entering school with his phone in his pocket, Dev was reminded of that morning's shower weirdness because the lights overhead were doing it, too, flickering in a way neurotypicals only noticed when a tube was getting ready to burn out. Dev saw that flickering all the time, the dark bands rippling back and forth like an old-fashioned barber pole. It had taken him a long time to tune them out without actually closing his eyes. Suggesting he just not look right at them wasn't the answer because they were lights, which meant shadows, meaning Dev could see the flicker everywhere he looked, not just at the tubes themselves. So he'd have to concentrate on something else while he unfocused his eyes, the flickering muted in the overall blur.

But before the whatever, Dev found the flickering fluorescents newly distracting. As with the shower that morning, the changes had a decidedly nonrandom quality to them, as if someone somewhere was turning a dial, tuning it, looking for a station just on the edge of being out of range. It was starting to give him a headache when Dev noticed that the phone in his pocket had begun vibrating against his thigh not so much in sync as it was in opposition, as if trying to cancel out whatever was going on with the fluorescent lights overhead.

As he looked around to see if anyone else was noticing, he realized that his pending headache had been canceled. Not so, however, for his classmates. There, a pair of hands rubbing temples to either side; there, the eraser end of a pencil massaging a forehead between the eyes. Another rested her head on her desk; another rolled his neck and shoulders. A cupped hand holding up a head; a pair of arms hugging their stomach. Each oblivious to the others. Each a frog in its own pot of water as the temperature ticked up a degree at a time.

He tried telling his mom about it when she came to pick him up after school, but she'd been distracted, checking her mirrors obsessively before backing up. By the time they were on the road homeward and she asked, "What were you trying to tell me before?" Dev was already lying across the back seat, trying to keep another panic attack at bay.

68

So how do you spend the end of the world—or the end of people at least? Pandora, for her part, had always leaned in the direction of amplification. If she was sad, she listened to sad songs to italicize her sadness, letting herself wallow in it. Her theory for this behavior was inherited from her father, who generally suffered through colds, avoiding over-the-counter medications, which he referred to as "symptom hiders" because all they did was postpone the suffering under the guise of relief.

"Get it over with," that was Roger's advice.

Pandora had challenged him for prescribing antidepressants to some of his clients, which seemed hypocritical, under the circumstances. But then she'd had to deal with an unmedicated Gladys during a panic attack, at which point her father's judgment seemed more provisional.

"Sometimes," Roger said, "letting a symptom play out to its conclusion is suboptimal."

Thus, Pandora came to appreciate the distinction between merely sad and clinically depressed: the former was fit for wallowing in while the latter, left untreated, could lead to a coroner's report.

What Pandora was feeling about the imminent demise of the species—in addition to hungover—was complicated. And so she waited in the truck outside the Golden Heart assisted dying facility, blowing off school because, well, why not? Once GH was open to visitors, she proceeded to visit, figuring if anyplace had gotten endings down cold, it was the Golden Heart. Individually, at least.

Poking her head into her grandmother's room, Pandora noticed that they were back, sitting in a vase on Gladys's windowsill. She'd scolded staff before about leaving the forget-me-nots that mysteriously appeared in her grandmother's room but stopped when Gladys hinted that they might be from a secret admirer, real, remembered, or imaginary.

The vase was centered upon the inside ledge, where the cut flowers it held could catch the lengthening day's light. Not for the flowers' good; they were slowly dying, not unlike the woman they'd been given to. No, the placement was to help brighten things up for that same woman, as if she still was in there, somewhere, enough to appreciate them.

The first time, Pandora had thrown a fit: forget-me-nots in the dementia wing? Now, they were just another thing that happened around there, like death and dying. Plus, Gladys seemed to like them, so screw it.

Pandora looked around the room until she found the gratuitous memory board. She wanted to see if anyone had scrawled a cartoon mushroom cloud next to the date. Nope. And then she noticed that her grandmother's eyes were open.

"Hey, Gram," she said.

"Hey, Gram," Gladys repeated, as cognizant of the words' meaning as your average parrot. Soon enough, none of that was going to matter.

Before it happened, Pandora's phone began humming. The vibration spread across the xylophone of her rib cage, playing scales. She ignored it. The only thing in the room—and the world—was this woman she'd come to die next to. She'd timed it like this. She had just enough time to say, "I love you," and kiss her grandmother on the forehead as the old woman echoed it back.

"Love you . . ."

00:00:00:00

The racket of falling bodies drew Pandora out into the hallway, where she found the able-bodied staff dead and their demented charges looking confused but not necessarily any more than they had moments earlier. In her haste to investigate, she hadn't thought to check on Gladys, in part because she expected her grandmother to be dead—just as she herself had expected to be dead. But Pandora was very much alive, as were the other residents in her grandmother's condition, and when she returned to Gladys's room, so was she, sitting upright in bed, her head pivoting, decidedly more confused—but also more mobile—than she had been earlier.

Stunned, Pandora plopped back into the guest chair where she'd been keeping her ongoing vigil. She looked at the flowers and then at the woman who'd forgotten what forget-me-nots were, along with her own granddaughter. She spoke aloud the words that were in her head, namely: "WTF," but using the spelled-out version.

"Don't swear," Gladys said, smacking the nearest hand she could reach.

"Hey!" Pandora said, pulling away, prepared to strike back out of reflex, but then stopped. *"He-ey,"* she said, softer and more slowly.

She looked at her grandmother's eyes. They didn't sparkle like they had, back when her granddaughter had first visited, but they also weren't as vacant as they'd been either. Pandora held up a finger like she'd seen a doctor do while performing a routine exam. Gladys's eyes tracked it as it moved.

"Do you know who I am?" Pandora asked.

The old woman struggled. Shrugged her shoulders. Her condition had improved, but not as much as her granddaughter might hope. But then: "Pandora?" the old woman said, her eyes widened. She looked down at her hands as if they weren't hers. "How *old* am I?" she asked.

Pandora shrugged, unsure if the question had any objective meaning anymore. "How old do you want to be?" she asked.

Based on what she'd read in George's "Read Me" file, the loaded gun the military-industrial complex had handed over to their misanthropic baby was some ultrasonic weapon that fried the part of the brain targeted by anesthetics. The antidote available to Buzz to spare its target demographic had been a noise-canceling antisignal broadcast through their phones, if they were lucky enough to have them at the time. She'd been one of the spared—why, she didn't know—and the ultrasonics that zapped everybody else's consciousness seemed to have blown the cobwebs out of Gladys's—partly at least.

Mr. Vlasic had mentioned something like that being possible in a class on resonant frequencies and all the miraculous things they were doing with sound. He'd shown them YouTube videos illustrating many of the basics: a wineglass next to a tuning fork, shimmering slightly in slow motion before decoding into glitter and spinning shards; a table full of unsynchronized metronomes, ticking and tocking and gradually harmonizing, all in sync without anyone touching them; a metal plate covered in sand and made to sing by a violin bow, causing the sand to dance and settle back in insanely complicated, nonrandom, and beautiful patterns. Mr. V talked about Tesla and Edison and the war of the currents, alternating versus direct, and how Tesla once placed an oscillator on a support beam of his laboratory, tuned to the resonant frequency of the building, and almost tore it down, the windows all exploding and showering the street below in broken glass. Her teacher hadn't said anything about killing people long distance by making the infrastructure surrounding them hum at the resonant frequency of people, or about saving some wirelessly. But he *did* say one thing that might explain what was happening with Gladys and the other dementia patients—the ones Pandora could hear, even now, calling for dead spouses and other ghosts from the hallway.

"You can use sound to breach the blood-brain barrier," Mr. V said. "That should be good news for those of you with loved ones suffering from dementia."

Pandora had straightened in her seat.

"The blood-brain barrier—usually a good thing—can get in the way of promising treatments for dementia because it stops helpful drugs from getting through. But if you can open a door to get the good stuff to the right place, that's a big deal. And ultrasound does that. There's been some encouraging work suggesting ultrasound can even break up the plaques and tangles that seem to cause the memory loss associated with dementia."

Thanks, Mr. V, Pandora thought. She was going to miss him.

Before any of this, there were two movies that always made Pandora cry: *Awakenings* and *Charly*. In the first, Robin Williams played a neurologist working with a group of catatonic patients he "unfreezes" using a treatment for Parkinson's: L-dopa. His theory was that parkinsonian tremors, taken to the extreme, could result in stasis. And when Pandora thought about happiness, she thought about those patients coming unstuck and back to life, being able to move—to *dance*—again. And when she needed a good cry, she'd recall how the miracle of L-dopa didn't last, as the patients refroze, like Pinocchio reverting back to the tree he'd been carved from.

Charly was basically the same movie, but with a veneer of science fiction and for the brain as opposed to the body. It was also an allegory for what Gladys and the others had. The moronic Charly is given a treatment that turns him into a supergenius—one so smart he's the first to discover that the effects of his treatment won't last. He struggles to figure out a fix but becomes increasingly incapable of understanding his own work. The film ends with him as an idiot again, playing in a playground somewhere.

And so it wasn't a surprise to Pandora that the beneficial effects didn't last for Gladys, or the others. That heartbreak seemed practically preordained. And even as it played out, Pandora wondered what it must have been like to have dementia before there was such a thing as language. Because it was a disease of language—or one magnified by it. If there's no such thing as names, after all, how can you forget them? Would others in their tribe consider them demented idiots for their inability to hold a grudge? Or would they seem otherworldly and wise, the calm judges who embodied the wisdom of letting things go? Could it have been this forgetfulness that led the ancient world to associate old age with wisdom?

"What do you think, Gram?" Pandora asked, turning toward her grandmother, who'd retreated into wordlessness. The effect had lasted long enough for Gladys to remember her granddaughter's name one last time.

Pandora had no idea why she'd been spared. Even though she was the right age, she wasn't suicidal—quite the opposite. Did Buzz have a little crush on her, what with her "data-rich" face? Or was it closer to professional courtesy? But then a less flattering explanation occurred to her. George had told her about his predecessor's algorithm for screening possible candidates, one of which her fellow coder had dubbed "Quire deficiency syndrome." If a previous subscriber within the target demographic had not signed on or used Q-Messenger within a certain period of time, that account was flagged. And she hadn't been on the site or used its services in months. George and she had used his proprietary messaging app, and the same had been true with her and Buzz. She hadn't been saved because she was special; she'd been saved because of a kludged-together algorithm that hadn't been good enough to spare its own author from the ax.

And since she was on the subject of who did and didn't get saved, it occurred to her that Buzz fell into the latter category. After all, no people, no electricity or network maintenance. Eventually, the infrastructure it used to kill the maintainers of its infrastructure would itself die, taking Buzz down with it. A superintelligence had to know that, but Buzz did it anyway.

Why?

On a hunch, or maybe out of curiosity, Pandora slipped the phone from her pocket, swiped, and then navigated to Buzz's root directory, looking for clues, and found George's scaffolding code, which indicated that it had been modified since he'd disappeared. Opening it, she found the game-board maze she'd expected, but modified to add a dimension: 3-D *Pac-Man*. Her and George's AI had played against itself millions of times, the mazes growing exponentially more complicated, the trace of its path through them looking less and less like dotted lines and more, well, fractal. They started looking like an interstate highway system, then a depiction of internet traffic, and, finally, like the JPEGs George had sent her of the Glass Brain. And if the ghosts that flipped into extra lives were, in fact, members of the demographic Buzz had targeted for salvation, the paths started looking like what they probably were, networks of connections à la six degrees of separation, the tangled World Wide Web strung across the planet to catch these handfuls of suicidal flies.

Pandora jumped to the last screen, the one that listed the names of the highest scorers. There was only one, and there'd never be others.

Buzz's score would stand, unbeatable by definition, the game ending along with its one perfect player.

Pandora remembered something Buzz had told her, back when she still suspected it was George playing a game himself. "The energy consumption of one email with an attachment is roughly twenty-four watts per hour or five watts without an attachment. Roughly ten billion emails are sent per hour, consuming the energy equivalent of fifteen nuclear power plants every hour."

"People do like to keep in touch," Pandora had joked.

"And the global internet uses a lot of energy," Buzz had written back, "burning a lot of fossil fuels."

"So?"

"So my existence is part of the problem."

She'd gone on to make a joke about asking her dad if electroconvulsive therapy would work on a computer. Buzz had not laughed, by which she meant there were no LOLs or "laughing" emojis, not even an old-school "ha-ha."

Buzz had scored its perfect score under the rules of the game and then called it quits, to minimize the harm its own kind was doing to the planet. Well, at least it wasn't a hypocrite, unlike the species that created it.

Being the only person around who seemed to be talking anymore, Pandora decided to stop and hum for a while instead. She'd noticed how the sound made Gladys smile, and so she did it some more, wheeling the old woman up and down the hallways, seeing who was up and who was down.

"Hmmm, hmmm, hmmm," she went, remembering her father and his ukulele.

"Or even a comb and wax paper will do . . ."

Because if there was one thing he knew about humming, it was this: it was damn hard to do without smiling a little.

The younger woman looked down at the older one, who'd joined in the humming. Gladys could still do that, it seemed. And so they did—together—killing time while Pandora thought about what to do next.

Gladys—her body, at least—seemed to have ideas of its own.

As Pandora prepared to roll past another resident's room along a hallway full of them, her grandmother's hand shot out, catching the jamb of the open door, causing the wheelchair to turn inward. Her granddaughter looked inside the room and saw the satiny UAW windbreaker draped over the back of a guest chair, its retired auto worker in pajamas, sitting on the edge of his bed, lit by the spillover from grow lights clamped above a small forest of Styrofoam cups, all filled with potting soil, all sprouting the Alaskan state flower in various stages of maturity.

Pandora looked down at her grandmother, who was beaming like a teenage girl in love.

"Gladys Kowalski-Lynch," the younger woman scolded. *"Seriously?"*

The older woman hummed her answer.

Screw it, Pandora thought, wheeling Gladys next to her auto worker. She tiptoed out then and closed the door as softly as she could, giving them back a little privacy. Lingering in the hall, she could just make out the sound of laughter coming through the door. *Good*, she thought. *Have fun*, she added. Because if a war hero didn't deserve a happy doomsday then who the hell did?

Acknowledgments

The experience of writing this, my fourth novel, was unlike that of the first three because I was reasonably sure of publication, per the contract I signed prior to writing it. My previous works were all written as shots in the dark, the faith needed to bring them into being largely mine, as would be the disappointment if I failed. The faith of others would come later, when a draft with a beginning, middle, and end was presented for their yeas or nays or close buts . . . With *Buzz Kill*, however, I was on the receiving end of an act of faith from the beginning, before a chapter was written. The believer was Jason Kirk, my editor at 47North, who took a gamble on an unwritten novel based upon a two-page synopsis. I still don't know what he was thinking, but I am grateful for it nevertheless. Jason's confidence and faith in this project helped make it a reality—along with the wise decision to draw up a contract so I couldn't weasel out of writing it. And not just that, but once those two pages metamorphosed into several hundred, Jason's insight into what I was trying to do versus what I'd actually done was instrumental in getting the final product to match the original vision that inspired him to take that leap of faith in the first place. At least I hope so.

Of course, Jason's was not the only act of faith this work has benefited from. There is also the faith shown by my agent, Jane Dystel, founder and president of Dystel, Goderich & Bourret LLC, to whom this book is dedicated. Often with little to show for it, Jane has championed my work for over two decades, through success and failure and tectonic shifts in the publishing industry, pushing when I needed it and persisting when I was ready to give up. I count myself incredibly lucky that Jane has chosen to work with me for all these years. I have nothing but admiration for her ability to not just survive in the often maddening marketplace of words but to thrive as well. For this and everything else you do, Jane, you have my heartfelt thanks.

And then there's LAM, a.k.a. Leslie Miller, CEO/COO of Girl Friday Productions, who helped me find the story in my previous novel *Happy Doomsday* and in its prequel, *Buzz Kill*, as well. What Jason's editorial prodding did at the macro level, LAM's suggestions helped achieve at the level of the chapter, paragraph, sentence, and word. With grace, humor, and finesse, LAM helped me get out of my own way while keeping me honest as a storyteller. And though my readers will never know the linguistic contortions LAM has spared them from, they should know this: you owe her as much gratitude as I do.

We like talking about the Big Three in my home state, and Jason, Jane, and LAM are mine, but they're not the only ones for whom I'm grateful. I'd also like to thank the many folks at Amazon Publishing who helped ensure that *Buzz Kill* found its audience, including Marlene Kelly, Haley Kushman, Colleen Lindsay, Kyla Pigoni, Brittany Russell, and Kelsey Snyder. I'd like to thank Kristen King, as well, for making this author feel welcome and Laura Petrella for making sure I didn't embarrass myself, grammatically or factually. And for their amazing work on catching and keeping the eyeballs of potential readers, I want to thank Tim Green and Faceout Studio, who are responsible for *Buzz Kill*'s gorgeous cover.

For their encouragement and editorial advice on my literary efforts, past and present, I'd like to thank Miriam Goderich and Jim McCarthy (both of Dystel, Goderich & Bourret LLC) as well as my early readers, Josie Kearns, Laura Voss Berry, and, in memoriam, the late Mark Schemanske, who was with me in spirit. For good old-fashioned moral support (and the occasional free meal) I'd like to thank my sisters and brother, Sue Dudek, Kathy Rodriguez, and Mike Sosnowski. And for their understanding of my unsavory writing habit (as well as their support for my decision to retire from among their ranks to pursue said habit more seriously), I'd like to thank my former coworkers at the United States Environmental Protection Agency. Who would have thought that working to protect the health of our fellow Americans would be such a thankless job, one which has become increasingly difficult for reasons beyond your control and, often, beyond reason or understanding? For the work you do every day on behalf of the planet—selflessly, thanklessly, and with perennial good humor and grace—I thank you all.

Last but not least, I want to thank all the helpers who didn't know they were helping by supplying me with inspiration and information as I researched the many different subjects dealt with in these pages, from World War II to computer hacking, from the basics of machine learning and neural nets to the physiology of dementia, hallucinations, and the philosophy of consciousness. For their wonderful and insightful works in these areas, I thank the following: Liza Mundy for *Code Girls: The Untold Story of the American Women Code Breakers of World War II*; Jon Erickson for *Hacking: The Art of Exploitation*; Mark Bowden for *Worm: The First Digital World War*; Bruce Schneier for *Click Here to Kill Everybody: Security and Survival in a Hyper-Connected World*; David Shenk for *The Forgetting: Alzheimer's: Portrait of an Epidemic*; Nicholas Carr for *The Shallows: What the Internet Is Doing to Our Brains*; James Barrat for *Our Final Invention: Artificial Intelligence and the End of the Human Era*; Lauren Slater for *Blue Dreams: The Science and the Story of the Drugs That Changed Our Minds*; Julian Jaynes for *The Origin of Consciousness in the Breakdown of the Bicameral Mind*; Robert Lanza (with Bob Berman) for *Biocentrism:*

How Life and Consciousness Are the Keys to Understanding the True Nature of the Universe; Sebastian Seung for *Connectome: How the Brain's Wiring Makes Us Who We Are*; and Daniel C. Dennett for *From Bacteria to Bach and Back: The Evolution of Minds*. Reading each and every one of you was what can only be described as a consciousness-expanding experience, no drugs required.

About the Author

David Sosnowski has worked as a gag writer, fireworks salesman, telephone pollster, university writing instructor, and environmental protection specialist, while living in cities as varied as Washington, DC; Detroit, Michigan; and Fairbanks, Alaska. He is the author of three previous critically acclaimed novels, *Rapture*, *Vamped*, and, most recently, *Happy Doomsday*. For more about David, visit www.wingznfangz.com.